# NEIGHBORS
## TO DIE FOR

# NEIGHBORS
## TO DIE FOR

## AN HOA MYSTERY

## LINDA LOVELY

*Author Photo Credit: Danielle Dahl*

*First edition*

*ISBN: 978-1-68512-190-7*

*Cover art by Level Best Designs*

*This book was professionally typeset on Reedsy.*
*Find out more at reedsy.com*

*For my nephew and nieces—Jim, Tammy, Brenda—and their delightful families.*
*Thanks for including us in so much fun.*

# Praise for the HOA Mysteries

"An excellent mystery written with charm, appeal and wry humor - and ex-Coast Guard Kylee Kane is a great main character."—Lee Child, #1 *New York Times* bestselling author

"Multiple mysteries converge as retired Coast Guard investigator Kylee Kane returns in this welcome second installment of Linda Lovely's HOA Mystery Series. Lovely excels at balancing the life-and-death stakes of her well-paced narrative with the character developments of her robust and memorable cast, all against the backdrop of the deceptively benign world of HOA machinations. A delightful, page-turner of a mystery, not to be missed."—Jonathan Haupt, coeditor, *Our Prince of Scribes: Writers Remember Pat Conroy*

"Linda Lovely delivers another nail-biting, edge-of-your-seat mystery that kept me reading late into the night to find out what would happen next in *Neighbors to Die For*."—Dorothy St. James, author of the Beloved Bookroom Mysteries

"*Neighbors to Die For* is filled with kidnappings, coastal intrigue, adrenaline-pumping action, and an intelligent sleuth—everything I need in my mysteries. Loved it!"—Melissa Bourbon/Winnie Archer, national bestselling author of the Book Magic and Bread Shop Mysteries

"Another masterful mystery by Linda Lovely. Filled with twists, turns, and interesting characters. Being part of an HOA can be dangerous business."—Dana Ridenour, award winning author of the Lexie Montgomery

FBI undercover series

"Linda Lovely delivers another twisty mystery with the perfect mix of wry humor and quirky characters. Anyone looking for a fun, fast page-turner, here it is!"—Tami Hoag, #1 *New York Times* bestselling author

"HOA communities seem deceptively safe, but the mix of gossip and politics in rule-bound groups can be a fertile breeding ground for murder. For the gutsy Kylee Kane, a fact-finding gig in South Carolina's Lowcountry turns increasingly complex and dangerous. *With Neighbors Like These* offers a distinctive setting, a tenacious female sleuth and captivating suspense."—Katherine Ramsland, bestselling author of *How to Catch a Killer*

## KEY CHARACTERS & ASSOCIATIONS
*(No worries. You'll meet them gradually.)*

### Welch HOA Management
- Ted Welch, owner *(retired U.S. State Dept.)*
- Kylee Kane, security consultant *(retired Coast Guard)*
- Grant Welch, Ted's son, *Citadel Cadet*
- Mimi Jones, Grant's girlfriend
- Myrtle Kane, office temp, Kylee's mom *(retired nurse)*
- Robin Gates, IT Specialist
- Frank Donahue, Maintenance

### HOA Client: Lighthouse Cove
- Ernie Baker, president *(owns right-wing media, wife Barb)*
- Carrie Sullivan, director
- Olivia Klaus, director
- Howie Wynne, Mr. Red Mulch
- Ed Hiller, son of late millionaire
- Sam Whitner, Q's golfing buddy
- Chief Vaughn, Head of Security

### HOA Client: Hullis Island
- Cliff Jackson, president *(wife Peggy)*
- Capt. Billy Stubbs, party boat *(daughter, Katie)*
- Chief O'Rourke, Security
- Martha Evatt & Ruth Leopard *(Myrtle's friends)*

### HOA Client: Jade Pointe
- Phil Graham, president *(billionaire developer)*
- Ashley Vogt, Phil's fiancée
- Saffron Adams, Phil's daughter by first wife
- Connor Cassidy, Phil's son by first wife
- Jim Savercool, Director Security

### Neuter1 Radicals
- "Quincy" or Q, the leader
- Matt, Red Mask
- Jacob, Blue Mask
- Ryan, Brown Mask, stutterer

### Law Enforcement
- Nick Ibsen, Acting Sheriff, Beaufort County
- Deputy Owens, Beaufort SWAT
- Capt. Harvey Reed, Coast Guard
- Lt. Johnson & Lt. Carter, Coast Guard officers
- FBI Special Agent Shirley Minton
- FBI Special Agent Lance Davis

### Spoonbill Island Development
- Ken Taylor, promoter

### Barrett's B&B
- Kay Barrett, owner (*attorney*)

### HOA Client:
### Crestway Plantation
- Lucille Sanford, president (*husband, Dan*)

### Former HOA Client:
### Satin Sands
- Roger Roper, president (*wife, Karen*)
- Donna Dahl, director (*nickname Freckles*)
- Alex Peters, master naturalist

### HOA Client: Sea Bay
- Evelyn & Gilda, opposing directors
- Janice Caldwell, Emotional Support claimant

### Pine Inlet
### Homeowners Association
- Owen Farash, president (*wife, Diane*)

### Florist
- Sally Wilson

# Chapter One

Kylee

*Saturday Afternoon*

A peek at my watch says the meeting's twenty-two minutes old. Feels like twenty-two days.

*Just shoot me!*

"Only wood-hued mulch is acceptable," Carrie huffs.

"I agree." Ernie strokes his chubby chin, his deep-thinker pose. "Homeowners know we have a nature-based color scheme. True, our documents only address paint colors, but red mulch violates the spirit of our architectural policy."

These two bozos on the Lighthouse Cove Homeowners Association board are determined to fine Howie Wynne big bucks for spreading red mulch in his flowerbed.

I imagine Carrie and Ernie would have an even bigger hissy fit had Howie installed black mulch, thinking it might be a Black Mulch Matters statement.

*Keep quiet. I'm here as a Welch HOA Management security consultant. Mulch color isn't a crime. Nonetheless, I've heard Ted's spiel on HOA fines and due process. An offense must be defined and publicized before a fine can be levied. And owners are entitled to a hearing to present their case.*

*Be patient. Surely another board member will object to Ernie's and Carrie's tirade.*

1

Keeping my lips zipped offers a secondary benefit. No deep breaths to inhale the mold-scented odor of the basement conference room. Lighthouse Cove is one of the South Carolina Lowcountry's many posh residential/resort enclaves. It boasts a championship golf course, swimming pools, tennis and pickleball courts, a fitness center, and other amenities. Yet, despite the HOA's deep pockets, its mold problem persists. If it's not solved soon, Ted suspects they'll tear down the fancy clubhouse and start over.

Usually, the board gathers upstairs, but the building's main floor is reserved for a golden anniversary wingding tonight. To ensure no one messes with the fancy decorations, even the HOA directors have been banished to the basement.

BAM! BAM! BAM!

*Oh, my God! Gunfire.*

"Everyone, get in the bathroom." As I leap up, my rolling chair crashes against the wall. The directors' eyes widen, and their mouths hang open. But their derrieres stay glued to their seats.

"Go. Go. Now! It's the safest place. Lock the door. Call 911," I order. "Tell them there's an active shooter. I'll guard the stairs and the door."

Ernie leaps up and scurries toward the outside patio. "No way I'm locking myself in a bathroom. I'm getting out while the getting's good. Y'all can listen to Miss Pretend Annie Oakley. Not me."

*Argh. Don't raise your voice. Project calm authority.*

"What if there's a shooter outside? I can't protect you out there. Only two ways to get inside the basement—the stairs and that back patio door. I can cover both."

To punctuate my promise, I extract my Glock from the pocket holster inside my purse. The holster ensures I don't accidentally put a hole in my foot while grabbing my Chapstick. A Glock doesn't have an external safety.

Olivia grabs Ernie's arm. "Don't be an idiot. Get in the damn bathroom. Kylee Kane is retired military. She knows a lot more about these situations than you. You own TV stations and a manufacturing company that churns out adult diapers. Not exactly combat training."

Ernie glares at Olivia, his sworn enemy where HOA rules are concerned.

2

Olivia is one of the three directors who feel colored mulch isn't a heretical, fine-worthy offense. Ernie's beady eyes narrow to a squint as he looks my way. "You better be right."

*Or what? You'll haunt me from the grave.*

BAM! BAM! BAM!

Three rapid shots. Gunfire does a terrific job of focusing the mind. Ernie and Olivia sprint to join their fellow directors in the bathroom. The door snicks shut; the lock clicks. Good.

*What in heaven's name is happening?*

I slip into a corner, back to the wall, gun ready. My gaze darts between the stairs and the patio door, covering both entrances. My pulse shifts into overdrive. I breathe deep; hold it for a count of three.

*Crap, I can practically taste the mold.*

BOOM! The whole building shudders. Not an explosion. A sharp, percussive crack. Wood splintering.

*Good grief, they've breached the front door. A battering ram?*

Heavy boots, a herd of them, vibrate the ceiling.

*Armed intruders? What in blazes?*

"This is the police! Put down your weapons! Show yourselves. Hands up."

The bellowed orders issued from a bullhorn. SWAT?

My brain stutters, beyond confusion. How could the police—let alone some flavor of SWAT—arrive within seconds of a 911 call? Could this be a trick? Anybody can claim to be "the police."

Yet, why would terrorists or armed robbers target a clubhouse where party favors and a couple cases of cheap champagne are the only booty? Well, unless someone thinks five Medicare-eligible directors and yours truly would make valuable hostages.

Overhead, footfalls cascade into a waterfall of sound. Shouts of "Clear!... Clear!" erupt every few seconds.

*If robbers or fanatics are masquerading as police, they're doing a bang-up job.*

The clomp of heavy boots echoes in the stairwell. Someone's headed

3

downstairs.

*Time to decide.*

I go with my hunch. The SWAT team's the real deal.

I summon my former Coast Guard command voice that Mom claims could wake the dead. "Don't shoot. There are no gunmen down here."

"Who are you?" the unseen SWAT leader demands from the stairwell.

"Kylee Kane, an HOA security consultant. When I heard shots, I told the directors to shelter in the bathroom. They're locked in. I'm alone."

"Are you armed?" he asks.

"Yes."

"Lay on the floor. Leave the gun in sight and out of your reach."

The drumbeat of boots signals the leader's arrival, and his buddies will join him in seconds.

"Understood," I holler back as I stretch prone and send my Glock skittering across the tile floor.

My face plant makes it tough to discern much about the officer who appears in my peripheral vision. The body shield he's carrying only allows glimpses of the man behind it. But he's definitely super-sized and has me clearly in the sights of the Glock peeking around the side of the large shield. A helmet and body armor hide all other details. He looks costumed to appear in a dystopian movie scripted with a dim view of mankind's future.

The Beaufort County Sheriff's Office insignia is emblazoned on the shield.

I should have known. Who else but the Sheriff's Office could field a local SWAT team? I groan.

*If my name's relayed to the Sheriff's Office, the acting sheriff will ID me as a public enemy.*

Two officers decked out in matching SWAT paraphernalia loom beyond the glass patio door. I lift my head enough to yell, "That door's unlocked."

No need to smash the glass. The brawny officers practically collide as they rush inside. I twist my neck to look back at the leader.

"Five board members are crammed in the bathroom and can't see what's going on," I comment. "All the yelling must be scaring the bejeesus out of them."

"They should be scared," he answers. "You should be, too."

"If you didn't find a shooter upstairs or outside, whoever fired the shots is gone. The directors are frightened seniors sandwiched in a one-holer restroom. Please tell them it's safe to come out."

"First, let's see your ID," the leader demands. "John, secure her weapon, and see if it's been fired." The leader never takes his eyes or pistol off me. "Need to make certain you aren't the shooter."

"My ID's in that black purse on the conference table."

He checks it.

"Can I get up now?"

"Yeah, but slowly. You say your name's Kylee Kane. I've heard of you."

*Crapola. He's probably one of Nick Ibsen's buddies.*

I levitate to something resembling a downward dog yoga pose, teetering on hands and knees, when Olivia bursts from the bathroom. The door bangs against a metal shelf, sounding like another gunshot. The SWAT leader's Glock swings up. Automatic reflex.

Olivia flings her pudgy arms above her head. "For God's sake, don't shoot. I had to come out. I think Carrie's having a heart attack."

"Keep watch," the leader tells his officers.

He lifts his helmet visor, lays down his heavy shield and gun, and heads for the bathroom. I scramble the rest of the way upright and follow.

"We put her on the toilet," Olivia explains, "only place to sit. Carrie's complaining of intense chest pains."

"Everyone else out of the bathroom," the officer orders. "You," he lasers me with a stern look, "come with me. The woman knows you. Help me move her into the conference room."

Carrie isn't a fan of Welch HOA Management, my employer, or me, but I don't argue with the deputy's logic. Negotiating the narrow doorways will pose enough challenges in extricating Carrie.

The woman's face is pasty-white, and beads of sweat dot her forehead. Smeared mascara clumps in black smudges beneath her eyes.

Yikes. And I thought she looked like a witch before.

*Not nice. The woman may be a pain, but now, she's in pain.*

5

Mr. SWAT and I drape Carrie's arms around our shoulders. Because the deputy is at least half a foot taller than my five-foot-seven, he stoops as we perform a shuffle duet, turning sideways to get through each door. When we deposit Carrie in a chair, her body oozes in a boneless melt, and her moans grow louder. Olivia holds her hand and whispers, "Hold on, dear. Help's coming."

"Call EMS," the SWAT leader barks at his men. "We need an ambulance. Tell 'em to bring a stretcher in through the basement door."

"What about the shooter?" Ernie's angry voice interrupts. He's huddled in the corner of the room farthest from the stairs and patio door.

"Your job is to keep us safe," he protests. "A crazed killer's hiding somewhere. Bring in more people, and the gunman can take advantage of the chaos to murder us all."

*Ten minutes ago, Carrie was Ernie's esteemed ally. Now, improving her chance of survival is the last thing on his mind.*

"You're safe," the leader snaps. "We searched the building and perimeter. There is no shooter."

Ernie glares at him. "You saying that gunfire we heard was a group hallucination?"

Before the leader can answer, two new SWAT officers enter from the stairwell.

"Think we discovered our *shooter*," one says, holding up a digital recorder. "We knocked down the door seconds after we heard the final shot, and there was nobody home. Looks like we were hoodwinked."

A siren's wail halts the speculation. In the moments that follow, EMTs lift Carrie onto a stretcher, give her aspirin, and check her blood pressure and oxygen level.

A woman EMT smiles and pats Carrie's scrawny arm. "Don't you worry, sweetie. You'll be at Beaufort Memorial Hospital before you know it."

After the EMTs whisk Carrie off, the tension in the room drops. Emotional exhaustion quickly defeats the group's adrenaline spike.

"I'd sure like to know if that gunfire was real or recorded," I begin. "Can you play whatever's on the tape?"

The SWAT leader shrugs. "Why not. By the way, I'm Deputy Owens. Deputy Pike's the fellow holding the recorder. Put it on the table, Pike. You're wearing gloves. No harm mashing some buttons."

The remaining board members and I shuffle toward the table. No one makes a sound. We barely dare to breathe. It is so quiet I imagine I could hear dust bunnies doing a dance routine.

The deputy hits "Play."

BAM! BAM! BAM! Then silence.

Deputy Pike fast forwards. BAM! BAM! BAM!

"A damn sick joke." Deputy Owens doesn't disguise his disgust. "If you folks had panicked, somebody might have been killed. As it is, that lady may have suffered a heart attack."

I frown. "Have you dealt with a hoax like this before?"

He sighs. "No. But swatter incidents are increasing across the country. Figured it would happen here, too. People call 911 and claim there's an active shooter."

"Surely, a well-trained SWAT team wouldn't just break down doors because someone makes a phone call." Ernie's innuendo isn't lost on anyone.

"No." Owens glares at Ernie. "But we do just that when there are exigent circumstances—like hearing gunshots inside a building. That's what happened today. If we wait, people can die."

"Did the caller give a name?" I ask.

"Yeah, said he was Ernie Baker."

"What!" Ernie explodes. "That's me."

Owens raises a beefy palm to silence him. "Let me finish. Let me finish. The caller claimed he was hiding inside the Lighthouse Cove Clubhouse. The signal told us the call originated in or very near the building. He said a killer was hunting down and murdering everyone trapped inside. We broke down the door when we heard shots. They sure sounded real."

"Howie Wynne did this." Ernie states his opinion like it's proven fact. "You need to arrest him. He knew Carrie and I planned to recommend the board hit him with a two-hundred-dollar fine for his ghastly red mulch."

"You have to be joking." Olivia snorts. "I know Howie. No way he'd pull a stunt like this. He'd never endanger others."

"It's him," Ernie insists. "No other violations were on the agenda. Remember how Howie retaliated when we chastised him for not edging the lawn next to his curb? This is just escalation."

I almost smile at Ernie's reminder of Howie's last—perfectly legal—up-yours response. He'd edged his lawn, then positioned a flock of thirteen pink plastic flamingos in his front yard. Lighthouse Cove covenants and rules are silent on the subject of yard art. I'm with Olivia. I doubt Howie's behind this. But whoever is, it's no laughing matter.

"We'll find out who did this," Deputy Owens promises. "And, when we do, the District Attorney will prosecute. Reckless endangerment. False reporting. He'll get real jail time. Especially if that lady the EMTs whisked to the hospital dies."

# Chapter Two

## The Leader

### *Saturday Afternoon*

To show off its proximity to the Atlantic Ocean, Lighthouse Cove built a hill to elevate the eighteenth golf tee. Too bad I have zero interest in the view of sandy beaches and glittering water. All I care about is what's happening—or rather, what's not happening—at the clubhouse.

*Hurry up! What's taking so long?*

Knowing when the raid would start, I insisted on a late tee time. I wanted to be on the back nine and close enough to hear, if not see, the action. Since those slowpokes let us play through, I fear we'll finish before the clubhouse show starts.

The commotion begins as my fraternity brother balances his ball on the tee.

"What on earth?" Sam's attention is riveted on the swarming SWAT team. His drive is totally forgotten, though if he misses the fairway, it's likely to cost him our hundred-dollar side bet. An unexpected bonus.

Once the club's front door is breached with a wood-splintering crash, shouts of "Clear...Clear!" ring out. The empty entranceway funnels the interior soundtrack outside, making it easy to follow the SWAT group's progress.

While the urge to chuckle is strong, I attempt to contort my features to appear shocked rather than gleeful.

The audible portion of the raid tails off as all but a few tactical-gear stragglers disappear inside. Wish I could see Ernie's face. Hope the blowhard pisses his pants. A big talker when tearing other people down and exposing their secrets, Ernie's a cowardly bully at heart.

Sam and I continue to watch as a few officers mill about the clubhouse exterior. I turn to Sam. "Whatever happened, the excitement appears to be over. Let's finish our game. Maybe someone in the golf shop can fill us in."

Sam nods and waggles his driver. His shot sails left and disappears in a palm tree and doesn't come out. Not the first time I've seen a palm eat a golf ball. Sam tees off again. He's lost our bet. Ought to use my winnings to reward my crew. Of course, they'd be horrified to learn I was golfing with a trust-fund buddy whose daddy owns a military weapons contractor.

I stripe my drive down the center of the fairway. Perfect.

As we finish putting, an ambulance speeds down a service driveway to the rear of the clubhouse.

My mental gloating ends. Did Matt or Jacob screw up? I made sure Ryan—the weakest link—stayed outside Lighthouse Cove. Assigned him to drive the getaway car. Of course, if Matt and Jacob followed my instructions, the getaway should have been a leisurely affair, completed long before the SWAT team arrived.

*Did something go wrong?*

I justified this exercise as a way to judge SWAT capabilities and response times. I lied. An unnecessary risk, especially with so much riding on what happens tomorrow.

Once we're inside the golf shop, I consider excusing myself to call Matt from the privacy of a bathroom stall.

*No. Don't be an idiot.*

Keep your nerve. Stay cool.

A stray thought worms into my brain. Maybe the ambulance was for Ernie. A heart attack?

I almost smile before I realize that would be a setback, not a gift. Ernie could survive a heart attack. I need him on the party boat tomorrow. I want his likelihood of survival to be nil.

# Chapter Three

Kylee

*Saturday Evening*

"About time you got here," Mom scolds. "Ted and Grant are practically faint from hunger waiting for your lazy behind."

I kiss Mom's cheek. "It's been one helluva day. Maybe you and my *boss* ought to hear what happened before I'm subjected to tongue lashings."

Ted peers around the wall that separates Mom's kitchen from the entry hall.

"What?" He smiles. "Did Carrie and Ernie want surveillance cameras installed in club bathrooms to catch nicotine addicts sneaking smokes?"

I shake my head and walk toward the kitchen. "No, last I saw Carrie, she was being carried out on a stretcher by the EMTs. Didn't you get my text?"

"No." Ted's smile disappears. "After Grant and I went for a run, we soaked in the club's Jacuzzi. Haven't looked at my phone since. What happened?"

"Did board members start duking it out?" Grant asks.

I give Ted's nineteen-year-old son a fierce hug. "So good to see you, Grant. No fisticuffs. I'll tell all over dinner. Ted should definitely reward his security consultant—me—with hazard pay for that meeting."

I'm working—temporarily—for Welch HOA Management. The owner, Ted Welch, was my late brother's best friend. The Kane and Welch families are related by geography, not blood. Ted was nine years old when his mother died, and Mom took him under her wing. She loves Ted as much as any flesh-and-blood son. Grant calls Mom "Grandma" and me "Aunt Kylee."

The family history makes Ted's and my newly-minted relationship … complicated. We haven't quite figured out how or when to share the news with Mom or tell Grant that Aunt Kylee is now his divorced dad's lover.

I'm helping Ted with security until his Lowcountry HOA clients become a little less skittish. Nothing like homicides and assaults in well-to-do HOAs to make homeowners nervous and testy. True, the crafty killer, who terrorized multiple South Carolina communities this fall, is now locked behind bars. But you can't turn off fear like a water faucet.

We queue up next to the stove, plates in hand, for Mom to dish out oversized portions of her chicken divan casserole—a one-dish meal. Then we take our usual seats at her cozy kitchen table. Since Dad died, Mom only uses the formal dining room when there are too many people to crowd around the kitchen table. I never host family dinners since Mom claims she gets seasick just looking at the boat I call home.

"So, spill," Mom commands.

With occasional pauses to wolf down chicken divan, I fill in my dining companions on my SWAT adventure. I'm relieved that my *boss* doesn't second-guess any of my actions.

I know it's an absolutely horrid idea to work for someone you sleep with. Lovers should limit potential territorial disputes to the equitable distribution of bed sheets. No point inviting work-related stress into a relationship. In my defense, the employee-boss part of our relationship came before I had an inkling we'd ever share sheets.

Grant, who's home for Thanksgiving break, jumps up to clear the table. No doubt the freshman cadet is eager to dish up Mom's carrot cake.

The doorbell rings.

"You expecting someone?" I ask Mom.

She shakes her head. "You're closest. Go see who it is."

I spot Nick Ibsen's hateful puss through the glass sidelight. I'm tempted not to answer the door. But, given that Ted's and my cars are in the driveway,

Ibsen might just use a battering ram if there's no answer. I take a deep breath, remembering he's not Deputy Ibsen anymore and is serving as acting sheriff until a special election can be held.

*Don't let him push your buttons. Stay cool.*

I open the door.

Before I can utter word one, Ibsen says, "Carrie Sullivan is dead." Then he delivers his verbal left hook. "And I firmly believe your actions were a contributing factor."

"What?" I'm flabbergasted. "Carrie's dead?"

It takes me a second to process the rest of Ibsen's accusation.

"I'm sorry Carrie's dead. But how can you possibly blame me for her heart attack?"

"Do you deny ordering five panicked seniors to crowd into a claustrophobic bathroom?" Ibsen brings his face inches from mine. "Those elderly folks were blind to what was happening, convinced they would die. A wonder more of them didn't have heart attacks. Yes, I blame you, and I've already told Ms. Sullivan's loved ones they should sue you."

"You're kidding, right? I went by the book for an active-shooter situation. Got people in the safest space available. Anyone with a brain would have done the same thing."

Ted's hand clamps my shoulder and exerts serious pressure to short-circuit my diatribe. "Deputy Ibsen, do you have a warrant? Are you here to arrest anyone? If not, you are not welcome. Get out."

"It's Sheriff Ibsen, to you," the bad news messenger snaps as he engages Ted in a glaring contest. Then, Ibsen does an about-face and heads to his SUV. He's left the roof lights pulsing to punch up the drama for Mom's neighbors.

The lawman swivels around to face us for his parting shot. "Imagine the lawsuit will include Welch HOA Management. Kylee Kane attended that meeting on your behalf, right, Teddy?"

Ibsen's smug smile makes me want to run down the drive and kick him where the sun doesn't shine. It won't cost the acting sheriff a penny to stir up legal trouble for Ted's company and me.

Grant has momentarily abandoned his carrot cake quest to join us at the door.

"Wow," he says. "That guy hates you two. Makes no bones about it. Guess he's still peeved you showed him up by catching that killer."

I turn toward Ted to judge his reaction. Grant's right, of course. We embarrassed then Deputy Ibsen by collaring a clever serial killer he swore was a figment of our imagination. Yet I know his hatred springs from a deeper, more personal well. I had a brief fling with Ibsen before discovering he was a misogynist dipshit. He didn't take my rejection well. Later, his assumption that I welcome Ted into my bed poked serious holes in his over-inflated ego.

"Hey, don't let that idiot ruin our dessert," Ted manages. "Go get the cake, Grant."

"Are you worried about a lawsuit, Ted?" Mom asks.

"Nope." He smiles and pats Mom's shoulder before he sits back down at the table. "Our company insurance covers us and anyone working on our behalf. Good protection against frivolous lawsuits. Not going to give Ibsen's temper tantrum another thought. It's Grant's vacation, and nothing's going to spoil it."

I applaud Ted's outward show of optimism. Yet his smile doesn't reach his eyes. We both know defending against a frivolous lawsuit costs money and can bump insurance renewal rates sky high. Even worse, you can win a case and still lose in the court of public opinion. Reputation is an HOA manager's most important asset.

# Chapter Four

## The Leader

### Sunday Morning

I wave at Matt as he enters the marina parking lot. He thinks I drove here. Actually, I walked over from my yacht. I reserved a slip a month ago. Reservations are a necessity around Thanksgiving. Seems like every yacht owner has a granny who lives in one of Hilton Head's upscale communities. I know. My maternal grandmother spent the last fifteen years of her life in Sea Pines.

"You'll find the Midnight Rum's spare key inside a purple koozie in the cupboard above the sink." I hand Matt a blue jacket and matching ball cap with the logo of a boat repair company.

"Keep the jacket on and pull the cap down to shade your face. The harbormaster's finished his morning check of slips to make sure no boats sank or disappeared overnight. The slips won't be checked again until nightfall. Just return the yacht before sundown, and it'll never be missed. The owner's staying at a relative's house in Bluffton until Friday."

"Got it." Matt grins and shakes his head. "Can't believe how easy it is to take a yacht for a joy ride. A lot simpler than boosting a Jaguar. Glad you found us a forty-five-footer. The bigger ones look tricky to maneuver in tight quarters."

"Don't worry." I motion toward the sound's calm waters. "You'll do fine.

Light winds all day. Just take it slow leaving the marina. I seriously doubt the harbormaster will radio you. But, if he does, say the Midnight Rum's owner asked you to take her for a sea trial to check recent repairs. Happens all the time."

Matt scans the busy marina. "Glad you know so much about boats and marinas."

I can tell he's dying to ask me how I know, but I've drilled the "no questions" mantra into the heads of all three of my worker-bees. They think it's to protect the group if anyone's caught. Not quite true. I just don't want them to learn who I am.

I squeeze Matt's shoulder. "Remember, the party boat will have a captain plus seven passengers aboard. Don't let anyone slip away. I'll meet you at the safe house after you return the Midnight Rum to her slip. Good luck."

# Chapter Five

Kylee

*Sunday Afternoon*

"Myrtle Kane, would you like to share?"

When the minister calls Mom's name, I squeeze her hand in support before she stands and walks to the front of the Hullis Island chapel. It's her turn to eulogize Gina, a down-the-block neighbor, friend, and frequent bridge partner.

The memorial service is packed, and Mom's the fourth person to share fond and often humorous memories of Gina, a classy lady I really liked. I should be thinking of her, but I'm not. I can't get Carrie's death out of my mind.

*Should I have done something else when the SWAT raid began?*

My rational mind says no. So, why do I feel responsible? Guilty?

I refocus on Mom and her tribute. I've accompanied Mom to three memorial services in the last year. Since private Hullis Island is heavily weighted toward retirees, the island flag, which is lowered to half-staff whenever a resident dies, droops way too many days.

Can't see much of Mom behind the lectern. Wish she'd put some weight back on and take it easier. Last year, I feared I'd be visiting her marker beside Dad's in the Hullis columbarium. A tough battle with breast cancer has transformed Mom's familiar soft curves into anatomical studies with her skeletal bones prominently on display.

Of course, if I voice any concern, Mom tells me to stuff it. Cancer did nothing to stifle her spirit or curb her willingness to share opinions.

Mom returns to her seat. "Nice job," I whisper. "Gina would be smiling."

Once the service ends, we hurry next door to the community center to dish up casseroles for the mourners. As I walk through the open breezeway, I glance at the sky. Despite a blanket of clouds, it's a nice, warm fall day. I envy Ted and Grant their hike in Pinckney Island National Wildlife Refuge. The Lowcountry offers so many amazing recreational options with its beaches, marshland, and maritime forests. Hope the weather's nice tomorrow for our sail.

As mourners pass through the buffet line, I hear way too much chatter about the SWAT raid at Lighthouse Cove. Spiraling gossip has transformed the incident into something just short of a nuclear detonation. One lady claims Carrie died after being trampled in the raid. Another speculates the "swatter" will target Hullis Island next.

"Good thing they don't realize you were there," Mom whispers. "You'd be a celebrity."

# Chapter Six

Kylee

*Monday Morning*

Grant looks sleepy as he comes aboard the River Rat, my thirty-eight-foot Island Packet. Makes me feel a bit guilty for insisting we depart at seven a.m.—sunrise. Since Grant spent the fall as a freshman cadet at the Citadel, I'm sure he'd have preferred to sleep in.

The sky is crystal clear. Yesterday's clouds are gone, and the warmth has vanished with them. A steady breeze makes the forty-two-degree temperature feel colder. The brisk weather whisks my fatigue away. Last night I mentally replayed the SWAT invasion and Ibsen's lawsuit threat ad nauseam. Didn't have a prayer of getting much sleep.

We all shiver a bit as I run down the basics of sailing the River Rat. Still, I'm glad I pushed for a dawn launch. The tide's going out and, as forecasted, a steady northwesterly wind is at our back. Looks like we'll exit the Beaufort River before boat traffic crowds the channel.

From the air, the aptly-named Lowcountry looks like someone scattered a land jigsaw puzzle onto a water canvas. Water—rivers, streams, estuaries, sounds—covers almost half of Beaufort County's nine-hundred square miles. By some counts, the county has more than three hundred islands. Owning a boat, as I do, open up a wealth of travel options. Today, I'll have Grant skirt deserted Spoonbill Island and head for open sea. That'll give him lots of variety.

"Grant, your sail is starting to luff," Ted comments.

"Don't forget to check the channel buoys," I remind.

Grant responds with good-natured eye rolls. "I'm used to hearing real pros bark orders." He laughs. "You two are rank amateurs."

Neither the early start nor our kibitzing seems to dampen Grant's fun. The handsome young man has Ted's thick black hair, hazel eyes, lean tall frame, and trademark grin.

The South Carolina Lowcountry's popularity as a Thanksgiving destination can translate into midday Intracoastal Waterway bottlenecks. Better if a first-time sailor isn't forced to play dodge boat with obese yachts or two-hundred horsepower fishing boats flitting about like annoying mosquitoes. Less traffic lets Grant focus on judging the wind and keeping the sails full.

Our first hour on the water flies by. Grant's doing great at the helm. The nineteen-year-old's concentrating hard, regularly checking the fluttering yarn telltales and ripples on the water for shifts in the breeze. He has a keen eye.

*Hmm. Wonder if he's noticed the new vibe between his dad and me.*

I glance at the cobalt sky. "Wish the sun would hurry up and climb high enough to warm us."

Ted hands me another cup of steaming coffee. "Lucky, you keep a twelve-cup coffee pot in the galley." The warm mug makes my hands feel downright toasty. I hold it next to my cheek.

"You weren't such a wuss when we were kids," Ted jokes. "Back then, you'd have ridiculed anyone who said a temperature in the mid-forties was cold."

I smile. Childhood was long ago. I'm fifty; Ted's forty-seven. A lot of years since we bare-handed snow and fired slushy ice balls at each other. A ritual whenever Keokuk, Iowa's first-of-the-year snowstorm arrived.

"Dad? Aunt Kylee? See those people hopping around and waving like mad. Should I sail closer?"

Grant points toward a beach on the southern tip of uninhabited Spoonbill Island. Situated near the Atlantic Ocean's two-mile entrance to deep Port

Royal Sound, the Spoonbill beach is a fragile, erosion-shifting ribbon, frequently battered by angry storms and high seas. The island's also an international lure for birders, since it's a migratory haven for many endangered species.

Grant's probably spotted a group of bird watchers. I pick up the binoculars I keep topside.

Six people. Three men, three women. Attempting pitiful jumping jacks to attract our attention. Their flailing white legs and arms are bare.

*Birders would dress more sensibly for an early morning outing.*

Behind them, gouges in the sand spell a giant SOS.

I hand the binoculars to Ted. "I don't see a boat anywhere. The skimpy clothes suggest they've been stranded since yesterday afternoon when it was in the mid-seventies. Wonder what happened."

Ted nods. "They're definitely frantic. Good grief, that pudgy guy on the left looks like Ernie Baker."

"Grant, head us into the wind. That'll make it easier to lower the sails," I say. "The fastest way to get to that beach is to motor over."

"Let Kylee take the wheel," Ted adds, "and help me look for sandbars. Don't want the keel to get stuck."

I bought the River Rat when I retired from the Coast Guard two years ago with dreams of exploring the Intracoastal Waterway's three-thousand-mile length. Life interrupted.

Aided by shouts from my sandbar watchers, I direct the River Rat on an ocean hopscotch toward the stranded beachcombers. Having sailed around Spoonbill Island at least a dozen times, I know these waters.

Once we're within shouting distance, I recognize Ernie, though fortunately, I'd never before been treated to a view of his flabby white belly. It flops as he slogs through the surf. He pauses when waves lap at his bare, pudgy knees.

"Thank God," he yells. "We've been here all night. About froze my nuts off. Can you get us off this god-forsaken island?"

Ernie raises a hand to shield his eyes from the rising sun, which has just cleared the horizon. He does a double-take. "Goddamn. Ted and Kylee?

What are you doing here?"

"Out for a morning sail," Ted answers. "How'd you get stranded, Ernie?"

"Son-of-a-bitch captain of some party boat deserted us."

*An argument? Given Ernie's personality, the idea's not a big stretch.*

"Go back to shore," I call to him. "I'll maneuver a little closer. Once we anchor, we'll ferry everyone to the boat in our dinghy."

As Ernie turns back to the beach, I lower my voice. "What are the odds?"

"Yeah, even before you had words with Ernie, we weren't buddy-buddy. The minute he became Lighthouse Cove's president, he started lobbying to dump us and hire a property manager who happens to advertise on his stations."

I smile. "Maybe saving Ernie's rather large, marooned ass will make you a little more popular with the prez."

My comment earns a snicker from Grant.

"I'll row over in the dinghy...alone," Ted says. "That'll let me ferry everyone over in two trips. Grant, you help hoist them into the River Rat."

"I'll get blankets and put on another pot of coffee before they get here," Grant offers as he heads below deck.

The dinghy slices through the surf as Ted's shoulders and arms move in a swift rhythm. Three women awkwardly straddle the gunnels to climb inside. Behind them, I notice the charcoaled remnants of a driftwood fire. Someone must have had a lighter or watched Tom Hanks in *Castaway*.

*Bet Ernie wasn't happy the ladies got the first ride.*

As soon as the dinghy arrives, Grant hustles topside to help lift the shivering women into the boat. I wrap blankets around their shoulders.

"I'm Kylee Kane. Welcome aboard. Go below deck to get out of the wind and claim a cup of hot coffee."

Teeth chattering, the women offer curt thanks as they clumsily shamble across the rolling deck. Only Diane, a beefy middle-aged woman, bothers to introduce herself. Her companions just mutter to themselves. "Damn, I'm cold."..."Last boat ride I ever take."

None of the women appears seriously ill. For a moment, I consider holding my hot coffee hostage while I play twenty questions. Instead, I keep my eye on the dinghy as Ted rows the male castaways to safety. Better believe I'll press for details later. If the party boat captain is licensed and deliberately stranded people, he'll pay a price.

Ernie is the first of the three men to heave his bulk into the River Rat. He waves Grant's offered hand aside, grunting as he gracelessly spills into the boat.

*Time for answers.*

I pull him off to the side while Grant helps the next man aboard. "Ernie, how did your party get stranded?"

He shakes his head, and his jowls jiggle. "That asswipe Ken Taylor invited us on a relaxing Sunday cruise. Basically, he trapped us in a confined space and forced us to listen to his pitch. Wanted investors or, failing that, he hoped we'd endorse his grand plans for Spoonbill Island. I said I wanted to go ashore and look for shells. Don't give a damn about shells. Just sick of his verbal spam. Barb, my wife, and two other couples jumped on my suggestion. The rest of the party sailed off. Captain said he'd be back in half an hour. Bastard never returned."

I give Ernie a withering look. "Since we don't know what happened to that boat, you folks may be the lucky ones. Can you describe the boat?"

Ernie returns my black look with interest. He's acting like a spoiled toddler...again. The boat could have capsized or sunk.

"Taylor chartered the party boat," he snaps. "We left from the Hullis Island Marina. The captain's name is Billy something."

"Billy Stubbs?" The name's a gut punch. "Was the boat the Hullis Hussy?"

My mind flashes on an image of the affable captain grinning as he greets local students for one of his pro bono environmental discovery cruises.

"Yeah, the Hullis Hussy, that's right."

"How many people were left on board besides Taylor and the captain?"

"Three other couples."

Ted joins us. "Grant's getting everyone settled below deck," he says. "I understand these folks left from the Hullis marina. Should we head back there now?"

"Not yet," I answer. "They were aboard the Hullis Hussy. The captain's an experienced, licensed charter captain. No way Billy'd leave folks stranded on a beach. If he'd had boat trouble, Billy would have made a Mayday call. Something's wrong."

I scan the calm sea. No storm to blame for a disappearance. "I'll call the Coast Guard to report the missing boat. Then we can do a quick search around Spoonbill Island until the Coast Guard arrives. They'll want to speak with our passengers."

"You saying you won't take us back until the Coast Guard shows up?" Ernie's voice shakes with anger.

"Don't worry. It won't take long. It's warmer below deck, and Grant's pouring hot coffee."

"Not the drink I have in mind." Ernie looks to Ted to veto my plan.

"It's warmer below," Ted suggests before Ernie wheedles any more.

Ernie's eyes narrow, and his jaw seesaws like he's going to say something. He doesn't. Just stomps away.

Once he's out of earshot, I whisper, "Bet Ernie's going to redouble his efforts to fire Welch HOA Management."

Ted smiles. "When Ernie was elected, I didn't realize he was *the* Ernie Baker, behind a coastal media empire. Of course, he made sure everyone knew at the first board meeting. I'd have resigned by now if it weren't for fervent pleas from three of his fellow board members."

I shake my head. Ernie's talk radio network, podcasts, and cable TV stations take pride in being the first to air every crackpot theory that comes along. Conspiracy connoisseurs. His company's also a big supporter of Nick Ibsen's election campaign.

"Wish you'd clued me in about Ernie's identify before yesterday. 'Course, if you had, I might have encouraged him to run for it when SWAT arrived."

25

# Chapter Seven

Kylee

*Monday Morning*

Ted and I stay topside as we cruise around the tip of Spoonbill Island. In less than ten minutes, we spot the Hullis Hussy anchored in a protected cove.

As we approach the party boat, I yell. "Captain Billy, can you hear us?"

No answer. Wind and waves provide a muted white-noise soundtrack.

Ted and I share a look. "Please don't let us find another dead body," I mutter.

"Amen," Ted replies.

As I edge alongside the ghost boat, our male castaways come topside.

"We heard you yell," Ernie says. "What's happening?"

When the men spot the bobbing Hullis Hussy, their mouths gape open.

Ted uses a grappling hook to cozy up close enough to tie off as I drop a couple of protective fenders over the side. Waves gently rock us, and the two boats thump together in a soft rhythm. I can't see a soul. The party boat looks more like a barge than a ferry or a yacht. The Hullis Hussy's designed to give passengers sunny—or moonlit—cruises on pleasant, calm outings. No below-deck quarters. A head and a small captain's cabin are the only fully enclosed structures.

"You're better at controlling the boat if the wind comes up," Ted says. "I'll hop over and check things out."

I nod and root around for the gloves I keep for working with palm-shredding lines. "Here." I toss them to Ted. "Gloves might be a good idea."

Having looked into my share of boating accidents—and fatalities—I know the Coast Guard will thoroughly investigate whatever the hell this is.

*Please, not multiple fatalities.* Though I can't conjure up an alternate scenario that would keep Billy from using his radio.

Ted dons the gloves and hops from the River Rat to Billy's charter. I bite my lip, waiting for his verdict.

"The cabin's empty," Ted calls. "Bathroom, too. No sign of a struggle, no blood. Wherever they went, they took everything with them—jackets, sunglasses, purses."

*A ghost boat.*

"Try using the radio. See if it's working."

A few seconds later, the River Rat's radio crackles as Ted demonstrates the one on Billy's boat is functioning.

I radio the Coast Guard.

What the hell happened? If Ernie's passenger count is correct, Billy and seven more people have vanished into thin air—or the deep blue sea.

* * *

The approaching Coast Guard cutter Oakum is out of Tybee Island, part of the Charleston district, my last duty post. *Wonder if I know the CO?* Duty postings change every couple of years. Doesn't really matter. Any commanding officer will order a search-and-rescue operation.

The cutter slowly approaches our two-boat flotilla, and I recognize Captain Harvey Reed. Seeing the competent officer's face loosens a knot in my stomach. He acknowledges me and salutes.

"Permission to come aboard, Captain Kane?"

"No need to salute." I smile. "I'm just Kylee Kane these days. Glad you were in the area. Didn't know who would respond."

Reed sends a team to search the abandoned boat, then asks, "What can you tell me?"

Ernie interrupts. "Hey, you two can jabber all you want *after* someone takes us to civilization. We're cold and hungry, and I have business to attend to."

"Quiet," Reed barks. "I'm speaking with Captain Kane." While the rebuke and stern look temporarily silence Ernie, the man's scowl says his trap won't stay shut for long.

The Oakum's captain takes my arm and walks me out of eavesdropping range.

"A party boat's not a promising prize for pirates," Reed begins. "People don't take a lot of cash and valuables on an afternoon cruise."

"Agreed." I share what I know about the Hullis Hussy and Billy Stubbs. "The captain's a retired Navy officer and doting grandfather. Not some drug smuggler or on-the-water coyote. I can't imagine what happened."

Reed nods. "Assuming you're right and this isn't drug dealers or human traffickers fighting over territory, what happened? Innocents in the wrong place at the wrong time?"

His suggestion chills me. Ocean-faring crooks have zero qualms about "disappearing" accidental witnesses of drug exchanges, human trafficking, or toxic waste dumps. They dispose of their victims by feeding the fish.

"It's possible. But Port Royal Sound seems an unlikely smuggling route. Too many recreational boats with potential witnesses."

Captain Reed frowns. "Could be they're using small fishing boats to ferry drugs, illegals, or weapons. Hiding in plain sight."

Hadn't considered that. "Maybe. But why use Spoonbill Island as a rendezvous or drop site? There's no land access. A second boat would need to transfer any cargo that's dropped, doubling the risk of being caught unloading and loading merchandise."

"Could be people on the party boat witnessed something unplanned," Reed replies. "A smuggler getting rid of a dead body? A trafficked woman screaming for help?"

One of the Coasties tasked with searching the Hullis Hussy approaches and salutes.

"What did you find?" Reed asks.

"No sign of a struggle or forced boarding, sir. The garbage container holds only what you'd expect, discarded food and drink, dirty paper plates, and plastic cups. And the radio's operational. Either the captain chose not to radio for help, or he was restrained from doing so."

Reed turns back to me. "I need to stay here to coordinate our search and rescue effort. Are any of the people you picked up seriously ill?"

"No," I reply. "Just hungry and chilled." I glance toward Ernie. "And some are quite cranky."

Reed looks over at the huddled trio of rescued men. "Did the boat leave from the Hullis Island Marina?"

"Yes, Billy always boards his passengers there."

"Okay. I'd appreciate it if you'd take them to Hullis. A Coast Guard investigator will meet you there. But, first, I need to find out who's missing."

Of course, makes it easier to identify any bodies that wash ashore.

I shudder. *Please don't let Billy and his passengers turn up as water-logged corpses.*

# Chapter Eight

Kylee

*Monday Morning*

Reed turns and walks toward the rescued men who stayed topside. "We're launching a search and rescue operation, and we need names and descriptions of the missing persons." He nods toward another Coast Guard officer. "After Lt. Johnson takes the information, Captain Kane will sail you to the Hullis Island Marina, where you'll be met by a Coast Guard investigator.

"Since there's no cellphone service out here, I realize you've been unable to let loved ones know you're safe. Once you regain a signal, please limit your calls to people who may be worried about you. We don't want to trigger a tsunami of rumors regarding the fate of your missing friends."

As Lt. Johnson starts jotting down the names the three men provide, Reed pulls me aside.

"Can someone else take the helm? I'd like you to get the survivors talking. See if you can gather some useful information while everything's fresh in their minds."

"Sure," I answer. "Ted can handle the boat."

\* \* \*

Once the River Rat is underway, I attempt to bond with the passengers. I'm hoping food will boost my popularity, though I'm quite sure even sweets won't win over sourpuss Ernie.

Grant handed out hot coffee, tea, and cocoa when the shivering castaways first boarded. Time for snacks. I scour my refrigerator and cupboards. Cheese, crackers, half a package of chocolate chip cookies, a family-size bag of potato chips, and one frozen Milky Way. Not much to feed the multitudes. My meager offerings disappear in one pass.

Diane's the first to quit munching and speak. "Kylee, let me introduce the folks you saved." She pats the arm of the man seated next to her. "This is my husband, Owen Farash, a retired radiologist. We retired to Pine Inlet in Bluffton four years ago. Glad to be here instead of Buffalo. It's probably thirty degrees colder where we raised our kids."

"Nice to meet you." Owen's bald head bobbles in greeting. His hatless dome and freckled scalp indicate he may have skipped some dermatology lectures in med school.

"You spoke with Ernie earlier. He's in the toilet," Diane continues, and waves toward a prissy woman with hair dyed an improbable henna shade. Her gray roots definitely need a touch-up. "This is Ernie's better half, Barb Baker."

I don't fault Barb's pinched smile. I'd have a hard time showing my gums, too, if I spent my days with Ernie.

"This is Phil Graham and his fiancée Ashley Vogt," Diane gushes.

Graham's manicured fingers massage the young woman's thigh near the cuff of her short shorts. I originally assumed Ashley was Phil's daughter. Glad I was wrong. The woman is much, much younger, closer to Grant's age than Phil's.

"Phil and Ashley are getting married next weekend in his gorgeous home in Jade Pointe," Diane continues.

Phil's jawline is firm, no sagging jowls. Cosmetic surgery? Men succumb, too. No matter how hard folks try to erase the signs of age, hands are mocking billboards. Phil's hands suggest he's closer to seventy than sixty. Buxom Ashley, on the other hand, hasn't escaped her twenties. A cuddle toy for old age?

Phil's silver eyebrows scrunch together as he focuses on me. Guess he's sorting through his mental index for the right card. "Kylee Kane, I've heard your name before." His expression brightens. "I know. You're the one who saved General Headley from some maniac. Hear the general's still in a coma. Wonder where that leaves ownership of his Jade Pointe estate."

Wish Phil hadn't brought up the harrowing showdown with a serial killer. Time to suggest a new topic.

"Sorry it's a little cramped in here. Never entertained so many people in my cabin. Were you all friends before the cruise?"

"No. Not everyone." Owen preempts his talkative wife. "Before we boarded, we only knew the Bakers by reputation. When we got our invite, we suggested the developer include the Ropers and Jacksons, if he had room for more HOA officers. We'd met them at Chamber functions and figured they'd be interested."

My breathing quickens. "I know a Cliff Jackson on Hullis Island and a Roger Roper who lives in Satin Sands. Are those the missing folks you mentioned?"

"Yes." Diane's upbeat tone sounds like I deserve a prize for correctly solving a social riddle. "Are they your friends, too?"

*Friends? Not exactly.*

Roger Roper is president of Satin Sands' HOA, and Cliff Jackson holds the same post on Hullis Island. Unfortunately, I know Ernie is the top honcho for the Lighthouse Cove community.

"How many of you are presidents of homeowner associations?" I ask.

"All of us." Phil's tone makes it sound as if I asked a really stupid question. "Each president brought a spouse or, in my case, my fiancée. Our host figured HOA presidents were good candidates to support Spoonbill Island development. Another exclusive international resort will boost all Beaufort County property values while spreading the tax burden. Who could object?"

Phil pauses. "I added the Sanfords to the guest list last-minute when I learned they'd returned from a trip to visit their children."

"What community do the Sanfords call home?" I ask.

"Dan and Lucille Sanford," Diane jumps in. "She's president of Crestway Plantation HOA. Nice to see a woman in the lead."

*Great. Three missing HOA presidents, and two are Ted's clients.*

Until a few weeks ago, all three of the missing HOA presidents would have been Welch HOA Management clients. That's before Roger Roper, Satin Sands' top honcho, gleefully fired Ted because his security consultant—me—dared critique his plan for twin electronic entrance gates.

Hope the Coast Guard quickly solves the ghost boat mystery and rescues Billy and the missing passengers. If not, their families and friends will be put through a living hell, and boaters, a superstitious lot, may think twice about entering a Beaufort version of the Bermuda Triangle.

I glance at Ernie and wonder what wild conspiracy theories his media empire will concoct. Given the HOA connection, homeowner communities will be primed to swallow whatever "alternative" facts Ernie's gelled-hair talk show hosts present. I don't envy Ted playing whack-a-mole as claims of alien abductions or secret Commie cells go viral.

I shudder, realizing Nick Ibsen, Beaufort's acting sheriff, will use the missing boat to gain exposure for his election campaign. I fervently wish Sheriff Conway hadn't decided to quit with two years left on his term. I understand it, though. Conway's wife was diagnosed with late-stage terminal cancer, and he wants to be by her side for the time that remains.

Since the Coast Guard works to maintain close relationships with local law enforcement, I'm certain the acting sheriff's been briefed.

I try to recall from the counterterrorism courses I've taken what circumstances might prompt the FBI to take over this investigation. Contrary to numerous thriller novels, the FBI isn't eager to take charge of a kidnapping case unless children are involved or there's a clear indication hostages were taken across state lines. Then, again, these people were snatched in U.S. territorial waters. Does that give the FBI jurisdiction?

Guess we'll find out shortly—if, indeed, this is a kidnapping. Even if the FBI takes charge, Ibsen will wiggle his way into the spotlight. He loves seeing his name in headlines even more than he hates me.

# Chapter Nine

Kylee

*Monday Morning*

Ernie keeps repeating there's no need to talk with another Coast Guard officer once we reach the Hullis marina. His constant carping is revising the group's reality. Instead of thanking blind luck they didn't vanish with their shipmates, they're bitching about talking with another Coast Guard officer when we dock.

Five minutes ago, the plump, loud-mouthed agitator slipped into the head for a third time. Does Ernie have diarrhea? One can hope. While I'm thankful for the quiet, Diane's fidgeting suggests she needs a bathroom break, too. Did Ernie fall in? Time to knock.

Before my knuckle raps wood, I hear Ernie's muffled voice.

Oh, crap. He's in the crapper on his cellphone, and he's not calling a loved one—if such a creature exists. We must have reentered a service area.

"Ernie, are you okay? I believe another passenger needs to use the facilities."

"I'm just dandy." His tone edges on swagger. "Be out in a second."

*Who did he call?*

I can't wait to reach the Hullis Marina so we can offload our human cargo, especially Ernie.

"Seems we have cellphone service again," I casually remark. "As Captain

Reed suggested, please limit your calls to family. Don't contribute rumors about the fate of your friends. You don't want to cause their loved ones unnecessary heartache."

My reminder has the same odds of success as Ernie deciding Howie's crimson mulch is A-Okay.

Phil's ingénue fiancée waves me over when Phil gets up to stretch his legs. "I told Phil we really must show our gratitude to you three good Samaritans. Something more personal than writing a check."

Ashley pauses and beams her full-wattage smile. "You're all invited to our wedding celebration. We reserved extra rooms at Jade Pointe Inn. I really want Ted, Grant, and you to join us for the weekend. Your formal invitation will have all the details."

*Wish she'd told Phil to write a check. Wedding extravaganzas aren't my thing. Be nice.*

*Ashley's actually sweet, and believes this is a special personal gesture.*

"Thank you, but Thanksgiving is Mom's favorite holiday. She's looking forward to spending time with Grant since his break from school is so short."

"Oh, no worries!" Ashley gushes. "The more the merrier. Bring your mother along. We've planned tons of fun activities, and the menus are to die for."

"You're very thoughtful. Let me see what Mom's planned. If we can't make it, I hope your wedding weekend goes perfectly."

Having brewed two more pots of coffee and dispensed every use-by-date-eligible morsel of comfort eats, I decide to give the passengers some privacy and me a little fresh air. Metal hinges creak as I lift the hatch. The freshening breeze is a welcome reprieve as I join Ted and Grant topside.

Ted glances my way. "How goes it below?"

"Ernie made a phone call while hiding out in the bathroom. Imagine he handed his TV and radio network a potentially viral exclusive. He flashed a big, gloating smirk when he swaggered out of the head."

Ted frowns. "Too bad. The Coast Guard should have a chance to break the news before the gossip goes viral."

Grant turns toward Ted. "Dad, were Ernie's stations the ones that blamed your company for the HOA murders this fall?"

"Yep, Nick Ibsen said only poor management could let HOA disputes reach the boiling point, and Ernie's on-air pundits endlessly parroted him."

"Wonder what Ernie's telling them to report this time?" I sigh. "Can't wait to hear how he theorizes his fellow passengers were captured without any sign of violence. I'm sure he'll come up with a humdinger."

Ted smiles at his son. "Grant's got that figured."

The young man grins. "I'd use a drone to deploy a paralyzing nerve gas. Once everyone's unconscious, I'd board the boat and haul off the unconscious bodies. Today's drones are quite capable of delivering that kind of payload."

I take a moment to let my imagination work through Grant's proposed scenario. Flying a drone is one of the young man's hobbies. Last summer, he captured spectacular aerial shots of HOA properties for Ted's website.

I nod. "Using a drone is feasible but risky. Wind's the first problem. An unexpected gust would disperse the nerve agent, leaving some or all targets unaffected. The second problem? How does the villain track the boat? Billy would notice another boat tailing him, looking for the right spot to launch a drone."

Grant chews his lip. "I'll concede wind could make things dicey. But the people on that party boat knew they'd be sailing around Spoonbill Island. They must have told friends. Probably bragged about the invite on Instagram or TikTok. Wouldn't take a genius to assume the party boat would hug the Spoonbill shoreline. Just anchor in a protected cove and wait for the party boat to come to him."

I smile. Grant's a smart cookie. "Using your logic, I'll propose a simpler strategy. The villain could have faked a boating emergency. Captain Billy wouldn't hesitate to motor over to help a boat in trouble."

Ted laughs. "Wouldn't Billy radio the Coast Guard the minute he saw a boat floundering? The Hullis Hussy's radio was working, and the Coast Guard would have come if they'd received a call."

"True." I raise my hands in surrender. "I'll wait for a few facts before I champion any new theory. I remain mystified."

Landmarks along the shore say we'll reach the Hullis Marina in ten minutes or less. The realization erases amusement at what-if theories. Some people are about to have their lives turned upside down. While Billy's a widower, his daughter, Katie, and young grandchildren live on Hullis. They'll be gobsmacked.

*Then again, they must be worried already.*

"I wonder if Billy's family reported him missing. When fourteen people fail to return from a Sunday afternoon cruise, you'd think someone would sound an alarm. I'm surprised no one was reported missing last night."

"That bugs me, too," Ted agrees. "Why didn't anyone notice Billy's slip was empty?"

Except for the captain and the outing's sponsor, all the passengers were accompanied by spouses or, in Phil's case, a fiancée. Who'd realize they were missing? No worried partners waiting for a front door to open. On a Sunday evening, they probably weren't no-shows for social outings. Even so, it's strange the empty boat slip didn't stir concern in the marina office.

*The Coast Guard should definitely talk with the marina staff.*

I suddenly realize Ted may not know some of the missing passengers are clients.

"Sorry, Ted. I've been so worried about Billy I forgot to tell you that Roger Roper, Cliff Jackson, and Lucille Sanford were on board when the Hullis Hussy sailed away from the beachcombers."

Ted's mouth falls open. "You're sure?"

"Who are they?" Grant asks.

"HOA presidents and clients—or former clients," Ted corrects.

"Are any of them celebrities or super rich?" Grant asks. "Would they be worth kidnapping?"

I seize the idea with a glimmer of hope. "Kidnapping sounds better than murder. If someone murdered those folks, they'd have left the corpses on the boat or dumped them in the sea. Why risk carting dead bodies away? Maybe they were kidnapped."

I turn toward Ted. "The Ropers and Jacksons don't seem to offer big ransom opportunities. How about the Sanfords?"

He shakes his head. "As far as I know, none of the missing couples seem like prime targets." He pauses. "Phil Graham and Ernie Baker are a different matter. Phil's a billionaire. While Ernie's wealth doesn't put him in Phil's league, his media network could probably raise money for a ransom—especially if it could spin his captors as evil, far-left terrorists."

He pauses and his eyebrows knit together. "They could have been after the developer," he adds. "I know next to nothing about Ken Taylor or the money behind his proposed resort."

"Taylor might be a prize for an environmental fringe group," I add. "Maybe someone's already claiming credit."

As we approach the marina, I spot a Coast Guard patrol boat in one of the transient slips.

"You want to dock?" Ted asks. "I remember you called me Captain Crunch after I plowed into a pier on my first attempt to dock the River Rat."

I smile. "Yeah, and we do have an audience."

I take the helm as Ted and Grant drop the River Rat's buoy fenders. A crowd has gathered in the parking lot beyond the pier. Reporters? Curiosity seekers? Family?

On the pier, a female Coast Guard officer's deep in discussion—arguing?—with a man. Can't see his face, just his waving arms. The Coastie moves to her right.

*Oh, hell. The acting sheriff is on the scene.* And, no doubt, creating a scene.

# Chapter Ten

The Leader

*Monday Morning*

J acob, Matt, and Ryan sport ear-to-ear grins.

*Can't let my anger show. They need to keep believing I'm a bad-ass mastermind dedicated to the cause.*

"Your plan was per…perfect." Ryan giggles like a schoolgirl. "Those fat cats didn't have a clue. Got…got 'em all without a struggle. Well, we did have to zaa…zap the boat captain once he cottoned on."

I want to yell. The idiots grabbed the wrong people. But it's my fault. I told them eight people would be on board, and they captured eight people. Imagine my surprise when I got a look at the captives and discovered Ernie Baker and Phil Graham—the only two I wanted—weren't there.

Questioning Ken Taylor, I learned he handed out last-minute invites to three couples. And Ernie and Phil jumped ship for a spur-of-the-moment shelling excursion. What are the freaking odds?

*Now what?*

My worker bees believe this kidnap operation is designed to gain headlines and start knee-capping the rich one-percenters, who hoard the nation's wealth. Can't have them start doubting. Too bad our captives are pretty much nobodies. A fact I've tried to finesse by revising the ransom note. Made HOAs rather than individuals the target.

The upside is Phil and Ernie must credit luck for sparing them from a random attack. As long as they're clueless, Phil will plow ahead with his reality-show wedding. Has to be eager to impress his big-tits, tight-assed young bride. And Ernie Baker's near the top of Phil's weekend guest list. That blowhard won't miss an opportunity to rub elbows with the beautiful people. Nobody will expect a ragtag Neuter1 group to strike again so soon.

*I have a second chance. Just need to conjure up a plan on the fly.*

I shouldn't have left the at-sea capture to three lugheads. If I'd been on board instead of establishing an alibi, I'd have scrubbed the operation the minute I realized Ernie and Phil weren't there.

"Can I send the text message now?"

Matt's question yanks me back from what might have been to what is.

I read the message to see if it needs additional HOA tweaks before Matt drives to Savannah and uses a burner phone to text the newsroom at Ernie's flagship TV station.

*We're Neuter1!*

*No longer will we wait for alt-right, white supremacists to rally around scumbag politicians, send thugs to beat up comrades of color, or rape our environment. We're going to neuter the one percent's hold on our people by going after their enablers—rich folks who write checks to dark-money political action committees. People who kowtow to the one percent, vainly hoping their offspring will someday join the anointed.*

*You gloat behind the gates of your exclusive compounds. Think your high-priced property can protect you from the people you help oppress? Wrong. Our hunt for fat-cat pigs has just begun. What becomes of the oppressors we captured depends on you. Time for your HOAs to renounce their collective sins and make reparations. You'll hear more soon.*

*Count on it.*

# Chapter Eleven

Kylee

*Monday, Noon*

I startle when Ted slips an arm around my waist. Focused on the pier and the crowd beyond, I didn't hear his approach. "A little jumpy, are we?" Ted whispers. "Something to do with the appearance of your favorite sheriff?"

"Could be. The man makes my skin crawl. What's he up to?"

Ted tilts his head in the direction of a TV camera crew elbowing its way toward the front of the parking lot crowd.

"No mystery," Ted observes. "It's a chance for Nick to get his mug on TV. He looks good till he opens his mouth."

Sadly true. Cameras love Nick's square-jawed, ruggedly-handsome face. After he left the Marines, he should have chosen modeling instead of law enforcement. His looks and ego would have made him famous hawking razors, hair gel, and condoms.

As Nick spots the River Rat, his cheeks grow redder; his jaw juts forward. A pulsing cord in his neck looks like it may pop through his skin.

*Fun and games. He might not have spotted me yet, but Nick knows the River Rat.*

During the brief period we dated, I took Nick for a sail. Once. He hated that I was in charge, telling him when to trim a sail or come about. Had I

41

been paying attention to more than his good looks, his attitude would have provided an early warning of his misogynist leanings.

When I dumped him, it shook Nick's worldview. He figured he set the terms for any relationship. If there was going to be dumping, he'd be the dumper, not the dumpee. For months after I bid him goodbye, Nick phoned me whenever he got tanked. Obscene suggestions and endearments like "bitch" and the "c" word peppered his sporadic calls.

A few months back, when Nick decided Ted and I might be lovers, he floated conspiracy theories to humiliate us and wreck the reputation of Ted's company. Now he's determined to get Carrie's relatives to sue me for shooing the woman into a bathroom when I heard gunfire.

*Be interesting to see how Nick'll try to cast Ted and me as the bad guys this time around.*

As we tie off, Grant goes below deck to help the passengers climb topside. I can't make out the words Nick is shouting at the Coast Guard officer. However, I'm pleased when she turns her back on him and briskly walks to the River Rat.

She salutes. "I'm Lieutenant Carter. Permission to come aboard?"

"Of course," I say, and we shake hands.

"Thank you, ma'am. It's an honor. Captain Reed told me you're a Coast Guard Academy alum, too. I can only imagine how tough it was for the first women cadets. Thank you for paving the way."

Her comment seems heartfelt, so I stuff my snarky reply. How many millennia ago does she think I graduated? I was in kindergarten when the academy admitted its first women cadets. My curly hair turned white at age thirty. Gives a first impression that I'm older and wiser than I am. Sometimes that's a blessing.

Lt. Carter is a knockout. A fit, curvy figure. Big brown eyes. A close-cropped Afro accentuates a perfectly-shaped head and long elegant neck. I swallow a laugh when Grant pops back on deck and practically face-plants, gaping at the lieutenant.

The newcomer—I'm guessing mid-twenties—has the nineteen-year-old's undivided attention. Maybe all Welch men have a thing for older women.

Lt. Carter clears her throat and steps forward as Grant helps the women passengers find firm footing on deck.

The male passengers are bunched in a tight group. They shuffle their feet and whisper, furtively glancing toward the lieutenant.

"I know you've had a traumatic experience. We will get you back to your homes as soon as we can," Lt. Carter says. "First, however, we need to ask a few more questions and get your contact information. If you'll follow—"

"This is ludicrous," Ernie snaps. "You're treating us like suspects. We were stranded on a beach when terrorists, pirates, or some other maniacs killed or kidnapped our friends. We didn't see shit. I refuse to be a captive a moment longer, and you best not argue."

He waves at the parking lot. "See that TV crew? Stacy Douglas works for me."

*Figures. Two peas in a pod, though Stacy is a much more attractive pea.*

Stacy is the confrontation queen. If the perky blonde TV reporter interviewed a nine-year-old selling Girl Scout cookies, she'd browbeat the child about promoting obesity. Of course, if the woman chats up anyone who espouses her cable station's right-wing philosophy, she fawns.

Ernie bulls past the lieutenant, and barks at his wife, "Barb, get over here right now."

*I should trip him.*

Owen Farash speaks up, and my fleeting opportunity to knock Ernie on his can disappears.

"Let them go," Owen says. "I'm sure we can answer all your questions."

"We'll come with you," Phil Graham adds. "Ernie's just being Ernie. Nothing to gain in making a scene."

Lt. Carter looks torn but makes no move to stop the Bakers from leaving.

*Smart lady. Ernie's probably hoping for a showy, don't-tread-on-me kerfuffle in front of the cameras.*

"Thank you," she says to the four passengers who remain. "We've arranged to use the marina office. This won't take long."

Lt. Carter turns toward me. "Captain Reed says he knows how to reach you. We'll call if we need anything else."

In the parking lot, Ernie Baker's arrival puts him center stage, and he's not shy about shouting his opinions.

"A wanton act of piracy in local waters left six of us perilously stranded on a deserted beach last night, and eight more Lowcountry residents are missing," he begins.

I glance at the lieutenant. "Want us to walk these folks over to the marina office so you can make a statement to the press."

"Yes, thanks." She smiles and hurries off the boat and onto the pier.

Ted turns to the four remaining passengers. "Follow me, if you're not keen on talking with reporters. The marina office isn't far, and Kylee, Grant, and I can block for you."

Phil nods. "Let's do it."

As Ted leads the way, the lieutenant's loud, clear voice commands attention, improving our odds of making it to the marina office unmolested.

"I would like to make an announcement on behalf of the Coast Guard," Lt. Carter says. "At 0800 hours today, the Coast Guard was notified the Hullis Hussy, a commercial boat licensed to carry up to twenty passengers and crew, failed to return to pick up six passengers who disembarked to collect shells on Spoonbill Island. The party boat left the Hullis marina Sunday at noon with the captain and thirteen adult passengers aboard.

"At 0830 hours today, the captain of the River Rat radioed the Coast Guard to report the Hullis Hussy had been found anchored in a Spoonbill Island cove with no one on board. We immediately launched an air and sea search for the missing passengers—"

"Have you found bodies?" Stacy yells. "Identified the pirates?"

The lieutenant ignores her. "At this time, we do not know what prompted the captain and his seven remaining passengers to abandon the boat. Meanwhile, our search and rescue efforts are continuing both on the water and in the air. We're hoping satellite imagery captured over the past twenty-four hours will help with the investigation."

Lt. Carter looks in our direction, and I give her an all-clear sign. Our wards are safely inside the marina offices.

"We have no other information at this time," the lieutenant concludes and turns on her heel to hurry our way.

"Thanks again," she whispers as we pass her on our return to the River Rat.

Ernie reclaims the spotlight.

"As soon as I could get a cell signal, I called Sheriff Ibsen," Ernie says. "I know we can trust him to move heaven and earth to find our friends and hunt down the terrorists who took them, undoubtedly thugs or extremist scum. I'm delighted to see he's already taking charge."

Stacy and her cameraman quickly shift and shove a microphone toward Nick.

"Sheriff Ibsen, what can you tell us about this horrific development? Do you think the missing people are in danger? Is this an act of high-seas piracy like we've witnessed in the Middle East?"

*Like Ibsen knows shit from shinola about high-seas piracy.*

"All the people who boarded that boat yesterday are Beaufort County citizens or visitors. On my orders, the Sheriff's Department has already launched an exhaustive investigation. As a former Marine, I know enemy sorties demand an immediate response. My first objective is to find out how the people aboard the River Rat just happened to find the people stranded on Spoonbill Island. I also want to know how they knew where to look for the abandoned party boat."

*Holy shit! The bastard's insinuating we're involved.*

We're back on board when Nick glares at the River Rat and starts strutting our way, the TV crew faithfully trailing him.

"Grant, untie us while I start the engine. We're not going to sit here and let Ibsen and his conspiracy theories aboard."

"You sure that's the right move?" Ted's calm voice doesn't lessen my ire.

"Even with sirens blaring, there's no way Nick can beat us to the Beaufort marina," I counter. "We can call our own press conference in Beaufort."

Ted frowns. "The press is here now. Nick will spin our hasty departure as evidence we're involved in some outrageous fantasy. He'll claim we ran off to gain time to make up a story. We might as well get this over with."

My shoulders slump. Ted's right. "Okay, let's make our conversation public. Grant, tell the press how the beachcombers grabbed your attention." I smile. "Wouldn't hurt to sneak in a mention that you're a Citadel cadet. The school's code of honor might boost our credibility."

As we exit the boat and step onto the pier, members of the press stampede our way. The reporter swarm temporarily shuffles Nick to the back of the pack.

Ted introduces us, and says, "We'll be happy to explain how we came to rescue the people on the Spoonbill shore. Grant?"

"Hi, I'm Grant Welch, home on Thanksgiving break from the Citadel, where I'm a cadet. My dad and aunt are teaching me to sail. We started early this morning, so I could practice tacking when there were fewer boats around."

Nick elbows his way to the front of the reporter scrum. The set of his jaw says he's furious. However, he knows better than to badger clean-cut, young Grant. Had it been Ted or me talking, he'd have ripped into us mid-sentence.

"I saw some people on the shore of Spoonbill Island doing jumping jacks to get our attention. Then I saw the big SOS in the sand."

"How did they get stranded?" Stacy calls out.

"They told us the captain of the Hullis Hussy was supposed to return for them in half an hour," I answer. "That was the last they saw of the rest of their party. We radioed the Coast Guard and cruised the Spoonbill coastline in search of the missing boat. When we found it, we contacted the Coast Guard again and waited for them to arrive."

"Nothing more to tell," Ted wraps up. "The commander of the Coast Guard cutter asked us to ferry the folks we rescued back to Hullis Island while they organized a search and rescue operation. We're happy we could help."

# Chapter Twelve

Kylee

*Monday Afternoon*

I'm famished. A mound of sizzling bacon within a fork's reach has me drooling. Can't imagine how vegans ignore bacon's siren-call scent. Not to mention the lure of fresh-from-the-bakery cinnamon sweet rolls practically oozing butter.

Grant carries a big skillet of scrambled eggs, the finishing touch, to Ted's dining room table.

"Dig in," Mom orders. "I know you must be hungry."

After leaving the Hullis marina, I phoned Mom to scrap our downtown lunch plans. She wasn't surprised.

"Been listening to the news," Mom commented. "Figured you wouldn't want half of Beaufort peppering you with questions between chews. Tell you what, I've got a key to Ted's fixer-upper, and figure he stocked his larder with Grant home. I'll whip something up. Have food on the table by the time you arrive."

"Bless you," I answered. "That means Grant can quit gnawing on the mast to quell his hunger pangs."

Thankful for Mom's home-cooked meal, I pile eggs and bacon on my plate and limit myself to one sweet roll. What discipline!

Grant snags three pastries. "Grandma Myrt, these are great," he manages

47

between bites. "I'm starved. Those people ate all of Aunt Kylee's food. Even the stale crackers and peanut butter."

Mom smiles at the young man she claims as a grandson. "Eat up. They're not feeding you enough at the Citadel. You're too thin. Need to put on a few more pounds."

"Speaking of food and splurging, I forgot to mention all four of us are invited to Phil and Ashley's wedding," I say. "Sounds like the celebration would offer Grant lots of opportunity to pack on more pounds. We could all stuff our faces with caviar—blech—and other exotics. Personally, I prefer turkey leftovers with Mom's gravy."

"Hold your horses," Mom says. "I can put those leftovers in a freezer. The society pages say this wedding celebration is gonna be waaaaaay over the top. I could entertain my friends with stories for months."

I groan. "Please, Ted and Grant, tell Mom she's the only one interested."

Ted's fork toys with the eggs on his plate. "Half the HOA presidents in the Lowcountry will be there. From a networking standpoint, it wouldn't be a bad thing. But Thanksgiving isn't about business.

"Grant, it's your vacation," Ted adds. "Would you want to go?"

"Fine with me, if we're all together." Grant laughs. "We can snicker and roll our eyes at the excess." He cuts a look my way. "Actually, I love caviar."

"Okay, okay." I succumb. "I'm outnumbered. Let's see if a formal invitation actually arrives. Phil may veto Ashley's impromptu invite. I get the feeling we're not among what Phil thinks of as his class of people."

Believing folks gathered around a dinner table should converse with each other, Mom normally enforces no cellphone, no TV, and no radio rules. Today, she's tuned Ted's radio to one of Ernie's talk stations. That spot on the dial has never been a pre-set in this house. She sees me eyeing the source of the soft background noise.

"I know it's against the rules, but I'm worried about Captain Billy," Mom explains, "I'm hoping a news bulletin will tell us the Coast Guard's found Billy—and the others, including Cliff and Peggy Jackson—safe and sound. Sure, Cliff called me everything but my given name after I sued the Hullis Island board. Doesn't mean I want him or Peggy to come to any harm."

"Did you get many calls from clients this morning, Myrt?" Ted asks.

After a key employee unexpectedly departed and left Ted short-handed, Mom started filling in four days a week. I fretted the schedule would wear her out. Her double mastectomy and chemo treatments aren't exactly distant memories. To my surprise, working the phones seems to boost my mother's energy and improve her mood.

No matter how old we are, it's nice to feel needed.

Mom grins. "At the start of the day, I handled the usual calls. Hysterical homeowners certain the world will end if their complaints aren't addressed instantly. Apparently, a bulldozer cut internet cable in Lighthouse Cove, and Becky couldn't connect to Facebook to find out what her friends ate for breakfast. Then, a Hullis Island newcomer demanded we get DNA samples from all the neighborhood dogs so we can finger the Fido pooping on his lawn.

"After thirty years of nursing, I can deal with all these namby-pambys. Tell 'em to take two aspirins and quit being a pain in the butt."

Mom laughs as she watches Ted's expression. "Just kidding, Hon. I pretend to care."

Her laughter dies quickly. "The calls changed after Robin told me the River Rat was making social media headlines. Didn't take long for clients to phone in, wanting the skinny on the ghost boat and the missing HOA honchos. I promised Welch HOA Management would keep them informed, though I stressed authorities were unlikely to tell us more than what they'd hear on the news."

The radio crackles with pretend ticker-tape clatter, signaling a news bulletin is about to air. Grant jumps up to boost the volume.

"Neuter1 terrorists are taking credit for the kidnapping of eight individuals who boarded a party boat at the Hullis Island Marina Sunday afternoon."

The newscaster's voice vibrates with excitement as he reads what he calls the "Neuter1 manifesto." The bulletin ends with the newsman's promise to stay on top of this "newest example of left-wing terrorism." He pauses, then adds, "It appears the terrorists could target more leaders of Lowcountry homeowner associations."

"Holy crap," I exclaim as Grant lowers the radio volume to a soft purr. "Neuter1? Really?"

Ted frowns. "The folks they kidnapped aren't members of the one percent. They're well off, but not mega-billionaires. Seems out of character for Neuter1. Yet crazies exist within both fringes of the political spectrum. Then, again, it could be a ruse. Wouldn't be the first time someone falsely credited a group with something it didn't do."

"I haven't heard of much Neuter1 activity in the Lowcountry," Grant adds. "And they're pretty unorganized. This kidnapping sounds too well planned."

"Whoever's behind this, I'm terrified for Billy and the other captors," Mom says. "Billy's no right-wing fascist. Why kidnap him? For that matter, the Jacksons aren't right-wingers either. True, they're ignoring Hullis Island's covenant voting requirements to greenlight a deer hunt, but if some group wants to punish right-wing politicos, they're off base. The bumper on the Jacksons' car still has Vote Clinton stickers."

Ted pushes his plate away. "Wonder what the kidnappers mean that the fate of the captives depends on HOA willingness to make amends and reparations. Do they think all HOAs are gated enclaves for the super-rich? Half of our clients are gateless, and the owners are solid middle-class.

"As soon as we finish eating, I need to head to the office. We're going to be flooded with calls from panicked homeowners. Especially given the implied threat that more HOA directors could have bulls-eyes painted on their backs."

He turns toward his son. "Sorry, Grant. I wanted us to spend the day together. Do lots of fun things."

Grant shrugs. "It's all-hands-on-deck, and cadets answer the call. Give me a little guidance, and I'll help with anything else you need."

"A family affair then," Mom says. "Of course, Kylee and I will help."

As usual, my mother volunteers me without asking if I have other plans. In this case, she's on terra firma. Helping Ted dismiss client fears about terrorists falls squarely within my security purview.

"Guess we'd better eat up," I say. "Have a feeling our workday will stretch into the evening hours."

# Chapter Thirteen

Kylee

*Monday Afternoon*

When we reach Ted's office, he huddles with Robin, the company's young IT wizard. He wants her to add a "News Update" section to the dozen HOA websites she manages. When, and if, there is good news to share, Ted wants to do it quickly.

While Robin works on the website, Grant will answer emails, monitor online HOA message boards, and keep an eye out for news and social media updates. Thank goodness, Grant's home. Online multitasking isn't part of my skill set.

Not sure answering phones is either. But flashing lights on all five office lines mean Mom and I are drafted. As I listen over and over to the same caller questions, I jot notes on ways to calm fears of Neuter1 vengeance against Lowcountry HOAs.

A hand grips my shoulder, and I look up.

"After you finish this call, we need to talk." Ted has a worried frown.

I hurry through my safety spiel and hang up.

Ted scoots a chair close to mine. "I just got off two disturbing phone calls. The Hullis Island board met—without their kidnapped president, of course. The four remaining directors said they didn't sign up to be kidnap targets and were resigning immediately. They drafted a resolution to transfer all policy and budget decisions to Welch HOA Management until the community elects new board members."

"Can they do that?" I ask. "Just resign en mass without appointing replacements?"

"No," Ted answers. "We are a management company. Our job is to manage the HOA according to policies and rules set by the board. While the directors aren't legally entitled to hand the mess over to us, that's what they've done. The deserters already sent a statement to owners and the press saying Welch HOA Management is now responsible for all decisions related to this attack and the Jacksons' welfare."

I roll my eyes. "I get it. They're scared. But it's unfair to put you in the hot seat when you aren't legally entitled to act without board approval."

Ted stands. "Tell me about it. The board members who abandon ship will be the first in line to sue us if we screw up."

Grant rolls his office chair in our direction. "Appears directors in different HOAs talk. Minutes after the Hullis Island board resigned, the Crestway Plantation directors did a copycat. Exact same statement except for the board member names. Guess you should add a new management service—negotiating with terrorists."

I shake my head. "There is one bright spot. Since Satin Sands terminated its contract with you, its board can't tag you to negotiate Roger Roper's release. You can thank me for irritating Roger enough to get you fired."

Grant chuckles. "Yeah, Aunt Kylee, prompting clients to fire Dad is a definite skill. Too bad you didn't irritate more HOA boards."

"Give me time," I mumble. "Never could keep my mouth shut if some SOB claims an entire community must accept his—or her—personal peccadillos as gospel."

"On the bright side, we won't have to sit through endless meetings with surly Hullis Island or Crestway Plantation directors," Ted snipes. "They've run for the hills. Hope those counterterrorism courses you took in the Coast Guard prove worthwhile, Kylee."

Mom clears her throat. I didn't realize she'd joined our circle.

"Ted, I know your code of honor won't let you shirk responsibility, but don't be a sucker. At the very least, cover your ass so ungrateful owners can't blame you after the fact for decisions they refused to make. Call Kay. Let's hear what a lawyer has to say."

# Chapter Fourteen

Kylee

*Monday Afternoon*

Kay Barrett is Mom's attorney and my best friend. We're single, independent women with decades of experience shrugging off chauvinistic snipes. While our professional careers could hardly have been more different, they spawned similar pet peeves. It didn't take us long to become fast friends after we met.

A year ago, the fifty-year-old attorney opted to shake up her life. She bought a B&B and quit accepting new legal business. However, old clients still count on her for help. In fact, Kay recently sued the Hullis Island HOA on Mom's behalf. That lawsuit paused the board's planned deer hunt in the island's nature sanctuary. A court has yet to decide if the directors exceeded their authority by making the decision without a community vote.

Kay answers my call on the first ring. "Barrett's B&B."

I chuckle. "Don't sound so cheerful. We're not about to reserve one of your high-priced suites. We need you to put on your lawyer hat."

"Kylee..."

My friend sighs. "Sounds like you and Ted are neck-deep in this hostage mess. I've been glued to the TV. Ken Taylor, the developer who chartered Captain Billy's boat, has been staying at my B&B for three weeks.

"Couldn't believe that last bulletin," she adds. "Looks like two HOAs have told the kidnappers Ted's in charge."

"That's why we're calling, Kay," Ted jumps in. "You're on speakerphone, and the whole crew is listening in."

"I'm the smart one," Mom pipes up. "Told 'em you'd know what kind of shitstorm Ted's walking into. I think he needs to put on a hazmat suit."

Kay chuckles. "HOAs are corporations, and every corporation is required to have a board. No board, no corporation. Ultimately, the South Carolina Secretary of State will dissolve the corporation. 'Course, a response takes time to snake through the bureaucracy. Even worse, HOA insurers can void liability insurance policies the moment the board vanishes.

"Wonder if the resigning directors understand their D&O protection may be gone," she adds. "Homeowners could sue the directors for leaving the association in the lurch. Bottom line, it'll be one hell of a convoluted, costly mess."

"What about us?" Ted asks. "Walking away seems cowardly. But how risky is it for Welch HOA Management to start making decisions on policies or spending money?"

"Let me put it this way," Kay answers. "When you're sued—and I can almost guarantee you will be—your defense attorney would need to be damned creative. Your company has no legal right to assume board duties. Unless…"

She pauses. "I could petition the court to name you as receiver until the association can be legally dissolved or a new board elected."

"Can the directors rescind their resignations?" Mom butts in. "If they realize their cowardice might cost them big bucks, a few might hang around long enough to appoint replacements. You know, brave old ladies like me!"

Kay laughs. "Myrt, you're such a creative schemer. Your new board will arrange a community vote on the deer hunt, right?"

"It'll be our first act. Well, not really. The first act would be dealing with the kidnapping. I'm certain I can round up two more appointees to give us a three-person, decision-making quorum."

"Mom! No! Those directors are fleeing for a reason. They don't want to be kidnap candidates."

"I'm not scared." She bats her eyes at Ted. "I have Welch HOA Management's superb services to protect me. Besides, Kylee, your dad and I always preached that when you see wrongs, keeping silent, doing nothing is the same as giving your blessing."

Grant laughs. "You're awesome, Grandma Myrt."

I give Grant the evil eye. *Don't encourage her!*

"Myrt, if you're serious, it's a possibility," Kay answers. "I doubt the directors officially approved any meeting minutes before they ran for the exit. They could correct their public statement. Say they intended to make clear they would be resigning *after* appointing replacements."

"All righty." Mom's tone is triumphant. "I'm off to recruit fellow septuagenarian and octogenarian troublemakers."

Mom waves goodbye and winks as she leaves the group huddled around Ted's speakerphone. She flips open her cellphone as she heads for a quiet corner of the office.

*Crap! Not a thing I say will change her mind.*

"Kay, could you prepare emergency receivership petitions for Crestway Plantation and Hullis Island?" Ted asks. "I don't share Myrt's confidence that the Hullis Island directors will appoint her and two more of her pro-vote buddies to the board. They hate Myrt for calling their arrogant no-vote bluff."

I hope to hell Ted's right. While I don't like seeing him squeezed in an ethical vise, it's not as bad as worrying about Mom becoming a kidnap target.

"I'll do what I can," Kay answers Ted. "I'll plead with Judge Glenn to act quickly. We've been friends since grade school, forty years, but I should warn you that even emergency petitions aren't answered instantly."

After Kay hangs up, Ted and I return to fielding calls from stressed-out clients who've been on hold. Somehow a mechanical voice periodically proclaiming, "Your call is important to us…" hasn't improved their moods.

Yep, when I'm waiting on the other end of the line, it torques me off, too.

* * *

Less than half an hour passes before Mom taps my shoulder. Her Cheshire grin tells me all I need to know.

"Who did you convince to play Russian roulette with Neuter1?" I ask.

"Martha Evatt and Ruth Leopard," she crows. "It's a done deal. Once the dear-departing directors understood their financial peril, they swallowed their spite and appointed us. I'm the new acting president since Cliff is unable to fulfill his duties."

I take a deep breath. *How am I going to protect Mom?*

If the kidnappers are truly anti-fascists, they need to get a look at my mother's Facebook page. It's plastered with pre-retirement photos of her in a nurse's uniform and my fire chief dad in full fire-fighting gear. If my parents' middle-class occupations aren't enough, Mom's caustic posts about billionaires not paying their fair share of taxes should convince them she's no HOA fat-cat.

# Chapter Fifteen

## The Leader

*Monday Afternoon*

"Did the boat captain drink all of it?" I ask.

"He did," Matt answers. "His brain's nicely marinated. He's hallucinating and meek as a lamb."

"Good. Nonetheless, keep him blindfolded, tied up, and out of sight in the back of the van. I checked a Google street view of that HOA management office. No close neighbors, and no sign of surveillance cameras. Still, make it quick. Dump the captain in the vacant lot. Then turn around. Don't drive past the HOA office. Can't chance someone looking out a window.

"Leave the van in the Westview Drive parking lot and jog to the Broome Lane lot," I add. "You'll blend right in with other runners on the Spanish Moss trail. I left a tan Prius at the Broome trail access. The car's unlocked, and the keys are inside a thermos on the passenger seat. We'll collect the van tomorrow once we're sure no one's connected it to the boat captain's express delivery."

Matt nods in agreement. "What about the note?"

"Put it in the captain's shirt pocket. Wear gloves the whole time you're with him," I stress. "Fingerprints can be pulled off most anything from belt buckles to eyeglasses. Stay vigilant, disciplined. I suspect the FBI will send agents in the next couple of days. We can't afford to get sloppy."

"Got it," Matt says.

I leave what I think of as our "unsafe" house as soon as Matt exits the room. The note in the boat captain's pocket should keep the sheriff—and the FBI, if it joins the hunt—quite busy and on the wrong track.

I'm off to Jade Pointe to devise my own weekend entertainment plans.

When I told Phil I'd lost the financial backing for my planned development, he shrugged. I thought if I begged, he'd cough up the dough I needed. Not even a month's expenditures for his multiple household accounts.

"You quit working for me, remember?" Phil said. "Thought you were ready to be a big-time developer. All developers are risk-takers, but the smart ones have bail-out options. You should have considered what would happen if Stan Hiller and his money disappeared."

I was dumbfounded. How did he know about Stan? I balled my fists, telling myself I had nothing to gain by using my fist to erase his smug smirk.

"Were you spying on me? How did you know Stan said he'd finance my project?"

Phil laughed. "No. I wasn't spying on you. Your career is of little concern since you quit working for Graham Enterprises. No, Stan was a potential headache, given my political aspirations. I asked Ernie to do some research to tarnish Stan's do-gooder image. Turning up your connection was an unexpected bonus."

I worked hard to control my rage. "Okay, Phil. Lesson learned. But I'm in a real bind. Will you help me out?"

Phil shook his head. "Can't. Am in a bit of a liquidity crunch. Already committed millions to this Spoonbill Island deal, and I need a healthy reserve for an election campaign. Just write off this deal of yours. I can give you your job back at Graham Enterprises. And, if you don't want to work for me, that Ivy League education I paid for should help you find a job somewhere."

Phil patted my shoulder. "Any developer worth his salt has been bankrupt at least once. Move on."

Well, Phil, I'm moving on, and I believe my creativity would impress even you. Too bad you won't be around to appreciate it.

# Chapter Sixteen

Kylee

*Monday Afternoon*

The weedy vacant lot beside Ted's office isn't ideal for a back-to-nature stroll, but I need a break. The outdoor air may not be fresh, but it's air.

My mind is reeling. Mom refuses to move in with me, and she's turned down my plea to bunk with her on Hullis Island.

I open my cellphone to call Chief O'Rourke, director of security for Hullis Island, to request extra patrols on Mom's street while the body-snatching maniacs remain at large.

Muffled noises distract me. A wavering clump of tall mare's tail grass hides the source. I approach the distressed sounds with caution. A homeless person?

"Oh, my Lord!" A man's splayed face down in the debris-strewn lot. Trussed like a turkey, his hands are wrenched behind his back, ankles crossed and bound with tough plastic rope.

I scan the lot and the street. Though the office is on a busy thoroughfare, there's not a car in sight. Not a soul around. No sign whoever tied him up is lurking nearby.

Incoherent mumbles assure me the victim's alive. An oily bag covers his head. A heaving chest suggests he's struggling to breathe. No time to worry about messing up a crime scene.

I slide my hands under the captive's shoulder and lift to ease his breathing, and find the edge of the makeshift hood. My touch—gentle as it is—ignites fury. His bound legs buck as his head snaps back and forth. Furious, ready to fight.

"It's okay. I'm here to help."

When I pull the hood free, I'm stunned. "Billy?"

Hearing his name calms him. I grab a corner of the gag stuffed in his mouth and wriggle it free.

"Kylee?" Billy's voice is sandpaper raw. "What?"

Can't see any visible injuries. No blood on his clothes. Billy's slender, but wiry. The hair on his arms may be gray, but he's kept his muscles toned.

Billy's pupils are dilated, and his eyes dart back and forth like a crazed metronome. "They gone? Where...I? Help...up?"

His confusion alarms me.

"You're safe," I murmur and gently lever him onto his side. Sitting him up straight isn't possible the way his hands are tied.

"Whoever left you here is gone, Billy. I'm calling for help."

I pull out the cellphone I dropped in my pocket while hurrying to investigate the noise.

"I need an ambulance," I tell the 911 operator. "I found a man bound and gagged in a vacant lot. It appears he's been drugged."

I give Ted's office address. Close enough for paramedics to find the vacant lot.

"I don' wan' ambulance." Billy's slurred objection confirms I made the right call.

His slow, tortured speech is tough to decipher. Drugs, dehydration?

"My hans hur'. Please...untie."

I nod. "Will do as soon as I can cut the ropes."

I don't want to untie the bowline knots. They might offer a tiny clue about the person who tied them. Besides, it'll be faster to cut the ropes.

I hit the preset for Ted's private cell.

"Kylee? Where'd you go?"

"Vacant lot next door. Kidnappers left Captain Billy here. Already called an ambulance, but hurry over with water and your Swiss Army knife."

I disconnect before Ted has time to ask questions.

"Bastards drugged…me." Billy's chapped lips compress. "Need water."

Ted and Grant sprint from the office. Mom follows at a brisk pace.

"Ted, can you cut the ropes around Billy's hands and feet and leave the knots intact?"

While he works on the ropes, Grant kneels beside Billy, supports his head, and holds a water bottle to the man's cracked lips. Billy's Adam's apple bobs as he greedily gulps water. A steady stream trickles down his whiskered chin despite Grant's best efforts to angle the bottle so the captain can drink without being waterboarded.

"Let me in," Mom demands in her head-nurse voice. She rests the back of her hand against his forehead to check for fever, then snatches one of his newly-freed wrists to take his pulse.

"We've been worried sick about you," Mom says. "Your pulse could outrun a speeding bullet. Not good. You're not exactly a spring chicken."

"Younger than you," Billy mumbles. "Hate hos…pitals. Be fine."

"Sure you will," Mom quips. "Just as soon as your scrawny ass is peeking out from a hospital gown, and we've anchored an IV in your starboard side. Case closed. I'll call Katie. Tell your daughter we're checking you into Beaufort Memorial."

We all jump at an ambulance's high-pitched wail.

"Oh, God, I'd better call the Sheriff's Office. There'll be hell to pay if Nick thinks we're keeping him in the dark. Of course, Nick will bitch regardless."

Stepping away to place the call, I watch two paramedics—one man, one woman—jog toward the captain.

An operator answers, "Sheriff's Department."

In no mood to speak with Nick, I speed through a curt message. "The kidnappers dumped Captain Billy Stubbs, gagged and bound, in a vacant lot. No visible injuries, but he says he's been drugged. Paramedics are loading him in an ambulance. He'll be at Beaufort Memorial in minutes."

I disconnect before the operator demands I stay on the line. As Billy's lifted onto a stretcher, the woman EMT's eyes rove between Mom and me. "He's pleading for Kylee to stay with him. Who's Kylee?"

Mom will be a nurse until the day she comes before the pearly gates. And then she'll want to take the temperature of whoever's manning them. I fully expect her to insist she's Kylee so she can stay with Billy.

"I'm Kylee," I answer. "Can I keep him company in the ambulance?"

"Okay," the EMT answers. "His agitation isn't helping his blood pressure and heart rate. Keeps mumbling somebody's stranded. Maybe you can calm him."

Ted grips my shoulder. "I'll follow you to the hospital as soon as I tell Robin where we're going. I sure hope Billy can tell us more about the kidnappers and what's happened to his passengers."

*Hope is nice. In this case, I'm a doubter.*

The kidnappers can't be dummies. If they were, they'd never have been able to capture Billy. And they wouldn't free him if they thought he could guide authorities to their door.

*So why did they let him go?*

The male EMT extends a hand to help me clamber aboard the ambulance. Billy's shoulders arch up as he fights the stretcher restraints. His fingers furiously scrabble at the edge of his oxygen mask.

"Can we remove the mask long enough for him to speak?" I ask.

"Just for a second," the EMT answers.

Billy looks frantic. "Three couples...got off...Spoonbill Island. Stranded."

"They're fine," I assure him as the EMT slips the oxygen mask back in place. "We spotted them on an early morning sail. After we rescued them, we found the Hullis Hussy, and the Coast Guard launched a search for you."

Billy's shoulders relax; his fingers still. He closes his eyes.

Exhaustion? Pray the drugs in his system have no lasting effect.

The ambulance jerks to a stop, and I look out the back-door windows. The Beaufort Memorial Emergency Entrance is a welcome sight.

Far less welcome is the sheriff's car streaking into the parking lot with lights flashing and siren blaring.

Ugh. Acting Sheriff Nick Ibsen.

# Chapter Seventeen

Kylee

*Monday Afternoon*

I trail the EMTs into the hospital as they roll Billy inside. A hand grabs my arm from behind and tightens its grip before I can wrench free.

"What are you doing here?" Nick demands.

The antiseptic hallway's acoustics amplify his barked command.

"Had a hunch you were involved, and not just as a Johnny-on-the-spot rescuer. If HOAs face trouble, I can make book they're clients of your lover's so-called management company. The Welch HOA logo should be a skull-and-crossbones."

I struggle to keep my mouth shut. *Don't give him the satisfaction.* My eye roll, however, escapes my control.

"I asked what you're doing here." Nick thunders. "Answer or I'll haul your butt in for obstruction."

I will myself to respond to his bellicose bleats in a serene, almost-whisper soft voice. I give a succinct summary of finding Billy, calling for an ambulance, and phoning his office.

"Ted cut the ropes used to tie Billy up," I add. "Left the knots intact. Maybe those knots and the oily bag used as a hood can provide some clues."

"I don't need you to tell me how to investigate," Nick growls. "Sounds like there's little point looking for clues since you and half of Beaufort tramped around where they left him."

I shrug. Refuse to be drawn into an argument.

"I'm going to question the captain," Nick continues. "You need to leave. I don't want you interfering."

Out of the corner of my eye, I spot Billy's daughter Katie rushing toward us. She works at a Beaufort bank, only minutes from the hospital.

Katie grabs me in a fierce hug. "Kylee, your mom called and told me you found Dad. How is he?"

"An ER doctor is with him in that first treatment room down the hall," I answer. "I saw no injuries, but he was drugged. Seems fuzzy-headed, but should be fine once they flush the drugs out of his system."

"I need to see him." Katie's eyes glisten with tears.

Nick thrusts out his chin. "I'm Sheriff Nick Ibsen, and you are?"

"Katie Stubbs," she answers. "Billy's daughter."

"Well, Miss Stubbs, I insist on questioning the captain before he speaks with anyone, even you."

The little putz again failed to mention he's the "acting" sheriff—at least until the election. When he wants to charm someone, Nick can be a gentleman. However, the sight of Katie hugging me must have put her in the enemy camp.

Katie glares at him. "It's Ms. Stubbs. I'll speak with the doctor. If he says it's okay for my father to answer questions, fine. But I damn well do have a say. While you may have a right to question him, I will be present. Whatever drugs he's been given may compromise his ability to understand and respond. If you want to argue about it, we'll wait for an attorney to decide the matter. In the meantime, I'm going to see Dad."

Nick's smile is predatory. "You afraid your father may incriminate himself? I do question how a captain could allow seven passengers to be taken off his boat without even sending an SOS."

"You bastard." Katie's face is scarlet. "You will not go near my father until I talk to his doctor."

She spins on her heel and heads toward the treatment room. "Kylee, come with me."

I have a childish impulse to stick my tongue out at Nick. I don't. The man has a gun on his hip.

The doctor and nurse look up as we walk inside the curtained space.

"I'm William Stubbs' daughter," Katie says. "Is Dad okay? This is my friend, Kylee. She found Dad."

The doctor allows Katie to come to the side of the examining table. She kisses Billy's cheek and holds his hand.

"I'm Dr. Wilkins. Your father's heart is racing, and his blood pressure is way too high. His pupils and speech suggest he's been drugged. Until we get blood test results, we can't be certain what he was given. Whatever it is, it appears to be gradually wearing off."

"The sheriff wants to question him," Katie tells the doctor. "Should I let him?"

I add my two cents. "Katie, Dr. Wilkins, Billy may be able to help authorities find seven hostages before they're harmed. The sheriff needs to know if Billy has any clues."

Billy raises his head. "Quit talking about me like I'm dumb as a stick." His voice already sounds crisper. "I want to talk. Just embarrassed I was hoodwinked."

"I'll allow it as long as his blood pressure doesn't soar," Dr. Wilkins says.

"I'll tell Ibsen he can come in." I can't bring myself to call him Sheriff Ibsen. "Katie, I'll be in the ER waiting room if you need me."

I walk down the hall to where Nick is pacing.

"The doctor says you can go in. But he'll kick you out if Billy's blood pressure climbs. Try not to be an asshole."

I take a seat in the waiting room. Any attempt to join the questioning would only bolster Nick's bullying tendencies. Not what's best for Billy. Nonetheless, curiosity about what happened on that party boat keeps my butt glued to one of the hospital's uncomfortable slick, plastic chairs.

Once Nick leaves, I'll chat with Katie.

# Chapter Eighteen

Kylee

*Monday Afternoon*

I 've been seated for less than ten minutes when Ted and Mom enter the ER. I stand to flag their attention.

"There you are," Mom says as she walks over. "Is Katie here? How's Billy doing?"

Before I can answer, Nick bulls toward us.

"Glad to see you here, Welch." Nick smirks as he greets Ted. "The kidnappers want you as a pen pal. Addressed a note to you and put it in the captain's pocket. If they try to contact you again, you *will* notify me immediately. In no circumstance will you interact with them in any way."

"What did the note say?" Ted asks.

"Not your concern," Nick replies. "I'll handle any communication with the kidnappers. You will play no role in negotiations, understood? None. Zero."

A flush creeps up Ted's neck as he glares at Nick. "If the note's addressed to me, I have a right to know what it says. Maybe I could answer, stall for time. I've worked at U.S. embassies around the world. I do know how to negotiate. I can help."

"No, you can't." Nick turns on his heel and struts off. "I'll make that abundantly clear at my press conference."

I put a hand on Ted's arm and whisper, "Katie will tell us what happened. She might even know what that note said."

* * *

I've barely finished telling Ted and Mom about Nick and Katie's heated exchange when Billy's daughter rushes to join us.

"They moved Dad into a private room," she begins. "The doctor says he can have visitors—as long as they're not as upsetting as that idiot Ibsen. I hope to hell someone runs against him for sheriff. How about you, Kylee?"

I choke out a laugh. "Not a job I'd want in my wildest dreams."

*But how I'd love to see a woman beat him out of his coveted sheriff's badge.*

"Katie, can you tell us about the note?" Ted asks.

"Wait till we get to Dad's room," she replies. "He hates being left out. The doc sentenced him to a minimum of twelve hours in a hospital bed. Dad isn't happy. Wants to break out and do something to help. He feels responsible, though he has no reason to feel guilty."

Katie leads us to her dad's room. To my relief, the patient's lost the deathly pallor he had when I found him. Though Billy's well-acquainted with Mom and me, he's never met Ted. Once I complete the introductions, the captain waves away all "how-are-you-feeling" inquiries.

"How do I feel? Like an imbecile. They suckered me." Billy wriggles to sit up straighter on the starched sheets. "Have to give the devil his due. The kidnappers were damned clever. We were cruising along the shoreline so the developer could point out locations for his planned marina and hotel. That's when a yacht came steaming our way with a big advertising banner draped over its side.

"The banner was plugging some wine. When the yacht—it was a power cruiser, forty-five or fifty-footer—got close, a guy dressed in a turkey costume yelled, 'Gobble, gobble. We're offering free samples of the very best wine for your Thanksgiving feast.'

"My passengers were gung-ho. Before I could object, the jerk in the turkey get-up and two other guys—one dressed as a pilgrim, the other as an

Indian chief—jumped on board and started passing out wine. The Indian chief—he had a Yankee-New England accent—tried to talk me into a taste, but I refused. That's when the passengers began getting woozy, slumping in their seats. When I reached for the radio to call for help, the pilgrim, who stuttered when he talked, zapped me. Made me helpless as a baby. They tied me up. Carried me along with the comatose passengers over to the yacht. Blindfolded me. Imagine they blindfolded the others, too."

"Pretty slick, using freebies and ad slogans for a con," Ted says. "When did they drug you?"

"Today. Forced me to drink something. Could have been whatever they put in the wine."

"Can you identify the men?" I ask. "Did you see their faces?"

Billy shakes his head. "No. They were decked out like characters on a parade float or greeters at a theme park. Full costumes with bigger-than-life plastic heads. I can't even tell you what color hair the men had. If they had hair. Hell, I *think* they were men. For all I know, they were women with deep voices. At the house, they wore ski masks."

"Their plan wasn't cheap," Ted comments. "Maybe the authorities can trace the yacht or the source of their costumes."

Billy shrugs. "Don't know diddly about procuring costumes, but I'm ninety-nine percent certain the captain of that yacht wasn't the owner. Didn't know beans about navigation. Nobody in his right mind would have rented him a yacht either. Whenever we changed course, he over-compensated. Almost took out the pier when we docked."

"When did they take you off the boat?" I ask.

"Soon as they docked. Packed us all into the back of a van. One of the kidnappers pushed me to the floor. We drove over backroads for maybe half an hour. Then they herded us into a house. Everybody could stumble along upright by then."

"Can you tell us anything about the house?" Ted asks.

"Pretty sure it was vacant," Billy answers. "Voices echoed like they do in empty spaces when there's no carpeting or furniture to soak up sound. Know it was in the boonies. We bounced over rutted roads getting there, and there were no city-type noises. Just birds, frogs. The house had two stories. They marched us up a flight of creaky stairs before locking us in a room."

I try to think of any way to narrow the location of the house. "How long were you on the boat before it docked? Did it pull in at a marina?" I ask.

"I may have been blindfolded, but there was nothing wrong with my ears. We'd been underway for a time when I heard the engine of a big boat nearby. It had throttled down. Sounded like a shrimp trawler coming into port. Swarms of seagulls were making their normal racket, diving on the trawler's discards. My guess is the trawler was approaching the Harbor River Bridge to put in at the commercial dock there. If so, we'd just skirted Hunting Island and were on our way to St. Helena Sound. Quite a bit later, I heard what sounded like jet planes taking off. Could be the yacht came close to the Marine Corps Air Station."

I try to recall any marinas near there. "What happened when you docked?"

"The pier swayed and creaked with every little breeze." Billy closes his eyes. "The dock was old. The boards felt kinda spongey when we walked on them."

Mom clears her throat. "Enough interrogation. Billy, you may feel fine, but you don't know what kind of poison they pumped inside you. You need to rest."

Billy rolls his eyes. "Myrt, you're no longer an active member of the bed-pan brigade. I'll rest as soon as I tell my new friend, Ted here, about the note the kidnappers sent him. Heard that addle-brained sheriff say he wasn't gonna tell you diddly. Plain foolish. What a jerk."

"What did the note say?" Ted's calm, even tone doesn't mask his frustration. The jumping-bean blood vessel thudding at his temple suggests the suspense is driving him nuts.

"The docs had already stripped me, and Katie was gathering my clothes when she found a note in my shirt pocket," Billy begins. "She read it out loud. Katie, help me out if I miss something. The kidnappers tagged you, Ted, because you manage the Hullis Island HOA. Gave you until Thursday to raise a half-million-dollar ransom to free Cliff and Peggy Jackson. Said

70

they'd contact you with exact instructions for the exchange."

Ted looks grim. "Did they say what would happen if the money isn't paid?"

Billy shakes his head. "Best I recall, they left it at 'or else.'"

"There was something about basing the ransom demands for the hostages on the number of doors in their HOAs," Katie adds. "Guess Hullis Island is a test to see if property owners are willing to pony up to free their HOA presidents. Though I'm not one of Cliff's fans, I'd hate to see any harm come to the Jacksons. Peggy's a real sweetheart."

Mom frowns. "Wonder if Nick will make the ransom demand public at his press conference."

"We'll find out soon enough," I reply. "He'll want the press to know he's in charge. That way, he can claim victory if the hostages are rescued. Of course, if things go sideways, he'll scapegoat someone else."

"Heaven help the Jacksons," Billy says. "He's gonna screw it up."

"And probably blame us," Ted says, "his favorite fall guys. Thanks for the heads-up, Billy. Time for you to rest and us to brainstorm."

# Chapter Nineteen

Kylee

*Monday Afternoon*

Back at Ted's office, five of us—Ted, Mom, Grant, Robin, and I—crowd around the scarred conference table primarily used for communal lunches. Frank, the only Welch HOA Management absentee, is dealing with an HVAC emergency at a client's clubhouse. While I'm surrounded by intelligent people, I'm not sure our brain trust can solve the knotty ransom dilemma.

"Grandma Myrt, have you taken over as Hullis Island's HOA president yet?" Grant asks.

She smiles. "Yep. Our press release should show up online soon. With Martha and Ruth, we have a three-person quorum for decision-making. My fellow directors elected yours truly acting president until we bring Cliff and Peggy home."

"Think the acting sheriff will consult with you since you're Cliff's official replacement?" Robin asks.

Mom laughs. "Before that happens, pigs would have to do more than fly—they'd need to become astronauts."

"So, what's the plan?" I look at Ted. "With your State Department assignments, you have some hostage experience. Do we raise money? Do we attempt to negotiate?"

Ted shakes his head. "No matter what we think of Sheriff Ibsen, we can't go behind his back. There can only be one hostage negotiator. Add a third party, and miscommunication and chaos always follow."

"We do nothing?" Mom looks aghast. "I can't sit on my hiney and trust Ibsen to outsmart the kidnappers. He's an imbecile. Cliff and Peggy don't deserve to die."

The iPad on the table in front of Robin beeps. "Hold on. The sheriff's started his press conference." She swivels her tablet and ups the volume so we can all see and hear the news conference.

"I have important news," Ibsen begins. "Neuter1 has claimed responsibility for the kidnapping. They're demanding a ransom to free two of the remaining seven hostages. It appears the terrorists plan to auction off the hostages one couple at a time. I've asked the FBI to assist in bringing the hostages safely home. However, the Sheriff's Department remains on point. My office will handle any negotiations with the terrorists. Any civilian interference will result in criminal obstruction charges."

Grant elbows his dad. "Think he means you."

"Shhh," Mom admonishes. "Ibsen's not finished."

The acting sheriff straightens his shoulders. "These Neuter1 terrorists should understand there will be no possibility of negotiation until we receive proof-of-life—proof that all seven hostages are alive and well."

Ibsen stares into the camera. "Here's my personal advice to these left-wing fanatics. Your few minutes of fame are up. Shut down your Commie circus. If you want to be alive and breathing when your little tent collapses, surrender. Now. Time is short. It won't be long before the Sheriff's Department, with the aid of the FBI, closes in."

\* \* \*

I feel like cheering. "Thank God the FBI's involved. Did you notice the somber-looking man and woman behind Ibsen? I'm betting they're special agents. Even if the FBI doesn't take charge, the agents can steer the investigation behind the scenes. Actually, the FBI's smart to let the acting sheriff strut around like he's big man on campus. That guarantees his cooperation. No who's-in-charge pissing contests."

Ted frowns. "Interesting that Ibsen didn't mention the Jacksons are the first hostages to be ransomed or the price the kidnappers are asking."

"Got to give it to old Nick," Mom adds. "Can't decide which tough-as-nails lawman actor he was imitating—Cary Grant, Clint Eastwood, or Bruce Willis—but he sounded good and looked the part. First time I ever heard Nick string five sentences together without his subjects and verbs engaging in mortal combat. Wonder if Nick had a ghostwriter. If so, I'll bet he adlibbed that bit about time running out for the villains."

I close my eyes and roll my neck to ease the tension. "Since every sentence didn't pat Ibsen on the back, someone else prepared the speech. If not the FBI, I'd nominate Stacy Douglas. Ernie's Big-Hair TV reporter. She only tossed Nick a few powderpuff questions. No obvious probes about what the acting sheriff didn't disclose—like what kind of help the FBI is providing or which couple is the first to be ransomed. The way Big Hair gushed over him, you'd think Nick just crossed the Beaufort River with no need of a bridge."

Ted raps his knuckles on the table. "Okay, we agree, Nick's an insect, and Ernie's media empire is using the hostage situation to boost Nick's political profile. But, let's dissect what the acting sheriff actually said. Does anyone believe Nick or the FBI is closing in on the kidnappers?"

I shake my head. "Doubtful. According to Captain Reed, satellite imagery was zero help in identifying the yacht or tracking where it took the hostages. Too many clouds Saturday afternoon. While there are high-tech ways to locate boats, they only work if you know the boat's identity. So far, no reports of a stolen yacht that matches Billy's description.

"I hope the FBI or the Coast Guard follows up with Billy," I add. "Ibsen never asked the captain's opinion of where the yacht put the hostages ashore."

"Can't you contact one of the FBI buddies you made during that counterterrorism course you took?" Mom asks. "Tell them to follow up."

I shake my head. "They're in Washington D.C. Even if they happen to know any of the details in this investigation, sharing them with a civilian would be against the rules."

Grant looks at me. "So, how would you find the kidnappers?" he challenges.

"I'd start with the details Billy shared and search for the yacht used to hoodwink the hostages. I'd check on all forty-five to fifty-foot yachts moored in nearby marinas to see who owns them. The Coast Guard is undoubtedly doing just that.

"I'd also look for vacant, two-story houses in the boonies beyond the Marine Corps Air Station. Of course, that covers one heck of a lot of territory."

Mom pushes back her chair and stands up. "Enough palavering. We're not solving anything. It's approaching five o'clock. The new Hullis Board is convening at my house at six-thirty. As president, I'm inviting our HOA manager and his entire team to join us. Lucky for you, I started chili in the crockpot this morning. Enough to feed everyone. Robin, that includes you."

The IT guru blushes. "I'm sure your chili is awesome, but I've made other plans."

"A date?" Mom probes.

"Uh, yeah."

"Good for you, Robin," Mom says. "Have fun. You've had a rough day. I expect the rest of you in my kitchen by six p.m."

# Chapter Twenty

Kylee

*Monday Afternoon*

**M**om assigns me to rustle up red-pepper flakes, cumin, and other condiments while Grant sets the table. Grant's speed-dealing silverware like playing cards when he stops to study one of Mom's plastic-coated placemats.

"Impressed with our high-class tableware," I tease. "I can get you your very own set of plastic placemats for Christmas."

"Come look," he says.

The placemat features an artist's rendering of a nineteenth-century map, picturing tidal tributaries near today's Marine Corps Air Station. Stylized white-columned plantation houses dot the lush green marshes crisscrossed by aquamarine tidal creeks.

"I've driven some of these backroads," Grant says. "Mimi, the girl I dated last summer, was into birding. We drove by at least three abandoned houses perfect for holding hostages. Almost invisible from the roads."

Ted clears his throat. "After tonight's chili-supper board meeting, we can look at Grandpa Hayse's historical documents. Should show the location of old plantations. I doubt Myrt has touched Hayse's moldy historical records."

"No, I haven't," Mom pipes up. "But while you look at dusty, crumbling records, Kylee and I can search Zillow. If the kidnappers are squatting in a vacant house, it may be listed for sale."

"Good thought," I agree.

The doorbell rings, announcing the arrival of Mom's two friends—Martha Evatt and Ruth Leopard. The Hullis board now has its three-person, decision-making quorum.

Martha crushes me in a bear hug. The seventy-four-year-old hasn't changed her hairdo or clothing style since college. Only now, the long braid that reaches almost to her waist is gray, and her loose tunic is plaid instead of tie-dyed.

The years haven't dimmed the woman's passion for causes. As soon as Mom sued the Hullis board to force a vote on a deer hunt inside Hullis's nature preserve, Martha arrived with a check to help pay legal costs.

When Martha turns me loose, Ruth smiles and pats my shoulder. The reserved eighty-year-old, a former CPA, is Martha's social and style opposite. Not a strand of the introvert's hair dares to stray from her tight, iron-hued bun.

Mom wastes no time herding everyone into the kitchen. Once we all have bowls of chili and drinks, Mom updates her friends on the ransom details Ibsen kept secret. Namely that the kidnappers are asking half a million dollars for Cliff and Peggy Jackson.

"The authorities may be within their rights forbidding civilians from interacting with the kidnappers," Mom says, "but there's nothing to stop us from raising funds. I doubt the Jackson kids can lay hands on half-a-million bucks by Thursday. We could help them find the cash."

Ruth frowns. "I don't like the idea of paying the kidnappers. Won't giving into their demands invite more attacks? Besides, our covenants are crystal clear. HOA funds can't benefit individuals, especially directors. I'm quite sure paying a ransom crosses that fiscal line. We were mad as heck when Cliff and his fellow directors exceeded their authority."

"I agree, Ruth," Ted says. "Paying a ransom is always risky, and it can backfire. Plus, nothing in the Hullis Island covenants gives you three the wiggle room to hand HOA funds over to kidnappers."

Mom awards Ted with a rare frown. He holds his palm up to ward off her objections.

"If you want to raise money that could *potentially* be used by authorities as a payoff, do it privately. Don't involve the homeowner association."

"Why not set up a Go-Fund-Me account?" Grant suggests. "People use that app for all kinds of fundraising. Just be clear what happens to donations, if…." His voice trails off. "Well, if something, uh, unfortunate happens, and there's no point in, uh, paying up."

"I have an idea," Martha says. "If the money's not needed for ransom, we could use it to fund humane measures to cull our deer herd."

"Right." Mom snorts. "That'll encourage Cliff's gun-toting fans to donate."

Ted clears his throat. "Don't mention ransom at all. Simply say you're raising money to support the families of the hostages. That gives plenty of flexibility."

Mom, Martha, and Ruth nod in unison. "Sounds reasonable. One decision down, and we don't even need to include it in our meeting minutes since it's not a board matter."

"But there is a topic the board needs to address," Mom says. "Fear. While I doubt the kidnappers will start snatching golfers off tee boxes or bridge players from our rec center, we need to make Hullis residents feel safer. That's especially true with all the vacationers arriving for the Thanksgiving holiday. Don't want residents eyeballing every stranger like they're Jack the Ripper."

Mom's right. Islanders still haven't forgotten an October murder a few blocks away. That killer posed the corpse to look like part of a Halloween display.

"It would help if residents see security officers patrolling more frequently," I suggest. "And you should tighten security at the gate. Let owners see officers look inside vendors' trucks to make sure they're not smuggling crooks in with a load of kitchen cabinets."

"Good idea," Ruth agrees. "I don't mind spending HOA money to tighten gate inspections or double security patrols. I move to authorize funds to pay security officers for overtime and to hire temporary help if needed."

Martha seconds the motion. Three "ayes" follow, and Mom turns to Ted.

"Will you make the necessary arrangements with Chief O'Rourke?"

Ted nods, and the board meeting concludes just before Mom serves slices of her apple-dapple cake. Once Ruth and Martha depart, we all waddle to the den. While Grant and Ted sort through Hayse's plantation history, Mom and I scan online for-sale listings and foreclosure notices. In less than an hour, our combined efforts identify a dozen vacant properties ideal for a criminal hideaway.

"Of course, there are probably a dozen more we're not seeing," Ted comments. "It's possible one of the kidnappers owns the house in question. In that case, it's not for sale or in foreclosure. It's just vacant."

I shrug. "Well, at least our list offers a starting place. Think it will do any good to share it with Nick?"

Mom laughs. "No way he'd take our suggestions. But he might listen to a respected real estate agent, especially one whose endorsement might sway votes. I'll ask Melissa Yantis to share the list. I'm sure she'll be glad to say it's her idea."

"Okay, settled," Ted says. "Kay just texted me that Judge Glenn can fit me in first thing tomorrow. Kylee, that means you need to be my stand-in at eight a.m. at the Sea Bay HOA board meeting."

I groan. "Why? Can't Frank go solo? I know nothing about the structural defects Frank investigated."

"Frank can handle that portion of the meeting just fine," Ted responds. "But one of the board members has more to say about the Emotional Support Animal—ESA—controversy. When Frank signed on, he did it with the proviso he'd only deal with construction and maintenance issues. Emotional support animals are way out of his wheelhouse."

I sigh. "Frank's not alone."

"Oh, buck up," Mom says. "Since I have volunteers to chop veggies and peel potatoes, I can wait until Wednesday to start prepping side dishes for Thanksgiving. I'll keep Robin company in the office tomorrow. Don't want her there alone."

Mom eyeballs each of us in turn. "Well…is it settled?" She stands on tip-toe to rub Grant's brush cut.

"Are you talking about Kylee attending the meeting or my mandatory KP assignment? How come I always have to chop onions?"

"We've shed a lot more tears than you," Mom replies. "Onions let you catch up without any of the heartache."

# Chapter Twenty-One

## The Leader

*Monday Evening*

"About time you got here, brother," Saffron says. "I thought you might be standing me up. Afraid you got a better offer."

I wink at my sister, two years my senior. "Not a chance. Thought I'd give your admirers a shot at charming you without a man at your table to discourage them. You've served the requisite six months as Mrs. Adams, grieving widow. Figure you're ready to move on."

Saffron punches my arm. "I have to make up for you—the perennially eligible bachelor. Are you ever going to stop shopping for a woman and take one home for keeps?"

Laughing, she inventories the posh club's dining room. "Too many geezers for me. My late husband cured me. Won't marry anyone old enough to be my father again. Not lonely enough for Metamucil cocktails."

"How's Mom?" I ask.

Saffron's smile fades. "Not good. I visited last week. She managed to drag her butt out of bed, though she never dressed. Doesn't even try to hide her addiction anymore. Her eyes never quite focus."

I frown. Our mother is not long for this world. Oblivion sits one handful of pills and a bourbon chaser away. Saffron and I tried. You can only save loved ones if they want to be saved.

"How's your big development project coming?" Sis asks, changing the subject. "Vineyards and thoroughbreds. Can't wait. Tell me there's going to be polo. I have a thing for strapping young men with charging stallions between their legs."

I chuckle. Saffron thinks she's introduced a cheerier topic. She's dead wrong.

A tuxedoed waiter arrives, buying me time to decide on an answer. I love my sister but she's a ditz, genetically incapable of keeping secrets. Not out of malice. Words just spill from her mouth before her brain has a chance to dam the flow.

Saffron orders seafood pasta with lobster, crab, and shrimp, and I get the same. I scan the wine list for a good Zinfandel. While Sis will swig down anything with alcohol, I've educated my palate.

"So, tell me what's happening?" Saffron prompts as soon as the waiter leaves. "Have you broken ground?"

"Not yet, but soon," I lie. "Had a little financing glitch that put the project on pause. Nothing to worry about."

Sis's eyebrows bunch. "Yeah, I did hear something weird about someone you mentioned as a big investor. What was his name? Stan something? Did he back out?"

"Stan Hiller," I keep my voice matter-of-fact. "Afraid Stan's not investing in anything these days. He's dead."

Saffron's smile contorts into a perfect O. "Was it sudden? A heart attack?"

"Something like that."

Actually, a drug overdose. Poor health had Stan on a life-and-death precipice, and I'm convinced Ernie's hounding provided the fatal push.

"I'm making new financing arrangements," I add. "Expect to be flush with cash in a month or so. Hey, new subject. What's the skinny on this weekend's nuptials? Are the soon-to-be bride and groom in residence?"

"Guess so. I'm staying in the west wing of Phil's mansion along with a dozen other wedding guests. I paid the expected peasant homage to our lord of the manor and his bimbo bride. She couldn't stop talking about their close call. Apparently, some weirdos kidnapped a bunch of old fogeys for ransom. Phil and Ashley got off that cruise to collect shells just before the kidnapping. Ashley raved about how she and Phil shivered on the beach overnight until some teenager taking a sailing lesson spotted them.

"I got the feeling Phil isn't pleased his dewy young bride invited sailor boy and his family to all the wedding festivities," she adds. "Phil was miffed she booked her 'saviors' into prime Jade Pointe Inn suites. He'd kept the suites in reserve for fat cats who hadn't decided yet if they could fit the nuptials into their globe-trotting."

*Maybe the bride wants the teen cadet nearby. One final good lay before sentencing herself to the bed of an aging Lothario.*

"Yeah, I heard Phil and Ernie both escaped the kidnapping," I say. "They're incredibly lucky. No matter what happens, those two keep breathing and soaking up money like thirsty sponges."

"Could be the bimbo bride will be Phil's undoing." Saffron raises an eyebrow. "His heart might not survive the honeymoon. She looks extraordinarily healthy."

Our food arrives. As we enjoy our entrées, I scan the room, wondering how many of our fellow dinners will attend Phil's wedding.

"Now that you're here, I assume you'll be staying at Phil's," Saffron comments. "Want to go horseback riding tomorrow?"

"Sorry." I shake my head. "I'm staying on my yacht. Meeting tomorrow with folks on my new financing. Might not be back to Jade Pointe until Friday."

"Hey, what about Thanksgiving?" Saffron pouts. "If you won't be around, I may be forced to hunt up a date. I don't want to gobble turkey with the bimbo bride and a bunch of geezers who'll tell me all about their arthritis pains."

"Things are rather fluid, but I'll try to wrap things up before Thanksgiving dinner," I say. "Definitely count me in for the Friday beach party. Never say no to a clambake. It's rain or shine, right?"

Saffron's fork hovers mid-air as she answers. "Yes. The weather forecast looks good. They're setting up poles so they can roll out canopies if it starts sprinkling, and they'll fire up portable heaters if it's cold. No real option to move that party inside."

"What's on your agenda for Saturday?" I ask.

"I signed up for the tennis round robin. I hear the bimbo plays. I'd love to kick her butt. You signed up for the golf tournament, right? You still have a two handicap?"

"Haven't played in months," I lie. "Afraid my official handicap will keep me out of the money."

"Hope Phil doesn't pair high handicaps with low ones. You could wind up with Ernie as a partner. He's not only a duffer; he cheats."

A hand settles on my shoulder, and I look up.

"Glad you could make it." Phil retracts his hand and circles the slim waist of the young woman beside him. "I'd like you to meet Ashley, my fiancée, and soon-to-be bride."

I rise to shake hands. Ashley crushes her body against me and puts a wet kiss on my cheek. I force a smile.

She's exactly what I expected. Generous lips. Toothpaste-commercial teeth. Tawny, carefully wind-blown hair. Big knockers. Long legs. And very, very young.

No deviation from Phil's prior spouse selections. Too bad Ashley will never be pronounced wife number four.

# Chapter Twenty-Two

Kylee

*Monday Night*

I slip into bed.

Alone.

I'm fifty years old, never married. Having the sheets all to myself isn't exactly a novel situation. Still, it's amazing how quickly sharing a bed with a lover becomes the new normal. I tug the blankets up around my neck to manufacture extra warmth. A sorry replacement for the man who's become my reliable heat source—in more ways than one.

Would I miss Ted as much on a mid-July night when the Coast's humid heat makes it feel like I'm trapped in a sauna?

Yeah, I'd miss him in July, too. *Got it bad.*

The phone trills. Ted's special ringtone.

"Miss me?" he begins. "I love my son, but spending hours with you nearby when I can't even kiss you is killing me. Maybe we should tell Myrt and Grant."

His mellow baritone urges me to agree. Panic intervenes.

What might happen to our makeshift family if whatever Ted and I have dies? It's awkward now, but awkward could morph into awful if we declare ourselves a couple and later split. That could strain Mom's ties with Ted and Grant. Not to mention my bond with both men. Mom, Ted, and Grant are my only family.

The silence stretches as I try to figure out how to explain my panic. Buck up. Ted deserves an answer.

"Tempting," I whisper as I try to rationalize stalling. "But let's allow Mom and Grant to enjoy the holiday without any complications. The two of us can make up for lost time when Grant returns to the Citadel."

"You're not having second thoughts about us, are you?"

"No, no," I answer in a rush. "I miss you. It's just…we're asking Grant and Mom to rewire their thinking, their relationships. I don't know how to tell them."

"Okay." Ted sighs. "But we can't keep this charade up forever. Think about when and how to break the news. It is happy news, right? They should be happy for us."

Ted's right. I *feel* it. What's my problem?

Is it because I've never managed a long-term relationship? Before Ted, the men I dated were friends and casual, no-commitment lovers. Dinner dates, bridge partners, a few weekend escapes. With Ted, that changed.

"I promise," I say and mean it. "We'll figure this out. Soon."

I clear my throat, ready to change the subject.

"Wish you were going to the Sea Bay meeting tomorrow," I say. "I'm not sure how effective I'll be at de-escalating the ESA free-for-all. Offering sage, calming counsel isn't one of my strengths. You, Mr. Patience, are the diplomat. Couldn't we postpone the meeting until this kidnapping crisis is over? Wait till you're available and things are normal?"

Ted laughs. "This is kinda normal. If it's not one crisis, it's another. I have to meet with the judge in the morning. You'll do fine. Just stick to the research we dug up and remind the directors they're likely to tumble into a money-pit if they abandon legally-proscribed procedures."

"Okay," I say. "Hope I don't alienate another board. You really need to speed up your search for some sort of mental-health guru to appear at potential HOA free-for-alls."

Ted laughs. "Mental-health professional, huh? I'm imagining the wording for the recruitment ad now. 'Must have experience soothing cranky retirees.

Wrestling skills a plus.'"

"Glad I gave you a laugh," I say. "Good night."

"Love you," Ted says. "Wish me luck with the judge. See you tomorrow."

# Chapter Twenty-Three

Grant

*Tuesday Morning*

Dad looks startled when I walk into the kitchen.

"How come you're up so early?" he asks. "It's your vacation. Figured you'd sleep in since Kylee and I rousted you at dawn yesterday, then made you work all afternoon."

My stomach's rumbling. I scan the kitchen counter and snag a banana and two left-over pastries.

"Can I use your truck today?" I ask. "If Grandma Myrt and Robin don't need me at the office, I'd like to ask Mimi out. Not sure she'll be interested. Didn't stay in touch after school started. Don't know if she's even home for the holiday."

"The truck's yours, though I'm afraid it's no babe magnet," Dad says. "Be sure and clean the garbage off the passenger seat before you take her for a ride. I forget. Where's Mimi going to college?"

"Cornell University. It's in Ithaca, New York."

Dad laughs. "I know where Cornell is. An old girlfriend went there. A food science major. Think I gained ten pounds while we were dating. Hope Mimi's home. Not every college has a weeklong break at Thanksgiving. Whatever you do, have fun today. Myrt and Robin can keep things down to a dull roar at the office without you."

I realize Dad's dressed up—suit and tie. "Looks like you're on your way to meet the judge."

"Yes, at nine a.m. Sorry I can't spend the day with you. No idea how long the meeting will last. Truth is, I kind of hope the judge doesn't make me Crestway Plantation's receiver trustee. Feel like I'm already hip deep in pluff mud with grinning alligators waiting for me to sink a mite deeper."

I raise an eyebrow, imitating Dad's expression when he's questioning me. "Maybe you should rethink your HOA gig. You were less wigged out in Saudi Arabia managing contractors who spoke three different dialects, none remotely related to English."

Dad smiles. "On days like this, I tend to agree. Spend some time outside today while the weather's good. Forecast is for plenty of sun and a high in the sixties."

*Oh, I plan to. Perfect conditions for conducting a little drone surveillance.*

Of course, I don't detail my plans. However, I did tell the truth about calling Mimi.

*It will be easier to navigate those tidal marshlands with a birder like Mimi riding shotgun.*

# Chapter Twenty-Four

Kylee

*Tuesday Morning*

The Sea Bay secretary hands copies of the meeting agenda to Frank, me, and the five directors. While this board normally opens all meetings to property owners, the directors opted to make this a closed executive session. They want to hear Frank's report and ask questions before sharing the expected financial shock with owners.

Since Frank's up to bat first, I mentally review Ted's notes on the Emotional Support Animal—ESA—quagmire. Given how I dread being Ted's stand-in at these meetings, maybe I need an ESA. Would I be more composed with one of Mom's cats in my lap?

*Just ignore any histrionics. Remember Ted's admonition—appear impartial. Do not roll your eyes.*

If I'm lucky, the debate over the aging condo's structural defects and the humungous repair costs will take so long the board will postpone the remaining agenda items to a later meeting.

*Yeah, right. Evelyn and Gilda, the directors prepping their ESA arguments, aren't even pretending to listen to Frank.* Based on their competing text messages, the women only agree on one point. Ted's cautious approach sucks.

Evelyn hates dogs and wants an immediate eviction. Gilda, a retired mental health counselor, thinks any ESA request should be granted, no questions asked.

The women should pay attention to Frank. Welch HOA Management is lucky to have Frank Donahue as an infrastructure expert. The minute he noticed signs of construction defects, he brought in a structural engineer to confirm his suspicions. Now the owners of this thirty-year-old mid-rise complex must make essential repairs, even though the projected costs are three times the balance in their reserve account. A big ouch but infinitely better than being buried in a building collapse.

Frank's encyclopedic knowledge of trustworthy companies will help, too. He owned a family roofing company until two years ago, when his wife insisted he quit scampering around chimneys like Santa. Claimed it would be the death of him. Ironically, two months after Frank sold the company, the missus tumbled down a flight of stairs and broke her neck.

I watch the sixty-eight-year-old widower's earnest face as he explains the problems. Decades of working in the sun have baked Frank's skin into Naugahyde territory, but he's still handsome with an aged-Marlboro-man vibe. Recently, I've noticed how his eyes light up whenever Mom enters the office. Maybe Ted and I aren't the only secret company romance.

The board president clears his throat. "I move that the board authorize Welch HOA Management to solicit bids for the repairs outlined by Frank Donahue," he intones.

The call for a vote snaps me out of my daydream. Three directors vote in favor. Evelyn and Gilda abstain.

"Evelyn, I believe you want to revisit our decision to postpone action against Janice Caldwell," the president says. He gives her the floor.

"Sea Bay has always prohibited pets—dogs, cats, birds, whatever," Evelyn begins. "It's right in our covenants—no animals, period. Now, Janice Caldwell has the nerve to move in with a one-hundred-twenty-pound dog that intimidates residents in the elevator and barks constantly whenever that fraud leaves the beast alone in her unit."

"One dog in our complex isn't going to hurt you," Gilda counters. "If you don't want to be in an elevator with the dog, wait for the next one. We can't know what emotional trauma Ms. Caldwell is dealing with. What's more, we have no right to ask her!"

"Rubbish," Evelyn's voice climbs two notches up the Richter scale. "The woman hands us a note from some quack, claiming her mutt is not a pet but an essential Emotional Support Animal. She flits off for entire weekends, leaving the creature with a pet sitter. Clear evidence she doesn't *need* the dog. I'm allergic to dogs and cats. It's the primary reason I chose Sea Bay. I move for the board to start eviction procedures. Today."

Have to admit my sympathies lean toward Evelyn's point of view. Janice knew Sea Bay was a no-pet complex when she bought her unit. Tons of dog-friendly condos in the area would have welcomed her. Janice's ESA letter was penned by an online "medical" mill that produces documentation of any malady for a hundred bucks. Another strike.

However, if the Sea Bay board tells Janice to either lose the dog or say adios without investigating and documenting the facts, it could give the woman an opening to sue. Evelyn needs to cool her jets. This association is already cash poor. Stupid to throw money away.

I raise my hand, and the chair recognizes me.

"As Mr. Welch already explained, the goal should be to settle this matter without a costly lawsuit," I begin. "Even condominiums with rules prohibiting pets are required by law to provide accommodations for service and emotional support animals."

"But she's lying!" Evelyn interrupts. "The woman's fit as a fiddle. Janice works out at a gym three mornings a week. What's her *alleged* dire condition?"

"Ms. Caldwell is not required to disclose her medical condition," Gilda growls. "You're one of those people who think someone who isn't blind or missing a limb can't be ill or suffering. Have you ever heard of post-traumatic stress, Evelyn?"

The chair slams his hand on the table. "You're both out of order. Ms. Kane has the floor."

*Time to try again. Mediation isn't my thing. Ted, you owe me big time.*

"Mr. Welch is exploring several options with our attorney," I reply.

"What about our rights?" Evelyn's not about to be silenced. "Neighbors who bought here never expected they'd have to listen to continuous barking or be forced to cower in our narrow hallways to stay clear of that police dog's powerful jaws?

"I understand—" I begin, when Evelyn's loud harrumph makes me stop and start again.

*Many more board appearances, and I'll have PTS.*

"While Sea Bay may be required to make ESA exceptions to its no-pet policy, the accommodation doesn't mean you must put up with a specific animal if it violates noise and nuisance covenants. If we document that this dog barks constantly or exhibits aggressive behavior, the board has a valid reason to say it must go.

"Mr. Welch also is researching how to question the authenticity of a letter from a doctor hundreds of miles away. He asks the board to delay any decision until he completes his investigation."

"So, why isn't Mr. Welch here?" Gilda asks. "Maybe Sea Bay should reconsider our contract with Welch HOA Management. Your company seems to be in constant crisis. How can Mr. Welch address our concerns when he's off negotiating with terrorists? Seems like being one of his clients makes us prime kidnap targets."

*Can't let Gilda paint Ted's company as incompetent.*

"Mr. Donahue's presentation offers an excellent example of how Welch HOA Management is dedicated to meeting Sea Bay's needs in a timely, professional manner." I counter.

*Geesh, I sound just like all the pabulum-spouting managers I used to ridicule.*

The board president bangs his gavel and tables any decision on the ESA matter until the board receives Mr. Welch's final recommendations.

I nod to the participants and rise to leave. Frank offers me a discreet thumbs up.

I'm congratulating myself on surviving another HOA meeting when my cellphone vibrates. I hate being required to leave the stupid hunk of plastic on when I'm playing HOA consultant.

Yet I smile when I recognize the caller—Freckles. I always think of Donna

Dahl as Freckles—Ted's nickname for the witty woman. Hope she's calling to suggest lunch—or a drink, even though it's not yet eleven o'clock.

"Hi, Donna." I slip into the Sea Bay hallway for a little privacy.

"Get your behind over here," Freckles orders. "Our board, minus our illustrious kidnapped president, just voted to re-hire Welch HOA Management."

She chuckles. "Bet you weren't expecting that. The two doofuses who voted with our president to fire you are gone. Ain't life a kick in the pants?"

"Ted can still say 'no,' right? You're a sweetheart, and so is…." Oh, crap, I can't remember Sparky's real name.

"Hey, let me buy you a drink and explain," Freckles says. "Meet me in the bar at the clubhouse quick as you can."

"Better make my drink a double," I reply.

"Why not? You'll recognize me by my shit-eating grin and the half-empty daiquiri in front of me."

# Chapter Twenty-Five

## The Leader

*Tuesday Morning*

I park in the rutted driveway and walk toward the sad-looking plantation house. The caved-in roof on the north side offers a clue to the water damage inside, while the rotted porch stairs suggest it's dangerous to enter.

The mortgage bankers knew the structure had a future date with a bulldozer. Building on the site wouldn't be cheap, either. Rising water tables already flood low spots in the dirt access road every high tide. The bankers thought I was a real pigeon for taking this dump off their hands.

I purchased it for cash three months ago through a shell company after I envisioned a multi-hostage scenario. No way to off Ernie and Phil by arranging fatal *accidents*. Forensic advances make it really hard to get away with one accident, let alone two. Authorities get obsessed about determining the cause when any of the super-rich kick the bucket.

A better option—given current political hysteria—seemed to be making their demise a tragic consequence of a random terrorist act. Shunt blame to Neuter1, and I'm nowhere on the suspect list. The *Patriots Unite* bumper sticker on my Porsche announces my political leanings are the polar opposite of the Neuter1 loonies.

This house's isolation made it ideal for stashing any number of bodies a

Neuter1 kidnap scheme might net.

*Damn Ernie and Phil for getting off that cruise.*

I sigh and carefully pick my way up the left side of the stairs where boards are the least decayed. I'll stay just long enough to arrange hostage proof-of-life for the sheriff and FBI. Need to keep everyone focused on our seven hostages with no thoughts about the two fish that wriggled off my hook.

"Hi, Q," Jacob greets me.

While his braying voice doesn't quite break the sound barrier, our hostages can catch every syllable. One of the many reasons I used a phony name while enlisting these pea brains. I still insist they address me as Q and not Quincy whenever the captives might eavesdrop.

As added protection, I wear a disguise when I'm around my peons. The disguise is simple, cosmetic lenses to change eye color, heavy, black-framed glasses, a high-quality wig, and a temporary tattoo. If any of my Neuter1 soldiers are caught, their descriptions will be wrong. My left forearm isn't inked with a spider's image. My eyes are brown, not blue. And I keep my almost-black hair cut close to my scalp. A far cry from the collar-length brown wig that covers my ears.

"Hi, Jacob," I reply. "Hope you're treating our fat cats right. Don't want them to complain when they're released. We need the public to understand Neuter1's word can be trusted, unlike the racist fascists we captured. I'm confident we'll collect our ransom in a matter of days."

Jacob rocks back and forth as he speaks. "That guy Roger's bitchin' about eating white-bread sandwiches. Told him he's lucky to eat. Ought to think about the little kids starving in ghettoes thanks to him and his fellow oppressors."

I stymie the urge to roll my eyes. "Anything beyond complaints? Hear any hostages trying to hatch escape plans?"

"Nope," Matt answers as he joins Jacob and me. "Placing baby monitors in the room was a great idea. We hear everything. Did like you said. Told our hostages we're negotiating their ransom, and they'll be released soon. Seems to be keeping them docile."

"Good. I brought copies of the Beaufort Gazette and Island Packet. We'll use a burner phone to photograph each couple, and our developer holding papers with today's date. Prove they're still breathing. Then, one of you can drive to Charleston and email the images to the Beaufort County Sheriff's Office."

Matt's forehead creases. "That's not proof these days. It's too easy to Photoshop digital images."

Matt's the smartest of my recruits. I'm cautious around him. Don't want to give Matt any reason to wonder if "Quincy" is truly a passionate Neuter1 crusader.

"Good point, Matt. It's harder to manipulate videos. We'll ask our captives to read the first line of a news story. Their voices will be part of the proof."

# Chapter Twenty-Six

Kylee

*Tuesday Morning*

Freckles, aka Donna Dahl, waves at me from a table at the back of the clubhouse bar.

"I ordered you a daiquiri. Hard to screw up. If you don't want it, it'll be my second, and I'll order you something else."

"A daiquiri's fine." I sit across from the chubby-cheeked senior. The spray of freckles across her pale nose and cheeks prompted Ted's nickname for her.

Before my first visit to Satin Sands, Ted described each board member. Knowing my difficulty remembering names, he gave each director a catchy nickname. Unfortunately, I remember the aliases, not their actual names. I only know Donna's real name because we've met for lunch a few times since Satin Sands terminated Ted's contract.

"Okay, Donna, since you're plying me with liquor, let's hear your sales pitch."

She quickly summarizes what's happened since Satin Sands' president, Roger Roper, and his wife were kidnapped. The two directors who always sided with Roger said they were resigning. Donna warned the fleeing directors she'd sue them unless they named replacements. Similar strategy to Mom's.

"Bottom line," Donna grinned. "Satin Sands now has four directors who are big fans of Welch HOA Management. Alex is one of our new directors, and I know you love her."

I smile at the thought of Alex, a master naturalist, being on the board. Roper would be apoplectic if he knew. Inappropriately, the phrase "turn over in his grave" sneaks into my brain. While I actively dislike the Satin Sands' president, I don't want him dead.

"Our board is offering Welch HOA a new two-year contract that includes a provision for a big payout if the HOA cancels the contract for any reason. However, Welch HOA can terminate it without penalty at any time. You can't lose."

"You fail to mention the wrath we'll endure when a rescued Roger Roper discovers it's too expensive to fire Ted. Not to mention his ire that new directors will likely veto his expensive makeovers."

Freckles laughs. "Hey, don't tell me you wouldn't love to see his face when he learns what we've been up to?"

She sets down her daiquiri and shakes her head. "I hope I do have a chance to see his face. I want Roger and his wife back, unharmed. This kidnapping is a terrible business. Do you think they'll release the hostages? What's happening with the negotiations?"

"I don't know." My answer's truthful. While I'm aware the kidnappers are asking a half-million dollars for the Hullis Island board president and his wife, I don't know if the kidnappers and authorities have had any added dialogue.

"If you're offering the HOA contract to Ted in the hope he'll be your go-between with the bad guys, forget it. You know my opinion of the acting sheriff, but Ted won't intervene. He thinks any involvement would create more confusion and could cost lives. Besides, the FBI is on the scene, and they do know what they're doing."

Freckles nods. "Got it, but the offer stands. No matter what happens to the hostages, Satin Sands needs wise counsel on how we move forward."

She frowns. "I do need to share one other piece of news. Some lawyer with a Charlotte firm called me, wanting details on the decision to fire Welch

HOA Management. He specifically asked about your competence, if I'd seen you act rashly. A fishing expedition. Said he was representing Carrie Sullivan's heirs, who plan to sue you and Welch HOA for creating conditions that led to the woman's death. The man contends you forced everyone into a tiny bathroom—without cause—and claustrophobia triggered Carrie's heart attack.

"When I told the attorney he was barking up the wrong tree, he claimed Sheriff Ibsen says different. In his version, you became unhinged when you were fired for incompetence. Sure as shoot, that blood-sucker will chat up Roger's disciples. The cowards who resigned will nod in agreement to whatever nonsense Sheriff Ibsen claims happened."

*Wonderful. Now Ted can add defending a potential lawsuit to his worries. Geez, what if it becomes common knowledge that Ted and I are lovers. That attorney would probably say Ted hired me—a hot head—for a little, well, hot head.*

# Chapter Twenty-Seven

Grant

*Tuesday Morning*

I roll down the truck windows. It's downright chilly, but Mimi insists it's the only way to hear birds singing. Bird calls clue her about which species are in the area.

"Hear those marsh wrens?" Mimi asks. "They're super chatty. The beginning of their song is sweet, then they spoil it with a bunch of static. Sounds like a cellphone vibrating on a table."

I laugh. "Speaking of cellphones, how come you're taking so many photos with your iPhone when you've got a Nikon with a honking big telephoto lens sitting in your lap?"

"The phone shots are for Dad. They show where we are each time I see or hear a new species. He's always on the lookout for cool backdrops."

I look out over the tans and browns of the winter marsh as I hear a series of cheeps. Not sure I'd agree they sound like a vibrating phone. "Marsh wrens look kind of innocuous. What makes them interesting?"

She grins. "The males don't have showy plumage, but they're horny buggers. Unrepentant philanderers. They mate with as many females as possible. They also build a half-dozen decoy nests for each mama in their harem. They try real hard to compensate for being tiny. They fight dirty, killing other rivals' eggs and hatchlings."

When Mimi first asked me to go birding last summer, I had zero interest. I just hoped the hot redhead's promise of a picnic lunch might end with us entwined on a beach blanket.

Her storytelling flare won me over. Mimi sounds like she's giving me the lowdown on naughty children, ruthless killers, or conniving thieves instead of birds.

"Is this the road you usually take to photograph the wrens?" I ask.

She shakes her head. "No. Marsh wrens are everywhere. Don't need to search for them. We're hunting American Bitterns—and, of course, your kidnappers' hideaway."

I was honest when I invited Mimi on today's scouting expedition. "While you photograph birds, I'll fly my drone to check out vacant houses. Hope to identify places where kidnappers might hole up."

I promised we'd only do long-distance snooping, not get close enough for kidnappers to see us.

"Put on the brakes," Mimi says. "We're within a mile of an old house that's been abandoned since Dad first brought me here—eight, maybe nine, years ago. A big wind gust could topple that dump. Let's not get any closer."

"Okay, we'll stop," I agree. "Can I help you search for the—what did you call them—Bitterns? What do they look like?"

Mimi laughs. "You'd never spot them. Bitterns aren't rare, but they're masters of camouflage. They have brownish stripes on pale bodies, sort of like vertical zebra stripes. To hide—from danger or prey—the birds stretch their necks and sway to look like marsh grass fluttering in a breeze."

I shut off the engine. "And do these masters of disguise sound like vibrating cellphones, too? Or are they the strong silent type?"

"Actually, I hear one now." She cocks her head. "Know the sound a dripping faucet makes when a drop hits a metal sink? Plink! There. That's it. Hear him?"

"That's a bird? Are you pulling my leg?"

"No," she chuckles. "Not even your ear."

Climbing out of the truck, I notice a muddy dip in the road and multiple tire tracks.

"Mimi, is there just one house on this dirt road?"

Her forehead creases in concentration. "Yes. The road dead-ends at that scrapheap."

I motion toward the low spot. "The last high tide was around three a.m., right? If that's when the tide last washed over that patch, these tire tracks are fresh. Makes me wonder who—besides us—is driving up and down a dead-end road. One vehicle with big fat tires; another with much skinnier ones."

Mimi gnaws her lip. "I vote we turn around now. If there's any chance the kidnappers are holed up around the bend, we need to get gone."

"Hey, I agree. One short flight, and we'll turn around. Maybe I'll get lucky and get photos of vehicles near the house. I'll call Dad with the location. He'll know what to do."

Mimi's worried expression tells me two minutes is too long.

"Listen, you can drive a stick shift, right? While I launch the drone, you turn this clunker around. We won't waste a minute that way. Okay?"

I hand Mimi the keys to the truck, and she hops into the driver's seat.

"Hurry, Grant," she says as I hoist my drone out of the truck bed. "I swear I'll take off without you if you're more than five minutes."

While Mimi says the house is only a mile away, I'm not sure how much the road twists and turns to reach it. I jog toward a raised hummock. I hope a little elevation will let me glimpse the house—or at least the roofline—so I can tell where to aim.

In the distance, I spot a ramshackle house and two vehicles—a panel van and a Jeep. I send up the drone. Watching my control screen, I wait for the vehicles to appear in the picture frame before I start snapping images.

A scream sends icy shards down my spine.

Mimi!

I almost drop the drone controls as I turn. The truck now straddles the road, which it no longer has to itself. A monster four-wheeler blocks Mimi's exit. It's inches from the truck's front end.

*Not the move of a Good Samaritan hoping to help.*

"Get away from me," Mimi yells.

A man tries to wrench open the driver's-side door. It inches open, then slams shut. But Mimi can't win this tug-of-war. Though she's strong, the bulky stranger outweighs her by at least seventy-five pounds.

I run toward them. The attacker lets go of the door handle. Is he giving up? No. He's freed both hands to reach through the open truck window. He grabs Mimi's shirt collar to pull her close, then seizes her by the throat. A stranglehold.

"Stop fighting," he yells, "or I'll choke you to death. Open the door and get out."

*He doesn't know I'm here. Creep closer. Don't yell. Wait till he has his back to me.*

Using the marsh grass as cover, I slowly inch closer.

*Blend. Make like an American Bittern.*

Too bad I lack the one-pound bird's stealth. No matter how hard I try, my two-hundred-pound frame rustles the brittle winter grass.

Mimi's out of the truck. The attacker's arm is tight across her chest, crushing her body to his. He's busy dodging Mimi's scissoring legs. She keeps trying to land a kick where it's most likely to get a man's attention. No luck.

*Do it now! Tackle him from behind. If he's surprised, he'll let Mimi loose.*

I'm primed to leap when the man turns ever so slightly. Sun glints off a hunting knife pressed against Mimi's neck.

Tackle him, and his hand might jerk. Too big a risk.

*Maybe I can bluff our way out—at least buy time to improve our odds.*

"Hey, let go of my girlfriend! We don't give a shit if you're growing weed out here or poaching alligators. Won't say a word. We're just taking photos for a nature documentary. No harm, no foul. Let her go, and you'll never see us again."

"A nature docu...documentary?"

The man's stutter gives me hope. He doesn't sound confident.

*If I could only see the face behind his brown ski mask.*

"You're no...no docu...no movie maker." He pauses. "You made the news, dude. Saw you on TV. You were on that sailboat. The one found those stranded pissants who jumped ship. And I saw the dro...drone up in the sky. Gotta call Q. See what to do with you."

"Who's Q?" I ask.

"Shut up. I gotta think. We're gonna...gonna walk back to my ATV, Cadet-boy. You gonna go ahead of me. I'll be right behind. Gonna keep my knife right next to this honey's neck. And, sugar pie, if you try to land one more kick, my hand is gonna jerk. My sister liked to cut herself. Never understood, but you don't look the type to be into carving up your skin."

As soon as we reach the ATV, the stutterer orders me to sit in the passenger seat.

*Why? He can't drive to the house with the truck blocking the road. What's he up to?*

"Eyes stra...straight ahead," he orders.

*He's going to slit my throat! Damned if I'll die without a fight.*

As I start to turn, my neck explodes in white-hot pain. A second poker-hot flash turns my body into a jerking pile of jelly.

Mimi's scream fades as I start to go under.

# Chapter Twenty-Eight

## The Leader

*Tuesday Morning*

A cellphone buzzes.

I give Matt the evil eye. "Who has your burner number?"

"Ryan," Matt replies. "So he could call if he got in a jam. He's not the sharpest knife in the drawer. Have to watch each other's backs, right?"

"Give me the damned phone." I grab the burner.

"Ryan, if you're calling for something stupid, like asking if Matt wants sprinkles on his doughnuts, I swear I'll tie you up with the hostages."

"We got troub...trouble." Ryan sounds like he's ready to pee himself. "Bad trouble."

"Calm down. Tell me what happened."

As he describes this latest cock-up, I fight the urge to shoot him, his new captives, and everyone in this god-forsaken place. Just what I need—two more pieces of unwanted human baggage.

I force myself to speak calmly. Ryan's rattled enough. No telling what the lunkhead might do if he's more stressed.

"Okay, did either of them see your face?" I ask.

"No, soon as I saw the truck blocking the road, I pu...put on my sk...ski mask. The girl was havin' trouble turning the truck around. Didn't see me. The cadet kid was out in the marsh, playing with his drone. No way...no way he saw me."

"Okay, here's what we're going to do. Matt and Jacob will come help you. Once you got the kids tied up and blindfolded, bring them here. Their truck, too. Then I'll tell you exactly what we're going to do with our teenage spies."

# Chapter Twenty-Nine

Kylee

*Tuesday Noon*

Ted, Mom, Robin, and Frank are attacking their sandwiches.

"I see you didn't wait for me to say grace." I lean over and kiss Mom's cheek. "Hope you ordered a sandwich for me."

Mom sniffs. "Kylee, is that alcohol I smell on your breath? Guess you'd better put something in your stomach if you've already started drinking. Bought you a tuna sub." She waves at a brown bag sitting at the end of the table.

I rummage through the sack, pull out the remaining sub and a bag of chips. "Given my morning, stopping at one drink was very disciplined."

Ted's eyebrows hitch up. "According to Frank, the Sea Bay meeting wasn't too bad. Where did you go after it broke up?"

"Satin Sands."

My answer prompts the expected ring of puzzled faces.

"Didn't they fire Ted's company after your last visit?" Mom asks.

*A reminder I don't need.*

"Donna Dahl phoned and asked me to drop by. They want to re-hire Welch HOA Management. After the kidnapping, Roger Roper's two Satin Sands director-acolytes resigned. Donna's friends filled the vacancies."

I make my hand into a gun shape and point my index-finger barrel at Ted.

"The new board wants you."

Ted groans and shakes his head. "Don't think so. Given our Satin Sands history, Roger will find an excuse to fire us once he returns. I like Donna, but we're slammed as it is. Judge Glenn made me trustee for Crestway Plantation. I can't see any upside in taking Satin Sands back as a client."

I explain the contract terms Donna proposed. Ted quits shaking his head, and takes a vicious bite out of his sub. Looks like he's chewing on both the unwanted offer and his loaded hoagie.

"Donna did share one other bit of news." I sigh. "A lawyer for Carrie Sullivan's heirs is quizzing Satin Sands directors about my 'reckless' behavior. The acting sheriff claims I went ballistic after he questioned my expertise at their board meeting."

"That bastard," Mom growls.

"The lawyer hopes to show I have a history of rash behavior. My reputation for hysteria would argue that—'absent any real danger'—I ordered Carrie Sullivan into a sardine-like box and precipitated her heart attack."

Robin fiddles with the Coke can next to her paper plate. "Guess now's as good a time as any to tell you Howie Wynne left an urgent message for you, Kylee."

Howie Wynne? It takes a second to place the name. Howie is Mr. Red Mulch, the fellow Ernie Baker and Carrie Sullivan wanted to fine for his flowerbed's colored mulch. Ernie immediately insisted Howie was behind the SWAT prank.

"Don't keep us in suspense," Mom prompts Robin. "What was Howie's urgent message?"

Robin swallows. "He wants to hire Kylee to investigate the SWAT debacle. Says he had nothing to do with it, but some lawyer's claiming he instigated the SWAT raid that led to Carrie's death."

I roll my eyes. "Oh, brother. I'll return his call, but Howie should hire a PI, who won't be named in the same lawsuit."

Ted puts down the potato chip he'd carried halfway to his mouth. "Maybe, maybe not. Carrie's heirs must be looking to get rich in a civil suit where the rules of evidence are less stringent. You can bet that lawyer's contacted Ernie. Maybe you should help Howie prove his innocence. No doubt Ernie's telling everyone that Howie arranged the SWAT raid, and you overreacted and forced the directors into a bathroom. Making Mr. Media appear a fool—always a win in my book—would discount his accusations against Howie and you."

"Are you confident Howie's innocent?" Frank's deep voice demands attention.

Frank's not a big talker, but when he speaks, I listen.

"What if Howie did engineer the SWAT raid?" Frank continues. "Working on his behalf could be seen as a conflict of interest and proof you act before you think."

"Talk to Howie," Mom suggests. "Get a read on the man, then make a decision."

I nod. "Okay, I'll give Howie a call after you update us on the kidnapping. Haven't seen or heard any news all morning. Anything new?"

Before Mom can answer, a chime alerts us to someone at the office door.

"Have a special delivery for Ted Welch," the newcomer says.

One look at his outfit tells me he's not with Fed Ex or UPS. A chauffeur? Ted gets up to greet the man. "That's me. Do I need to sign for something?"

"No, sir, my instructions were simply to see that this envelope is delivered into your hands."

The man leaves without another word.

"Phew." Ted mimics wiping sweat from his brow. "Figured the special delivery might be a subpoena, but doubt they come in envelopes with gold-embossed seals."

"Bet it's our high-society wedding invite," Mom guesses.

"And you'd be right," Ted answers as he rips open the large cream-colored envelope. "Two Jade Pointe Inn suites are reserved for us Friday through Sunday. There are cards for each event, and we can call the wedding planner with any questions."

I sigh. "Like what to do if your closet holds no designer gowns? You sure you want to go to this?"

"Don't worry." Ted lifts an eyebrow. "Except for Saturday night's dinner and Sunday's wedding, noted as cocktail attire, all events are casual dress."

"Yeah, somehow my definition of casual—a T-shirt and jeans—may not be what they have in mind."

"Quit whining," Mom says. "It'll be fun. Before the special delivery interrupted, you asked if there was any kidnapping news. Melissa Yantis, my real estate buddy, called our acting sheriff and suggested he check out the vacant house list we put together. Ibsen was courteous. Thanked her for the call but dismissed her suggestion. Said he had good reason to believe the hostages were taken off the boat on St. Helena Island."

I frown. "Wonder what his 'good reason' could be? Everything Billy remembered pointed to the hostages being shuttled to an old house in a marshy area beyond the air station."

"I've been monitoring the news," Robin says. "Ernie's outlets are running 'in-depth'—quote, unquote—reports on Neuter1 extremism and the need for tough local lawmen like our own Sheriff Ibsen to crack down on suspected Lowcountry extremists."

She rolls her eyes. "Ernie's definition of extremists probably includes me. After all, I helped register voters and gave folks rides to the polls if they needed them."

I smile and finish my sub. The daiquiri hasn't spoiled my appetite.

"I'm surprised Grant isn't here—at least for lunch. What's he up to today?"

"He hoped to see Mimi, a nice college girl he dated last summer," Ted answers. "Grant admitted he's been lax about staying in touch, so he wasn't sure Mimi'd be enthusiastic."

Ted whips out his cellphone. "I'll call and see if he got a date and, if so, tell him she's invited to join us for dinner."

He walks away from the table to make the call. His cellphone etiquette earns him brownie points. Like Mom, I hate it when people take and make calls at a dinner table. Do they really think their in-person companions want to sit like mute dummies while they talk into a hunk of plastic?

A few minutes later, Ted returns. "Not answering. Left him a voice message to call and let us know if we should set one or two extra places at supper."

Mom laughs. "You'll hear back. That boy always responds to a question if food's involved."

# Chapter Thirty

The Leader

*Tuesday Noon*

The teens may be tied to chairs, but they're giving me a throbbing headache.

"Want to video them, too?" Jacob asks. "Two more privileged prima donnas to ransom."

Sounds like he believes the bothersome spies are gifts from the gods.

"No," I bark. "Think. One—maybe both of them—confided where they planned to hunt for hostages. Teenagers can't keep their mouths shut. If we show their faces, it'll lead authorities right to our door. And now is not the time to move our seven—no, make that nine—captives. The entire Lowcountry is on alert. Too risky."

"So, what do we do?" Matt asks.

"Convince the parents that Superboy and Lois Lane decided to wander about somewhere else—miles away. You found their cellphones, right?"

"Yeah. Sure...uh, sure did." Ryan titters like he's been named terrorist of the year. "Found hers on the truck floor. She must of dro...dropped it when I grabbed her. The cadet kid had his in a back pocket."

"Good. Give them to me."

I smile. Both phones have fingerprint scanners. They're kids. Impatient. Need instant gratification. Scanners unlock phones faster than entering passwords. No need for threats to coerce these two into spilling their passwords.

The boy stares daggers at me as I approach. Guess he's trying to convince me he really *is* Superboy, and his X-ray vision can see through my scratchy ski mask.

Zip ties secure his hands, palms down, to the chair arms, making it hard to access his fingers.

I wiggle my own fingers impatiently at Ryan. "Give me your knife."

I'm tempted to laugh at his fumble-bumble hurry, but I don't need him cutting himself and dripping blood. I grab the knife handle. Before I insert the blade between the chair and the tie to free the boy's right hand, I wave the knife in front of his face.

"I'm going to free your right hand, don't try anything stupid, or this knife gets an up-close introduction to your girlfriend's face. Be a shame to scar her pretty skin."

I slice through the tie. The kid balls his fingers into a fist. Guess it's his way of resisting the urge to try and land a punch.

"Which finger do you use to unlock your phone?" I ask.

His jaw seesaws, and he shakes his head.

"Okay, don't answer. I'll saw off your fingers one at a time. Hope I won't have to chop off all five before one works."

"His thumb," the girl blurts out and awards Superboy an apologetic shrug. "Not worth losing a finger."

I press the kid's right thumb to the scanner. "Okay, let's see who you've been chatting up."

I check his texts and voicemail. Hmm. The latest voicemail arrived a few minutes ago. I play it.

"Were you able to catch up with Mimi?" asks a deep male voice. "Not sure what your plans are, but you're welcome to bring her to dinner tonight. Let us know."

Undoubtedly the kid's father. Hope the old man reads texts and isn't one of those voice-only dinosaurs. Not gonna give the kid a chance to choose his own words and send some sort of code to his dad.

"Okay, Mimi, is it? You're up," I free her right hand. "Open your phone." With a surly look as her only protest, she complies.

Her phone shows lots of recent activity. She's snapped tons of photos in the last couple of hours and forwarded them. My heart beats faster. Has she been photographing vacant houses as they're crossed off a possibles list?

I open her photo gallery. A relieved sigh escapes. Not a single picture of a structure. The photos are all birds or landscapes. I show her the screen.

"Why'd you take these photos?" I ask.

"We told you. We're working on a nature documentary."

I laugh. "Don't think so. Just heard Superboy's dad wondering if he was able to connect with you. Kind of doubt you two have planned a documentary since breakfast. But I'll grant you, nature seems to be your thing. All these stills and videos of birds. There was snow on branches in earlier shots. Clearly not taken in Beaufort County. What's the deal?"

"I'm a birder," she mumbles. "Studying to become an ornithology researcher."

I laugh. "Well, well, good for you. Nonetheless, I don't think you two accidentally stumbled on the rare birdies who captured you. We found Superboy's drone. He's been filming old, decrepit houses in the marsh. Not sure how or why Superboy decided to search this area, and I'm betting he isn't willing to share."

I turn to Matt, my brightest collaborator. "Mid-afternoon, drive the kid's truck to Botany Bay. It'll take over an hour. It's been quite a while since I've been there, but it's a popular ACE Basin nature preserve. Take their cellphones. Since their thumbs won't be handy to reopen the phones, I'll make sure they stay on.

"When you get to Botany Bay, send texts to the most recent phone numbers. Superboy's dad and probably Mimi's mother or father. Text they've decided to do some birding at Botany Bay before Superboy takes Mimi to dinner in Charleston. Say they'll be home late. No need to wait up."

Matt nods. "Will Ryan or Jacob follow and give me a ride back?"

"Yes, Ryan can handle that while Jacob stays with the hostages," I say.

"This is important. After the texts are sent, smash the phones and bury them in marsh mud. If the parents start to get worried—hopefully not until morning—we want Botany Bay to show as the last place they used their phones. Oh, and wipe the truck down. No fingerprints."

Matt nods. "Got it. Smart. When and if their folks start a search, they'll have no reason to look in our direction."

He frowns and motions toward the teens. "What are you going to do with them?"

Matt's not only smart, he's the most principled of my three disciples. I promised him we wouldn't kill any hostages—even if our ransom demands failed.

"Don't worry," I reply. "They'll join our other guests for tonight's dinner. Baloney sandwiches are on the menu, right?" I smile. "The kids give us two added bargaining chips. They could come in handy as part of an exit strategy. Two hapless teenagers are infinitely more sympathetic than any number of over-the-hill, right-wing capitalists."

Ryan's forehead wrinkles. "How do we find this Bod...Bod...Any Bay?".

I resist the urge to slap my head—or his. "There are plenty of road signs to Edisto Island and the preserve. Just follow Matt's truck. He can use the GPS on his phone."

*You have it under control. Everyone's tied up. Jacob can hold down the fort. Time to get on with surprise wedding plans.*

# Chapter Thirty-One

Grant

*Tuesday Afternoon*

The kidnapper in the brown mask cuts the zip ties binding my feet to the straight-backed chair. He has zero worries about me kicking him. Can't even feel my toes, so I'm not up to channeling Jackie Chan.

Red Mask cuts the ties that still bind my left, mostly-numb, hand. Before I can flex my fingers, he and his buddy yank my arms behind my back. Jeez. Pain shoots up my arms to my shoulders. Leather cuts into my biceps as a belt winds around my upper arms, wrenching them backward. Do they want my elbows to touch?

The pair frog-marches me toward a flight of rickety steps.

*Can I head-butt one of them? Kick the other in the shins?*

Might work in a movie, not with my arms almost pulled out of their sockets. I'm having a hard time staying upright. My handlers pick up the pace and jerk me forward. My feet stumble. The thugs' iron grip is the only thing keeping my chin from whacking the floor.

I twist around for a final look at the leader. I want to memorize everything about him. If I survive, what could help authorities catch him? He's tall. Over six feet. Glasses don't camouflage the cruel ice-blue eyes. Pushed-up sleeves reveal a spider tattoo on his left forearm. Bushy light-brown hair.

Left-handed. Feet crossed at the ankles. Leather deck shoes.

The man notices me studying him. He leans back in his chair. A picture of casual disdain. He seems amused. Does he wonder what I'm thinking? Oh, God. What will he do to Mimi once he's alone with her? My anger yields to fear.

"Don't you hurt her," I yell.

"Don't worry." The captor holding my right arm snickers. "We'll bring your little girlie upstairs next. Put her close enough for you to plan your escape."

The men dragging me upstairs laugh uproariously. Why is the idea that we might hatch an escape plan so funny?

*Damn them. We're smarter than they think. They'll pay.*

On the second-floor landing, I'm shoved through a door. Three couples slump against the front wall. Duct tape binds the twosomes together at their waists. The ubiquitous sticky adhesive also immobilizes their hands and feet. There's no tape over their grim mouths, and they aren't blindfolded. They look to be about Myrt's age. But, unlike my grandma, their heads hang in defeat.

A single, middle-aged man has no companion. The developer? He's duct taped to a rusted patio chair.

The captives barely look up as I'm thrust inside.

My arms ache. Makes me wish the thugs would undo the belt and turn me into another duct-taped mummy. At least their hands are bound in front.

When the kidnappers leave, I start asking questions. "Are you all okay? Is there always someone on guard?"

The single guy—Spoonbill Island's would-be developer—shakes his head.

"They hear every word we say through those baby monitors. They don't have to be in the room to listen. Made that clear the first day. Came upstairs with a tape recorder and played back our conversations. Not much reason to talk."

"Who are you?" a plump woman across the room asks me. "Doubt you're the head of an HOA." She actually smiles.

"Grant." I only give my first name, thinking I shouldn't let the kidnappers know I'm Ted Welch's son. Then, I remember the stutterer saw me on TV. The video when we dropped the castaways at the marina included close-ups of me, Dad, and Kylee.

*They know who I am.*

"I'm Ted Welch's son," I add. "My friend Mimi and I were out exploring the marsh. Mimi was taking photos of birds when they nabbed us. She's downstairs. I'm scared what they might do to her."

"Don't fret, dear," the woman says. "Those men don't seem into torturing or, uhm, involving themselves in any other kinds of funny business. I'm Lucille Sanford, by the way. Your dad manages our HOA, Crestway Plantation."

Lucille's barely finished her introduction when Mimi arrives. She looks unharmed, but outraged at being manhandled.

# Chapter Thirty-Two

Grant

*Tuesday Afternoon*

O nce the kidnappers duct-tape Mimi and me together and leave, the developer asks some questions of his own.

"How did you stumble on this property? Are the authorities searching for us in this area? They keep telling us we'll be released as soon as their ransom demands are met. What's happening?"

I'm unsure how to answer. Every piece of information I share will be overheard by the kidnappers. I squeeze Mimi's hand, hoping she'll take it as a signal not to contradict my half-truths.

"Mimi's a birder," I reply. "While she was taking pictures of marsh birds, I flew my drone. Last summer I took aerial shots of properties for Dad's website. I was just playing. We had no idea the kidnappers were here."

The developer hangs his head. "Guess the authorities have no clue where to look for us. Tell us about the ransom negotiations. Are our friends and families raising money?"

I don't answer instantly, afraid the truth may deepen the hostages' despair. "The sheriff held a press conference. Said he needed proof of life before taking negotiations any further. That's all I know.

"Yesterday, we found your boat captain in the vacant lot next to Dad's office," I add. "He was real messed up. The kidnappers left a note in his pocket. Since my father manages some of your HOAs, the kidnappers tagged him to handle ransom negotiations. But the sheriff said Dad would face criminal charges if he lifted a finger. He's out of it."

Another hostage clears his throat. "I'm Cliff Jackson, president of the Hullis Island HOA. Did your father say how much money they want for our release?"

I shrug. "If Dad knows, he didn't tell me."

Mimi twists to bring her mouth close to my ear. "Good job," she whispers. "My photos of those elusive Bitterns may save us."

It takes me a minute to grasp Mimi's meaning. Just before I left to launch my drone, Mimi forwarded her father a picture of a Bittern along with a location panorama. She must think her dad can figure out where she took her last pictures.

"Love those Bitterns," I reply and nudge her shoulder with mine.

What more can I say? I hope Mimi's father questions the fake text from Mimi's phone. Perhaps he'll wonder why she isn't sending any bird or location photos.

I attempt a little mental telepathy.

*Dad, no way would I take Mimi to a Charleston restaurant. Not when I can order a big plate of Frogmore Stew on Lady's Island. Please don't buy the BS the kidnappers are selling.*

# Chapter Thirty-Three

Kylee

*Tuesday Afternoon*

Howie Wynne must be watching for me. A curtain twitches as I exit my car, and the front door opens before I'm halfway up the path. Lighthouse Cove is one of the wealthier HOAs that Ted manages. The homes, most with more than five-thousand-square-feet and three-car garages, sit on multiple-acre lots. Howie's sprawling three-story brick and stone home is typical. Can't help but notice the red mulch cozying up to the evergreen shrubs that bracket the front entry.

*While it's not my taste, the mulch doesn't offend me.* I'm continually amazed that some HOA boards want their personal taste in landscaping forced on their neighbors.

"Miss Kane, so glad you decided to come. I'm Howie Wynne. Please come in."

My hand's lost inside his oversized mitt as he welcomes me with a firm handshake. Howie's tall, maybe six-foot-five. Don't know why I expected him to be elderly, small in stature, and a little stooped.

While his hair's streaked with gray, I know first-hand that hair color's not a reliable indicator of age. Muscled forearms say he lifts weights. He's maybe late forties, early fifties. In other words, about my age. Definitely not elderly.

He ushers me down a long hall. "Let's talk in my office. It'll be easier to share my research."

Howie's home office/den could be a Scandinavian furniture showroom. Again, a surprise. Guess I figured a man of his considerable size would favor a massive oak desk and sturdy side chairs with claws for feet, not lean, sculpted wood rockers.

*Maybe I should quit guessing and just see what Howie has to say.*

"Mr. Wynne," I begin. "I'm not a licensed private investigator, which is what it sounds like you need."

He waves a hand in dismissal as he sinks into a seat behind a glass and chrome desk. No clutter, just a computer keyboard and oversized screen on the polished surface.

"Call me, Howie. I'm more impressed by results than licenses. Your takedown of that serial killer this fall was nothing short of amazing. Also, we share a stake in this. From what I hear, the attorney hired by Carrie's heirs is gunning for you, too."

"You're right about that," I answer. "What exactly are you hoping to do—prove your innocence or someone else's guilt?"

"My innocence. While I really don't give a flip who made the call, I need to counter that turd of an acting sheriff's contention that I'm the only person with a motive. Ernie has Ibsen in his back pocket. Ibsen takes that right-wing zealot's accusations as gospel."

I nod. *Can't disagree.*

"Did Ibsen ask if you had an alibi?"

"Yeah. That's a problem. No alibi. I was home alone the entire afternoon. I'm a financial advisor and work out of the house. Unfortunately, the day of the SWAT raid, I had no client conferences to confirm I was in my office—which I was. Just catching up on bookkeeping."

I frown. "An alibi isn't essential. You know the old 'innocent until proven guilty' thing. The Sheriff's Department requires actual evidence—something more than Ernie's accusations—to charge you."

"Again, Sheriff Dickhead claims I'm the *only* person with a motive." Howie snorts. "Like half a dozen neighbors wouldn't love to put a scare into Ernie.

He's changing our neighborhood, and not for the better. Ever listen to the broadcasts on his stations? Victims of his vicious smear campaigns would love to see him dead."

"Believe me, I'm not one of Ernie's fans," I say. "But, let's look at this objectively. The SWAT team was sent to the clubhouse when the board was in session. Would a neighborhood outsider know when and where the board meets? The circumstances suggest whoever set this up lives in Lighthouse Cove."

Howie's shoulders slump. "Great. Your reasoning tightens the noose around my neck."

"No, it just means whoever arranged the fake SWAT alert knew about the board meeting. Even so, Ibsen has zero evidence you recorded the gunshots, stashed the recorder in the clubhouse, or made the 911 call."

"They found my fingerprints on the table where the tape recorder sat," Howie continues. "Given my motive and opportunity, Ibsen thinks the prints clinch my guilt. While I haven't been charged yet, I suspect I will be soon as Ibsen gets a breather from this kidnapping case."

Howie raises his eyes to mine. "Even if my attorney clears me of criminal charges, you and I will both be defendants in a civil suit."

*Crap.*

"Can you explain why your prints were on that table?"

"Sure. Look, I'm gay, and my husband's a gregarious guy. We regularly attend social get-togethers at the club. Before Ernie arrived, everyone—well, almost everyone—in this neighborhood seemed to welcome us or, at least, accept us.

"I'm sure my fingerprints weren't the only ones on that table," he adds. "The cleaning service isn't *that* thorough. Besides, if the recorder had fingerprints on it, Ibsen would have said so. If I'm the guilty party, why would I wear gloves to plant the recorder and then take them off to leave my prints on the table?"

"Good question," I agree. "Everything you've told me suggests you need a good attorney more than a private investigator."

"I have a good attorney." Howie smiles for the first time. "Mike Jones, my husband. We talked this over. He agrees there's merit in showing Ernie has a slew of enemies who might be responsible."

He glances at a computer printout on his desk. "We started a list. We'd like to hire you to determine if one or more have opportunity as well as motive, demonstrating the sheriff focused on me without investigating other possibilities."

"You want me to investigate your neighbors? I'm a consultant for your HOA manager. Isn't that a potential conflict of interest?"

Howie shakes his head. "Mike doesn't think so. Ted's company works for our community as a whole. Not Ernie or any individual owner. Whoever tried to terrorize the board represents a security threat for all of Lighthouse Cove. Who says the culprit won't do something more drastic next time?"

"Let me talk this over with Ted. I'll give you my answer by tomorrow."

"That's fair," Howie says. "Take the printout. I'm sure Ted knows a number of people on the list."

We shake hands, and Howie walks me to my car.

*Wonder if I should pencil my name on the list. Ernie clearly considers me an enemy.*

# Chapter Thirty-Four

Kylee

*Tuesday Afternoon*

I use the office copier to duplicate the Ernie Baker enemies list. Then I head to Ted's cubicle to discuss the pros and cons of helping Howie uncover more information about potential suspects in the active-shooter hoax.

"Can you spare a moment to talk over Howie's plea for investigative help? My instincts tell me he's innocent. But if Ibsen learns I'm working on Howie's behalf, it'll only harden his resolve to nail the poor guy."

Ted switches off his computer screen and focuses on me. "Are you confident Howie's innocent?"

I fill Ted in on the flimsy fingerprint evidence Ibsen's using to place Howie in the clubhouse. I add that Olivia, another director, ridiculed Ernie's immediate accusation that Howie arranged the SWAT raid. On the flip side, I note the timing and location of the SWAT prank argue a Lighthouse Cove neighbor's responsible.

Ted taps a pencil on his desk as he stares off in the distance. This means he's thinking and isn't suffering a stroke. Unlike me, Ted thinks silently. He'll answer when he's ready.

"If Ernie wants the acting sheriff to charge Howie for suckering the SWAT team, you can bet Ibsen will do his bidding," Ted says. "Ibsen needs Ernie's support to get elected. Your involvement won't matter one way or the other."

"Think there's a conflict with my investigating owners in an HOA you manage?"

Ted shakes his head. "Howie's argument is solid. Whoever's behind this prank is a threat to the community as a whole, to everyone who lives in Lighthouse Cove."

He pauses. "However, limiting the suspect list to Lighthouse Cove owners might be a mistake. True, it's a gated community. But we both know how easy it is to bypass guards. And, when's the last time the clubhouse keypad code was changed? Even I know it's 1234—not exactly high-level security."

I nod. "True. But how would an outsider know when the board was meeting? This HOA doesn't post meeting times on its website's public face."

Ted laughs. "Simple to hack into the member section, and directors don't keep their meetings secret. Maybe Carrie asked her hairdresser to change an appointment so she could attend. Or Ernie might have bragged about teaching Howie a lesson for putting in red mulch. Any of the directors could have mentioned the meeting on social media."

I smile. "Guess I've been a bit myopic. I focused on Ernie's claim the SWAT team was called to intimidate him for trying to stamp out colored mulch. It could have been anyone with a beef against one director or the entire board."

"Right you are," Ted says. "Though Ernie's the most pugnacious director and easiest to dislike. Plus, whoever called 911 identified himself as Ernie Baker. That suggests he was the target. Show me Howie's list."

Ted scans the names, placing dashes, checkmarks, or question marks next to each.

"What's the code?" I ask.

"Checkmarks by owners I can see thinking up a stunt like this. Dashes by folks I can't imagine venting their ire this way."

"What about the two question marks?"

"I've never met Desi Darling in person, and Stan Hiller died months ago. Yet, I get why Howie put their names on the list."

"Let's start with Desi," I say. "Why is she on the list?"

"An on-air talent, Desi filed a lawsuit against Ernie that has yet to go to trial. She claims Ernie fired her after she rebuffed his proposition."

"Euww." I shudder. "The thought of Ernie coming on to some poor girl gives me the willies."

Ted laughs. "Desi's not exactly a 'poor girl.' She quickly landed a job hosting a talk show on another outlet. Her sharp tongue shreds unprepared guests in minutes. And she lives in Lighthouse Cove."

"What about the man who died?" I ask. "What's the sense of leaving him on the list?"

"The coroner ruled Stan Hiller's death an accidental overdose—prescription drugs. Imagine Howie included Stan since his family might seek revenge for the hell Ernie put Stan through in his final months."

I hear Mom's voice even before I realize she's joined us.

"Hell is right," Mom says. "Stan was a decent man. Well-liked and respected. He founded a successful hedge fund and was a big-time donor to liberal causes. That's why Ernie went after him."

Ted picks up the thread of the story, "Stan was a practicing Catholic. Ernie first used his media pulpit to pressure a local priest to refuse Stan communion because of his pro-choice abortion stance.

"When Stan didn't back off, Ernie hunted for dirt," he continues. "Discovered Stan belonged to a sexual-abuse recovery group and paid a member to break the group's confidentiality pledge. Ernie's headlines claimed Stan was mentally unbalanced because an uncle sexually abused him as a child."

"A very nasty campaign." Mom's voice is practically a growl. "I won't listen to Ernie's broadcasts or subscribe to any paper he owns. I can't fathom how his stations get away with violating people's privacy like that."

"Ernie argued Stan was a public figure," Ted replies.

"While Ernie can't be held responsible for Stan's accidental overdose, his family must be plenty angry."

"True." Mom shakes her head. "Doctors had Stan on a dozen meds for his cancer. I know what chemo brain's like. Easy to get mixed up and take a double dose. That said, Ernie's smears didn't do Stan's mental health any good. A widower, he lived alone. Son lives in Chicago. Lots of Stan's friends felt Ernie Baker deserved a swift kick in the keister for picking on a sick man. If I'd been his son, I'd have sued Ernie."

"And you'd have smashed right into a First-Amendment brick wall," Ted says.

"Does Stan's son have ties to Lighthouse Cove?" I ask.

"Yes," Ted answers. "Ed Hiller inherited his father's three-million-dollar mansion. Ed uses it as a second-home retreat when he can get away. Lives in Chicago with his wife and kids."

"Sounds like I should chat with both Desi Darling and Ed Hiller."

# Chapter Thirty-Five

## The Leader

*Tuesday Afternoon*

T hank God for a little peace and quiet. I do my best thinking alone, gazing at the water. My yacht, *Seaduction*, is the only thing I own free and clear. Dear old Mom gifted me the fifty-eight-foot flybridge yacht six years ago. Or rather, I guilted her into giving the boat to me.

It was an easy sell. Mom's a recluse. Never steps foot outside the Savannah mansion her parents left her. She's become a pharmacological zombie. Her interest in the living doesn't extend beyond a prescription score.

Except for Saffron and me, Mom only allows two people to visit. One is a "doctor," who functions as her drug dealer. Then there's an eighty-year-old cleaning lady who looks in on her employer a couple times a week to see if she still has a pulse.

My sister didn't begrudge me the yacht. Saffron prefers horseflesh and men—in that order—to boating. Sis had just tied the knot to the first of three wealthy husbands and had bought her very own racehorse.

I fetch a cold beer from the galley and sit down with a pen and paper to list the venues for Phil's show-off wedding for a hundred and fifty A-list guests. All Jade Pointe Inn rooms are reserved for the wedding party, and a dozen of the island's palatial houses are rented for overflow. According to

Saffron, the groom's hosting a dozen or so houseguests at his mansion, too.

I make three columns and label the first "Friday Night/Beach Clambake." I scribble Ernie's name under my clambake header, then cross it off as irrelevant. Ernie will be at every event. Never passes up hobnobbing opportunities. I add fireworks and draw a star. The gossips claim the fireworks display will rival Boston's Fourth of July blowout. Media insiders urge ordinary mortals—uninvited guests—to crank up their motorboats, head to the Jade Pointe harbor early, and drop anchor for a front-row seat.

I draw another star. Friday's beach party has strong appeal. It'll be dark, and fireworks are noisy. Multiple bangs will help disguise a gunshot or one big bang. Everyone will be looking at the sky, not paying attention to folks on the ground. At least until people die. An explosion fits nicely with my Neuter1 theme.

I drain the last swallow of my beer and write "Saturday Activities" as the next header. The pre-wedding crowd can choose to sign up for a tennis round-robin, a golf tournament, or a complimentary day at the Jade Pointe spa.

Phil and Ernie will be on the golf course. I signed up, too. I pencil golf accident on the paper. But being one of the golfers would move my name up any suspect list.

Under Saturday Activities, I list the evening's formal dinner at the Jade Pointe Club. This will be the biggest gathering—besides the wedding—and there's no guesswork about Phil's whereabouts. He'll be at the head table. Will Ernie be close by? Wonder if there's a way to get my hands on a seating chart. Something to consider...

I write "Sunday" atop the last column and mark the two o'clock wedding. Sunday's out. I can't wait until the last minute. Phil must be dead before he says "I do" to wife number four.

I'd prefer to strike when Ernie and Phil are within a few feet of each other. But I can't pass up my best opportunity to kill Phil just because Ernie isn't nearby. The timing of Ernie's death can wait, though I like the symmetry of the pair dying the same day. Apropos, since they collaborated to ruin my life.

Okay, I have the opportunities. What about means? A shooting? Poisoning? A bomb?

A small bomb would be ideal. A Neuter1 fanatic would never gun down an individual target. A bomb makes a statement. Placing an explosive entails risk. Need a small, easy-to-conceal explosive with a guaranteed kill zone. Remote control is a must. Can't have anyone see me trigger the blast. The charge also needs to be shaped so I can control the blast direction. I'm not overly squeamish about collateral damage, but I'd prefer not to blow up Sis.

Too bad I have zero weapons expertise. I'd self-destruct if I tried to concoct some homemade IED. No choice. I need the help of a terrorist or criminal, either of whom would happily slit my throat.

I sigh. My kidnapping plan was so perfect. Ernie and Phil would have been unlucky casualties in a captivity screw-up. I chose my hapless Neuter1 recruits because they weren't on any law enforcement radar. I had to convince them to step up and actually do something for the cause. Neuter1 would be blamed. Never in this world would anyone consider me a suspect.

My radicalized Neuter1 followers are of zero help with my wedding surprise. I might sell Jacob and Ryan that a deadly explosion at a billionaire's bash would serve as a Neuter1 exclamation point—another signal Neuter1 won't tolerate rule by the one percent. But Matt wouldn't go along. He's all about using ransom money for the cause, not killing.

I underline explosives. Before hatching my kidnap scheme, I asked an old Boston buddy if he could put me in touch with someone who knows how to blow up things. Didn't mention people. My friend's family's "connected." I never hinted what I wanted blown up, and he was smart enough not to ask. He gave me a phone number. I figure connecting with this guy is a lot safer than risking being caught in an FBI sting operation on the dark web. But my contact information is months old. Hope he hasn't been arrested.

*Time is short. Do I dare make the call?*

# Chapter Thirty-Six

## The Leader

*Tuesday Afternoon*

I glare at the number displayed on the throwaway phone. Watch it vibrate its way to the edge of the galley table. What the hell's gone sideways now?

Don't bother with a hello. "What?" I bark.

"Botany Bay was closed with a beefy wood gate blocking the road. No way around it," Matt answers. "I'd already sent the phone texts, so I left the truck on the side of the road near the gate. If we're lucky, no one will notice it till morning. Or maybe they'll think the kids snuck inside for a little hanky-panky."

*Probably not. Given my luck, someone will spot the truck and call a park ranger. Could those photos the girl emailed lead back to our safe house, to the hostages?*

I grit my teeth and fight the urge to scream.

"You wiped the truck down, right?" I ask.

"Of course," Matt answers. "Ryan and I are heading back to the house. Should be there in an hour to relieve Jacob."

My brain's grinding on all manner of end-of-the-universe calamities. I want to yell in frustration, but I'm the one who screwed the pooch this time. Had a vague recollection of an open gate and no park ranger. Why didn't I check the Botany Bay website?

"You still there?" Matt asks.

"Yeah, just thinking. Don't go back to the house. If someone studies the photos the girl took, they might use visual breadcrumbs to backtrack where the kids were earlier. Check into that same sleazebag I-95 motel where we met up before. The hostages aren't going anywhere. Jacob can feed them, sanitize the place, and join you at the motel. Meanwhile, I'll figure out how to move the hostages to a new place."

"Okay," Matt answers. "Hate leaving Jacob alone to do all the work."

"Not a big deal," I answer. "We wore gloves in the house, haven't left fingerprints. Shouldn't take long for Jacob to cart off items that could tell authorities where we shopped.

"The hostages won't know Jacob's gone," I add. "That's the beauty of those baby monitors. They think there's always someone downstairs listening."

# Chapter Thirty-Seven

Kylee

*Tuesday Evening*

"Choose your poison—chicken divan or chili," Mom orders. "You can nuke your choice in the microwave. Since Thanksgiving's only a day away, I'm putting all my cooking mojo into making sides. No entrées. Besides, the twenty-three-pound turkey thawing in the refrigerator doesn't leave much room. Need you to eat up these leftovers."

"Not a problem," Ted answers. "I'll go for the chicken divan."

"Make mine chili," I reply.

Once our food's warmed, we sit at the kitchen table.

Mom eyes Grant's empty chair. "Kind of disappointed Grant didn't bring Mimi to dinner. Enjoyed chatting with her last summer. Nice, bright girl."

I grin. "Maybe Grant decided microwaving leftovers wasn't the best way to impress a date."

"Could be," Ted says, "but I'm surprised he's taking Mimi to Charleston for dinner. He loves that seafood joint on Lady's Island, and he's never mentioned any Charleston restaurants. The Citadel doesn't give freshman cadets much free time to explore urban dining options."

Ted frowns. "Sorry. My cellphone's been vibrating constantly. It's going to wear a hole all the way through to my underwear if I don't answer. I'll be back in a minute."

Abiding by Mom's iron-clad policy on cellphones at the dinner table, Ted leaves the room to answer.

When he returns, Ted looks sick. "That was Carl Jones, Mimi's father. Carl got a similar text about dining out in Charleston and coming home late. He's convinced Mimi didn't send it. She'd made six-thirty dinner plans with two high school friends. Mimi was a no-show and never called her friends. They texted Mimi and left voicemails. Concerned they couldn't reach her, one of them called her parents.

"Carl tried to reach Mimi, too," he continues. "No reply. He's worried, and so am I. Carl says Mimi would never go to Botany Bay today since she knows it's always closed to the general public on Tuesdays. Even if she forgot, he says Mimi would have checked the South Carolina Department of Natural Resources website this time of year to see if they'd authorized any hunts. It's currently closed for a three-day teen archery hunt."

"You tried to reach Grant, right?" I ask. "Nothing?"

Ted's dejected look is my answer. "No luck. It's not like him to ignore my texts. The 'Send Last Location' app on Grant's phone shows Botany Bay. Of course, he could be anywhere if the battery's low. The app doesn't work then."

"Grant never turns his phone off," Mom's voice jumps an octave higher. "Why did they go there? What could have happened? A truck accident?"

Ted shakes his head. "I don't know. I'm meeting Carl in Beaufort, and we're driving to Botany Bay. Maybe one of them fell or twisted an ankle, and it's taking them time to get back to the truck in the dark."

"I'm coming with you," I say. "On the way, I'll check accident reports in Colleton and Charleston counties."

"I'm going, too," Mom says.

Ted holds up his hand. "No. Myrt, you need to stay here in case Grant shows up or phones. Maybe cell service is out in the area, or both Grant and Mimi let their phones run out of juice. Who knows?"

The set of Mom's jaw says she's not happy. "Okay. But you'd better phone the minute you have news. Any news."

"Promise," I say and kiss her cheek.

# Chapter Thirty-Eight

## Grant

*Tuesday Evening*

The sun's set, but enough murky light leaches through the filthy windowpanes to read the distress on the faces of everyone huddled in the room.

*Do they leave us in the dark all night?*

Can't imagine this dump has any electricity.

Blue Mask arrives with a lantern and trash barrel and sets both in the center of the room. He reaches inside the barrel to extract a 12-pack of water bottles and a large plastic bag crammed with sandwiches.

*Will he untie us to eat? May be my chance.*

No dice. The captor methodically feeds one couple at a time. Never unties a man's hand. Instead, he frees the left hand of each woman so she can feed herself and her husband. When each couple's time is up, Blue Mask tosses leftovers and the empty water bottles back in the trash barrel. After re-securing the woman's hand, he moves to the next couple. A no-nonsense assembly line.

Blue Mask watches each couple eat, giving them not quite three minutes to wolf down the shared white-bread sandwich and take a few swigs of water.

Since the developer has no partner, Blue Mask holds the doughy bread to his mouth. The developer turns his head.

"I'd rather starve. Even pigs won't eat that shit."

I hold my breath, thinking Blue Mask will smack Ken across the mouth or mash the sandwich in his face like some madcap scene in the old Three Stooges movies Dad watches.

Blue Mask laughs. "Getting irritable, are we? Well, if you don't eat shit, it means you don't need to shit. No bathroom visit for you tonight."

Mimi and I are the last to be fed. Left-handed, Mimi holds the sandwich to my lips. I shake my head. "Not hungry."

"Me either, but eat anyway. No telling when we'll have another chance."

"Well, well." Blue Mask's tone hints at a smile. "At least one of you has an IQ above eighty."

I take a big bite. The spongy bread imprisons paper-thin slices of baloney slathered with a thick layer of room-temperature mayo. Chewing turns it into a hard-to-swallow paste.

"Water?" Mimi asks.

I nod and gratefully gulp enough to wash down the edible glue.

Blue Mask's comment about bathroom visits makes me wonder how that works for couples. Anger surges at Mimi's potential humiliation.

The kidnapper snatches what's left of our sandwich. I got two bites. Two too many. We drain the water bottle before he can grab it.

When Blue Mask leaves, he takes the lantern, plunging us into a gloomy twilight.

"Nighty-night, now." He chuckles as he closes the door. "Sleep tight."

# Chapter Thirty-Nine

Kylee

*Tuesday Evening*

C arl's easy to spot. Dressed in a black puffer jacket, Mimi's lanky father paces beside his white Corvette at the designated used car lot entrance. A fluorescent streetlamp tints his bald scalp a ghastly green. The shade seems to suit his sickly expression.

Ted rolls down the window as his Lexus pulls alongside. "I'm Ted Welch. Sorry we're meeting this way." He tips his head toward me. "This is Kylee Kane, a retired Coast Guard investigator. She has contacts if we need to call in law enforcement. Hop in."

I trade my passenger seat for the back so Carl can ride shotgun. I barely get my seatbelt snapped before Ted stomps on the gas like someone dropped a checkered flag.

"I've spent time with your son," Carl begins. "A good kid. Want you to know I'm not out to blame Grant for anything. Hope the kids simply turned off their phones. But I can't imagine Mimi heading to Botany Bay on a Tuesday or blowing off a get-together with her girlfriends."

Carl shifts slightly in his seat to address me as well as Ted. "I feel like I know both of you. Mimi raved about how much fun she had when you took them sailing last summer."

I smile. "We had a good time. Mimi told us you own an IT company.

Information technology covers a lot of ground, but I assume you're savvy about smartphones. Ted checked Grant's 'Last Location' app, which pinpointed Botany Bay."

"Same result for Mimi's cell," Carl says.

He pauses. "Deciding to drive to Botany Bay seems very odd even if Mimi somehow forgot the park closes on Tuesdays."

"How so?" Ted asks.

"All afternoon, she emailed me pictures of birds—Roseate Spoonbills, Northern Flickers, American Bitterns," he explains. "We're both avid birders. She also sent panoramas showing where she found each species. All were in Beaufort County spots we visited together. From a birder perspective, Mimi was having real luck. No reason to suddenly head to Botany Bay."

Ted nods. "That is strange. Being so late in the day, they wouldn't have had much light left for photography either. And Botany Bay's an out-of-the-way detour if you're heading to a Charleston restaurant."

The hour-long ride to Botany Bay turns quiet. Each of us lost in thought about what might have prompted the teens' side trip. I use my cell to check on accidents and breathe a sigh of relief when nothing beyond a few fender benders has been reported in Beaufort, Colleton or Charleston Counties.

I share the information with Ted and Carl.

"One less worry," Carl says.

After we turn onto SC Hwy 174, all manmade sources of light seem to vanish. The rural two-lane spans vast stretches of coastal wetlands with only scattered human habitation. While the clear sky showcases millions of stars in the Milky Way, the slender new moon does little to illuminate the narrow ribbon of highway.

When we finally turn onto Edisto Bay Road, I hold my breath. The moss-draped, live-oak canopy blots out the pale moon's watery light. Our headlights unveil a long dark lump in the road. Ted stomps on the brakes.

"Alligator," he says. "A big one. Taking his time crossing the road."

I've visited Botany Bay's four-thousand-acre nature preserve many times. Its boneyard beach, filled with bleached serpentine tree limbs, is an awe-inspiring tribute to beauty and death. Trails through its marshes and maritime forest provide glimpses of alligators, raccoons, and other inhabitants. Though there's no fee, the entrance is manned. When it's open, a guide greets visitors and hands out maps. But, even during prime tourist season, the public can only visit between dawn and dusk. When closed, an impressive gate bars the entrance.

We've almost reached the gate when our headlights pick up a truck's off-kilter silhouette. "Ted, it's your truck!" I shout.

Parked on a slant, the truck tires nearest the road sit a foot uphill from the ones on the opposite side. Ted's headlights pierce the truck's interior. No one's inside.

"Damn," Ted says. "Where are they? No way Grant would risk his cadet status to sneak into Botany Bay after hours."

A chill runs down my spine. *No, Grant wouldn't do that, unless they were being chased.*

"Same goes for Mimi," Carl says. "Especially in hunting season. If the kids got here before dark, going inside Botany Bay could risk an arrow in the chest."

I voice my fear. "What if they were being chased? Entering the park might have seemed the lesser of two evils."

"Oh, no! I hadn't thought of that," Ted swears.

"We need to call the sheriff," I suggest.

"What if we're wrong and the kids snuck in as a prank?" Carl asks. "The authorities could arrest Grant and Mimi for trespassing."

Ted shakes his head. "An arrest is preferable to other alternatives. What if someone *is* chasing them? What if they slipped inside for some unknown reason, and one of them had an accident? Kylee's right. We need to make the call."

Carl frowns. "Shouldn't we search the truck first?"

"No," I reply. "If it turns out to be a crime scene, we can't risk contaminating evidence."

"Crime scene?" Carl chokes on the word. "Evidence?"

# Chapter Forty

Kylee

*Tuesday Evening*

Having worked with George Ellis, the Charleston County Sheriff, on joint Coast Guard-law enforcement exercises, I trust the man. He's smart and a team player. Nothing like Beaufort's acting sheriff, Nick the Asswipe.

I phone George and explain our worries. He agrees to send deputies and contact Jack McVea, Botany Bay's park ranger. "I'm on my way, too," he adds. "We'll coordinate with Jack if we need a search team."

I'm surprised George is coming. Not standard procedure, given the size of the county and his responsibilities. Our friendship is definitely a factor.

Ted, Carl, and I stamp our feet to stay warm as we fidget outside the gate. We only need to wait ten minutes for the park ranger to appear.

After we exchange curt who's-who introductions, Jack motions toward the entrance. "The sheriff tells me you're worried two young folks left that truck and went into the park. And you think it's possible they were chased or forced inside. Any idea when they arrived?"

"Text messages were sent from here around five-fifteen," Ted answers. "While we have serious doubts our children sent those texts of their own accord, they came from their phones."

Jack doesn't speak as he drags the toe of his boot through a hump of gravel. "We're hosting a teen bow-and-arrow hunting event." He looks up to meet our eyes. "If your timing's right, you needn't worry about your young people being injured by a wayward arrow. I personally checked all the hunters out before five."

"Our kids could still be inside and injured," Carl says. "Especially if someone was after them. It's already dark. We should start a search now."

"Let's wait for the sheriff," Jack answers. "He'll be here soon. If he agrees to a search operation, I'll call in park staff and folks from the Department of Natural Resources. We need people who know how to safely search in a wild area after dark."

I walk toward Ted's abandoned truck and use my cellphone flashlight to study the ground near it. Faint shoe prints are visible in the damp earth.

"Do you know what shoes she was wearing when she left home?" I ask Carl.

He frowns. "Mimi always wears hiking boots to go birding. Never know when you're going to step in pluff mud to get the photo you want."

"Does she have big feet?" I press.

"No, just the opposite. When our boots are sitting side-by-side in the mudroom, there's no chance I'll pick the wrong pair. Doubt I could get my big toe inside her boots. Why?"

"Come look at these footprints," I invite the men. "Impressions from two different shoes and both sets are big."

"I wear a size twelve," Ted comments. "Both prints look about my size, and the soles have shallow treads. I'm no expert, but I doubt boots made these prints."

"Definitely not Mimi." Carl's shoulders slump. "We shouldn't wait any longer to search the truck for clues."

As he lurches forward, I grab his arm. "Carl, we need to wait for the sheriff. We don't want to mess up any evidence."

The color drains from his face. "Are you talking about blood?"

"No." My answer is emphatic. "Fingerprints. If the kids were being chased, their pursuers may have left prints on door handles when they looked in the truck. There's also the possibility Grant and Mimi were never here.

Someone could have driven the truck here to throw us off base. Maybe that's the reason for those weird text messages. Somebody leading us on a goose chase."

"Look." Jack motions us to join him on the opposite side of the dirt road. "More fresh tire tracks. Someone recently parked across from the truck. A single set of footprints leads from this missing vehicle to the truck."

My mind buzzes with possibilities as two Charleston County Sheriff SUVs arrive. Ted hustles into the road and waves to prevent the vehicles from pulling onto the shoulder and obliterating the mystery vehicle's tire tracks.

The sheriff looks slightly peeved until we explain that a second vehicle, now vanished, might have interacted with the abandoned truck.

The sheriff nods his understanding. "We don't know if there's been a crime, but two kids have gone missing under suspicious circumstances. I'd rather go overboard than fail to act. Scott, bring an evidence kit. Let's make casts of the tire tracks and footprints. We also need to dust the truck handles, steering wheel, and dash for fingerprints."

While the sheriff and his deputies work the scene, I pull Ted aside and share my growing conviction. "If Mimi climbed out of the truck, we'd see small boot prints. Since there are none, Grant and Mimi didn't leap from the truck, running for their lives.

"And I can't come up with a scenario that concludes with Mimi and Grant being carried into the park." I choose my words carefully to avoid conjuring up images of thugs disposing of dead bodies. "Sure, if someone carried Mimi, it could explain the absence of small boot prints. Yet the prints suggest two males. If one set of footprints belonged to Grant, we're left with a single bad guy. Grant would never saunter alongside a single kidnapper with Mimi in danger."

The sheriff shouts, "Come here. Don't know what it means, but this truck's been wiped clean. Not a single fingerprint on door handles, steering wheel, or dash."

"No reason for Grant to erase his fingerprints," Ted says. "I loaned him the truck."

The sheriff shrugs. "Have to consider your boy might want us to believe he wasn't the driver."

"That makes no sense," I complain. "Not with text messages sent from his phone that claim he drove here. Those texts were meant to lead us astray."

"So, what's your theory?" the sheriff demands.

"Mimi and Grant were never here." I quickly explain my reasoning before anyone can interrupt.

Carl shakes his head. "I get your logic. But what if you're wrong? Mimi could be in the park, praying someone will save her. I can't let your hunch stop us from looking, not if it might cost Mimi's life."

The sheriff huddles briefly with the park ranger.

"Okay," George says. "We'll call in a K-9 search-and-rescue team. We found a red-and-black plaid scarf in the truck. Is it Mimi's?"

Carl nods.

"Good," the sheriff continues. "If the dog can pick up a scent, we might have some luck out there in the dark. If not, we'll decide on next steps in the morning."

# Chapter Forty-One

Grant

*Tuesday Evening*

A car engine coughs. Is another kidnapper leaving? How many are left?

When they dragged me inside, my brain was mush. How many cars do they have?

*Duh. What an idiot!* Two plus two is four. My drone pictured a panel van and a Jeep parked outside the house. The stutterer who zapped me drove a four-wheeler, and he stole my truck. That makes four vehicles.

*Think.* The leader told Red Mask to drive my truck to Botany Bay and ordered another guy to follow in the van. A little later, I heard a third car leave. The leader's Jeep?

Does the departure of a fourth vehicle mean we're alone?

Maybe. Though it doesn't say they won't be back soon. The two thugs headed to Botany Bay had orders to return. How long have they been gone?

"I think all the kidnappers left," I whisper to Mimi.

"Why?" she whispers back.

"All four vehicles have left," I answer, "and that means four people drove them away. We've only seen four kidnappers. Could there be others?"

"Might be. We've only been here a few hours."

Abandoning her whispers, Mimi speaks up. "Grant and I have seen four kidnappers. Are there more we haven't seen?"

"Are you nuts?" Cliff Jackson, the Hullis Island HOA president, complains. "They warned us not to talk about them, to say anything that might be interpreted as planning an escape."

"But, if there are only four," I reply, "no one's listening. I think we have an opportunity."

"We've only seen four," Lucille pipes up. "If someone's listening, they'll show up soon enough to end our little chat. If not, we're alone. What do you have in mind?"

"Are you crazy?" Cliff persists. "The kidnappers will let us go as soon as they get their ransom. You want to risk getting killed because two teenagers think they can outsmart them?"

"What if the ransom negotiations stall?" Lucille replies. "Think our captors would hesitate murdering one or more of us to show they're serious?"

The developer's head snaps up. "Suppose you're right, and they've all left. We don't know how soon one of our keepers will return. Even if we manage to get free of this duct tape, we have no phones, no cars. And we're in the middle of nowhere. You better believe they'll retaliate if they find us stumbling down the road."

Lucille nods. "Ken's right about a mass exodus. Impossible for nine of us to free ourselves and hoof it any distance before someone returns. But Grant and Mimi can move a lot faster. If they make it to the highway, they can flag down help, tell the sheriff and the FBI where to find us."

Cliff snorts. "You think these kids are little Houdinis? They're bound together like contestants in a potato sack race. How are they supposed to sprint away?"

"I may be able to solve that little problem," says Cliff's wife, Peggy. "There's a fingernail file in my fanny pack. They relieved me of my wallet and cellphone. Didn't bother to take my nail file and lipstick. Grant, honey, if you and Mimi can scoot over here, Cliff and I can wiggle around so you can reach in my fanny pack."

I smile at Peggy. Cliff looks peeved.

"Mimi, are you game?"

"Yes, let's try to stand."

Pressing our backs against the wall, we slowly inch upwards. Once we're standing, we clumsily hop across the room to Cliff and Peggy. They skootch away from the wall so we can access Peggy's hidden treasures.

"If we slowly bend over, I can unzip her fanny pack and get the file," Mimi says. "But we need to move together or we're going to topple."

"Got it," I answer.

Thank goodness they didn't bind our hands behind our backs.

Once Mimi retrieves the file, she starts sawing the tape binding my wrists together. With my hands free, I tackle Mimi's bonds.

"Should we sit again to undo our feet?" I ask. "Hard to keep our balance otherwise."

Mimi agrees. This time we have a better option than using the wall as a backstop. I hold on to a chair arm as we lower our bodies.

"Will you hurry it up?" the developer complains. "You'll still be screwing around when the sun comes up."

"Shut up, Ken," Lucille's husband says. "Like you've been a big help. We wouldn't be in this predicament if you hadn't invited us on a cruise to pitch your investment."

"I didn't invite you," Ken snipes. "Phil ordered me to include you."

"Hey, we're free," I announce, in part to end the bickering. "We can untie all of you now."

"No," Lucille says. "No time. Go on. Get to the road. Get as far as you can. That matters more than untying us. Good luck."

"We'll need it," Mimi whispers. "Let's go."

While the kidnappers didn't provide so much as a space heater to keep us warm, the rotting clapboards offered at least a little insulation from the cold. Outside, moist night air boosts the chill factor, and goosebumps race up my arms. The thick fog makes it tough to see more than a few feet ahead. I wrap an arm around Mimi.

"Wish I had a coat to give you," I say.

"Shut up and start running. That'll warm you right up."

*My kind of girl.*

We're only ten feet from the porch when gauzy headlights dance in the fog. *Well, shit.*

Maybe the fog's a friend. I grab Mimi's arm and tug her toward overgrown bushes at the side of the house.

"We've got company."

# Chapter Forty-Two

Grant

*Tuesday Night*

C rouched in the bushes, we hold our breaths as two men jump from the panel van. No masks. They're not expecting captives to be wandering around outside. Unfortunately, the swirling fog and darkness combine to create a different kind of mask. The best I can do is guess at hair color. The bigger guy's shaggy hair is light. Dirty blond?

The minute the big jerk opens his mouth, I recognize the stutterer.

"I don...don't like this. Q told us not...not to come back here. Jacob's car is gone. I wan...wanna get back in the van and go."

"In a minute." The abrupt no-nonsense reply indicates the stutterer's companion makes the decisions. "I want to make sure everything's secure. Asking Jacob to sanitize this place alone was a mistake. Jacob sounded stressed out when he phoned me."

"I don...don't blame him. Remember the SWAT team? They busted in Saturday just minutes after you phoned in a report of an active shooter."

"No one's calling them tonight. Don't sweat it." The in-charge kidnapper's voice is calm. "I'll make sure Jacob tidied up and do a quick check on the hostages. Shouldn't be more than ten minutes."

When the stutterer gets back in the van, I whisper to Mimi. "Let's get as far as we can before that guy returns."

"Couldn't agree more. Let's keep to the verge so we can jump in the marsh to hide if they come looking for us."

We trot down the edge of the road for about a quarter mile when we hear a yell.

I look back. A light in an upstairs room silhouettes the man leaning out the window.

"The kids split," he shouts to the stutterer. "The hostages won't tell how they got free or how long they've been gone."

"What about the res...rest of the hostages?" the stutterer yells. "Should we take them or may...maybe make sure they can't talk."

I suck in a breath. Guilt churns my stomach.

*What have I done? Please don't let them kill anyone because we left.*

"Too risky to move them," the decision maker's voice booms. "Those kids may already have contacted the cops. What if they stop our van? Can't have hostages inside. No, we leave the hostages. They're clueless. Can't describe us. We always wore masks and gloves."

"But they might have heard our na... names."

"Just shut up. Start the van. I'll be out in a second."

"Thank God," Mimi whispers. "They aren't going to harm those people."

"Yes, thank God," I add. "I'm hoping they won't waste time searching for us either."

Too soon, we hear the in-charge man's voice as he hops off the porch and heads to the van. "Phoned Jacob. Took him a long time to feed the hostages. He left less than an hour ago. No way those stupid kids could have freed themselves and reached the main road by now. Drive real slow. We'll catch our runaways in no time."

# Chapter Forty-Three

Kylee

*Tuesday Night*

Ted's fist pounds the wheel. "I should have guessed. Grant was way too interested in the areas with vacant houses suitable for stashing hostages. He didn't take Mimi birding. Sure, she snapped some bird pictures, but they had nothing to do with what my son was up to."

Unfortunately, I agree. "At least we have a starting point since Carl recognized a collapsed shed in the last photo Mimi sent."

We left Carl with the park ranger and the sheriff, waiting for the K-9 search team to arrive. Carl wanted to stay even though the sheriff nixed any civilians joining the search—"too dangerous in the wild at night."

At Botany Bay, Ted and I could do nothing but wait and worry. Better to spend time checking out the houses we identified as potential hideaways—starting with the one nearest the site of Mimi's last bird photo.

"Tell me again why Beaufort's astute acting sheriff ignored the realtor's tip on vacant houses in this area," I grump.

"After the initial press conference, the Sheriff's Office got multiple calls from people who sighted a yacht tied to a ramshackle dock on St. Helena Island. Authorities focused the search there because Nick discounted Billy's statement. Said being tased and blindfolded made Billy an unreliable witness."

We're barreling down the highway in an almost total white-out. Ted's foot is mighty heavy on the gas pedal. "Could you slow down a little? How can you even see the road?"

"It's fine. I can make out the center line. We're almost to our turn-off."

I shine my cellphone flashlight on the Beaufort County map in my lap. "You're right. Take the next left. It's a dirt road, and I doubt it's very wide."

# Chapter Forty-Four

Grant

*Tuesday Night*

Mimi and I can't stop shivering. My water-logged shoes and socks serve as icy weights sucking me deeper into the goo that's better known as pluff mud. Why did I wear tennis shoes? *Because I'm an idiot. Never considered I'd be hiding in marsh soup with an incoming tide.*

The van glides to a stop.

*Crap.* They're way too close. Mimi and I attempt statue mode, but our chattering teeth defy our efforts. Hope nature's white shroud mutes the faint sound.

The van's passenger door opens, and the wiry one hops out. He's put his red ski mask back on, which gives me a little hope. Would he bother, if he planned to kill us?

"Grant, Mimi," he shouts. "Might as well come out. We won't let you make the main road. Tide's coming in. It'll be like wading in molasses. You can't move fast. When the fog lifts, we'll see you. Are you listening?"

He pauses. Waiting for a reply?

"We can park by the main road and wait for you to come to us," he continues. "You can't escape. So how about we drive you back to the house, give you a towel, dry clothes. Maybe a cup of hot chocolate. Sounds good, doesn't it?"

Mimi shakes her head. Like me, she's not buying Mr. Reasonable's come-on, though the thought of a steaming mug of hot chocolate sounds mighty tempting.

Time's on our side even if the tide isn't. The kidnappers talked about sanitizing the place. That says they're worried about hanging around. Do they think someone's on to them?

Mr. Reasonable stalks the verge. He's little more than a shadowy shape in the fog. His flashlight does little to penetrate. It just gives the gauzy mist a yellow glow. If we can keep our distance, he'll never spot us. I hear a tiny noise. Mimi's pinching her nose. Her eyes scrunch shut.

"Ah choo." She fails to stymie her sneeze.

"Ha! They're really close." Mr. Reasonable's shout is triumphant. "We have them. Get your butt out of the van and help me round them up."

My heart thunders against my ribs. We need to put more distance between us and our pursuers. I grab Mimi's arm and push ahead. *Damn it.* The marsh sucks my left shoe into the muck, and my sodden sock is about to join it. *Shit!* Pain erupts as some sharp object pierces my instep. Broken glass? A crab's claw?

I bite my lip to keep from yelling. I suck in a deep breath to calm down, but there's so much water in the air, I feel like I'm being waterboarded. The fog absorbs the smell of decaying marsh grass. I can almost taste the rot.

Mr. Reasonable's dropped his game-show emcee persona. He curses at the top of his lungs as he and his stuttering pal thrash our way. They obviously feel no need for stealth. Their desire to catch us seems a lot stronger than their need to flee the scene.

*Think!* I try to imagine some evasion tactic. Crouch and hide? One sneeze and we're dead meat. Outrun them? Right, shoeless and dehydrated with a punctured foot. I'd be a real speed demon.

Mimi's an arm's length ahead of me. When she unexpectedly stops, I nearly bowl her over, trying to brake. She grabs my arm and points to the road. An envelope of murky yellow light is moving toward us from the main road. Headlights!

"Someone's coming," she whispers. "If those thugs don't know who it is, maybe they'll get spooked."

"And if it's their friends, they'll have reinforcements."

"C...car," the stutterer shouts. "Let's go."

Thanks to the fog, every noise seems to ping-pong within our cottony cocoon. The men run, breaking reedy stalks as they race through the marsh. But which way are they running? I hope my ears aren't playing tricks. I think they're running away from us.

I wrap my arm around Mimi's shoulders. We need to find out who's in that car. A returning kidnapper? I squint. Blink. Squint again.

"My God! It's Dad's Lexus."

# Chapter Forty-Five

Kylee

*Tuesday Night*

"Ted, slow down. Those headlights in the middle of the road aren't moving."

"I see them." He slows the car to a crawl. "Carl said no one lived on this road, right?"

"Right. It's supposed to dead-end at a derelict house."

I free my Glock from the pocket holster inside my purse. Ted raises his eyebrows. I shrug. "Believe in being prepared. Can you tell what kind of car it is, or if anyone's inside?"

"Not till we get closer."

I roll down my window. The damp fog instantly invades. A frog croaks, and something sizeable splashes in the brackish water. No helpful clues as to what—or who—lies ahead.

"Dad, stop! Two of the kidnappers are outside."

Grant's excited shout is both a relief—*He's alive!*—and a gut punch—*the kidnappers are here!*

"Call for help!" Grant yells.

Ted brakes. The engine's still ticking as he leaps from the car. "Where are you, son?"

I dial 911 and park my cellphone on the car seat, hoping the emergency operator will hear whatever happens next. I hesitate. Should I bring my Glock? I can barely see the end of my nose, and Grant's out there—somewhere in this dismal soup. Hopefully, Mimi is, too. Not knowing where they are, I can't risk firing a gun.

But what if the kidnappers start shooting at Ted? He might as well have painted a bullseye on his back, standing in front of the car's headlights. Concern for Grant has erased any thought for his own safety.

I grab the damn gun. My pulse jackhammers in my neck. What now?

"Grant, are you okay?" Ted shouts.

"Yeah, I think they're running to their van." The disembodied voice quavers. "Watch out. They may be coming for you."

*My thought exactly.*

I glance toward the distant vehicle's stationary headlights. Helpful to know it's a van. Did the headlights just move closer, or is it my imagination? No, it's coming our way—and picking up speed.

The dirt road is barely wide enough for two compact cars to inch past one another. The van speeding toward us is no compact, and neither is Ted's Lexus. Good God, are they going to ram us? They'll run Ted over if he doesn't move.

"Ted, jump! Get off the road,"

I heed my own advice, sprinting to put as much space as possible between me and the impending crash site.

Metal screeches as the van rams the left front fender of Ted's Lexus. The impact muscles the car sideways. The back right wheels teeter on the edge of the verge. Then gravity does its work. The rear of the Lexus plunges into the tidal marsh with a resounding splash.

My feet slide out from under me as I twist to watch the aftermath of the van driver's kamikaze attack. I skid on my stomach in the mud. It takes two attempts to scramble upright.

At least I have my Glock. Can I risk a shot at the van? I know Grant and Mimi are out of range. But I'm not sure if Ted's clear.

The van's stopped though its motor's running. Why don't they gun it? Having bulldozed the Lexus out of the way, their escape path is wide open.

Are they hoping to track us down and kill us before they flee?

A figure jumps out of the passenger side and disappears. Where did he go? The fog's his collaborator, masking all movement. I know he didn't run behind the white van. If so, I would have seen his silhouette. He's vanished. A ghost in the night.

"Kylee, are you okay?" Ted shouts.

"Yes. Stay off the road and take cover. One of the men jumped out of the van. He could be sneaking back. Don't be a target."

A second later, a dark shape materializes, and yanks open the van's driver-side door. What now?

The kidnapper pulls a bulky package toward him. He wheezes as he hefts the object and heaves it into the ditch. A second later, he's inside the van and speeding away.

The adrenaline coursing through my veins fuels my run toward the discarded bundle that resembles a body. I pray it isn't the corpse of some hostage the kidnapper decided to jettison before fleeing.

*Oh, God. It is a body.*

Face down. Big, muscular. And very still. Is he alive?

"I'm here," Ted says, his breathing ragged from the run. "Keep your gun trained on the guy. Has to be a kidnapper. Too young to be a hostage."

I keep the still body's center mass in my gun sights as Ted rolls the man onto his back. Ted's fingers scrabble over the man's neck, checking for a pulse. He shakes his head. "Dead."

The cause of death seems clear. His head's oddly angled. The idiot didn't buckle his seatbelt before he rammed Ted's Lexus. His forehead resembles ground beef. Tiny bits of glass are embedded in his blood-matted hair from a header into the windshield. The impact must have broken his neck.

Grant limps toward us, hand-in-hand with Mimi.

"Glad to see you, Dad."

Except for Grant's limp, the mud-splattered teens appear unharmed.

"What happened to you?" Ted asks. "Did they do something to your leg?"

"No. Managed that all on my own. Stepped on something sharp right after the marsh mud swallowed one of my tennis shoes."

"That's why I know enough to wear boots when I'm around tidal marsh." Mimi grins.

"I'm overjoyed to see both of you," Ted says. "I'm also mad as hell. Grant, why didn't you tell me what you planned to do?"

*Gee. I can answer that. Once upon a time, I was a teen.*

I keep my lips buttoned tight. I love Grant. But he's not my son.

"I'm sorry," Grant apologizes. "We'll fill you in on everything. But first, we need to call the cops and rescue the hostages."

He points down the road. "They're inside."

"All alive?" I ask.

Grant suddenly finds the ground at his feet extremely interesting. Won't meet my eyes.

"They were when Mimi and I left. But later, two kidnappers returned, and one went inside. He told his buddy the hostages were okay, but he could have been lying. I don't know for sure."

"The sheriff should be on the way," I note. "I dialed 911 and left my cellphone on. It was on the car seat when the Lexus took part in the demolition derby. The operator had to hear the crash. I imagine at least one deputy is en route to investigate."

Ted pats his pants pocket. "I still have my phone. After we see to the hostages, we can call the Sheriff's Office again. Can't waste time now. A hostage might be hurt."

"We do need to waste a few seconds to move this body off the road," I say. "If a deputy roars in here, he'll run right over this corpse."

I tuck my Glock in the back of my waistband to free my hands. Ted and I take the corpse's feet. Grant and Mimi grab its arms. Huffing and puffing, we shuffle what feels like a five-hundred-pound dead weight onto the verge. Duty performed, Ted, Mimi, and I jog toward the house with Grant hobbling a few paces behind.

I call to him over my shoulder. "Don't run. You'll only make it worse. We'll fix your foot after we get to the house."

Wincing, Grant keeps up a hop-run motion as he tries to keep up.

*Why did I waste my breath?*

# Chapter Forty-Six

## The Leader

### *Tuesday Night*

I snatch the phone the instant it rings. I'm expecting a call from—what should I call him, termination professional or terminator? I need the expert's help to secure a small yet deadly device. My pre-nuptial gift to the groom. Arranging communication has been a circuitous process. While I thoroughly approve, time is getting tight.

"Quincy, I'm scared. Not sure what to do, where to go."

Matt's frantic conversational launch is quite inopportune. Need to get him off the line. Can't miss the arranged call. Doubt my terminator would have much patience if my phone goes repeatedly to voicemail. My burner phone doesn't have call waiting. Not designed for chewing the fat.

"What now?" I bark. "Are you at the I-95 motel?"

"No, had to ditch the van. It's damaged. Parked it at the back of a used-car lot. Called Jacob to pick me up. Ryan's dead.

"Dead? What? How?"

Matt delivers his FUBAR tale in staccato bursts. Wish I hadn't answered the phone. Periodically, I stop Matt to ask questions. Guess I'm lucky Ryan's the one who bought the farm and not Matt. Ryan would be a stuttering basket case, screwing things up even more.

"I need to get off the phone. But let me make sure I understand," I say.

"You took Ryan's cellphone and his wallet before dumping his body, right? No one will be able to identify him immediately, and there's nothing on the body to tie him to any of us?"

"Right," Matt affirms. He seems much calmer now that he's handed me the mess to straighten out.

"I also wiped the van down and removed the plates," he adds. "The van might go unnoticed for a day or more."

"You're sure those kids and the two in the Lexus never saw your face?"

"I'm sure," Matt replies. "The fog did us a real favor. What do I do now?"

I close my eyes. Control my breathing. My plan has progressed to the point where I don't need—or want—Matt and Jacob anymore.

*Should I kill them? Eliminate all loose ends. Need to think about that.*

"Are you still checked into the I-95 motel we met at earlier?"

"Yes."

"Okay, stay there until morning. Don't go outside. Make sure no one sees you. Understood? By tomorrow, I'll have a definite plan."

Less than five seconds tick away between the time I hang up and a new incoming call.

"Here," I answer. I don't say another word as the caller spells out the details of tomorrow's ten o'clock meet at the always-crowded Charleston City Market. His fee will totally wipe out the last of my financial reserves.

*Think of it as an investment. You'll reap millions in return.*

# Chapter Forty-Seven

Kylee

*Tuesday Night*

Almost wish I'd waded into the marsh to reclaim my phone from the smashed-up Lexus. Ted's wavering cell flashlight provides meager light as we climb the rickety porch stairs.

As soon as we're inside, Ted shouts, "You're safe. Your kidnappers are gone. The authorities are on their way."

Good plan, reassuring the captives. Had we burst in without letting them know we're the good guys, they might have assumed their captors were back to do heaven knows what.

On the ground floor, Ted sweeps his cellphone light around the foot of the stairs. "Looks like our helpful kidnappers left a camp lantern. Hope the batteries hold."

A super bright light flicks on. I blink furiously to adjust to the blinding change. Ted tosses his cellphone to me. "Call 911 again. Tell them the hostages are safe. Let them know we're at the end of Dunhaven Road."

A cacophony of male and female voices spills from the second floor. Cries of "Thank God" mix with "Who are you?" and "What's happening?"

I make a repeat call to 911 and convey the relevant information. Namely that the hostages are safe, and the kidnappers have fled. No armed hostiles at the scene.

Staying on the line won't accomplish a thing, so I end the call. I want to help Ted tend to the hostages.

As I enter the lantern-lit upper room, I realize why the hostages' voices were so clear. No gags. While their mouths aren't covered, they resemble partially-wrapped mummies. Yards of tape wind around their hands, legs, and torsos.

Maybe the kidnappers bought stock in duct tape before they began their crime spree. At least twenty spare rolls are neatly stacked in the middle of the room. Is some big box store now out of stock? No, the kidnappers aren't dumb. They'd have spread their purchases over multiple outlets.

"Please hurry and get this tape off me," pleads a woman I've never met. "Those men didn't give us our nighttime bathroom visit. My bladder's about to burst."

"Sure thing, Lucille," Ted answers as he moves to her side. "Got my trusty Swiss Army knife. Are you okay otherwise?"

*Okay, got it, Lucille Sanford, the president of Crestway Plantation.*

"She's not the only one suffering. Hurry it up!" grumps Roger Roper, the Satin Sands prez who fired Ted's company.

*Don't imagine his mood will brighten when he learns his HOA inked a new contract with Ted while he was indisposed.*

The voices blend into a noisy din as the hostages talk over each other. Visiting a bathroom is clearly the most urgent need. Is there actually a working toilet in this dump?

Nick will have a conniption—and the FBI agents might join him—that we're undoing all the hostages' gummy restraints. But it's the only humane option. Except for a lone guy in the corner—the Spoonbill Island developer?—the folks are in their sixties or seventies. And lengthy immobility can lead to blood clots in people of any age.

Cliff and Peggy Jackson are the nearest couple. I kneel beside Peggy and start picking at the edges of the tape binding her hands. Once I free her hands, she can work on her husband's tape, and I'll move on to help the next couple.

"Sorry I can't do this faster, Peggy," I apologize. "Have nothing sharp to cut the tape."

"I'm just grateful you found us, Kylee." Peggy smiles.

Her forehead creases. After a pause, she adds. "Those men used garden shears to cut our hands free to eat and use the bathroom. Last time I came back from the toilet, those shears were sitting on the hall floor."

"I'll take a look," volunteers Grant, who just arrived at the room's doorway.

I wince as I notice Grant's bare left foot is leaving bloody tracks.

"How did you find us?" Cliff asks. "Did Grant call his dad instead of the authorities? Why aren't deputies or FBI agents here?"

I bristle at the Hullis Island president's tone. It hints at rebuke, that Grant did something wrong. I'm about to spout off when Peggy uses one of her newly freed hands to pat my arm.

"Clifford, don't start," she warns. "Ted told us the authorities are on the way. I, for one, am eternally grateful to that brave boy and girl for saving us. Without their help, we'd still be shivering in the dark, wondering if we'd live through another night."

Grant hands me a pair of garden shears. "Looks like the sheriff's here," he says as sirens blare.

# Chapter Forty-Eight

Kylee

*Tuesday Night*

I move to a window. The SWAT team's arrived. Either the 911 operator didn't share my message that no armed hostiles are here, or the Sheriff's Office didn't trust the information. Guess I get it. Why take chances?

As the first officers burst into the downstairs, Ted calls out, "We're all upstairs. Everyone's safe. No hostiles."

Boots thunder up the stairs as the commanding officer yells. "Everyone on the floor. I want to see everyone's hands, wide open and visible."

I recognize Deputy Owens' voice, and hope he'll recognize mine, too.

"Deputy Owens, it's Kylee Kane. Everyone will comply, if they can, but a few of the hostages are still tied up."

"Kylee Kane?" The deputy sounds puzzled. "What are you doing here?"

I slowly inch up to a sitting position with my hands high above my head. "Okay, if I lower my hands?"

Deputy Owens nods, and I briefly summarize how Ted and I came searching for Grant and Mimi and found the hostages plus two fleeing kidnappers.

Once I share our story with Owens, I ask permission to call the Charleston Sheriff so he can call off the Botany Bay search for the teens and let Mimi's dad know she's safe and unharmed. Owens agrees.

While SWAT team members finish freeing hostages from their bonds, Ted, Grant, Mimi, and I are banished to a corner to await the acting sheriff's arrival.

*Oh, goody.*

Now that the hostages are convinced they're safe—protected by a dozen heavily-armed officers—they can't stop talking and sobbing. Only natural. Had to be stressful, wondering if they'd die in this rotting house. Their raised, overlapping voices make it impossible to pick up the thread of any single conversation.

While Mimi and Grant occasionally whisper to each other, Ted and I stay mum. No need to add to the bedlam. Figure Nick will demand we do plenty of talking once the hostages are whisked away to Beaufort Memorial for health evaluations and interviews.

I hear the acting sheriff's angry bluster long before his dour puss appears in the upstairs doorway. I'm surprised. Nick doesn't have any media in tow. Then I realize this isn't the investigative triumph he envisioned. We found the hostages in a location he rejected as a possible search area. The fact that we led him here is beyond embarrassing.

When Nick enters, I'm happy to see he's flanked by two individuals I'm sure are FBI agents. Naturally, the acting sheriff doesn't bother to introduce them.

"Kylee Kane and Ted Welch, you are under arrest for obstruction of justice," Nick barks. "You were warned not to communicate with the kidnappers or interfere with our investigation. If you'd called the Sheriff's Office instead of barging in here, the kidnappers would now be in custody."

"Right, I'm sure you would have listened," I scoff, "even though you dismissed out of hand a suggestion the kidnappers might be holding hostages in this area."

Nick's fingers ball into a fist. For a moment, I think he might actually punch me.

The lady FBI agent places her hand on Nick's arm and asks if she can have a word. While the two move out of earshot, the youthful male agent introduces himself. "I'm Agent Soper, FBI. I believe my colleague Agent Minton is reminding the sheriff we need your cooperation to help identify and apprehend the remaining kidnappers. Threatening charges before we begin our interviews probably isn't going to help."

"You think?" Grant chuckles.

Nick and Agent Minton return.

"Although it goes against my better instincts, I will not press charges as long as you willingly provide the Sheriff's Office and FBI with any information that will help us apprehend the kidnappers." Nick ejects each word like a bullet. Conceding to the FBI agent's request costs him big time.

"Of course, we'll cooperate," Ted answers. "No one's safe until you catch the kidnappers. But Kylee and I came in late. You need to start with Grant and Mimi. We don't even know how they found the kidnappers—or how the kidnappers found them. They spent hours as captives before they escaped."

The FBI agents turn toward Grant and Mimi. "Okay," Agent Minton says. "Start at the beginning and try to recall every detail of your interaction with the kidnappers."

As the teens share the horror of their capture, Ted and I shudder. Grant and Mimi could easily be dead now instead of sitting here talking to the FBI and Nick.

While listening, I repeatedly resist the urge to interrupt and pose follow-up questions the agents and Nick fail to ask.

I listen as Grant recalls the stutterer's panic, urging his partner to flee the safe house as quickly as possible. "He was afraid the SWAT team might arrive any minute like it did last Saturday."

*Wow! What did I just hear?*

"Grant, what were the kidnapper's exact words? You said he mentioned a day?"

"Yeah," Grant replies. "The stutterer said the SWAT team busted in last Saturday just minutes after the other kidnapper called to report an active shooter."

I'm stunned. "Good grief. That means the kidnappers were behind Saturday's SWAT raid on the Lighthouse Cove clubhouse."

Nick waves his arms. "Just hold on a damn minute. You rehearsed this with the boy, didn't you, Kylee? Coaching him to conveniently recall a conversation no one else can verify. You want to blame that SWAT raid on kidnappers who are either dead or in the wind so you can shift attention away from your role in that woman's death."

The acting sheriff's heated accusations prompt blank stares from the FBI agents. They came on the scene in response to a hostage situation with terrorist overtones. No reason the sheriff would have told the agents about Saturday's swatting incident.

"Sorry," Agent Soper says. "You've lost us. What swatting incident? And who died?"

The acting sheriff eagerly launches into his version of the SWAT debacle. He repeats Ernie's suspicion that Howie Wynne made the fake active-shooter call in retaliation for directors trying to fine him for putting red-dyed mulch in his garden.

Nick then proceeds to describe how my "overreaction" in herding directors into a "coffin-like" bathroom resulted in Carrie's heart attack and subsequent death.

"There is no earthly reason to connect these Neuter1 terrorists to a silly HOA dispute about mulch," he concludes with triumphant flair.

Though I'm seething, I refrain from interrupting while Nick holds the floor. Shouting over each other will do nothing to convince the FBI agents there's a link between the SWAT incident and the kidnapping.

"Are you sure you heard the terrorist mention Saturday in connection with the SWAT raid?" Agent Minton asks Grant.

"I'm sure," he replies.

"Mimi, did you hear the kidnapper indicate the SWAT raid was this past Saturday?"

She bites her lip and shakes her head. "I wish I could remember. I can't." Her voice is soft. "I'm so sorry. I was frightened, only half-listening. My brain was too busy wondering how hard and fast we'd need to run to escape."

"Told you." Nick's tone is triumphant. "The boy's lying to help that woman he calls his aunt. That's perjury, son."

"I'm not lying." Grant's voice is ice.

"My son doesn't lie," Ted adds.

"Yeah, right, and he was totally upfront with his *daddy*. Told you he was coming out here to hunt terrorists and endanger his girlfriend," Nick sneers. "What an honest teen. Not a deceptive little sneak."

I grasp Ted's hand and squeeze. "Don't."

While Ted's far more easy-going than I am, the set of his jaw says the attack on his son has raised his temper to a boil.

Ted responds to my whispered caution and takes a deep breath. He glares at Nick with unblinking hatred, but he keeps his mouth shut.

I really don't care what Nick or the FBI agents think. I'm convinced. There's a link between the SWAT raid and the kidnapping, and I'm going to find out what it is.

# Chapter Forty-Nine

Kylee

*Wednesday Morning*

It seems to take forever for the EMTs to doctor Grant's foot while our FBI interrogators keep coming up with new questions. When Agent Minton finally dismisses me with a handshake, she slides a business card into my palm. A personal cellphone number is penned on the back. Her voice is just above a whisper, "Contact me if you think of anything else."

*Maybe she believes me.*

I'm impatient. Can't wait to get out of here. But we're stuck until AAA finds someone to rescue us in the middle of the night. Hard enough to arrange spur-of-the-moment rentals and towing in the daytime. Ted's Lexus is toast for the foreseeable future.

Mom must be pacing the floor. When I called, she insisted the three of us spend whatever's left of the night with her on Hullis Island.

* * *

It's really late—actually early morning—when we arrive. The sound of our car pulling in the driveway is enough to alert Mom. She's outside in a flash, hugging Grant.

"I should shellac your behind for taking the risks you did. But I'm too happy to see you alive and, for the most part, in one piece. Anyway, I need more time for a proper scolding. I insist you get to bed this instant. Now go! You're in the guest bedroom. You know better than to argue with me. Nurses never retire."

Inside, she shepherds a limping Grant down the hall. Over her shoulder, she calls, "Coffee's ready, and the whisky bottle's right beside it."

Ted and I are sipping Irish coffees when Mom returns. Her steaming mug waits at the head of the table.

She blows on her drink before taking the first sip. "You think I'm being silly, insisting you stay with me. But those terrorists may want revenge. The three of you royally screwed their plans. Ted, your historic house has more holes than a hunk of Swiss cheese with all the renovations. And, Kylee, your boat's an easy target from land or water. At least Hullis Island has a gate, and Chief O'Rourke is sending regular patrols to check on this house."

"Too bad you don't have more guest rooms," I grumble. "Not that I begrudge Grant the spare bedroom. About two seconds after we piled into the rental car, Grant was snoring in the backseat. I love you, Mom, but you're no treat as a bed partner. Your snore sounds like a contrary lawnmower, and you hog the blankets."

Mom lifts an eyebrow. "Well, now, there's an easy solution to your *terrible* misfortune. You and Ted can share my king bed, and I'll sleep on the couch."

Ted spews a mouthful of Irish coffee as the meaning of her suggestion registers.

Mom chuckles. "I'm old, but I've had cataract surgery. I'm not blind. I've seen the way you look at each other. You're sleeping together. Fine by me. You're consenting adults. I have no problems with you canoodling under my roof. Nonetheless, you really should let Grant in on your new relationship before I sacrifice my bed."

*What the heck? We've been so careful.*

I'm flummoxed. Potential responses stick in my throat.

Having wiped the hot spray off his chin, Ted laughs along with Mom. "Can't put anything over on you, Myrt."

"Better believe it," she answers. "When are you going to tell Grant?"

"It's too soon," I sputter. "It would be confusing for him."

"Hogwash," Mom replies. "Kylee, you surprise me. Never known you to be shy about letting people know what you think or feel, who you are. Grant will be happy for you. I'm guessing he already has a fair idea of what's going on."

"Exactly what I've been telling Kylee," Ted concurs. "We should have a sit-down with Grant before his vacation ends. Okay with you, Kylee?"

*No. I don't want to jeopardize my relationship with Grant. He loves me as an aunt.*

Yet I see no way out. Not with both Ted and Mom pushing full disclosure.

"You two win, though the timing stinks. Grant has enough on his mind, what with fanatics on the loose who may be interested in disposing of any and all witnesses."

Mom's hand waves like she's shooing away a pesky fly. "No worries. Grant talks to me, you know. Told me he wishes his dad would find someone to love. Thinks it's high time you get on with your life, Ted."

He smiles. "My son's a smart kid."

"On that, we agree," I say. "So, let's focus on how to keep your smart son breathing. Is there anything we can do to help catch the terrorists?"

Ted nods. "The acting sheriff dismissed the notion the kidnappers were involved in the SWAT raid. Since Nick's not going to investigate a potential link, it's one place to start."

Mom frowns. "What could possibly tie that SWAT raid to the kidnapping?"

"Ernie," I answer. "He was in the board meeting when the clubhouse was raided, and he was supposed to be on the party boat when the passengers were taken. He's the only common denominator. Yet, for the life of me, I can't fathom why Neuter1 would want to trigger a SWAT raid the day before a big kidnapping operation."

Ted leans back in his chair. "We can't know Neuter1's motives. However, since Carrie's heirs have hired a lawyer to pin the SWAT raid on Howie Wynne and Carrie's heart attack on your poor judgment, we have ample incentive to figure out who engineered that raid. It would help if we were certain Ernie was the primary target. That list of his enemies may help. Maybe one of them has ties to Neuter1."

I yawn. "I agree. But not tonight. I'm exhausted." I tilt my head toward Mom. "And since Grant isn't in the loop yet on his dad's new relationship, I hope you'll leave me a quarter of the bed tonight."

# Chapter Fifty

## Kylee

### *Wednesday Morning*

While strong coffee helps, my brain feels like it's cocooned in cobwebs. Can't seem to seize a single idea and hold on to it. I need one good night's sleep, preferably spooning with Ted instead of clinging to the edge of Mom's bed. Her frigid feet have built-in radar for finding warm flesh to torture.

*Need to suggest she's due for a pedicure. The woman's nails are sharper than talons.*

"Morning." Ted leans down to kiss me.

I jerk back to scan the hallway. Is the coast clear?

Ted grins. "Don't worry. Grant's a teenager. He won't get up until he has to. He's not due at the Sheriff's Office until ten. And Myrt said she doesn't mind us canoodling."

"I'm all for canoodling—in private. Not sure I'll ever feel comfortable kissing you in front of Grant, even after we have 'the talk.'"

"It'll be fine." Ted walks to the kitchen counter to pour a cup of coffee. "Is Myrt up?"

"In the shower. She hopes to schmooze her way into the hospital this morning to visit Cliff Jackson. Wants to advise him that the Hullis Island board was reconstituted while he was literally 'tied up.' Should be an

175

interesting meeting. You joining as a referee?"

"Thankfully, no," he replies. "I'm already over-committed, starting with meetings I set up after the court-appointed me trustee for Crestway Plantation's receivership. I want to exit that job ASAP. Never planned to charge for my services. Unfortunately, it'll take time to elect a new board. Lucille Sanford's a good egg. She'll understand why I pressed ahead with a receivership. I'm certain she'll work with me to extract her HOA from its legal quagmire.

"Besides dealing with the Crestway Plantation mess, I promised Donna Dahl I'd meet with the new Satin Sands board today. Of course, that get-together pre-dated Roger Roper's rescue. I'm sure he'll pretend the directors he had in his hip pocket never resigned. Should be a fun day."

Ted serves himself a big chunk of Mom's homemade blueberry coffee cake. "What about you?"

"Heading to Lighthouse Cove to start checking out folks Howie thinks are Ernie's enemies. Ed Hiller has an iron-clad alibi—he was taking part in a live stockholder Crowdcast during the SWAT raid. Nonetheless, I'm hoping his father told Ed about like-minded neighbors with a dim view of Ernie's HOA dealings."

I bite my lip. "Should I call for an appointment or simply ring Hiller's doorbell? If I were Stan's son, I'd be skittish about talking with a stranger."

"Make an appointment. Emphasize you realize he had zero to do with the SWAT raid, but need insights into how Ernie's high-handed tactics could have enraged other Lighthouse Cove residents. While it's easy to sympathize with I-hate-Ernie club members, let's hope Ed's empathy doesn't make him want to excuse whoever instigated the SWAT raid."

"Got it. Tact isn't one of my strong suits. But I'll try."

"Let's meet at the office for lunch and compare notes," Ted suggests.

"Sure, though I want to leave by one-thirty to join Desi Darling's live audience. Found out her TV talk show, *No Lies*, is shot in a Savannah studio. Desi must hate Ernie for calling her a whore and employing every conceivable roadblock to derail her sexual harassment lawsuit."

Ted frowns. "Isn't Desi a waste of time? While Grant can't ID the kidnap leader, we know it's a man."

"Desi's fiancé, Larry Zebley, is a guest on her show today. News reports indicate he didn't take kindly to Ernie depicting Desi as a slut. Want to get a look at him. Maybe Desi can also share the names of other former employees with a reason to hate Ernie."

"I smell coffee and schemes brewing." Mom sounds quite chipper as she enters the kitchen. Dressed in navy slacks and a matching jacket, she's accessorized her outfit with a red silk scarf and hoop earrings.

"See you're wearing your power suit," I comment.

"Yep, meeting Cliff at the hospital in an hour."

"Wow, I figured you'd have a hard time contacting him," I say. "Thought he'd be incommunicado, resting up from his hostage ordeal."

Mom laughs. "Cliff actually beat me to an email exchange. Demanded I meet him today. Said he was certain I'd want to resolve what he called the board 'fiasco'. Cliff had the gall to stress no one voted for me and my friends. Says we seized power. That's rich given Cliff's refusal to let our community vote on a deer hunt in our nature sanctuary."

Ted lifts an eyebrow. "Do I hear a possible trade? Might you resign and reappoint the people you replaced if he agrees to a community vote?"

Mom grins. "I might have hinted at that option. I get angry when people ignore or bend rules so they can shove what they want down people's throats. I'll accept whatever the majority decides, if—and only if—there's a fair vote. That said, being an HOA director isn't my thing. Who enjoys spending hours debating how tall a homeowner's grass can get before it violates upkeep standards?"

Grant rubs his eyes as he shuffles toward us in a pair of Dad's pajamas. While Mom gave away a lot of my late father's clothes, she couldn't part with some of his favorites. Since Grant's skinnier than Dad was, it's a good thing the oversized PJs have a drawstring waist. The high-water, hand-me-downs give Grant an orphaned look.

"Morning, Son," Ted says. "Figured you'd sleep until nine, then dash out the door to make your meeting at the Sheriff's Office."

"You're forgetting the sheriff kept your truck, Dad. Need one of you to drop me in Beaufort. Got up since I knew you'd be leaving early. If I'm a minute late, the acting sheriff will probably put out an APB on me."

"I didn't know you had to return to the Sheriff's Office." Mom frowns. "They interrogated you for hours last night. What more can they want?"

Grant shrugs. "I'm going to work with a forensic artist. The kidnappers wore ski masks inside, but Mimi and I saw two of them outside without masks. The FBI hopes we can help create a sketch of the terrorist who lugged his dead buddy out of the van before rocketing away."

"Before you do anything else, you should send Mimi flowers," Mom says. "Least you can do to apologize for dragging her into danger."

Grant's forehead wrinkles. "Flowers? What kind of flowers?"

"Myrt's right," Ted adds, "Mimi deserves a forgiveness offering. Doesn't have to be flowers, though. If you know Mimi's favorite candies, send a box of treats from The Chocolate Tree. That'll make it personal."

"Will do." Grant grins. "If you loan me the money. Need to replace my cellphone and drone, too. Those thugs took my phone and smashed the drone to smithereens."

Ted pulls out his wallet and extracts five twenties. "This should more than take care of a gift for Mimi. You can use your charge card to buy a new phone."

"So, who wants to give me a ride to town?" Grant asks.

"I'll drop you in Beaufort," Ted says. "Uber over to the office after you finish at the Sheriff's Office. Kylee and I are meeting there for lunch. Myrt, why don't you join us and then bring Grant back to Hullis? That'll ensure you have custody of your onion-chopper and potato-peeler for the afternoon."

Mom smiles. "I like it. It would be a real tragedy if there was a shortage of mashed potatoes to go with my famous gravy."

# Chapter Fifty-One

Kylee

*Wednesday Morning*

The bell only chimes once before Ed Hiller whips open his front door. The man's an unexpected surprise. Shorter than me and almost as round as he is tall. His large apron is speckled with blobs of gooey batter.

I looked up the hedge fund founded by his billionaire father. It included a number of photos of his dad. Even in the formal portraits, Ed's father looked thin, almost gaunt. His long narrow face and scrawny neck gave no hint of extra padding. In contrast, Ed's cheeks would make a chipmunk proud, and his neck is next to invisible behind his double chin.

"Come in." Ed grins. "Follow me, and there will be a reward. The oven bell's dinging. Got to get this batch of muffins out before the bottoms burn."

I follow Ed as he hurries down a hallway. The backside view shows me the clothes hidden by his large apron when he faced me. His dingy athletic shorts are topped by a hole-riddled T-shirt that reads, "Vertically Challenged."

"Thanks for seeing me, Mr. Hiller," I say to his back.

"Glad to. Call me Ed. Testing a new recipe. Always like to have an unbiased taster. Hope you're not allergic to nuts."

"No. Love 'em."

I assume Ed's kitchen would be any chef's dream. I do know how to cook, but I'm no chef. That makes the acres of granite countertops, multiple ovens, and forest of copper-bottomed pots hanging overhead look like way too much upkeep. Of course, if you're a billionaire's only child, hiring someone to polish countertops and scrub pots probably isn't a concern.

Ed pulls a tray from the oven, flooding the kitchen with a warm chocolate aroma.

"Is cooking a hobby?" I ask.

He looks up as he turns the tin upside down and shakes the muffins loose on a plate.

He laughs. "More like a passion. I own a restaurant chain. Guess you aren't into celebrity chefs. I have my own syndicated show, *Eats with Ed.*"

Howie had told me Ed was in Manhattan doing a live Crowdcast with stockholders at the time of the SWAT raid. I jumped to the conclusion Ed was meeting with hedge fund stockholders, not investors in a restaurant chain.

"Sorry, bad assumption. I figured you were an executive in your father's hedge-fund firm."

"Heaven's no. Never had a bit of interest in high finance. I'm lucky. My parents encouraged me to pursue whatever interested me, to find a career that makes me happy. I did. Sit down, please. Coffee?"

"Sure. Black would be great."

A minute later, Ed treats me to a mug of coffee and a dense chocolate muffin venting steam and heavenly scents. Though I ate a slice of Mom's blueberry coffee cake less than an hour ago, it would be rude not to indulge, right? Chalk up the extra calories as a job-related expense.

After a couple of bites, I share my thumbs-up on Ed's recipe. Delicious. We continue with food-related small talk until we've vacuumed every crumb off our plates.

I take a deep breath, knowing the coming conversation will be hard for my jovial host.

"My condolences on losing your father. As I explained on the phone, your neighbor, Howie Wynne, and I are in a bit of a jam regarding the Lighthouse

Cove SWAT raid. Ernie's convinced the acting sheriff and the dead woman's heirs that Howie planned the raid in retaliation for his objections to colored mulch."

Ed waves a hand. "I know the background and the cast of characters. I spoke with Howie, a good guy and one of dad's true friends. Howie explained you need to show Ernie has enemies aplenty."

"Correct. There may also be a link between whoever sent the SWAT team to the clubhouse and the kidnappings. Ernie was supposed to be on that party boat when its passengers were taken."

Ed's eyebrows jump. "Wow. Howie didn't tell me that."

"We had no reason to connect the two incidents before last night," I continue. "So, one goal is to show there are a number of people besides Howie who had motives to launch the SWAT raid. The second is to figure out who's behind the kidnappings."

"Glad I have solid alibis. I was in Manhattan until yesterday. Though I suppose someone might argue I could have hired pros to carry out my wishes. But, wait, didn't some Neuter1 group claim responsibility for the kidnappings?"

"The ransom demand communiqués were credited to Neuter1," I agree. "For all I know, the leader really is a rabid Neuter1 fanatic. Yet, Ernie's the common element in the SWAT raid and kidnapping. That suggests the motive may not be politics. Maybe it's personal."

I take a few minutes to explain how Grant "met" the kidnap leader, along with his vague impression that the man was over thirty. In Grant's lingo, an "older" guy.

"Did Grant see his face?"

"No, he always wore a mask. Grant could only describe his build and how he moved—lean and athletic. He thinks he'd recognize the man's voice if he heard it again. Cultured, no strong accent. Maybe a hint of New England in the guy's speech."

Over the next hour, Ed rehashes dozens of conversations with his dad's neighbors and associates when they arrived to offer condolences. Together, we narrow neighborhood suspects to two men who peppered their sympathy calls with diatribes about Ernie. One, Andy Shepherd, ran against Ernie to become a Lighthouse Cove director. Shepherd's in his mid-thirties, grew up in Maine, and is a marathon runner.

"Shepherd's convinced Ernie was behind a malicious whisper campaign that cost him the election," Ed says. "He circulated a rumor his opponent was under investigation by the IRS for tax fraud. What a crock! Ernie's own financial shenanigans probably gave him the idea for the gossip."

The second HOA resident who satisfies Grant's age, build, and speech criteria is Larry Crooks.

"How would you like to be stuck with that name?" Ed asks. "Larry invested heavily in a REIT—a real estate investment trust—touted by Ernie as a deal tastier than my triple-chocolate muffins. It went belly-up right after Ernie pulled out all of his money. Funny how Ernie knew when to pull the plug, but didn't share his 'intuition' with anyone he talked into investing."

Ed says he can name one more Ernie hater though he doesn't live in Lighthouse Cove.

"The day after Dad's funeral, Connor Cassidy showed up on my doorstep. Told me Dad promised him major financing—we're talking multi-millions—for some development in Upstate South Carolina." Ed shrugs. "Dad never mentioned it to me, but we never discussed his investments.

"I told Cassidy I couldn't help him. Explained my hands were tied. Years ago, Dad created a philanthropic trust to fund his favorite charities. When he died, all his assets—except this house—went into that trust. Over the years, Dad gifted me plenty of money, and my restaurants are a success. I had no problems with the bulk of his estate going to charity."

I frown. "I understand your father's death put this Cassidy fellow in a financial bind, but why would that cause him to single out Ernie for vengeance?"

"The way Cassidy reacted gave me the creeps." Ed shivers. "Got this distant look in his eyes, like he'd gone far away, and his tone turned robotic. When he repeated he was sorry for my loss, he vowed to personally see to it that Ernie and his friends would pay for tormenting Dad. He referred to them as people who enjoy torturing others and playing God. Then he shook my hand and left."

"And he mentioned Ernie by name?" I ask.

"Yes, and Cassidy said his friends would pay, too," Ed replies. "Since the man didn't make fiery death threats, I never told anyone about our conversation. Figured the guy hoped to publicly humiliate Ernie and whoever else he blamed for causing Dad anguish. Truthfully, I hoped he'd succeed."

"Did Cassidy call you before he showed up at your house?" I ask. "Since he's not a resident, I wonder how he got through the Lighthouse Cove gate. Not exactly a tough proposition, but maybe security has a record of his visit."

Ed shrugs. "Never occurred to me to ask how he got in. A friend could live here. Any neighbor could have called in his pass. Or he could have booked a lesson with our golf or tennis pros. Then again, Cassidy might have schmoozed his way past the guard. Security officers don't look too closely at well-heeled visitors. Cassidy dresses the part of a guy with dough. When he left, I watched him get into a Porsche."

\* \* \*

Knocking on the doors of the two neighbors Ed singled out as suspects gets me nowhere. Neither is home. I check my watch, plenty of time to pay a visit to the HOA's security office. Since Ted's company manages Lighthouse Cove, I've already taken part in a couple of sit-downs with Chief Vaughn, a fellow service veteran. After the SWAT raid, I defended Vaughn and his officers when Ernie—who likes to cast a wide net in his blame games—bad-mouthed them. One reason Vaughn views me as a helpful friend.

"Hi, Chief," I call to Vaughn as I knock on his office door. "Got a minute?"

"Sure." The ex-Army sergeant squares up the papers on his desk. "What can I do you for?"

"Could you search your guest database for the name Connor Cassidy?"

Earlier, when Vaughn walked me through his operation, I was impressed with the HOA's gate-credentials system. When a neighbor requests a gate pass for a friend or vendor, the request's processed electronically. Emails go to the guests with confirmation copies to the requesting owners.

The guest email features a barcode that the guard at the gate scans when the guest arrives. The scans record exact entry times. The database is easy to search by guest or owner name or by date and time.

Vaughn swivels to face the computer terminal sitting on a desk extension. "Do you have a specific timeframe?"

"Nothing exact. Is the past twelve months too long?"

I know Stan Hiller died less than a year ago, but can't remember which month.

"A year it is." The chief uses his index fingers to hunt and peck info into the search screen. Once he's finished, Vaughn turns to me. "Should I know about this Cassidy? Is there a problem?"

I see no reason to hide why I'm interested. "It may be nothing. I've learned plenty of people had potential motives to call in that SWAT team. Cassidy's name came up. Thought I'd see if he's a frequent visitor."

"Well, if you can get a lead on whoever did the swatting, I'm all for it." Vaughn glances at the screen. "Hmm. This bloke's no stranger. He's visited Lighthouse Cove eight times this year. Holy crap, his last visit was the day of the SWAT raid. Every time he visits, Samuel Whitner the Third calls in the pass."

"Do you know this Whitner fellow?"

"He's around forty. Rich. Lives in Atlanta, but spends long weekends here. Sometimes the wife and kid stay longer. Whitner's an avid golfer and the current Lighthouse Cove club champion. Heard some residents grouse about that. They think Whitner should only be allowed to play in his Atlanta club's championship, not here."

"Can you give me Whitner's address and phone?"

"Yes, but promise you'll let me know the instant you firm up any information on the SWAT raid. I'll feel a lot better when the putz who pulled that prank is wearing handcuffs. Made us look bad."

Back in my car, I use my cell to call Samuel Whitner III. Naturally, I get an answering machine. What to say? Don't want to imply we're suspicious of his buddy Mr. Cassidy.

"Mr. Whitner, this is Kylee Kane. I'm a security consultant for Welch HOA Management, and Lighthouse Cove is one of our clients. As part of the investigation into the recent SWAT raid, we're checking every guest pass request on the day of the raid. Want to make sure the passes weren't fakes.

"I'd appreciate it if you would call our office to let us know if you actually requested a guest pass for a Connor Cassidy and, if so, confirm that your guest used it. We want to rule out the possibility that the email and its barcode weren't stolen."

Probably won't call back, but it's worth a try.

# Chapter Fifty-Two

The Leader

*Wednesday Morning*

Before heading to Charleston, I make the promised phone call to Matt and Jacob. Killing them is too risky, and it would mess up my plan to credit Neuter1 with the bombing at Phil's wedding.

Matt sounds breathless when he answers. Must have been on pins and needles waiting for my verdict on what they should do next.

"Given Ryan's death, I think it's best if you and Jacob temporarily disappear. Do you have enough cash to drive to Nashville and stay in motels for the next week?"

"Think so," Matt answers. "But what's in Nashville, and when do we hook back up with you?"

*Nothing and never.*

"Drive the backroads and stay off the interstates," I continue as if he hadn't asked his questions. "Let me know when you get to Nashville, and I'll wire you more money. By then, I'll have a new plan to put Neuter1 on the map."

\* \* \*

Parking in Charleston is always a challenge. I walk several blocks to reach the open-air market. Is it always this crowded?

As I thread my way down the center aisle, I recall the myth that it was once a slave market. Not true, though slaves were sold just down the way at the water's edge. Today, the descendants of former slaves and slave owners hawk wares in adjoining booths, selling tourists everything from hand-woven sweetgrass baskets to made-in-China trinkets flaunting Confederate flags.

The day's warm for November. I'm sweating, and it smells like I'm not alone. Body odor wafts from the shoppers, mixing with smells of burnt coffee and urine. Horse-drawn carriages are popular downtown. Unfortunately, the diapers attached to equine hind-ends may prevent tourists from stepping on turds but do little to eliminate the eye-burning odor of their pee.

My nerves feel like tightly-stretched guitar strings one turn away from snapping. *Relax.* This is a simple and sensible first step to protect both of us. I spot the booth where I was told to stop. Its wares include fancy works of wrought iron, cornices, plaster rosettes, and other architectural bric-a-brac scavenged when 17th and 18th-century plantations were razed.

As instructed, I spend several minutes browsing through the offerings. My assumption is this required pause is meant to assure some watcher that I haven't acquired a police tail.

"I'm in the market for a wrought-iron gate for my garden," I tell the fellow manning the booth. He looks as ancient as the artifacts. "I'm looking for one with a cherub in the center."

The old guy's bloodshot eyes bore into mine. "Got what you're looking for. But it's at my warehouse."

He hands me a scrap of paper with an address.

"Thanks," I say. "I'm not in town for long, kind of in a hurry. When can I come by to see the gate?"

"Two o'clock," he rumbles. "That gate's mighty expensive, and I don't accept no checks. You'll need to wire the money or bring cash."

I nod and walk away. Once I'm inside my car, I use GPS to locate the meeting site. A street view shows the building at this address is indeed a warehouse in a rather seedy area.

Wonder if the go-between has a clue about how much I'm paying for the merchandise?

I swallow. Not sure I want to park in that neighborhood. I certainly won't be stupid enough to walk down an alley with a hundred thou. Bad enough risking a burner phone to wire money.

I straighten my shoulders. *Buck up!*

What does my father always say? "Fortune favors the bold!"

# Chapter Fifty-Three

## Grant

### *Wednesday Morning*

I'm about to give the deputy at the front desk my name when he says, "Take a seat, Mr. Welch. Agent Minton will be right out."

*Mr. Welch?*

I glance around to see if Dad's walked in, then realize he means me.

Is Agent Minton the female FBI agent? I think so. Her partner's last name started with an "S," sounded something like Soap. Last night's a little hazy.

I've barely completed my memory check when Agent Minton appears. "Follow me."

No hello, how are ya's. All business.

"Our artist's ready for you. I'll sit in on the session," she adds.

"Is Mimi here already?"

"No, we need you to work with the artist independently. Recall is tricky. It's easy for one person's memory to sway what another witness remembers."

"Okay." I'm disappointed. Wanted to make amends and invite Mimi to lunch. Since The Chocolate Tree was closed when Dad dropped me, I haven't bought her candy yet. Walked along Waterfront Park to kill time until my ten o'clock here.

Agent Minton introduces me to the artist, a middle-aged man with a long face, bird-beak nose, wispy blond hair, and a goatee with two gray curls that look like commas.

*Would be easy to describe him to a sketch artist.*

The artist begins trying to coax details out of me, visual clues to help identify the leader and the two other kidnappers still at large. I'm sure the FBI is busy checking Brown Mask's fingerprints. He's the dead stutterer Red Mask tossed out of the van before rocketed away.

The artist suggests I mentally zoom out and try to picture each man from a distance. "What can you tell me about their builds…how they move… how they're dressed?"

"The leader—I heard them call him Q—is tall. Maybe six-three or four? Red Mask—the one Q ordered to drive my truck to Botany Bay—is at least six feet but not as tall as Q. The third guy, Blue Mask, is quite a bit shorter. Perhaps five-nine."

After a number of comparative prompts, I finalize a description of Q as six-three or four, lean and athletic. His shoes are the only item of clothing I clearly remember. Much of the time he was questioning me, the leader sat with legs extended, feet crossed at the ankles. Think his posture was meant to intimidate, to make it plain, "You're a nobody. You don't worry me."

Nonetheless, the pose left me staring at his shoes. Deck shoes, brown leather. Just like the ones I remember a wealthy ex-pat classmate wore at the American school in Egypt. The kid bragged his shoes were some high-end brand, Bruno something or other.

My recall of the physiques of the leader's two surviving thugs is less clear. I think of Red Mask as wiry. Everything about Blue Mask seemed average. They both wore jeans and tennis shoes.

The artist and FBI agent don't bother to quiz me about Brown Mask, the stutterer. They have his actual corpse to help with an ID.

When the artist suggests I zoom in on the leader's face, I remind him the guy's ski mask hid everything except what I could see through holes for his eyes and mouth.

"That's why I haven't a clue about the size of the guy's nose or the shape of his cheeks. He did have dingy brown, shoulder-length hair. Could see it creep out from under the ski mask on the back of his neck."

My skimpy recall doesn't discourage the artist. And I find I can provide a few added clues. The leader wore Clark Kent-style black-frame glasses on top of his ski mask. While the glasses made it harder to see his eyes, they were an unnatural shade of blue, almost turquoise. If it weren't for those ugly glasses, I might have thought he wore tinted contacts to make his eye color more dramatic.

"Hmm. Funny, but I recall the leader's eyelashes were long and dark, almost black. So was the hair on his arms. Not the same color as the hair on his head. He wore disposable, see-through gloves that matted dark curls of hair against his skin."

"What about his skin?" the artist asks.

"He was definitely White, but a deep summer tan hadn't faded. His lips were neither plump nor skinny. Oh, he had a green-ink spider tattoo on his left forearm."

"How about his teeth?" the artist asks.

"His smile showed super-white teeth. Looked like he took bleaching them seriously."

When the artist turns to Red and Blue Masks, I fail miserably. Can't provide comparable eye, lip, and hair detail. Guess because I was forced to sit and stare at the leader a lot longer.

Agent Minton's face shows her disappointment. "After you and Mimi escaped and were hiding outside, you said you saw the man you call Red Mask without a mask. Can't you tell us anything about his hair or face?"

I shrug. "Sorry. It was dark and foggy. I heard Red Mask refer to the kidnapper who fed us—the one in the blue mask—as Jacob. As I said earlier, Red Mask was wiry and maybe six feet tall. Hard as I try to picture his face, I only see a pale oval through the fog. He's definitely White. No suntan like the leader. He had light hair. But I can't tell you if it was blond or gray. Oh, I did see him in profile once. His nose jutted out. Had the impression it was long and thin."

Despite more coaxing, I remember nothing more.

I hope Mimi was more observant. Can't imagine the scant details I've provided will help ID the terrorists.

# Chapter Fifty-Four

Kylee

*Wednesday Noon*

Grant's the first person I see when I walk into Ted's office. He's at a keyboard typing away.

"Hey, how'd it go at the Sheriff's Office?"

"Okay. Never saw the acting sheriff, thank God. Just worked with Agent Minton and the artist. Got to say, I was surprised how much I remembered with their prompting. I'm typing up my own notes before I forget anything."

"I'm eager to hear the details, but let's wait for Ted and Mom, so you don't have to repeat everything."

"Dad should pull in any minute," Grant says. "Since Dad doesn't know I bought a new cellphone, I haven't heard from him, but he texted Robin thirty minutes ago. Said he was leaving Crestway Plantation and would pick up lunch for the whole crew. Grandma Myrt should arrive about the same time."

Ten minutes later, the entire Welch HOA gang is seated at the conference table and chowing down. I smile at Grant's plate, which sports a foot-long sub, chips, and cookies.

*Oh, to have a teen's metabolism.*

By popular demand, Grant is forced to interrupt eating long enough to describe his meeting with the FBI agent and sketch artist. While he couldn't provide enough information for the artist to create any composite drawings, I'm fascinated by what he's able to recall.

I scribble notes. Tall, athletic. Hair color uncertain since the hair that escaped his ski mask was brown, and his eyelashes and body hair were much darker, maybe black. Could he dye his hair? Blue eyes. Wears glasses. Bleached white teeth. Suntan. Generous lips. No wisps of hair near his lips to suggest a moustache or beard. Well-educated. A modulated newscaster-type voice. Wealthy? Wears expensive boat shoes.

I'm hoping these scattershot clues will help me decide which suspects to prioritize.

When Grant finishes, Ted calls on me to share my conversation with Ed Hiller, the convivial chef. I report he singled out three men as suspects.

"But Grant's description may eliminate one of the Lighthouse Cove residents, even though I haven't met either of them," I add. "Andy Shepherd is pictured in the HOA owner directory. He's quite short, blond, and pale as a ghost. No way he could be the leader Grant met."

"Who's left?" Mom asks.

"Larry Crooks, another Lighthouse Cove owner, could be a visual match for the leader. And then there's non-resident Connor Cassidy, who doesn't own property in Lighthouse Cove. That prompted me to initially move Cassidy to the bottom of my suspect list. But I've since learned his good buddy Samuel Whitner III arranged a guest pass for Cassidy the day the SWAT raid went down. Haven't had a chance to see if Cassidy's appearance meets Grant's general specs."

Robin picks up her smartphone and starts tapping. "Give me a sec. Maybe I can call up a photo of this Cassidy fellow."

Robin worries her lip as she studies the screen. "Found his website. He's tall, has a runner's build, and his website works hard to suggest he's an in-the-know-big-money guy. He rocks quite the tan and has a killer smile. He's in the age ballpark, too…maybe mid-thirties? Dark hair and brown eyes. No way to mistake them for any shade of blue. And he isn't wearing glasses in any picture."

Robin passes her phone around the table. Grant tilts his head as his finger flicks over the screen to page through the suspect's website.

"I don't know." He shakes his head. "Height and build match. Wish the site included video. Would like to see him walk; hear him talk. His poses in the still shots suggest the same kind of arrogance as the leader. Unfortunately, there must be thousands of well-off, clean-shaven men in their thirties with athletic builds. And, you're right, Robin, the eyes are the wrong color."

"You can change eye color," Mom points out. "Just pop in some colored lenses. Actors and actresses do it all the time."

When the phone reaches me, I scan Cassidy's website to see what he's hawking. He has plans for a mega resort-residential club in South Carolina's Blue Ridge foothills. The project and how it's promoted ooze with snob appeal. The site layout shows vineyards, a winery, and a palatial clubhouse the developer promises will boast a five-star restaurant. Owners will be able to choose from several layouts of five-and-six-bedroom "cottages." There's also a polo field, miles of riding trails, and stables for owners' horses.

"I can see why Ed added Cassidy's name to the Ernie enemy list," I begin. "He was counting on the senior Hiller to finance this project and blamed Ernie for tormenting Stan and causing stress that might have exacerbated the confusion that led to his drug overdose."

"Did Cassidy find another source of funds?" Ted asks. "If so, that may have eased any initial rage he felt toward Ernie."

"His website suggests the project is steaming ahead," I note. "It shows an aggressive construction schedule and offers price breaks to charter members who sign on before the clubhouse opens. I'll keep Cassidy as a suspect, though he doesn't appear to be a hot prospect. His current official address is in Greenville, South Carolina, though his bio cites Boston as his hometown. Other than his buddy who owns property in Lighthouse Cove, he has no obvious ties to the Lowcountry. He's also a developer—not a likely Neuter1 devotee."

"Any suspects who weren't on Ed's list?" Frank asks.

"Only one. Desi Darling's fiancé. Lance Zebley, a pro golfer on the PGA Tour. Came here from South Africa to go to college and stayed. He lives on St. Simmons Island. They met when Desi covered the RBC Heritage Golf

Classic on Hilton Head two years ago."

Ted nods. "Lance's definitely a hothead. I watch golf, and he has the opposite of the calm demeanor you expect from a pro golfer. Throws clubs, yells at spectators and volunteers, and can't keep a caddy for more than a season. But Lance's damn good. Shows steely concentration when he needs to make a putt. Can see him going after Ernie for calling his fiancée a liar and a slut. But kidnapping HOA bigwigs to raise money for Neuter1? No way. Doesn't fit."

I sigh. "Lance does have black hair and blue eyes, and he's tan and athletic. I can't make any of this fit. Easy to see why the authorities are scoffing at any link between Saturday's SWAT raid and Sunday's kidnapping. They chalk up Ernie's dual connection to coincidence. Maybe they're right. Maybe I'm chasing a red herring."

Ted clears his throat. "Remember those potential civil lawsuits against Howie and us. Your efforts can still help discredit the acting sheriff's claim that Howie's the only person with a motive to scare the Lighthouse Cove board. I know you're discouraged, but there's good reason to keep at it."

I nod and pass the update baton. "Mom, let's hear about your hospital visit with Cliff."

"It went about as you'd expect." She smiles. "Cliff wanted me and my friends to resign and reappoint the *elected* directors we'd ousted. Not so fast, I told him. Said there was no assurance the four who vanished at the first whiff of danger would want back on the board. Reminded him that three of the terrorists who publicly expressed a desire to make HOA directors pay for their sins are still at large. Also pointed out that a quorum of the new board had already passed a motion to let the community vote on various options for culling the deer herd."

Mom chuckles. "When Cliff's neck and face flushed crimson, I reminded him I was a retired nurse. Out of concern for his blood pressure, I said our conversation was over. Suggested he call me when he was feeling less peevish. Then we might negotiate a compromise."

I roll my eyes. "Mom, maybe visiting Cliff in the hospital wasn't quite fair. Does he really suffer from high blood pressure?"

She waves away my concern. "Naw. Chatted with two nurses caring for the hostages. Authorities had them all housed on the same floor with guards on duty. According to the nurses, everyone's doing fine. Just dehydrated. I specifically asked after Cliff. Nurse said his ticker looked good for another decade or two."

"When will the hostages leave the hospital?" Frank asks. "Will the authorities provide protection for them once they're back home?"

"The hospital may have already discharged everyone," Mom answers. "That was the plan. Don't know a thing about protection for anyone besides Cliff and Peggy. Chief O'Rourke will have officers watching their house as long as the terrorists are at large and conceivably lurking in the Lowcountry."

Ted nods. "I talked to Lucille Sanford today. She and her husband will return to Crestway Plantation this afternoon. Must say Lucille was most gracious. Thanked me for taking the situation in hand when her board resigned. Working together, we've already put out a call for nominations. Lucille shares Myrt's view that the directors who ran for cover may not run again. What's more, she thinks her community may not be inclined to re-elect them. Lucille's always been level-headed and a pleasure to work with. Not surprised the kidnapping hasn't soured her positive outlook."

*Wonder what it would take to unsour mine?*

As the thought flits across my brain, Grant provides the answer.

"What we all need is a generous helping of turkey and Grandma Myrt's magic gravy," he says. "I'll contribute by peeling a peck of potatoes before supper."

"Do you even know what a peck is?" Ted asks.

Grant laughs. "Enough for me to have seconds of mashed potatoes and gravy."

# Chapter Fifty-Five

## The Leader

*Wednesday Afternoon*

Sweat beads on my forehead, and my scalp itches under the damned wig. Can't wait to jettison it. My contacts and glasses, too. The frames keep slipping on my nose, irritating the crap out of me.

I park a block from the address. A compromise. If this encounter goes sideways, I want the car close enough to make a run for it. Yet I refuse to be a sitting duck on display for anyone watching the warehouse.

Does my contact have a lookout? Someone who might sabotage my car or put a tracker on it?

*Paranoia? You betcha. For good reason.*

The warehouse entrance is a mammoth sliding door. Its right edge has been left ajar, wide enough to slip inside.

I pause in the bright sunshine. Do I really want to enter that black hole? Can't make out a single detail.

I step inside. "I'm here."

"So you are," a deep voice answers. "Since you're not carrying a suitcase full of cash, I hope you're ready to make a wire transfer."

"I am. I'll transfer funds to your offshore account, right after you demonstrate your device works."

I take a few more steps, and my eyes start to adjust. I make out the man's burly shape. Big, broad shoulders. Pumped-up biceps. Hope he's not a hopped-up, anabolic-steroid fiend. A person with a hair-trigger temper and explosives makes for a dicey combination.

I straighten my shoulders, stand tall. Can't let Muscle Man think I'm intimidated.

"Pay attention," he says. "You said you wanted something small enough to easily hide. How's this?"

He reaches out a beefy hand. The device inside his paw looks like it could be one of those magnetic desk toys that let bored workers assemble small, shiny balls into any shape. Its phallic shape brings a dildo to mind.

"The plastique core is about the size of a golf ball," he says. "But the ball bearings on the top add punch. Point the ball-bearing tip up and angle it, so the full force of the blast is aimed at your target. Should kill anyone within ten feet. A radio signal triggers the explosive."

I nod. "That should do."

"If you stay twenty-five feet away, you won't die unless you're very unlucky. A ball bearing might ricochet off course and reach you, but it won't have enough juice to do much damage." He laughs. "Hope you're a good judge of distances."

My vision's improved enough to make out his beady eyes. Like me, he's taken precautions to hide his identity. A kerchief covers his entire face below those eyes. Given the size of his gargantuan head, the checkered kerchief might actually be a tablecloth.

"I placed this baby's little brother inside a crate at the back of the warehouse," he continues. "We're fifty feet away, and, to make you rest easy, I set up this shield to protect us. The demo's activated by the same frequency as your custom-built bomb. Here, it's yours to test."

He hands me what looks like a slim cellphone. I note he's wearing gloves, so he won't leave fingerprints.

"It's not really a phone but a clone that looks like one," he adds. "Get behind the shield. Then use the start button on the side to turn the fake phone on. It'll ask for a password. It's a no-brainer. B-A-N-G. No extra numbers or special characters. Go ahead, turn it on."

I follow his instructions. The clone's screen populates with symbols for popular smartphone apps.

"Choose the phone app. Then go to contacts. I only loaded one choice. Click on it, and mash Send. Should have named the contact Smashto Smithereens. Go on, do it."

"What if someone hears the explosion?"

Muscle Man smirks. "In this neighborhood? It's being gentrified, don't you know? Developers use dynamite and bulldozers to demolish buildings every day. My demo is your device's little brother. Won't bring down the ceiling. Go on, mash the damn button."

My finger hovers over "Send."

*You've come this far. Do it.*

The next instant, a blinding flash lights the rear of the empty warehouse. Splinters of wooden crate bombard the ceiling and walls. Potentially deadly shrapnel for anyone nearby.

"Satisfied?" my termination expert asks.

"You're sure about the kill zone?"

He scratches an earlobe that peeks below the side edge of his kerchief. "Nothing's ever certain with explosives. Depends on which way you direct the force and ball bearings. A device the size of yours is comparable to a twenty-millimeter cannon round. It'll definitely make a mess of your target if you angle it right. Whether it will wound or kill someone five or ten feet away is less certain."

*Have to make sure Sis stays off the stage.*

"Any possibility of an accidental detonation?"

"Not unless you start believing this sleek little number is actually a cellphone and try making a call." He chuckles. "The clone packaging ensures security won't jump you when you whip it out of your pocket. Even someone standing right beside you will think you're on a real phone."

"I've showed you mine, now you show me yours. Where's my money? Here's my bank routing number for the transfer."

When the exchange is complete, Muscle Man turns his back on me and walks toward the rear of the warehouse. No handshake. No nice doing business. Fine with me. I'm sure he has an accomplice, eyeballing me from somewhere inside the musty warehouse.

I go outside and fast-walk to my car. Try to appear casual yet in a hurry. If authorities have been tipped about illegal activity inside this vacant warehouse, I don't want to be seen slinking away like a low-life crook.

I've driven past the Charleston city limits before I feel relatively safe. I pull on to the verge to rip off my wig and remove the irritating contacts. I consider throwing them out the window. But I'd probably be reported for littering.

Will I need a disguise again? Can't imagine why. Then again, I didn't plan on Ernie and Phil jumping ship to go shelling when I needed them on that party boat.

Best to leave all options open.

# Chapter Fifty-Six

Kylee

*Wednesday Afternoon*

T he studio where Desi Darling shoots her talk show isn't exactly cavernous. My guess is there's audience seating for forty. Most people are older or younger than me—either retirees or twenty-somethings who set their own hours working from home.

I grab an aisle seat in the third row. About ten minutes before show time, Desi comes out to warm up the audience. As she strolls across the stage cracking jokes, she periodically calls on audience members, asking their names and where they're from. She's good at connecting, suggesting she really cares. I slouch in my seat, hoping she won't single me out. I have no desire to announce my name.

If she points at me, I'll say I'm June Bug from Spirit Lake, Iowa. That's the first stupid alias that comes to mind. Fortunately, Desi's gaze slides right past me.

The theme of today's talk show—how the media covers professional athletes—is no surprise, given her fiancé's guest spot. In addition to Lanny Zebley, she welcomes Toni Camp, a seventeen-year-old rising star in the WTA, the Women's Tennis Association.

Lanny quickly makes it clear he has no sympathy for Toni, who's just described the mental anguish she suffers from constant media bombard-

NEIGHBORS TO DIE FOR

ment. Toni doesn't feel tournament sponsors or professional organizations should require her to sit for interviews.

"Hey, it's part of your job," Lanny says. "Don't like it, find another profession."

Lanny brags he's learned enough French and Spanish to say a few sentences and charm fans in other countries.

My attention wanders after Lanny mentions he flew in from Japan last night. The black-haired, blue-eyed athlete just took himself out of the running as the Neuter1 leader.

After the show, Desi agrees to speak with me. I'd sent a note explaining my interest in former disgruntled employees of Ernie's media-verse.

Desi laughs. "Sure you have enough time? What's your angle? Are you trying to help some attorney put together a class-action lawsuit?"

"No, I want to help Howie Wynne defend against a different kind of lawsuit. Acting Sheriff Nick Ibsen is encouraging the heirs of a woman who had a heart attack during a SWAT raid to sue Howie. Ibsen suggests Howie sicced the SWAT team on a Lighthouse Cove board meeting to freak Ernie out. Apparently, the sheriff thinks no one else has a motive to wish Ernie harm."

"What a laugh. Okay, I like Howie. But you'd better not imply I think any of my cohorts would call in a SWAT team. I'm just saying Howie's not the Lone Ranger when it comes to thinking Ernie's a slimy, misogynist bully."

She grins. "Glad I was on-air for the SWAT team's matinee performance. An excellent alibi."

\* \* \*

My return to Beaufort carries me across the long bridge spanning Port Royal Sound. It's a beautiful day. Sparkling water. Blue skies. A breeze tickles the tops of the trees but lacks enough muscle to dust the waters with whitecap lace. A yacht motors toward one of the Lowcountry's many ports. It's a big mother. Must be headed to a marina with slips that can accommodate a one-hundred-twenty-foot yacht.

*Maybe I should switch tacks.*

When sailing into the wind, as I seem to be with this investigation, coming about—changing direction—is the only way forward. Perhaps it's time to focus on the yacht used to scam the party cruise passengers.

While my Camry has Bluetooth, I've never married my phone to it. Don't believe in making or taking calls when I'm behind the wheel. In minutes, I'll drive by Ted's office. Might as well pop in and call Coast Guard Captain Harvey Reed.

The parking lot at Ted's office is empty. Not a surprise. We told clients the office was closed for Thanksgiving weekend, starting this afternoon. Of course, Ted promised an answering service would forward emergency calls. *Please, no more emergencies.*

I use my key to enter and grab a seat at Ted's desk. Wonder if I'll be able to reach Capt. Reed. Given the number of boats pouring into the area for the holiday, Reed and his crew may be swamped responding to accidents or distress calls.

After five minutes on hold, I'm ready to give up when an operator says she's connecting my call. "Hope you're not reporting another ghost boat," Capt. Reed begins.

"No, just wanted to see if you're following any leads on the yacht used in the kidnapping. Billy was certain it was forty-five or fifty feet, a white power cruiser. Any stolen yacht matching the description?"

"No. Lt. Carter—you met her—checked every marina in the region. No boats have gone missing. She also compiled a list of yachts matching Billy's description. She's calling owners, but it's a slow go. Think she's less than a third of the way through the list."

"Did she share her list with the sheriff?"

"Yes," he answers. "If anyone turned up anything hinky, we weren't told."

"Mind if I check out possibilities in nearby marinas? I promise to share."

"Sure, why not? I'll send you the list. Give me your email."

I thank the captain and leave the office. My stomach rumbles. Can't wait for tomorrow's turkey. But first, another come-about tack. Wonder if Ken Taylor, the Spoonbill Island developer, is still staying at Kay's B&B.

# Chapter Fifty-Seven

## The Leader

### Wednesday Afternoon

I t's nice Sis pays attention to details when it comes to parties. Going through the notes of Saffron's ramblings, jotted down from memory, I circle the names of the caterer and florist chosen for Phil's bash.

I phone the caterer first. Tell him I'll soon host a lavish celebration for area investors, and Phil recommended him. I ask him to walk me through his preparations for the weekend wedding.

The caterer puts me off. Pleads he's up to his elbows in cornbread and casseroles for a Thanksgiving buffet. He'll be glad to meet me after Thanksgiving. Too late.

I spin the same tale for the florist with much better luck. Even though I phone rather late on Thanksgiving eve, Sally Wilson invites me to come ahead. She gives me an address in Beaufort's tony historic district.

Since there's no need for disguise, I drive my Porsche. With my two remaining Neuter1 dupes banished to Tennessee, I can chill. The only remnant of my Quincy persona is the green henna tattoo on my forearm. While it's temporary, it hasn't completely disappeared despite serious scrubbing. Not a problem. A long-sleeved shirt isn't out of place in November.

I'm surprised when the address the florist gave me turns out to be a carriage house tucked behind a stately mansion. A walkway paved with oyster shells winds through a garden holding jealously to late fall blooms.

I knock, and Sally opens the door. Her big smile's the first thing I notice. China-blue eyes and flushed cheeks grace a face that must have had boys panting before the wrinkles arrived. Her curly black hair is streaked with gray. I'm guessing she's in her sixties.

"Come on in." Sally's drawl tells me she's a native Southerner.

"When you rang me up, you asked to speak to the florist. I'm a flower arranger. Buy flowers from wholesalers and prepare arrangements for special events. Weddings are my mainstay. But I do displays for corporate events, baby showers, funerals. You name it."

*Hope funeral arrangements will bring you some business soon.*

"Thanks for seeing me."

What was intended as the carriage house's living room is all workspace. Its two long tables are blanketed with flowers, branches, foliage, and stems to be mixed in bouquets. A vast collection of vases fills one corner of the room. The heady blend of scents makes my nose twitch. Hope I don't start sneezing.

Sally motions me to a settee at the back of the workroom. The large coffee table in front of the settee holds a pitcher of lemonade, a plate of cookies, and what looks like scrapbooks.

"Have a seat, and I'll pour you some lemonade. The cookies are homemade, white chocolate macadamia nut. Help yourself."

Sally opens one of the scrapbooks. "What kind of statement do you want your arrangements to make? Formal, whimsical, a salute to native plants? Browse through these pages. I've photographed a variety of arrangements to help people visualize possibilities."

"What did Phil choose?" I ask.

Sally laughs. "Phil didn't choose a thing. His sole contribution was a promise to pay for whatever Ashley picked. The bride is a delight. She wants the flowers to be memorable; the arrangements to be, well, unexpected. That got my creative juices flowing. Too bad I don't have pictures yet. Won't assemble the arrangements for the first event—the beach party—until

Friday. Has to be last-minute to keep the flowers fresh."

*I need to know placement.*

"Give me a feel for how you approach an event like Friday's beach party when you've got a client like me who knows nothing."

Sally smiles, showing off her dimples. "It's not rocket science. The beach party will have a stage—the focal point. My plan is to twine flowers and shells around the podium. That way, they won't block anyone's view of the speaker. I'll place small arrangements in the center of the buffet tables and drink stations. Plenty of surfaces to decorate."

The woman's quite pleased to walk me through her decision-making. Her enthusiasm is contagious. If I *were* planning an event, I'd hire her. In fact, when it's time for my Upstate wine and equestrian club's grand opening, maybe I'll fly her in.

When it's time to leave, I tell Sally I'll be in touch soon.

"I'll see you this weekend, right?" she asks. "I try to stay in the background. But since you're a guest, you'll probably catch me flitting to and fro with posies and checking details."

My visit helps me visualize a plan. Two options. Friday night's beach party during the fireworks display or Saturday's formal dinner. I prefer Friday if Phil will cooperate. I feel confident he'll climb on stage and grandstand as part of the fireworks finale. But, if Phil disappoints me, I can retrieve my little toy and play for keeps the next day. The small bomb would also fit nicely inside the head table's centerpiece.

I'm congratulating myself on my research when my car's Bluetooth plays Princeton's fight song. The ringtone's assigned to Sam Whitner, my fraternity and golfing buddy.

"Hey, Sam," I answer. "How are they hanging?"

"Lower every day," Sam answers with a chuckle. "But that's what happens when one's burdened with such a big package."

"What's up? Didn't expect to hear from you until after Thanksgiving. Didn't you say your wife carries on the family tradition of inviting every second cousin within a hundred miles?"

"Correct," Sam says. "But had to share a message on my answering machine. A broad called, said she was a security consultant, and wanted to know if I'd called in a guest pass for you the day that SWAT team descended on the clubhouse. Sounds like she's checking out all the guest passes for that day to see if one of them is bogus. I called back and said she could take you off the suspect list, that you were only guilty of stealing a hundred bucks from me with a sucker bet on the golf course."

I force myself to laugh.

"Sounds like they have no clue who played that prank," I say. "But I appreciate the alibi. What are fraternity brothers for?"

The call disconnects, and I pound the steering wheel with my fist. Why aren't they leaving that SWAT business alone?

Guess it's because some old biddy had a heart attack. My bad luck.

# Chapter Fifty-Eight

Kylee

*Wednesday Afternoon*

I call to warn Kay I'd like to stop by.

"Not exactly in the mood for company," she answers. "How about you keep going and send a plumber instead?"

My friend sounds a tad harried. I warned her owning a B&B might be more stressful than practicing law.

"I know how to work a toilet plunger, if that'll help."

"Possibly. If you bring a plunger. Can't find mine, and the crapper in Ken Taylor's room is plugged up. I'm not kidding."

I chuckle. "Perfect. You've given me an excuse for a face-to-face chat with the gentleman. Expect me and my plunger in fifteen."

I buy my save-the-day plumber's weapon at the nearest grocery and head to Kay's.

"Guess you'll use any ruse to interrogate unsuspecting folk," Kay comments as she opens the door. "Ken's in his room. Top of the stairs, first suite on the left. Do knock. I don't want any flack about a strange woman invading a guest's privacy."

I knock as instructed, then sing out, "Your friendly plumber's here."

Ken's jaw drops when he sees me on his doorstep hoisting a plunger like the sword of Damocles.

"Kylee? What the heck are you doing here?"

I chuckle. "Your hostess, Kay Barrett, and I are good friends. When I phoned a bit ago, Kay told me she was having zero luck finding a plumber who'd answer his phone on Thanksgiving eve. To make things worse, she couldn't find her toilet plunger. So, taa-daa, Kylee Kane to the rescue. Which way to the cranky commode?"

Ken leads me toward a closed door. I can hear the exhaust fan cranking, presumably to reduce odor in the unoccupied bathroom. He looks embarrassed. I consider reminding him that everyone's poop stinks. But decide the less said, the better. Ken stands in the doorway while I do battle. In short order, the trouble's flushed away. Too bad it isn't as easy to flush terrorists into the sewer.

I turn toward Ken. "I'll leave the plunger near the commode. The plumbing in these historic mansions can be finicky, but it's all good now. While I'm here, can you spare a couple minutes? I have a few questions about your cruise and how you picked the invitees."

Ken frowns. Looks like he's contemplating a run for the bathroom where he can hide and bolt the door.

He motions toward two club chairs in the suite's bay window sitting area. "Have a seat. What exactly do you want to know?"

"I believe the kidnappers targeted your cruise—at least in part—because Ernie Baker was scheduled to be onboard. If I can figure out how they knew Ernie was invited, it might help identify the leader. Did you make your guest list public?"

"Absolutely not. Only the passengers knew who all was invited."

Ken's expression shifts as his indignant denial gives way to puzzlement. "I don't understand how Ernie fits in. If the kidnappers were after Mr. Baker, why'd they bother to kidnap the rest of us once they discovered he wasn't on the boat?"

"I think I know the answer," I say. "The leader didn't take part in the capture. Remember, you were introduced to him after you were taken to the house."

Ken nods. "You're right. That's when he separated me from the group.

Badgered me about last-minute additions to the guest list. That means he knew who was coming before the last three couples were added. I told the man I had zero to do with the invitations. Phil Graham decided who to invite. Originally, it was only going to be Phil and his fiancée, Ernie Baker, and his wife, and Owen and Diane Farash.

"Phil's primary objective was to ensure Ernie would be all-in and use his media outlets to urge public approval of the Spoonbill development. He also wanted Ernie to work behind the scenes to strong-arm politicos. Phil included the Farash couple to make the cruise seem more like a party. The Farash woman's an heiress. So the invitation also opened possibilities her family would invest."

I frown. "I'm a little unclear on Phil's role. Did you tap him to be an advisor for your project?"

"Phil's a primary investor." Ken mumbles, then abruptly zips his lips.

*His expression tells me Ken won't elaborate.*

"What prompted the spur-of-the-moment invites to three more couples?"

"Phil suggested adding the Sanfords. Said they'd have been included on the original guest list, but he thought they'd be out of town. The Farash woman asked to add the Ropers and Jacksons. Phil okayed it."

"When did you first make plans for the party cruise?"

"Late October, about a month ago. That's when Phil set the date. A business trip was going to keep him away from the Lowcountry until mid-November, and he didn't want the cruise to interfere with his fiancée's plans for their wedding weekend. That's why he picked the Sunday before Thanksgiving."

"Any theories to explain how the kidnappers learned about your cruise? Their planning must have started almost as soon as you picked a date. An elaborate scheme, complete with costumes, a yacht, and a safe house can't be put together overnight."

Ken shakes his head. "Someone could have overheard anyone on the original list talking about it. Hell, could have been me. Phil never suggested it was some big secret. Billy Stubbs, the captain, might have blabbed, too. I booked the Hullis Hussy as soon as Phil gave a thumbs up on the date."

I decide Ken's told me everything he's willing to share. Our little chat gives me the distinct impression Ken's a shill and not the actual developer. Nothing to gain in asking him point-blank if he's Phil Graham's front man. He'd never admit it. Also, if I press the issue, he'll feel compelled to tell his boss every word of our conversation. That, in turn, could prompt Phil to let Ernie know I'm nosing around. No sense making the job of unraveling this rat's nest even more difficult.

Is Phil's behind-the-scenes control of the Spoonbill project related to the kidnapping?

If so, how does it connect?

# Chapter Fifty-Nine

Kylee

*Wednesday Evening*

"Hope you have some cash," Mom says as I enter the house. "Grant ordered a pizza. Should arrive any time. Unfortunately, I can't find where I put my purse. Chemo brain. I refuse to believe it's dementia. Just those left-over drugs playing pinball with brain cells."

"I can pay for the pizzas," I reply. "But why didn't you hit Ted up for the money. He's here, right?"

"Didn't want to interrupt him while he's on the phone with some client." Mom pauses and takes a deep breath. "Ted wants to spill the beans about your relationship tonight. Asked me to wish him luck. He's planning to talk to you before dinner. I'm pre-empting Ted to give you time to think. Don't overreact, Kylee. Keeping your relationship a secret from Grant is eating at Ted."

My shock turns to anger. *How dare Ted spring this on me now?*

Mom cups my chin in her palm and squeezes. "I know that look of yours. Don't you do it—allow your anger to obliterate common horse sense. Grant is Ted's son. He knows him better than either of us ever will. Since Grant's mom flew the coop, Ted's been mother and father to that boy. If you want to be angry, be mad at yourself. By pussyfooting around, refusing to acknowledge you're a couple, you've been forcing Ted to lie to his son."

I feel as if I've been slapped. Mom always could deliver a mental smack when deserved. She's forced me to realize my reticence is a slow-acting poison.

I exhale. "Okay, Mom. Message received and accepted. I won't screw up."

\* \* \*

I'm tipping the pizza delivery kid when Ted emerges from his client confab and stops to wait for me. When the pizza guy departs, I turn to Ted.

"Let me go first. Mom told me you want to tell Grant about us tonight. I'm fine with it. You're right. It's past time. I love you, Ted."

Ted crushes me in a fierce hug. "I love you, too. Grant will be happy for us."

As soon as we grab slices of pizza and claim our usual seats at Mom's kitchen table, Ted lifts his beer bottle—what else do adults drink with pizza?

"Here, here," he says to segue into a toast.

My innards do a somersault. Is this it?

"Here's to the three people who mean the world to me," Ted begins. "Tomorrow is Thanksgiving, and Myrt's tradition is to ask everyone at the table to name one thing they're thankful for. Well, I'm going early.

"Grant, I couldn't love you more, son. You make me proud every day. And, Myrt, you didn't need to formally adopt a motherless neighborhood boy to make him feel as loved as your own son.

"And then, there's Kylee. When we were kids, she tormented her little brother and his best friend—me. But I knew, if either of us needed her, she'd be there. What I never dreamed is that she'd change my life once we reconnected as adults. Kylee, I'm head-over-heels in love with you."

Grant grins. "Dad, that's one long-winded toast. You could have shortened it to one sentence. 'I love Kylee.' I'm more than happy to add to your toast. 'To Dad and Kylee.'"

Tears dribble down my cheeks as Ted reaches for my hand. For once, I have no smart comeback. I smile and try to refrain from outright blubbering.

"Can you pass the red pepper, Kylee?" Grant asks. "Don't look so surprised. It's not like I didn't suspect there was something more than security consulting between you two."

I laugh, and all my tension evaporates.

"So, Kylee, let's hear about your afternoon," Mom says. "Did you uncover any new clues taking in Desi Darling's talk show?"

"Enough to scratch Desi's handsome golfer beau off the suspect list," I answer. "An unexpected opportunity to brace Ken Taylor proved more interesting."

"Where did you catch up with him?" Mom asks.

"In his bathroom." I chuckle. "His toilet was plugged, and I came to his rescue—and Kay's—by supplying a plunger and some DIY know-how. Once the toilet was unplugged, I guess Ken felt he had to answer a few of my questions to show his gratitude."

"Don't keep us in suspense," Ted says. "What secrets did he share?"

"Phil Graham appears to be Spoonbill Island's real developer. Front-man Ken is shilling for him. Phil calls all the shots and planned the cruise primarily to woo Ernie. He wants his pal's media-verse to give its full-throated support of the controversial project."

"I don't get it." Ted wipes his mouth with a paper towel—an essential throw-away napkin for pizza consumption. "Everything I've seen says Ernie's in Phil's thrall. Don't see why Phil needed the cruise charade to get Ernie's endorsement?"

"Beats me," I answer as soon as I polish off my first pizza slice. "For some reason, Phil doesn't want it publicly known that he's behind the controversial project. Maybe he feared Ernie would let the secret out of the bag and prompt environmentalists to go after him. Who knows? What matters is the kidnapping was planned when only six people had been invited on the cruise. The same six who got off the Hullis Hussy before its capture. Whoever came up with the elaborate scheme must be one unhappy camper. He failed to get the hostages he wanted."

"Does that mean the folks stranded on the beach are still in danger?" Grant asks.

"Could be," I admit. "We should warn them, though Ernie will call us lunatics and alert the acting sheriff we're continuing to muck around in his investigation."

"Doesn't matter," Mom says. "It's still our duty to warn them."

"I agree," Ted says. "I'll call Ernie, Phil and Owen later tonight, when it's less likely I'll be interrupting their suppers. How they respond is beyond our control."

Grant grabs the last slice of pizza. "How many people are coming to Thanksgiving dinner?" he asks. "Hope the hungry hordes will leave us leftovers."

Our Thanksgiving feast is always shared with friends who would otherwise be alone for the holiday.

"There'll be eight," Mom answers. "The four of us, plus Martha and Ruth—I owe them for stepping up to replace the directors who hightailed it. And Billy Stubbs coming since the captain's daughter and brood are going to the in-laws.

"I also invited Frank Donahue," she adds. "Now, having one more Welch HOA employee at the table doesn't mean I'll put up with business talk. Don't bore our other guests with chatter about the pitiful size of Sea Bay's reserve fund or how much it'll cost Lighthouse Cove to resurface its tennis courts."

I smile. "Fine with me, Mom. I've noticed how Frank perks up when you walk in the office. I'm sure you two will find more interesting topics to discuss."

Mom harrumphs and shoves her chair back from the table. Grant, Ted, and I snicker at her flustered response. Tomorrow should be interesting.

"How about an after-supper walk to compensate for those pizza calories?" I suggest. "I spoke with Captain Reed today, and he gave me a list of area yachts that potentially fit Billy's description of the kidnappers' boat. Six of his matches are anchored at Seaside Yacht Basin. It's a nice night, relatively warm, and the marina's well-lit. Why don't we take a stroll and snap pictures of the candidates? We can show them to Billy tomorrow."

"Okay by me," Mom says. "Lucky for you that Grant and I slaved all afternoon. Nothing more to prep for Thanksgiving. Just need to put the turkey and sides in the oven tomorrow. Can't make the gravy till the bird's done."

"I'll drive," Ted volunteers. "My oversized rental buggy seats six."

# Chapter Sixty

Kylee

*Wednesday Night*

Strings of lights weave through the bare branches of trees surrounding the protected cove. Reflections on the dark water mirror the twinkling aerial displays, transforming Seaside Yacht Basin into a fairyland.

While this marina isn't the region's largest, it has just over a hundred slips. Tonight, it looks as if every one of them is occupied.

Though the temperature is still above fifty, Mom shivers and zips up her fleece jacket. "Let's start walking. I'll freeze my derriere off if we stand around like bumps on a log. How do you propose we find the six yachts we need to eyeball?"

"Easy. A boardwalk circles the cove. We start at one end, walk to the other. In Seaside, the average yacht is sixty-feet. Our targets are bigger than my thirty-eight-foot River Rat and smaller than the sixty-footers. Plus, if a boat has a sail, it's not a candidate. Billy described the scam yacht as a power cruiser."

Ted and I take the lead; Mom and Grant follow. Our pace is slow, nonchalant. We chat as we saunter, laughing at witty names stenciled on boat sterns. We also award oohs and aahs to the few relics sporting gleaming polished mahogany from bow to stern. We want to appear as if we're out for an evening constitutional, not casing the marina for easy pickings.

Ted takes my hand. My initial startle evaporates as he tugs me closer.

I smile. *It's okay. Grant and Mom know. We're officially a couple.*

The first forty-five-foot candidate is dead ahead. "Ted, how about taking a picture of Mom, Grant, and me with the marina behind us?" I suggest.

"Glad to."

He directs us to huddle in a pose that puts the suspected yacht in the center of the frame.

He shows me the screen on his cellphone. "Happy with everyone's expressions, or do I need to take another photo?"

"Perfect," I answer.

We've strolled past and photographed three scam candidates when Grant grabs his dad's arm. "Hold up. We need to stop," he whispers.

To provide an excuse for our abrupt halt, I ask to scan Ted's photos.

"I heard his voice," Grant whispers. "I swear it's him. The leader."

We hardly breathe as we strain to hear the voice Grant believes belongs to the Neuter1 leader. I tune into nearby conversations. Poker players sitting on a boat deck alternate ribbing each other and swigging beer. A little farther away, a woman's voice climbs in pitch as she castigates her husband for saying he'll wear jeans to her mother's house on Thanksgiving Day. Courtesy of an open cabin window, I hear the loud swell of dark music building up to some TV drama catastrophe.

"Do you still hear him?" I whisper.

Grant shakes his head, then clasps my hand. "There! That voice, it's him."

A cultured baritone floats down from a yacht moored two slips away. The talker's on his cell, chatting with someone he calls Saffron. He's pacing the flybridge of a sixty-foot yacht named *Seaduction*. The yacht's too big to have been used by the kidnappers.

"Time for another group picture." Ted's attempt at jolly chatter sounds forced. He suggests we slide to our right for the best light. He wants to get as much of *Seaduction* in the frame as possible. Too bad the man on the flybridge is in shadow. I doubt Ted's cell camera can capture any facial details.

"We'd better move on." I try to sound as chipper as Ted. "Let's finish our walk."

I don't want to give that man more reason to notice us. If he is the leader, our picture-taking might arouse concern. And he could recognize Grant.

My allegro heart rate makes it hard to maintain a slow stroll. A necessity until we're beyond the suspect's hearing range.

"I swear it's him," Grant says. "I'll never forget that voice. His laugh is unmistakable."

"What should we do?" I ask. "Call the sheriff?"

Ted shakes his head. "Wouldn't do a bit of good. Ibsen would laugh off an ID based on Grant thinking he recognizes a voice. I have a good shot of the yacht. Kylee, can you check the *Seaduction*'s ownership with the Coast Guard or the marina?"

"Can do," I answer. "Should we finish the walk and photograph the three remaining forty-five footers?"

"You two go ahead," Mom answers. "I'm ready to call it a night. Grant, why don't you walk me? I spotted a little café near where we parked. You didn't get any dessert. Let's see if we can buy something sweet while Ted and Kylee finish the photo shoot."

Ted hands Grant the car keys. "Okay, see you back at the car."

Is Mom tired or worried about Grant being too close to a clever terrorist? I suspect the latter.

After three more yachts are duly photographed, Ted and I return to the parking lot. The aroma of hot chocolate and baked cookies assaults me—in a good way—the minute I open the car door.

"We bought you hot chocolate and a cookie," Mom says. "Ted, hope you can drink and drive. I'm ready to get the heck out of here. That man's carefree laugh gave me the willies."

# Chapter Sixty-One

## The Leader

### *Wednesday Night*

In any marina, you expect a background hum of noise. People chatting as they walk along the piers. Drunks whooping it up before the liquor knocks them down for the count. Open windows allowing arguments and amorous murmurs to escape nearby cabins.

Boat slips are sized to provide just enough room to dock. Your neighbors are never more than a few feet away. Cheek to jowl, as my mother liked to complain. It's never bothered me. In some ways, the extraneous noise provides its own kind of privacy. There are so many conversations floating in the air that people seldom make an effort to eavesdrop on any one.

Taking advantage of the mild evening, I phone Saffron from the flybridge. The elevated view lets me survey neighboring yachts and new arrivals.

"Glad you called," Saffron says. "Do I have a story for you!"

I want to know who'll be eating turkey with Phil tomorrow before I decide to attend. Also need an update on wedding plans. But, before I can get down to business, I need to let Sis tell her story. She loves to share funny gossip, especially at the expense of someone she detests. This story's about the clueless bride's first encounter with a bidet. I laugh as Saffron delivers the punch line.

I'm still laughing when I happen to glance toward a group strolling the pier. That's when the kid's head snaps up like he's heard a gunshot.

*My God, is that the stupid teen with the drone?*

I grip my cell tighter. Tell myself I'm mistaken. I make a concerted effort to relax my body and my voice as I continue chatting with my sister.

*Shit!* It's the same kid. He's with three adults. The well-lit pier lets me get a good look at their upturned faces as they look up at me. I've never seen the old lady before. But I recognize the man and woman. Despite having no personal encounters with Ted Welch or Kylee Kane, I've seen their mugs prominently displayed on every TV report on the freed hostages.

Almost in unison, the four abandon their visual search of my boat and bow their heads as they clump into a loose circle. Welch pretends to pose the other three for a photo op. Right. He's taking a picture of my boat.

*Dammit.* What's happening?

They can't see my face. Not enough light on the flybridge. And, even if there was a spotlight on me, the snot-nosed teenager couldn't recognize me. Never saw my face. So, what made them focus on me...on my yacht? What brought them here?

Ah, maybe it's a scouting trip.

They could be searching for the yacht borrowed for the kidnapping. Lots of luck with that. Dozens of forty-five-footers have the same silhouette, and Matt covered the boat's name with a vinyl ad banner for our fictitious wine.

My reasoning doesn't make me feel better about the kid. I was laughing at Saffron's joke when the teen acted like he had a cattle prod shoved up his rear and lasered a look my way.

Could he recognize my voice? My laugh? Did I laugh while he sat across from me in the safe house? Yeah, so what? It's not like the cops have a voice print to compare. I have a rock-solid alibi for the day of the kidnapping.

Still, I can't shake my unease. The foursome tried too hard to hide Ted Welch's effort to photograph my yacht. My ownership isn't a secret. If they learn my name, does it make me a suspect? The Kane woman already called my friend Sam to verify my use of the gate pass he arranged on the day of the SWAT raid.

*Oh, shit.* Saffron told me the bride invited the kid and his family to stay at the Jade Pointe Inn for the weekend and enjoy all the wedding events. That's totally unacceptable. Especially if they're already suspicious. Can't have anyone watching my every move. Wish I'd told Ryan to permanently dispose of the teens.

Like I don't have enough worries. Now I have four more problems to eliminate. Do the busybodies need to be removed temporarily or permanently?

# Chapter Sixty-Two

Kylee

*Wednesday Night*

Back at the house, Mom announces she's ready for bed. "Had all the excitement I can stand for one night. I'm plain tuckered out. Plus, I told our Thanksgiving guests we'd sit down to dinner at noon. My cooking method shortens oven time but the turkey needs to go in the oven by seven a.m."

"Don't think any of us will stay up much later, Myrt," Ted says. "I'll set my alarm for six-thirty. Your bottom oven rack never wants to slide out, and I don't want you leaning inside an oven, holding a roaster with twenty-plus pounds of turkey and fixings inside."

I'm surprised no one's mentioned it's past time for Ted to call Ernie Baker, Phil Graham, and Owen Farash. Even for people who dine fashionably late, suppertime is over. We need to warn these HOA presidents the terrorists targeted them.

After I remind Ted, he puts the phone in speaker mode so Grant and I can eavesdrop.

Ernie's immediate dismissal is predictable. "So what if the Neuter1 scum planned the hijacking when only three couples had invites? They got wind the cruise would promote the Spoonbill Island development. The idea of another ritzy resort stuck in their craw. But, since their little plan blew up, they've crawled back into their hidey-holes. Nothing to fear. Goodnight."

Owen Farash's response is more cordial but equally skeptical. "I appreciate the warning. Diane and I will remain vigilant. However, I can't envision the perpetrators trying something new anytime soon. One of them died, and they can't have an endless supply of money. They invested a substantial sum in the kidnap scheme. No. I'm certain they'll lay low and lick their wounds for the time being."

Ted tries in vain to get a phone number for Phil. Unlisted.

"Wait a minute. There was a phone number on our invitation to the wedding bash."

Having been nominated to hold onto the invite, I know right where to find the sucker. I open my purse and hand Ted the fancy card. A phone number is prominently listed.

"This is the Graham-Fletcher wedding planner," a recorded voice informs.

An answering service. Should have guessed.

Ted hangs up. "Not going to leave a warning on some answering service," he says. "We'll find another way to reach Phil tomorrow."

Grant smiles. "Guess it's bedtime. Do you two want the guest room? I don't mind sleeping on the couch."

*Good thing I love the smart-mouthed little twit.*

"Uh, good night, Grant," I say. "See both of you in the morning."

# Chapter Sixty-Three

The Leader

*Wednesday, Midnight*

C an't sleep, thinking about my problems. I get up and turn on my computer. Turnabout is fair play. Need to learn more about Kylee Kane, Ted and Grant Welch, and whoever the old lady might be. It may be midnight on Thanksgiving eve, but the Internet never sleeps. While I visited the Welch HOA Management website earlier, it was a cursory look to determine where to dump Billy Stubbs and start a ransom dialogue. Time now for a deep dive.

The website's "About" section lists the company's employees and their credentials. *Hmm.* Didn't know Ted was a former State Department employee who managed facilities in a dozen countries before he retired. Obviously, no dummy.

Kylee Kane's background is more worrisome. A retired Coast Guard investigator, her bio says she completed courses in counter-terrorism and cyber warfare during her career.

*Shit!*

The old lady who works as the Welch HOA receptionist is Kylee Kane's mother. A registered nurse from Keokuk, Iowa, she retired to Hullis Island twenty years ago. Organizations in need of volunteers certainly have her number. What a sucker. Blah, blah, blah. Who cares?

Curious that Ted Welch also lists Keokuk, Iowa, as his hometown. Wonder how they all wound up here.

The only mention of Grant is tucked inside Ted's bio. Simply says he has one son. Of course, having met the Citadel brat, I know a good deal more about him. His cameo appearances on TV news reports about the kidnapping made a nauseating big deal of his clean-cut cadet status.

I glean only one added piece of intelligence from the website. The firm counts Thanksgiving as an official holiday. The office is closed. If there's an emergency, clients are told to call an answering service, which will forward their calls for help.

Hmm? Could I report an emergency? One that requires Ted and Kylee to respond. No, that still leaves Grant and the old lady as loose ends. And Grant seems to think he can identify my voice.

No, need them gathered in one spot. Like around a Thanksgiving table? Their surnames don't suggest the Welch men and the Kane women are related. Still, they act like family. I check out the old lady's Facebook posts. Yep, she brags she got the last twenty-three-pound bird at Publix. She's cooking, but where?

I turn to the web's White Pages. Ted's home is listed with a Beaufort address and Myrtle Kane's digs are on Hullis Island. I chuckle to learn Kylee's address is listed as the Downtown Beaufort marina. I could sail over to pay her a visit.

I rule out Kylee's boat as a likely Thanksgiving Day venue. They'll gather at Ted's house or Mama Kane's. Come on, Google maps show me what you've got. Ted's house is in Beaufort's historic district. Well, well, pricey real estate. Did the man take some under-the-counter bribes to award State Department contracts?

I zero in on a street view of Ted's abode and chuckle. Nope. He didn't diddle with accounts after all. It appears Ted bought a rundown money pit. Looks like the historic home's prior owner left no history of repairs.

Mama Kane's house is modest, mundane, a one-story structure. Its style and low-slung profile say it was built a few decades back. To get flood insurance, the living space now has to be a lot higher off the ground.

The house resides on one of the Hullis Island golf course's interior holes. I played there once. Looks like the sixth hole. The property is heavily wooded. A drainage ditch and trees hide it from its right-side neighbor. The adjacent lot to the left is vacant. I zoom in on the Google image. A small fenced enclosure hides something with a white top. Okay, a propane tank. Interesting.

I can't think of a single excuse to visit Hullis Island at one in the morning, but Beaufort's a different story.

Even with zero traffic, it takes over an hour to drive to Ted's address. By water, the route's a lot shorter. But, sailing over, I'd have needed to dock at the Beaufort marina, and a nocturnal visit by a strange yacht would definitely pique curiosity.

Though my Porsche is noticeable as well, it doesn't have a name plastered on its backside. I drive by the house and park two blocks away. Even the dog-walkers have turned in for the night. I don't encounter a single resident.

At Ted's house, I bend and pretend to tie my shoe. Once I'm certain no one's near, I edge to the side of the house. No lights. Shades drawn. House is as still as a grave. Total silence, though there are ample signs a plumbing service will be making plenty of racket after the holiday. The plumber left a pull-behind tool trailer, emblazoned with his name and phone number, parked in the yard. Highly doubtful his men will work Thanksgiving Day.

Given the reconstruction mess, Ted is unlikely to be hosting Thanksgiving dinner. They'll all be mooching off old lady Kane, who's probably roasted fifty turkeys in her day. Should my Welch-Kane solution look like an accident?

Not necessary. Neuter1 can once again claim responsibility, revenge for Welch-Kane interference. After all, the Neuter1 team is mourning one of its members, who died for the cause.

A fire, preferably one that consumes the house in seconds, would be great. That propane tank a few feet from Mama Kane's house might help. Too bad my youth did not include a pyromaniac phase. Have no notion of the best arson techniques.

But I do know the tools plumbers use when sweating copper pipes. That tool trailer undoubtedly holds at least one propane torch, and I know just where to find bolt cutters to slice through the trailer's padlock.

That's if the van that was damaged plowing into Ted's car is still parked where Matt left it. If no one's noticed it, I can rescue bolt cutters and a few other tools. Checking it out is a calculated risk, but worth it.

# Chapter Sixty-Four

Kylee

*Thanksgiving Noon*

I hurry outside to help Martha up the stairs. She's the last of our Thanksgiving guests to arrive. Only five stairs to reach the porch, but that can be a chore for an eighty-something like Martha, especially since she's carrying her famous pecan pie. Good thing Mom's house is grandfathered. Newer homes have lots more stairs or pricey elevators since they're built to higher elevation minimums.

Inside the house, my nose became numb to the heavenly aroma of roasting turkey. As I reenter, the overpowering scent practically brings me to my knees.

"Glad everyone's here," Mom says. "Kylee, hang up Martha's coat. Then, everyone put your cellphones in the basket and out of reach for the duration. Hurry up and take your seats. It's no mean feat getting all the dishes ready at the same time. Let's enjoy this feast before anything gets cold."

Following Mom's orders, we head to the dining room. The table is lovely. While paper-towel napkins are our norm, Mom insists on cloth napkins, her grandmother's china, and crystal water goblets for the three big holiday gatherings—Thanksgiving, Christmas, and Easter.

Grant follows the lead set by Ted, Billy, and Frank and waits to sit until Ted pulls out Mom's head-of-the-table chair. My seat's closest to the kitchen so I can scurry to the stove and bring back refills as serving dishes empty. The gravy boat always requires multiple refills.

Mom whips up her legendary gravy to taste—no measuring. Add-ins to the turkey drippings include pureed cooked veggies, red wine, heavy cream, and sherry.

Keeping with tradition, Mom asks everyone to share at least one thing they're thankful for. Since Ted's toast last night prepared me for his words today, I'm able—just barely—to keep my cheeks dry. Except for one stray tear.

However, Grant's words threaten to unleash a torrent.

"I've never been more thankful to be alive," he says. "Knowing your life may end at any second forces you to appreciate life and everything that makes you happy. I have the best dad in the world. I love him, Grandma Myrt, and Aunt Kylee more than I can say."

Usually, when my time comes, I attempt to be clever. An inexplicable aversion to sounding sappy. Today, my words are plain and heartfelt. "I'm thankful all of you are part of my life, and, Mom, Ted, and Grant, I couldn't love you more."

I've devoured every morsel on my plate—which could only be cleaner if I lick it. I'm stuffed. My fellow diners and I plead to postpone dessert for a bit, despite the lure of Martha's pecan pie and Ruth's coconut cream wonder. Frank volunteers to help Mom clear the table. Hmmm.

"Ted, before any of us succumb to naptime, why don't you retrieve your cellphone long enough to show Billy last night's photo shoot. Maybe he can ID the yacht used to scam his passengers."

The captain scrolls through the images. "I'll be damned," Billy says when he reaches option three. "That's her, Midnight Rum."

"What makes you so sure?" Ted asks. "This boat looks almost identical to the last one I showed you."

"That's because you're a landlubber." Billy laughs. "See the mahogany trim on the cabin? Mahogany costs big bucks, and it's a pain to maintain, but it's gorgeous. Us old salts love it. Too bad it's all but disappeared on newer yachts. Everything's plastic these days."

"Okay," Ted says. "We have a potential winner. Now all we have to do is have a little chat with the owner. Who is it, Kylee?"

"Hang on. I need to call the harbormaster at the Seaside Yacht Basin."

As soon as I have the owner's name, I announce it. "Midnight Rum belongs to Mel Weiss, and the yacht's registered in South Carolina. Maybe the owner's local."

"Possible, but he could live anywhere in the state and keep his boat here," Billy says. "Or, maybe his home marina is up the coast near Myrtle Beach."

"Well, wherever he lives, it sounds like you've identified one of the terrorists," Ruth comments. "Nick Ibsen will be apoplectic that you broke the case."

I shake my head. "The owner may know nothing about the kidnapping," I say. "Been asking myself, would a kidnapper use his own yacht—even disguised—to snatch hostages? Made me recall a 'borrowed' boat incident from my Coast Guard days. Two kids, who knew where their granddad kept a spare key, took his yacht for a sail without his permission. Nobody blinked an eye when the yacht left the marina, and the kids returned the boat before dark with no one the wiser."

"Then how did they get caught?" Grant asks.

"While they were out, they hit a rock and gouged the bow. Granddad raised a ruckus about the damage, accusing the marina of scraping it while cleaning the pier. Finally, his grandkids confessed."

Grant's eyes light up. "I get it. If the leader knew an owner wouldn't be around on a given day, he could borrow the yacht for the scam, return it undamaged, and the owner would never know."

"We need to ask Midnight Rum's owner his whereabouts that day," Ted says. "If he was nowhere near his yacht, we start looking at people in a position to know an unoccupied craft was there for the taking."

Mom returns from the kitchen. "You're not going to track down that owner today," she says. "So, let's forget about terrorists and hijackings for a while, shall we? How about we play cards. Tripoli's a great game for a group. Once I win all your chips, it'll be time for dessert."

"You wish!" Grant says. "I've gotten a lot better at cards since you used to sucker me."

Judging by their initial expressions, Martha and Ruth, bridge fanatics, view playing Tripoli one step up from a visit to the dentist. Nonetheless, they manage smiles and agree to a game that novices can learn in minutes.

We set up two card tables. My table includes Ted, Billy, and Ruth. Mom, Frank, Grant and Martha make up the other foursome.

As we sit down, Ted whispers in my ear. "That fellow on the big yacht. The one Grant's convinced is the leader. His yacht practically sits next door to Midnight Rum, the scam boat."

"My thought exactly. Bet he knows the owner. First thing tomorrow, I plan to put that gentleman under a magnifying glass."

# Chapter Sixty-Five

## The Leader

### *Thanksgiving Noon*

Getting a gate pass for Hullis Island proved child's play. I rang the golf shop on my remaining burner and requested a tee time. Private residential resorts seldom turn away paying guests, who shell out the outrageous greens fees that subsidize owner memberships.

When I called the golf shop, I introduced myself as John Reeder. If I put all members of the troublesome foursome out of commission, a phony name might not be necessary, but why take chances? I claimed to be a Beaufort visitor who needs a break from my in-laws. A round of golf seemed just the ticket.

"Do you mind joining a trio of ladies?" the staffer replied. "We have a threesome teeing off at two o'clock. Best I can do. We're booked solid before and after."

"Two o'clock will be fine," I answered. "It's always fun to meet other golfers, and ladies are such good sports. Do I just give my name at the gate?"

"Yes, sir. A pass will be waiting in your name."

And it is. I arrive two hours early, driving the clunker Jeep I bought to use around my Neuter1 idiots. A cash transaction. No fooling around with title transfers. I smile, thinking how Matt, Ryan, and Jacob would have reacted to seeing me in my Porsche. Would really have messed with their

233

screw-the-rich mentality.

I'm glad Phil's Thanksgiving feast isn't until this evening, a fashionable seven o'clock feeding time. I promised Saffron I'd be her date. Should make it to Jade Pointe on time if things "fire up" as I hope.

I studiously avoid the golf club parking lot attendant, who offloads golf bags, signs folks in, and provides golf carts. I park my clunker as far away as possible and remain on the pavement. My golf bag is oversized, but only a few of my clubs currently sit inside. The rest will wait in the trunk until I show up for my tee time.

At the moment, the two propane torches liberated last night from the Handy Plumbing trailer make my golf bag heavy enough. Hoisting the bag over my shoulder, I walk briskly toward the tree line on the ninth hole. Guests are required to drive carts as it increases revenue. However, Hullis Island lets club members walk the course. That means it's not out of the ordinary to see a man shouldering a golf bag. Just need to keep out of sight of players.

Having golfed here before, I know the layout, including a shortcut across a waste area that will put me directly behind the Kane house. The tree line offers cover all the way to the side of the house. When I reach the Kane property, I swing a golf club back and forth in the grass, pretending to search for an out-of-bounds ball. The charade lets me creep around the side of the house to see the driveway. Two golf carts and three cars. Bingo. It's turkey time.

Conversation drifts through an open window. Women's voices and at least two different males. Okay, time to add a bit of excitement to the festivities. Spent two hours this morning watching videos and reading everything I could about propane gas explosions. Contrary to the ease with which propane gas explodes in movies, it's not easy to trigger a big boom—well, at least without blowing yourself up in the process. The gas-to-air ratio has to be just right, more than five percent and less than fifteen percent. Sort of hard to control if you simply cut a hose. Not going there.

I continue my pretend ball search, and use my three-wood to whisk pine straw, available in copious quantities, into a loose pile against the house.

Some straw settles inside the crawl space. Excellent.

I repeat the tinder-building process in a spot about eight feet away. Here the combustible clump sits against the house and next to the propane tank's latticework enclosure. Who knows? Maybe if the fire gets hot enough, I'll get lucky, and KABOOM!

Why did I lug propane torches here when I could have just brought a book of matches? Ever tried to light a campfire? A propane torch stays lit till it runs out of fuel. Little vagaries like wind or a damp spot in the tinder won't snuff out the flame.

I stand still and attempt to control my breathing. Adrenaline is urging me to run like hell. I twitch at every sound. A dog barking two blocks away sounds like a bloodhound on my trail. Stop it! I stand very still and listen.

Any sign someone inside heard me mucking about? No, they're talking, laughing, and moving around. When I first arrived, I heard the occasional clink of silverware. The sounds are different now. Have they already finished the meal?

I check my watch. Just after one o'clock. These folks sure eat early. Wonder what time the old bat got up to roast the bird. Wish she'd slept a little later. Would be better if they were still stuffing their faces when the fire starts. More chance a good blaze can get underway before they wise up to what's happening.

Well, it is what it is. Best I can do spur of the moment. They'll probably escape. I just hope smoke inhalation and house fire damage will move investigating me to the bottom of their to-do lists. Dealing with the fire's aftermath should discourage them from popping over to Jade Pointe for the wedding gala.

I snug on my golf gloves and retrieve the propane torches from my golf bag. Once lit, I gently deposit them on the dry straw piles. Flames blaze instantly in the tinder, licking up at the structure's wooden framing. Drought should help. It's been a dry fall.

Shouldering my golf bag, I walk briskly away. The urge to look back is strong. I fight it.

# Chapter Sixty-Six

Kylee

*Thanksgiving Afternoon*

"**M**om, did you leave the stove on?" I ask. "I smell something burning."

The words barely escape my mouth when the kitchen fire alarm's ear-splitting wail begins. Tendrils of smoke snake along the ceiling, moving from kitchen to dining room.

"Everybody out the front door, hurry!" Ted yells. "Grant, grab a cellphone and call 911, then help everyone outside. I'll get a fire extinguisher."

"Ted, don't try it," I shout. "The extinguisher's in the laundry room. You can't go through the kitchen. Better to use the outside hose until firemen get here."

I glance toward the front door. As Billy and Grant shepherd Martha and Ruth outside, Miss Issippi, Mom's oldest cat, streaks past them. The black cat's definitely spooked. Her exodus a charcoal blur.

Frank puts an arm around Mom's shoulder, urging her to move. She's rooted to a spot in the foyer, scanning the hallway and shouting, "Keokuk, come here. Come now. Don't hide."

While the shrieking alarm prompted Miss Issippi to make a break for it, Keokuk, Mom's younger cat, decided to hide.

"I won't leave without Keokuk," Mom protests.

"Go!" I yell. "I promise I'll find her."

Frank practically wrestles Mom out the door.

*How long before the fire reaches the living room?*

I race to the powder room. Grab two hand towels and douse them with water, then run to the living room where Ted's lifting a large canvas off the wall.

"Can't leave this." The words hardly leave his lips before he starts coughing.

I toss a wet towel to Ted and clamp the other over my mouth to hunt for Keokuk. My best guess is Mom's bedroom. In the past, I've found the skittish cat curled in the closet when something's frightened her.

Thick smoke is boiling down the hallway stinging my eyes. Can't feel the heat but know the flames must be moving fast. I race to the bedroom. The closet door's partially open. "Keokuk, come on, sweetie."

She's scrunched in a back corner. An afghan's on the shelf above her. I snatch it and attempt to bundle her inside. Frightened, Keokuk claws my arm as I make my grab. But I have her firmly imprisoned.

"Come on! Kylee, get out!" Ted pleads as he waits by the front door.

We stagger outside and down the front porch steps with our respective bundles. Mom stretches out her arms to take Keokuk. "Careful," I say. "She's in tiger mode."

The scream of sirens announces the fire trucks are almost here. The fire station's less than a mile. I turn toward a sizzling sound. Grant's manning the garden hose. Flames lick at the roof above the kitchen. The puny stream of water isn't enough.

"Get the cars out of the drive," Frank shouts as he backs Martha's golf cart out of the way. "Ted, do you have car keys? Let's clear the way for the fire trucks."

Ted shoves the oil painting of Mom, Dad, my little brother, Barry, and me into my arms and sprints toward his rental.

I awkwardly juggle the family portrait in its heavy frame as I shuffle toward Frank's car—the only one left in the drive. Opening the door to the backseat, I muscle the oil painting inside.

"Keep your Mom at a safe distance," Frank orders as he climbs in the front seat. "Get everyone clear."

Like a practiced ballet, Frank's car pirouettes out of the drive and moves left as the first fire engine pulls in from the right.

BOOM!

A heavy pressure knocks me backward as a vertical fireball roars skyward. An instant later, the fiery column collapses. The propane tank.

Hullis Island firemen rush forward with hoses. I hear shouts. Can't make out the words, but waving arms make their meaning clear. Get the hell out of the way.

I spot our Thanksgiving gathering huddled across the road. Ted runs to meet me as I cross the street. He crushes me in a hug. "Everyone's safe. Thank God."

I glance back at the house. It won't be recognizable, if it survives. Bright embers dance toward the dry palm fronds, stubbornly clinging to nearby trees. Neighbors join our anxious cluster, fearful the fire will spread.

Tears stream down Mom's cheeks.

I grab her shoulders. "Mom, look at me. It'll be okay. We can replace everything. It's just stuff. We're safe. The cats are safe. What else matters?"

"I know, I know," she sobs. "But that fire's stealing my history. When we moved to South Carolina, I made Hayse pack the china in the backseat of our car. Wouldn't trust it to movers. Your great, great grandmother's china. Now it's gone."

Her words loosen my own tears. Mom's told the story a hundred times. How my great, great grandmother was forced to part with her china during the Great Depression. But, later, my great-grandmother saved a few pennies every week until she could buy it back.

The china set isn't worth much. Would probably sell for under a hundred dollars at a thrift resale shop. Young people don't care about fine china or silver service anymore. I still mourn the loss for Mom. One more severed link to memories, to family, long gone.

Ted puts an arm around my shoulder, the other around Mom. The comfort is immediate, real.

# Chapter Sixty-Seven

The Leader

*Thanksgiving Night*

D read. It floods my body as I stand in front of the massive oak door.

*You can do this.* Paste on a smile. Think of a favorite place. Pretend I'm sailing there.

I square my shoulders, push the bell. A deep sepulcher echo within the mansion does little to lessen the feeling I'm walking straight into hell.

A uniformed functionary opens the door and asks my name. "You can join the others in the sunroom for cocktails," he intones.

I scan the faces inside. Only twenty people? Small potatoes for a Phil Graham event. He prefers an adoring crowd to swoon at his every utterance, no matter how asinine. Saffron spots me, rushes over, and takes my arm.

"Thank goodness. I've run out of things to natter on about with these old farts. Where have you been? Looks like you got a little sun today."

"Yeah, played golf on Hullis Island," I answer as Sis walks me into the lion's den.

Her eyebrows bunch. "Why on earth did you go there when you could play the Jade Pointe ocean course?"

"Jade Pointe's guest fees would have been too steep for my foursome. Not all my friends are billionaires."

While I'd never laid eyes on the new "friends" who made up my two o'clock foursome, I leave out that small tidbit.

"Besides, if I hadn't played Hullis, I'd have missed the excitement," I add. "A big house fire. By the time we reached the sixth hole, the house was reduced to smoking timbers, but firemen were still scurrying about like ants at a picnic."

"Was anyone hurt?"

*I wish.*

"No. But it caused plenty of excitement. Seems everyone on the island knew the house belonged to Myrtle Kane. I hear she and her guests had just finished Thanksgiving dinner when the fire broke out."

"Kane? Is that the woman who rescued Phil and Ashley when they got stranded overnight on Spoonbill Island?"

I feel a tap on my shoulder. "Sorry to interrupt, but I just heard my name. Your father introduced us at the club the other night. You're Connor, right?"

"That's right." I manage a smile. "And you're the blushing bride-to-be."

Ashley giggles. "That's me. Just caught a snatch of your conversation. Were you talking about Kylee Kane?"

"Her mother, Myrtle Kane. Her house was destroyed by fire this afternoon. Everyone got out in time."

"How horrible—and on Thanksgiving." Ashley grimaces. "I've never met the mother, but we invited her and Kylee, and Ted and Grant Welch to join us this weekend. A thank you for getting us off Spoonbill Island. Plus, we owe them thanks for rescuing Phil's friends who were taken hostage by that Neuter1 rabble."

I try on a pensive face. Sad, concerned. "I doubt the Kanes will be joining you this weekend. Tragedies have a way of altering plans. Imagine Kylee and her mother will be focused on what they can salvage from the ruins, not to mention finding a place to sleep tonight."

Ashley's eyes light up. "Oh, we'll bring them here. Tonight! We reserved Jade Pointe Inn suites for them this weekend. I'll just have the Inn add an extra night. Since it's a holiday weekend, they wouldn't be able to accomplish much. They might as well come and have some fun. Take their minds off their worries."

*I have a sudden longing to wrap my hands around Ashley's throat and choke every ounce of bubbly goodwill out of her over-endowed body.*

"I'm sure they've made other plans. According to the golf club chatter, the Kane women and Ted Welch are really close. I'm sure he'll put them up tonight."

"Oh." Ashley's deflated one-word response signals disappointment. She can't play beautiful, benevolent princess and wave her money wand to whisk all sorrows away.

In less than a second, the ditzy blonde re-animates, her lashes, which could pass for furry Black Widow spider legs, bat furiously as if she's transmitting Morris code. "I'll call this minute. Invite all four to come early. Arrange carte blanche for the mother at the Jade Pointe Inn boutique. Even if the poor lady rescued some clothes, they'll stink of smoke. The boutique has such lovely options. Can't think of a better way to lift spirits."

*Ah, yes. New duds are a surefire antidote to finding yourself homeless. Maybe you should buy the woman a mink coat.*

Ashley touches two fingers to her pouty lips, then presses the lipsticked digits to my cheek. "See you later. So glad I overheard you. I *really* want to help that poor woman."

Saffron chuckles as Ashley dashes from the room. "Quite the introduction to our future stepmom. While I'm uncertain of her IQ, she's an improvement over Phil's last two wifely discards, better known as the Wicked Witch and the Psycho Bitch."

I scrub Ashley's pseudo kiss from my cheek. "What's your pet nickname for this one?"

Saffron lifts an eyebrow. "Still contemplating. Need more time to decide if she's unbelievably naïve, has perfected a clueless act to charm old men, or she's plain stupid."

*Was our worn-out mother as naïve once upon a time?*

I give Saffron my arm. "Past time to head to the bar. Your glass is empty, and I can use a drink. Think I'll make that a double."

*Surely, bubbly Ashley will strike out.*

When normal people find their lives in disarray, the response isn't, "Let's go party."

\* \* \*

As always, I find no fault with the food or wine Phil serves. The conversation is another matter. Ernie's regurgitating all his political platitudes. Though the South Carolina governor is to the right of MAGA world on most issues, Ernie's bad-mouthing him for backing away from a new religious rights bill that's panicking businesses. He turns to Phil. "Now, if Mr. Graham were in the governor's mansion, he'd have stood up to these woke businesses, and the Neuter1 scum would all be in jail."

Suddenly, the light dawns. Phil's rehearsing. He's running for office. That's why he's hoarding cash…why he couldn't spare me a few million or whisper to a few of his cronies to invest with me.

I want to beat my head against the table. My Neuter1 nonsense is tailor-made to give Phil exposure and a national platform. I can hear him now. "I never wanted to be a politician. I'm just an ordinary American, a self-made businessman. Then my good friends were captured and held hostage by scum, terrorists America never should have tolerated."

*Ad nauseam.* Maybe after the final bomb goes off, I'll claim responsibility on behalf of some white nationalist group instead of Neuter1. Give the lefties some headlines to rally the troops.

# Chapter Sixty-Eight

Kylee

*Thanksgiving Night*

"Y ou're welcome to spend the night," Frank says. "Myrt, I know your aversion to sleeping on Kylee's boat, and my house is safer than Ted's. His place may be the next target for whoever set the fire."

"A generous offer, Frank," Ted answers. "Kylee's friend, Kay Barrett, issued the same invitation. But we talked it over, and we're not going to endanger any of our friends."

"I still can't believe those Neuter1 bastards set Mom's house on fire with all of us inside," I say. "And they gleefully texted the Hullis Island fire station to say it was repayment for their comrade's death. Like we made that lunatic ram his van into Ted's car without his seatbelt buckled."

"Do you think arson investigators will find any clues?" Grant asks. "Hard to imagine that no one saw the person start the fire. He walked up to the house in broad daylight carrying a pair of propane torches."

"We can worry the 'who did this' and 'why' to death," Mom interrupts as she cuddles Keokuk on her lap. "But where are we going to spend the night? Seems wise to leave Beaufort County and check into a hotel in Charleston or Savannah. Of course, we need to find one that allows pets."

I nod. "Good idea. The creep who set the fire figured out where we'd be on Thanksgiving and somehow got through the Hullis Island gate. He's smart. But I doubt he's hanging around to see where we head next."

The corners of Ted's mouth turn down in a scowl as he pulls his cellphone from a pocket. When Grant left Mom's house, he carried the cellphone basket with him. Wasn't about to lose his brand-new phone.

"What now?" Ted wonders. "It's the answering service. Someone called in an emergency. Terrific. Just terrific."

He stalks out of the room to discover what new calamity awaits.

"Is anyone hungry?" Frank asks. "If you won't stay the night, I can at least feed you before you leave. Won't be the turkey leftovers you craved, but I have sliced ham, cheese, bread, and ice cream."

"I'm in," Grant says. "Only wish you'd brought a homemade pie and baked a second to keep. Destroying pecan pie is downright criminal."

Frank laughs. "I don't bake, but I can offer multiple flavors of ice cream."

"Frank, you're a wonderful friend," Mom says. "Can't begin to thank you. I'll help you rustle up some eats for our young'un's bottomless pit of a stomach."

*Mom's amazing. Already regaining a sense of humor.*

Ted returns. His irritation—evident when he took the call—is replaced with a puzzled expression.

"There's no emergency. Ashley, Phil Graham's fiancée, somehow learned about the fire. She insists the four of us boat over to Jade Pointe tonight. Says she can send the inn's water taxi to collect us. Ashley adds that our suites at the Inn are prepared, and someone will meet Myrt at the boutique in the morning to outfit her for the weekend. All gratis, of course."

"Are we going?" Grant asks. "You were thinking of a hotel anyway. This is free, and probably very nice digs."

I frown and lower my voice to a whisper to keep Mom out of the debate. "It's a nice gesture, but don't forget who else will be at Jade Pointe—Ernie Baker, Phil Graham, and Owen Farash. Neuter1's targets from the get-go."

"What a great opportunity!" Grant's all in for the challenge. "We'd be right there if Neuter1 shows up. If I hear the leader's voice, we can catch the bad guys before anyone else gets hurt."

"That's one possibility," I answer in a fierce whisper. "But if Neuter1's planning something at Jade Pointe, we're making it easy for them to finish what they failed to do today. Eliminate you, Grant, as well as Ted, your Grandma Myrt, and me. Mom's suffered enough. I'm not going to gamble her life or yours. This isn't a game."

Mom announces her presence with a loud harrumph. The woman has to be part bat. How did she hone in on our whispers from a room away?

"You're wrong, Kylee, it's a game, and we've been drafted. We're playing, want to or not." Mom's tone has pivoted from grief to anger. "We've been dancing to Neuter1's tune. They came after us today. Who says they won't be back tomorrow? Time to do the unexpected. Go on the offensive. Catch them unprepared."

Frank shakes his head. "Want me to keep your kitties? I'll take good care of them."

"Thanks," Mom answers. "They'll be happier here than being carted around in a cage."

Grant laughs. "You're my hero, Grandma Myrt."

*Mine, too. But I prefer my heroes and heroines to stay among the living.*

\* \* \*

I let Ashley know we've accepted her kind offer, except for the water taxi. We'll sail the River Rat over to Jade Pointe. Gives us the flexibility to skedaddle whenever we want. Ferry schedules and water taxis may not be available if you're fleeing terrorists.

Ted drops me at the marina to ready the River Rat for our short sail and to pack clothes and incidentals for the weekend. Mom opts to keep Ted and Grant company while they pack bags at Ted's house. Mom doesn't enjoy boating anywhere, which is why I'm surprised she accepted the Jade Pointe offer. Maybe that medical catch-all she keeps in her purse—which Ruth luckily snagged while exiting Mom's house—has Dramamine.

I check my closet and sigh. Nothing appropriate for Saturday night's cocktail-attire dinner or Sunday's wedding. Fancy clothes were seldom needed in the service. For any formal Coast Guard event, I could slip into my trusty dress uniform. I throw two slinky pantsuits in my bag. Have to do. Too bad Ashley's boutique shopping spree offer doesn't include me. Maybe I can afford a scarf to dress up the pantsuits, though imagine I'll choke at the price.

I exit the River Rat and walk down the pier toward the marina parking lot, figuring I'll help my passengers with their bags. Ted pulls up before I reach the end of the pier. Men can throw clothes in a suitcase with amazing speed. Mom looks a little less feisty. Guess she's finally realized accepting the Jade Pointe invitation requires a sail. The private enclave, about half of Hemp Island's land mass, can only be reached by boat.

Fortunately, calm seas allow me to whisk us smoothly across the sound. The trip's short enough to keep Mom from turning green. Ashley arranged a slip for us at the private docks, and a jumbo eight-seater golf cart is waiting when we tie off. Looking at the gussied-up, limo-style cart brings back a few nightmares of my own. The last time I was at Jade Pointe, the cart's twin carried a passenger intent on killing Ted and me.

I shudder. Memories of that horrifying night have since discouraged me from setting foot on Hemp Island and its ritzy Jade Pointe millionaire's-club compound. However, I have had a couple of friendly phone chats with the new head of security, Jim Savercool. He's been working to plug the security holes Ted and I exploited to sneak inside the HOA to thwart a killer.

*Forget that night.* Tonight, you're invited. Be happy the private enclave's security is tighter. Harder for Neuter1 to attack.

# Chapter Sixty-Nine

Kylee

*Friday Morning*

Ted's already seated in the Jade Pointe Clubhouse dining room. The inn's connected to the clubhouse by a glass-enclosed breezeway. He's claimed an oceanview table, not a big challenge since the dining room's outer perimeter is all glass and less than a third of the tables are occupied.

"Hi. Is Grant still sleeping?"

"Of course." Ted smiles. "I assume Myrt is, too."

"Yes. Can't remember when she's slept this late, but that fire exhausted her emotionally. Whoever started it may not have known Mom's husband and son were firemen, but his choice for revenge couldn't have been crueler since Barry died fighting a fire."

"I know. Myrt was stoic at Barry's funeral. Almost as if she weren't there, only an empty husk. I worried she'd never come back. That losing her only son was too great a burden."

"But Mom did come back," I reply. "God, I want to find out who set that fire. Think I could kill him."

Ted motions toward my laptop. "Counting on your computer to help you find who did it?"

"Maybe. Didn't want to wake Mom, and I'm eager to see who owns

*Seaduction.* If we have a name, we can research the man Grant thinks sounds like the Neuter1 leader."

Ted rights the over-turned china cup at my place setting and serves me from our table's carafe. I take a sip.

"Thanks. Needed that. I have the guest password for the Jade Pointe Inn internet. Let me send my query about *Seaduction* to the Seaside marina. Then I'll give you my undivided attention."

Ted laughs. "Could have used your undivided attention in bed last night. A shame I couldn't share our suite's comfy king bed with you."

"Remember, half the HOA presidents in the area are here. One of your motives for wanting to come. Wouldn't do to have them tutt-tutting about you shamelessly sleeping with your consultant and setting a bad moral example for your son."

As soon as I email the Seaside harbormaster, I close my laptop and study the menu. Eggs Benedict—why not?

Ted orders the same. "What are we going to do today? Can we find out what Ernie, Phil, and Owen are up to? If there's a chance Neuter1 is coming after them, we need to keep watch—even if they don't believe they're in danger."

"Ernie's of special interest to Neuter1," I agree. "He's the link between the group triggering the SWAT raid and kidnapping the people off that cruise. But it's not clear if Phil and Owen Farash are also Neuter1 targets. Though, if I were a terrorist looking to ransom the filthy rich, Phil would be my number one prize."

Ted nods. "Diane, Owen's wife, is an heiress, but her family's not in Phil's league. While we can't rule out Neuter1 going after the Farash couple, I think we should focus on Ernie and Phil."

When the waiter brings our breakfasts, the plated treats deserve our total focus. Between forkfuls and contented sighs, I gaze around the sumptuous dining room. Despite the fact that one-hundred-and-fifty guests will attend the Graham wedding, the club's posh eatery is far from packed. This morning's patrons are predominately couples, middle-aged and up. Their dress is casual but expensive. Collared polo shirts for men. Swanky sports outfits for women.

One man sits alone. While he looks familiar, I can't place him. I'm certain we've never met, but I've seen his face—in the newspaper, a magazine? He's handsome. Somewhere between thirty and forty. Tan, athletic. The stranger glances my way, and I quickly look down at my plate. Don't want to be caught staring. *Where have I seen him before?*

I nudge Ted's leg under the table and whisper. "Casually glance toward the left side of the dining room and see if you recognize the fellow who's sitting all by his lonesome. I know the face but can't place it."

The napkin on Ted's lap just happens to slide to the floor. He reaches to retrieve it, and, as he slowly rises back up, he studies the man.

"Remember the fellow Ed Hiller told you about? The one desperate to get money to replace the funds Stan Hiller pledged to invest before his death. Robin found the guy's photo on the internet."

"Yes," I interrupt. "That's him! What was his name?"

"Connor Cassidy. Because the leader always wore a mask, Grant never saw his face. Only remembered he had striking blue eyes. We dismissed Connor as a prime suspect because he has brown eyes."

"Wonder why he's here?"

Ted shrugs. "His website implies he's a high-roller. Probably wangled an invitation to hit up other rich folk to make up for losing Stan's backing."

Once we finish our breakfasts and completely empty our table's coffee urn, Ted gets out his wallet and signals the waiter. When he holds up his credit card, the waiter shakes his head.

"No, sir. No charge. You are Phil Graham's guests this weekend. Anything you want."

Ted smiles. "How about your tip? Guess I'll have to leave cash on the table."

The waiter frowns. "Oh, no, sir. A generous gratuity is included. Cash could get me canned."

Exiting the dining room, we walk directly past Connor Cassidy's table. A raven-haired bombshell has joined him. The woman's a live wire, talking with her hands, practically bouncing in her seat. Still, Connor's eyes—dark brown eyes—leave his companion long enough to laser Ted and me. His look is anything but friendly.

*We know who you are. Do you know us?*

"Think I should check on Mom," I say as we walk toward the elevators. "Does your suite have a balcony? If Mom's sleeping, we could talk on the balcony without waking either sleeping beauty."

"Good idea," Ted says. "No way we'd disturb Grant. Don't know what time he turned in last night, but I'm betting it was late. He was texting with Mimi when I nodded off. Both of them made getting replacement cellphones a top priority."

I try to be quiet as I slip into the suite assigned to Mom and me. My stealth entrance is a bust. As soon as I close the door, Mom calls out. "Kylee? Assume you went off to breakfast, so I ordered room service. Nice to be waited on."

I smile when Mom comes into the sitting area from the bedroom. She's wearing one of my Coast Guard sweatshirts and a pair of my drawstring pants. I packed a few one-size-fits-all options so mother would have a change of clothes before Jade Pointe's boutique opens. Having lost thirty pounds fighting cancer, Mom's rail thin, much thinner than me, and several inches shorter. The drawstring waist is the only thing preventing the loaner pants from slithering to the floor. Rolled-up cuffs keep her from stepping on the excess fabric.

"Bet you wish you looked this good in these." Mom slowly twirls like a fashion model. "I called the number Ashley wrote down for the boutique. Turns out the phone belongs to the manager, not the store. Though the boutique doesn't open until ten-thirty, the manager insisted I meet her right away. Told her I'd be down in a few. I'm still uncomfortable about accepting charity. But I'd stand out like a ragamuffin at the palace ball wearing your loaners."

"Glad to see you're up and dressed. More importantly, you've had coffee and breakfast. I'll phone Ted and tell him to come over. We were going to meet on his balcony if you were snoozing. Didn't want to deprive you or Grant of extra Zs."

250

When Mom opens the door to leave, Ted's in the hallway, hand raised to knock.

Mom wags a finger at Ted. "Just put a 'Do Not Disturb' on the door if you plan to play kissy-face or kissy anything else."

Ted shakes his head, but can't keep from grinning. "You're incorrigible, Myrt. Have fun in the boutique. Don't tease the manager or try to pay. At breakfast, we learned our money's no good. Our waiter freaked at the prospect of me leaving a cash tip. Appears the staff's been put on notice."

# Chapter Seventy

Kylee

*Friday Morning*

"I left Grant a note," Ted says. "Told him to come to your suite when he wakes up."

I stake my claim on a club chair in the suite's compact but comfortable living room while Ted opts to sit at a corner desk. When I log onto the inn's internet service and check my emails, a reply from the Seaside harbormaster is waiting.

His answer's a stunner.

"The yacht *Seaduction* is owned by Connor Cassidy," I blurt out. "Good God!"

"What? Are you kidding me? Looks like Grant did recognize the leader's voice and Connor's the leader. He was at Lighthouse Cove the day of the SWAT raid."

Ted shakes his head. "But it makes no sense. The man owns a yacht. He's a developer. It's highly unlikely he's a closet Neuter1 leader and commander of some secret militant cell. He's playing a game."

"It's time to follow all the cyber crumbs Connor's left on the internet," I say. "Need to find out who he is, his friends, his family, his education. You name it. Hard to hide anything from a determined researcher, and I'm beyond determined."

We divvy up search tasks and the myriad web resources available for spying on complete strangers.

Forty-five minutes later, there's a knock on the door. "Kylee, Dad? It's Grant. You guys decent?"

*Another comedian.*

Ted opens the door. "Come on in. We have a lot to tell you."

"Can I get breakfast first?" Grant asks. "I'm starving."

"Of course you are," I answer. "Order from room service. Believe me, you want to hear what we've learned, and it's best if we tell you in private with no chance of people eavesdropping."

As Grant devours a "Farmer's Breakfast"—pancakes, eggs, sausage, and fried apples—Ted and I tag-team reports, describing everything we've dug up on one Phillip Connor Cassidy. Grant squeezes in questions between bites.

Finally, he pushes away his room-service dishes. "So, let me get this straight. Phillip Connor Cassidy is Phil Graham's son by his first wife. He goes by his middle name. His last name's Cassidy because a stepfather adopted him. His mom, a widowed recluse, had a daughter with Phil before Connor was born. The girl, Saffron, is a couple of years older than her brother. She's been hitched three times, and her late third husband left her enough to continue hobnobbing with celebrities. Connor's a Princeton grad. He worked for his father until he struck out on his own with this vineyard-equestrian project."

Ted smiles. "You seem to have inhaled the salient facts along with your eight-thousand calorie breakfast. You're convinced this guy's voice is a dead match with the Neuter1 leader who questioned you?"

"Yes. One-hundred percent. It was his voice."

"One thing is *not* certain," I interrupt. "Since you never got a look at the man you overheard on the yacht, we can't be certain it was Connor Cassidy. In all likelihood, the shadowy silhouette we saw talking on a phone was the yacht owner. Still, there's a chance Connor loaned *Seaduction* to a friend or the person sauntering around the deck was a visitor."

Grant pushes back his chair and stands. "Okay, let's eliminate that possibility right here, right now. We find this Connor character, and I ask him a question. The minute he answers, I'll know."

"And how do you propose we find him?" Ted challenges. "Right here, right now?"

"We ask around," I reply. "It's clear the staff's been put on notice that we're royalty. Our poop doesn't smell. Might as well take advantage. We mingle. Get 'creative'—that's what Mom calls it when she's caught in an exaggeration. We mention Connor's real estate project and say we're thinking of investing. Or we dream up a Princeton friend who suggested we look Connor up."

"Good idea," Grant says. "If we split up, we can cover more territory. Jade Pointe isn't that big. There's a clubhouse, a fitness center and spa, a golf course, tennis courts. Oh, and stables and riding trails. That development he's pitching includes a polo field, right? He probably rides. I could head to the stables."

Mention of the Jade Pointe stables jolts me. My heart races as I flashback to my middle-of-the-night bareback ride along Jade Pointe's beach. My brain stalls on that terrifying gamble.

"You are not going anywhere by yourself, son." Ted's pronouncement brings me back to the present. His tone indicates he'll brook no argument.

"If Connor *is* the leader, you're a loose end—someone who can help identify him. Let's assume it is Connor. If so, Connor or one of his followers torched Myrt's house when we were all inside. This man has no compunction about killing people. You are not going anywhere on Hemp Island without me."

I nod. "Your dad's right, Grant. But your idea of visiting recreational venues is a good one. It's a gorgeous day. The man probably isn't locked away in his room. Connor had breakfast with his sister, not a date. Saffron's easy to recognize since her picture pops up all over the web.

"Why don't you two try the stables and the golf shop? I'll head to the boutique and collect Mom. We'll stay in pairs. Mom and I can visit the spa and the tennis courts."

# Chapter Seventy-One

## The Leader

### *Friday Morning*

Saffron is relentless. Always gets her man. As her brother, I should be immune, but she wears me down. Besides, she supplied an excellent argument for joining her on a trail ride. "I know you're dying to spend more time with dear old Dad, his giggly bride, and Ernie of the Half-Baked Bakers, but I can assure you none of those asses will grace saddles today."

I do need time to think. Riding a horse isn't quite as conducive to brainstorming as riding ocean swells on *Seaduction*. But it's up there. What should I do about that pesky teen and his nosy family? How much do they know, and what do they suspect? Is there a way to eliminate them before tomorrow night? I don't think they can stop me, but I can't afford for them to point fingers in my direction after the fact.

Inside the stables, a horse stretches his neck over the stall's Dutch door and neighs. Saffron tosses her long black hair as she rubs his silky nose. "Meet Tactical. Always ride him when I visit. Tactical reminds me of Gerald, my late third husband. Sweet but old. Gelded by age rather than a knife."

She turns toward me and arches an eyebrow. "Too bad we can't geld Phil. Maybe that would make him easier to handle. I'm sure it would make life more pleasant for Ashley."

Her comment earns a chuckle. Sis and I share a long history of animosity toward our father. From the time we were toddlers, Mom insisted we "behave" around Phil. She was terrified Phil would boot her off the gravy train if he decided his kids were brats. He only had use for us at command performances when he'd trot us out to demonstrate his familial loyalty and generosity.

Saffron's sole duty was—and is—to look beautiful. A testament to Phil's outstanding genes and his ability to get knockouts to screw him. When I was younger, my job was to appear smart and athletic. Later, Phil cast me in the role of dashing young executive, serving time in low-level Graham enterprises executing any order he gave me.

Then, I did the unthinkable. Struck out on my own. Phil is one vindictive SOB. I know he egged Ernie on, encouraged his buddy to go after Stan Hiller for backing my "ungrateful" show of independence.

"Hey, Connor." Saffron pushes my arm. "You off to another galaxy again? I'm talking to you. Saddle up Marshmallow. Despite the name, she's young and spirited. That's how you prefer your women, right? And, you can dump Marshmallow after an invigorating ride, just like your girlfriends. Come to think of it, you do have one thing in common with Our Father in Humping."

"Not nice, Sis. I'm just dating until I find the right woman. I don't use a diamond to lease a wife, then ditch her when a new model catches my eye. Phil's prenups only cut one way. No penalties when he bails, but the Mrs. misses. If she wants out before he's bored with her, she gets zip."

A young stable hand greets us. "Hi, Miss Saffron. Always nice to see you. Would you and the young man like me to saddle horses for you?"

"That would be great, Steve," Sis answers. "We'd like to take Tactical and Marshmallow out for a couple of hours. How's the Marsh Tacky breeding program going? Expecting any new colts this spring? I've talked a few more equine enthusiasts into contributing to our efforts to save the Marsh Tackys. These horses are magnificent survivors."

The groom leads our horses outside the stables. He saddles Tactical first, then Marshmallow. As I swing into the saddle, I hear a familiar voice.

*You have to be kidding me! What's the brat doing here?*

"Want to head to the beach first?" Saffron asks as she leads Tactical in a prancing circle waiting for me.

The teen and his father round the corner of the stables and come into sight.

"Hi, there!" The father hails us like we're long-lost friends. "We love to ride. Were wondering if any of your famous Marsh Tackys are available for guests."

"Yes," Saffron answers as the man walks up and strokes Tactical's neck. "Steve's inside. He can fix you up with two of our beauties. Have you been here before? Know the trails?"

The father's lips quirk up slightly. "Just one impromptu ride on the beach. Maybe you could show us the trails, if you can wait a few minutes."

I want to shout, "NO!" Then I force myself to calm down.

*Consider this an opportunity. A chance for a threat assessment. If nothing else, Saffron will wrap the man and boy around her little finger. They'll answer any question she poses. By the end of our ride, I'll have a second-by-second preview of their weekend itinerary.*

# Chapter Seventy-Two

Kylee

*Friday Morning*

I find Mom in one of the boutique's sizable dressing rooms, and she's not alone. Bride Ashley is perched on a stool in the corner. "You just have to get that dress, too," Ashely coos. "You can wear it to the Saturday night dinner, the other one to the wedding. You're a perfect size six! Hope I'm as trim when I'm your age... Uh, not that you're old."

"Huh, don't kid a kidder. I have underwear older than you," Mom says. "At least, I did before the fire. And be careful what you wish for. I was a less-than-perfect size twelve before I got cancer."

Ashley's mouth opens in a perfect O.

Mom laughs. "Hey, don't go all pity-party on me. I'm in remission. Life doesn't suck. Especially when someone insists on buying you a new wardrobe."

I knock on the dressing room's wooden frame. "Hi, Mom. Hello, Ashley. Based on the overflowing piles of clothes, it looks like you two have been busy. Are they all rejects?"

"No, we're keeping the stack on the right." Ashley beams. "We've had such fun shopping. Wish I had a mother to shop with."

I frown. "I'm sorry. Did you lose your mother recently?"

"No. Years ago. My grandmothers are all gone, too. You're so lucky,

Kylee."

"That I am."

Mom peels off the dress she's been modeling. The exposed body looks anything but a perfect size six to me. Her ribs stick out. She needs to put more meat back on her bones.

"I think I've had all of the retail therapy I can handle. What are Ted and Grant up to?"

"They went to the stables, hoping they could go for a trail ride," I answer. "They really got into the equine scene when Ted was working in Saudi Arabia."

"Oh, how exciting," Ashley says. "Since they're off doing their thing, how about us girls head to the spa? They'll be gone for hours. We can be pampered while you tell me all about your lives. So much more exciting than mine."

*Hope your life stays nice and boring, especially this weekend.*

Mom looks a question at me, and I nod my okay.

"Sounds like a wonderful idea, Ashley," she says. "We want to learn more about you, too, and your handsome groom. Nice to see that Phil has so many friends and his children have come for the wedding. A real blessing."

Mom's piling it on by the shovelful, but Ashley doesn't seem to detect any sarcasm. Wish I could remember being that open and naïve.

* * *

The spa proves to be what I expected in a tony resort, though I've never actually visited one before. While I'm a huge fan of massages, the masseuses I engage tend to operate in the backrooms of hair salons or work as contractors in franchise operations.

We've been anointed with oils, massaged, and steamed. Frozen tropical drinks kept us cool in the sauna. Now, I nibble on strawberries, kiwi slices, and melon balls as a young lady paints my virgin toenails. A first. I'm very relaxed since Mom's deftly handling Ashley's interrogation. The blushing bride doesn't seem to realize she's being pumped for insider info.

Among other tidbits, we've learned Phil's prior brides signed nondisclosure agreements to get whatever financial considerations they could squeeze from their ex post-divorce. We also learn Phil is disappointed in Saffron and Connor, his only offspring. Ashley confides her hope she can beget children more deserving of Phil's love. I refrain from pointing out that by the time said offspring graduate high school Phil will either be dead or too old to recall their names.

"Where's the handsome groom today?" I ask. "Surprised he'd let you out of his sight. He's obviously crazy about you."

*I am my mother's daughter. I know how to lay it on thick.*

"Playing golf with Ernie Baker." Her face crumples. "Ernie was so rude to you on your boat, Kylee. I don't know what got into him. I mean, you and Ted and Grant rescued us from Spoonbill Island. He should have been grateful."

"Well, we all handle stress differently." I pause, wondering if I can push Ashley into revealing why her husband wanted to keep his Spoonbill involvement secret and who knew about the party cruise in advance. *Worth a try.*

"Phil must have been more upset than Ernie about the kidnapping," I begin, "since he's Spoonbill's primary investor and arranged the outing."

Ashley's head bobs up and down in agreement. "You're right." Then, the lightbulb over her head blinks. "Oh, my, guess the cat's out of the bag. Phil's trying to stay under the radar. A few misinformed birdwatchers oppose the island's development, though I'm sure Phil will only make it more beautiful. A place people can enjoy along with the birds. Since Phil's getting involved in politics, he doesn't want to upset any potential voters."

*Aha! On a roll, might as well go for the gold.*

"I'm still puzzled how the kidnappers found out about the party cruise early enough to make such elaborate preparations."

Ashley nods. "Me, too. At the start, Phil only invited two other couples. Oh, and Connor, but he had other plans, so he couldn't make it."

*Yes, other plans, like arranging a kidnapping.*

"Thought you said Phil was disappointed in Connor, at least in his business judgment. Sort of surprised he'd want his son along when he's trying to woo investors."

"Oh, that's exactly why he invited Connor," Ashley says. "Wanted to show him how it's done. How to be a success."

*Also, wanted to rub his nose in his failure.*

Ashley bolts upright. A move only twenty-somethings can pull off when they're stretched out in a lounge chair.

"Look at the time. It's been such fun chatting with you two. Feel like we're old friends. But I must run. Have a late lunch with the cool lady handling our flower arrangements. She couldn't get a few of the flowers we picked and wants me to approve her substitutes."

"Thanks so much for your generosity," Mom says. "You're a doll. Look forward to seeing you and your dashing husband-to-be at the clambake tonight."

"Same here." I smile. "Loved the chance to get better acquainted."

*And the opportunity to pick your brain.*

# Chapter Seventy-Three

Grant

*Friday Noon*

I feel like I'm in a movie—or in an alternate reality. The four of us are galloping along the beach. Wind whipping through my hair, foamy waves breaking on the white sand, clear blue sky, even a pod of dolphins demonstrating aerobatic leaps near the shoreline. Should be exhilarating.

Except the man on the horse at my side wants to murder me. Keep expecting him to whip out a gun, though I'm sure he's planning something more subtle. When our horses were meandering down forest trails, he talked and asked questions incessantly. Kept his eyes on me the whole time, weighing my answers. He seemed to be gauging my physical responses, too. Maybe we've read the same detective novels. Do a person's eyes shift to the left—is it left?—when he's lying? I sense he's egging me on, hoping I'll scream he's the Neuter1 leader.

Dad and Saffron, in the lead, suddenly rein in their horses, forcing Connor and me to follow suit.

"Guess we can't go any farther down the beach," Saffron says. "They're setting up for tonight's clambake and fireworks. I do hope you're coming."

Geez, the woman's practically purring. Does she flirt with every male she sees? Hope Dad's only playing like he's gaga to pry information out of her.

She points at a mansion, poised on a rise above the beach, where workers are stringing lights and muscling portable gas heaters into place. "That's Phil's house, where Connor and I are staying. Come on, let's go up. Grab a cold drink. Let the horses rest a spell."

"Sure," Dad answers. "Why not?"

*Why not? How about we can't make a run for it after we exit our saddles? How about we don't know if Saffron's in on Connor's schemes? How about they might poison us?*

Dad glances my way. "I'll just give Kylee a call. Let her know we've made some new friends and may be a little late since we're stopping by Phil's house."

Saffron looks unhappy at the mention of another woman's name.

We dismount and walk our horses up a narrow trail that winds through the dunes. At the house, Saffron calls the name Carlos repeatedly until a stooped man working in the backyard comes running.

"Carlos, can you see to the horses while my friends and I take a rest on the porch?"

"Yes, Miss Saffron, of course."

The wide front porch includes at least a dozen cushy chairs with stone-topped tables scattered about. "Sit, sit," Saffron commands. "Tell me your poison, and I'll order our drinks. Beer, wine, warm mulled cider—with or without a little kick?"

*A poison kick?*

"Mulled cider sounds great," Dad says. "I think my horse will appreciate it if I forgo any alcohol. Don't want to fall out of the saddle."

"Same for me," I mumble.

Connor laughs. "I wouldn't mind a little kick, Sis. Okay, make it a big kick."

*Damn him.* Connor seems to laugh every chance he gets. I sense he realizes its effect. I long to reach over, grab his throat, and choke him.

"Connor, I hear you're in real estate development, like your father," Dad says. "Seems like Stan Hiller told me about a project of yours in the Upstate. Sounded interesting. Imagine Phil is behind you one-hundred percent."

Connor's not laughing now. The mention of Stan Hiller and his father dissolves the remnants of his smile. He stares at Dad, looks daggers at me. Before he speaks, Saffron slithers back on the porch and curls in a seat between Dad and Connor. A young man scoots out after her and hands around steaming mugs.

"What were you all talking about?" she asks. "Connor, it looks like someone just walked over your grave."

"No one's put me in the ground yet, Sis. But Ted here brought up Stan Hiller, which made me think about his death. A real tragedy. How well did you know him, Ted?"

"Not well. My company manages Lighthouse Cove, his HOA, and Stan was appointed as a director to complete the term of another board member who died."

Saffron frowns. "Isn't that where Ernie lives? Didn't I hear him bragging about being elected president of that association?"

Dad nods. "Right you are, Saffron. Though it's not much of a trick to get elected in most HOAs. It's often tough to get anyone to serve in unpaid volunteer positions unless they have a pet peeve they want to address. Probably a good thing Stan's stint as director ended before Ernie's began. Those two didn't see eye-to-eye on a lot of things."

Connor's face looks like a death mask. I wonder if the rictus act hides a very real emotion. His chin moves a little. Grinding his teeth?

Saffron chuckles. "I keep my opinions to myself around Ernie. The man must stay up at night thinking of ways to slime anyone who crosses him—or Phil. Sometimes I think Ernie will morph into a pit bull before my eyes. 'Course, he always licks his master's hand. He's Phil's lapdog."

A door creaks. Barb Banks, Ernie's wife, stands rigid, half in and half out of the open front door. I jump to my feet.

"Mrs. Banks, can I offer you a seat? I'm Grant Welch. We met on my aunt's boat when we picked you and your husband up from Spoonbill Island."

"I remember." Her tone says she wished she didn't. "I just stepped outside to check the weather. A little too chilly. I'm going back inside."

As the door closes, Saffron swipes the back of her hand across her forehead—shorthand for being saved from a fate worse than death. "And, here, I'd been hoping the sun would warm things up. Thank you, November weather. Chilly saves the day."

I've stayed quiet, let Dad carry the conversational ball. In part because adults are more apt to listen to him and respond. I'm also afraid my voice will betray my anger. Confirm I know who Connor is and that I'm determined to prove it. But I need to ask a question. "Tonight's clambake is on no matter how much the temperature drops, right?"

"Of course." Connor smirks. "If Phil makes a plan, he delivers on it. No excuses. Just ask him."

"I assume you'll both be there tonight," I continue.

Saffron bats her eyes at Dad. "Wouldn't miss it. If it gets chilly enough, we can share a blanket."

*Yeah, and Aunt Kylee will provide a companion pillow to smother you.*

Connor stares at me as he fiddles with a button on his left shirt sleeve. Pushing up his sleeve and V-neck sweater, he bares his forearm. He casually scratches his arm as he continues to stare at me. The spider tattoo is faint, but the green ink hasn't disappeared. He's daring me to say something, blurt an accusation.

I keep my lips sealed tight. Refuse to play his game.

"Will you be there, Grant?" Connor finally asks. "If so, I'll be sure to look for you."

# Chapter Seventy-Four

Kylee

*Friday Afternoon*

"Q uit looking at the time, Kylee. You may think you can move
mountains—and I love you for it—but mind-control is beyond
you. Staring won't keep the hands on that clock from advancing.
Don't worry. Ted and Grant are fine."

I stand and walk to the wall of windows. If Mom begrudges my clock-
watching, maybe it's time to pace. "I expected them to show up by now.
True, Ted texted that they were going horseback riding with 'new friends'
and weren't sure when they'd get back. Doesn't stop me from having visions
of those new friends chasing Grant's and Ted's horses over a cliff."

Mom laughs. "Well, that's one more thing to love about the Lowcountry.
No cliffs. Can't you find something more productive to do? Worry solves
nothing."

I return to my chair and pick up my cell. "Thanks, Mom. You're right. I
have yet to reach the guy who owns Midnight Rum, Billy's candidate for the
scam yacht. I put the man's number in my contact list. Tried him repeatedly
yesterday, but he didn't pick up, and voicemail wasn't set up. Time to try
again."

After six rings, I hear heavy breathing, then a "Hullo. This better not be a
damn marketing call. Practically broke my neck getting the phone."

"Uh, no. Is this Mel Weiss? This isn't a marketing call. My name is Kylee Kane. I'm a retired Coast Guard officer and a friend of Captain Billy Stubbs. He owns the party boat boarded by kidnappers last Sunday."

"And you're calling me because…."

"Because Captain Stubbs and I visited Seaside Yacht Basin, and he identified your boat, Midnight Rum, as the one the kidnappers used to waylay him."

*Okay, not quite true. Billy wasn't at Seaside Yacht Basin, but I showed him pictures. Keep it simple.*

"Is this a joke? If so, I'm not laughing. Maybe your captain's been drinking too much rum—before, during, and after midnight. I haven't taken Midnight Rum out of her slip for ten days. Been staying at my mother-in-law's house in Bluffton. If you don't believe me, ask my wife. We've fought every damn day. Me pleading to escape, her enforcing her annual prison sentence. She claims hanging with her family one week a year isn't too much to ask."

"No, no, please listen. I'm not implying you were aboard Midnight Rum. Just the opposite. I think someone knew you wouldn't be anywhere near her the day of the kidnapping. I think the terrorists borrowed Midnight Rum for the day. Returned her before nightfall. And no one noticed."

Silence on the other end. "Could explain it. When I came aboard today, I knew I should gas her up first thing. Remembered she was near empty. Then I discovered the tanks were full. Made me think I was losing my mind faster than my mother-in-law."

"That raises another question," I continue. "Did you tell anyone at the marina about your holiday plans?"

"Just complained to a few folks when I was shooting the breeze with them."

"Can you tell me their names? I'm not accusing your friends of anything," I add hastily. "But they may have innocently passed the information along."

*Innocently like hell.*

I hold my breath until Weiss utters the third name. The one I expected. "Then there's Connor Cassidy. He owns *Seaduction*, a real beauty. Wish I could afford her."

"Thank you for your help, Mr. Weiss. I'll share our conversation with my friends in the Coast Guard and the FBI. Let them take it from here."

I hang up. "Yeeeess!" I gloat. "Knew it."

"What did you know?" Ted asks as he and Grant enter the suite. We've exchanged keys so the four of us can come and go in either suite without loitering in the hall.

I gleefully answer, "The owner of Midnight Rum, the yacht Billy swears is the scam yacht, told Connor Cassidy he was staying with in-laws and would be away from the marina for days."

Mom shakes a scolding finger at the newcomers. "Where have you two been? We've been worried, since we assumed one of your 'new friends' was Connor Cassidy. He doesn't appear averse to kidnapping and arson. Murder's a very small next step."

"Sorry." Ted holds his palms up to slow Mom's tirade. "Should have called to let you know we stopped for a bite after escaping the evil clutches of Connor and his sister, Saffron."

"And Saffron made it clear she wanted Dad in her clutches." Grant laughs. "The woman's a human piranha. A sexy piranha, but I'd be very wary of her teeth."

*Okay, another reason not to like Phil's offspring.*

"Guess it's time to compare notes," I say. "You first. How dangerous are Saffron's clutches?"

\* \* \*

Our shared information erases any doubt that Connor Cassidy arranged the SWAT raid, planned the kidnap operation, grilled Grant after he was captured, and torched Mom's house.

But I'm most alarmed by Grant's description of the man's taunts. "Connor pulled up his sleeve so I'd see the remnants of his spider tattoo. He knew I'd remember it. He lounged in a chair less than three feet from me during my interrogation. He seemed amused I was making an effort to study every visible inch of him, including his inked arm. At the time, I wondered if he was trying out the design. Green ink can be permanent or a temporary henna trial. A friend tried out a design with the green henna ink before he committed to a bunch of needles making it permanent."

Ted shakes his head. "Whatever Connor's motive for taunting might be, he's aware Grant knows who he is. That means Grant's in danger. We should leave Jade Pointe, immediately."

"No, Dad." Grant shakes his head. "You're forgetting Connor isn't alone. He has followers. Men the police haven't caught. These men do his bidding. We know who Connor is. We don't know who his followers are or where they're hiding. Maybe Connor goaded me to get us to flee. That way, his buddies can come for me—for us—when he's nowhere in the vicinity."

I nod. *Smart kid.* "Grant's point is valid. Connor undoubtedly has an alibi for the time of the kidnapping. He lets his followers do the heavy lifting. I seriously doubt the men who pulled off the kidnapping are inside Jade Pointe. Your stereotypical Neuter1 devotees would stick out like sore thumbs in this crowd. No hiding inside costumes like they did when they snatched the hostages."

"What do we do then?" Mom asks. "We owe it to Ashley—really a sweet kid—to warn her that she and Phil may be in danger. We need to wise up the authorities, too. Someone with a badge should know what we know."

"I'll take care of the authorities," I say. "Know just who to call. Mom, you spent plenty of time bonding with Ashley. Maybe she'll heed a warning from you. Convince her. It's our best bet to make Phil pay attention."

# Chapter Seventy-Five

## The Leader

### *Friday Afternoon*

Back in my room, I tear off my clothes and head to the shower. Fortunately, all of Phil's guestrooms have ensuite baths. No sharing.

I turn the water as hot as it will go; put the shower on full force. Perfect. No water-saving shower heads for Phil.

I brace my hands against the tile wall opposite the shower array and hope the pounding heat on my neck and back will clear my brain.

Did I play it right—letting the snot-nosed kid know I have his number?

Maybe, maybe not. If he and his old man are scared—as they should be—they could leave the island pronto and take Kylee and her old lady with them. That would eliminate worries about them watching me. I can't let anyone see me place my bomb bouquet.

Still, even if they run, they remain a threat. Soon as they hear Neuter1 has managed to kill Phil and his bride, they'll finger me. And this time, I have no alibi. The flower lady might blab, too, if anyone thinks to interview her. Shit!

Okay, time to reset. Phil impressed on me that there's always a need for backup plans. What are my options, given my goals?

Goal one, prevent the wedding. In South Carolina, a widow's Right to

Election means she has the right as surviving spouse to one-third of her husband's estate. Doesn't matter a bit what any existing will says or how long they've been wed. Ashley's share would definitely cut into Saffron's and my take.

Goal two, kill Phil before he gets a bug farther up his ass and decides to disinherit me. Who knows what might prompt him to cut me out of his will? Plus, I need the money yesterday.

Goal three, send Ernie Baker to hell. While his death will bring me great pleasure, there's no ticking clock deadline for his time of death. If it's this weekend, great. If not, there's always next week or next month.

So, back to goals one and two. The meddlesome Kane/Welch foursome must be handled. They know too much. Post explosion, their accusations could lead authorities to my doorstep. Grant's the primary worry. The only one who can connect me with the kidnapping. The rest is conjecture.

I can't use my only bomb to blow up the Kane/Welch foursome. Need it to do away with Phil—and maintain my Neuter1 ruse. Plus, disposing of the meddlers with a bomb would lock down Jade Pointe tighter than a drum. Phil would probably fly in bomb-sniffing mutts and hire tasters to sample anything he eats or drinks.

*Hmmm.* Eats and drinks. Maybe the clean-cut Cadet can suffer a drug overdose. It's a shame today how even kids we think of as all-American get hooked. Bet Ernie would love to run that story.

I can pay a quick visit to Mom. Her pharmaceutical cornucopia surely offers interesting options. Then, I'll only need to figure out how to dupe Grant Welch into eating or drinking himself to death.

# Chapter Seventy-Six

Kylee

*Friday Afternoon*

I rummage through the side pocket in my purse for the card FBI Agent Minton slipped me the night our search for Grant led us to the hostages. She penned a private cell number on the back of her card.

I dial it, hoping to get a live person and not a recording.

"Hello."

I'm briefly thrown. I expected Agent Minton to answer with her name and title. Then I remember it's her private cell. "Uh, hello. This is Kylee Kane. Am I speaking with Agent Minton?"

"Good to hear from you, Ms. Kane. Let's dispense with the formalities. Call me Shirley. Hope you're calling with new leads on our kidnappers. We surely could use some. The terrorists were exceedingly careful. No fingerprints. CSI teams found random hairs, but DNA is only useful if we can match it to suspects."

"What about the dead kidnapper? Have you identified him?"

"Yes, he's from Boston, a dock worker whose job was loading freight on container ships. We talked with his co-workers and regulars at his favorite bar. He had drinking buddies but no real friends. Often went off on rants about rich people after he'd tipped a few. A month ago, he didn't show up for work. No one knew why or where he went."

"I have a lead on a new suspect, who happens to hail from Boston," I say. "The suspect's name is Connor Cassidy, and I think he plans to strike again this weekend. Grant's life may be in danger. Phil Graham's and Ernie Baker's, too."

It takes thirty minutes to share all our suppositions with the agent. Shirley promises to come to Jade Pointe before tonight's clambake and bring at least three agents with her.

"I'll try for a search warrant for *Seaduction*," she adds. "But I doubt a judge will grant one based on a teenage hostage's belief he can ID a kidnapper's laugh. The tattoo might help if other hostages noticed it. However, Grant admitted it was already fading. Connor may succeed in removing it before we can get corroboration from other hostages."

I thank Shirley. We've definitely progressed to a first-name relationship. I head to our suite's kitchenette for a glass of water before making my second call. Shirley suggested the delay to give her time to contact Jade Pointe's Director of Security and suggest he hear me out. Her blessing may make the security chief more inclined to listen—if not believe.

I'm alone in the suite, having stayed behind to make the calls. Ted and Grant accompanied Mom to the clubhouse to meet Ashley.

I gulp down an entire glass of water and make a few pacing loops around the suite. Enough time for Shirley to get through?

I dial Jade Pointe Security and hope whoever answers isn't one of the officers I decked on my last visit to this rich-folk sanctuary. At least the head of Jade Pointe security is a newcomer. He won't be nursing a grudge about Ted and me kicking his officers' butts. Not our preference, but we needed to escape the HOA security to catch a killer who'd convinced authorities Ted and I were the real threat.

I punch in the phone number. Apparently, I waited long enough. The minute I identify myself, I'm put through to Director Jim Savercool. He listens without interruption.

"I'm not sure what more we can do," he says. "With all the bigwigs here this weekend and the wedding hype encouraging every yahoo with a boat to sail into our harbor, all our officers are on duty and hyper-alert.

"Phil Graham also beefed up his personal security. He hired a number of off-duty deputies to be on guard at every wedding event. I can't imagine how any strangers could sneak through the double security to cause trouble. But, from what you've said, the threat could come from a guest, maybe even a member of the Graham family. That's a tougher problem. I doubt Mr. Graham would take kindly to us frisking invited guests."

I thank Savercool for taking the threat seriously. We sign off, agreeing to keep each other posted. I'm taking a risk, making accusations against Graham's son. If nothing happens this weekend and Connor's involvement can't be proven, he'll sue me up the wazoo for defamation.

*If that's the outcome, so be it. Rather go to court than a funeral.*

I step to the window and put my cheek against the cool glass. My view of the harbor lets me see a portion of the docks. The River Rat is tucked in a transient slip at the very edge of the suite's view. My boat may be dwarfed by the yachts surrounding her, but she's my pride and joy.

Oh, shit! There's *Seaduction*. I didn't realize Connor's yacht was here. *Seaduction* is leaving the marina, heading southwest. Where's Connor going? Did we frighten him off? Somehow, I doubt that. Maybe he's off to pick up Neuter1 followers and smuggle them on the island. That would be one way to bring terrorists in under Jade Pointe's security radar.

# Chapter Seventy-Seven

## The Leader

*Friday Afternoon*

Glad I sailed *Seaduction* to Jade Pointe instead of taking the island ferry or the inn's water taxi. Makes my spur-of-the-moment trip to Savannah easy and quick. Since I visit the city often, I know where to tie up for a short spell. My drop-in won't take long. Pour my mother a double bourbon, and she'll be unconscious in minutes.

I feel as much dread entering her Savannah house as I do on Phil's doorstep. Different reasons, though. Once upon a time, my mother was a beautiful Southern belle. Her family Savannah aristocracy. She met Phil a year after her coming-out debut. While the marriage lasted three years and produced Saffron and me, Phil's fidelity survived less than six months.

Mother remarried and moved to Boston, where I grew up. Hope she had a couple happy years before my stepfather died. Too young to remember him. The mother I knew was always scared. Now pills and booze offer a hazy comfort. Killing Mother might be a kindness. Inheritance is of no concern. Only thing she has left is the antebellum family home moldering around her.

I let myself in. No need to pour Mom a drink. She's passed out on a settee. A kiss on her cheek doesn't elicit so much as a facial twitch. Out cold. I rummage through the cabinet in the master bath as well as her "secret" sitting room stashes. Find exactly what I need.

Sailing back to Jade Pointe, I still have no concrete plan. My supply of sleeping pills, oxycodone, and anti-depressants could becalm a charging herd of wildebeest. But how can I get them in the pesky teen's bloodstream?

# Chapter Seventy-Eight

Kylee

*Friday Afternoon*

The River Rat provides an ideal, though unconventional, hunting blind. From my port-side cabin window, I can keep watch for *Seaduction*'s return without the risk of Connor spotting me lurking about the marina.

I send a quick text to let Ted know my plans and location should anything go awry. Once *Seaduction* docks and Connor leaves, I'll visit his yacht. Need to make sure he isn't importing Neuter1 followers to crash tonight's party. Also plan to search for some personal items to serve up Connor's DNA. Unlike Agent Minton, I have no worries a warrantless search might jeopardize my career. One more point in favor of my retired Coastie status. Even if what I find can't be used as evidence, I know the FBI will be able to show a judge that discovery of Connor's DNA would have been inevitable.

I brew a pot of coffee to stay alert. The sun sets around five-twenty tonight. Hope the SOB returns before dark. While the pier's lighted, daylight would sure help if someone besides Connor steps off his yacht. I need to see and memorize the faces.

Ted hasn't responded to my text. Probably switched off his phone to avoid distractions. Convincing Ashley that one of her husband's guests intends to kill the bride and groom will be a hard sell. Before leaving to meet Ashley, Ted insisted we keep the suspected terrorist's ID secret. He argued that pointing a finger at Connor would make Ashley and Phil less inclined to believe they were truly in danger.

At four-thirty, I spot *Seaduction* approaching the marina. The man is a competent mariner. He deftly throttles down his engine, reverses, and glides backward into his allotted slip. Doesn't so much as graze a fender.

Connor hops from stern to pier carrying a medium-sized dry bag. *Wonder what's inside?* He wastes no time. Speed walks to a waiting golf cart, Jade Pointe's favored transport. It's impractical to ferry personal cars to the island unless you intend to leave them here permanently.

I wait—impatiently—ten minutes before I slip my Glock in the back of my waistband and pull on a jacket to hide it. I take my backpack, too. Might come in handy if I discover any treasures of interest to the FBI.

I stroll along the finger pier where *Seaduction* is moored in the next-to-last slip. I saunter past it and pretend to enjoy the view as the sun's slow descent tints the clouds a faint pink. A noisy squadron of seagulls arrives to dive on fish entrails jettisoned by some fisherman. Not exactly a soothing serenade.

I turn, scan the pier. *Okay, no one's watching.*

Glad Connor reversed into the slip, easier to board *Seaduction* from her stern. My tennis shoes barely make a sound as I hit the deck. The boat's a beauty, and its owner hasn't neglected her upkeep, all spit and polish.

First priority. Make certain I'm alone. I loudly call Connor's name, acting like a friend hoping to find him aboard. Figure if terrorists are lurking inside, they'll be reluctant to shoot one of Connor's girlfriends loudly announcing her presence. I call Connor's name repeatedly as I move from one section of the yacht to another. Given *Seaduction's* size, it takes several minutes to explore all the yacht's potential hideaways.

*Okay, I'm alone.*

I return to Connor's master cabin. The luxurious stateroom's king-size bed is positioned to provide its occupants panoramic views through a long, horizontal window. The adjacent master bath is a study in white marble and gold fixtures. The long vanity's shaped like a canoe. Plenty of marbled space for all of Connor's toiletries, including a razor. *Perfect.*

The hairbrush sitting on the counter surprises me. Connor's hair—almost a buzz-cut—doesn't require a brush. I pick it up. Long brown hairs are wedged between its bristles. A girlfriend?

My mental lightbulb slowly flickers on. Grant said the leader's dingy brown hair was shoulder-length. He wore a wig! Maybe it's here, too. I bet the CSI team retrieved a few hairs from the wig in the hostage house. I won't remove the brush or the wig and compromise their use as evidence. But I can photograph them and steal a few strands of hair from the brush. *Eureka.*

The wig's tucked inside the bottom vanity drawer. I slip off my backpack to get my cell and take a picture. I'm quite pleased with myself. Can't wait to report my finds. Didn't even need the Glock tucked in my waistband for protection.

As I straighten, my eyes come level with the mirror. *Oh, shit!*

# Chapter Seventy-Nine

Grant

*Friday Afternoon*

Ashley's out of breath when she arrives at the Clubhouse. Seeing three of us waiting for her, the bride's face scrunches in puzzlement. Guess Grandma Myrt didn't offer any clues about why she needed an emergency meeting.

"Myrt, what's happened? Did that arsonist discover you're here? Did he threaten you again?"

Myrt shakes her head. "Sit down, dear. It's going to take some explaining. I'm not worried about *my* safety. We believe you and Phil are the ones in danger. Ted and Grant came along to help explain. Kylee would be here, too, but she's in our suite, phoning the FBI and Jade Pointe Security to bring them into the picture."

Ashley's pale face blanches. Her blue eyes and red lipstick look like they're pasted on white cardboard. "What? I don't understand."

Myrt motions toward me. "Grant, tell Ashley how you learned the Neuter1 leader is one of her wedding guests."

I take a deep breath. Need to offer enough details to explain why I'm sure the terrorist is a guest. Just can't blurt out his name. Dad wants to hold off revealing Connor's identity until Phil agrees to a sit-down with the FBI.

"I'll never forget the leader's voice, especially his laugh," I tell Ashley. "I met him today at the stables. He deliberately taunted me, laughing and rolling up his sleeve so I'd be sure to notice his spider tattoo."

When I finish, Dad takes over, describing how online research and interviews documented our suspect's animosity toward Ernie. "We have proof he was at Lighthouse Cove the day of the SWAT raid," Dad adds. "We also know how he may have arranged for the kidnappers to 'borrow' a yacht undetected."

Ashley looks shaken. "I'm no brainiac, but you've lost me. Why would this terrorist want to harm Phil or me? I get it that Phil's one of Ernie's friends, but so are a lot of people.

"I know the three of you mean well and have our best interest at heart. But, if you're certain of this man's identity, tell me who it is. Then, Phil can have our private security force boot him off the island. End of threat."

Myrt sighs. "Wish it were that simple, dear. Phil has a very close relationship with our suspect. We fear your fiancé might dismiss our warning as nonsense if we name a person he believes he has every reason to trust. This terrorist has a knack for camouflage. If the suspect gets wind of our suspicions, he might even speed up his attack."

Ashley bites her lip. "Yet, you have no idea what kind of attack the man might try. Would he gun us down, poison us, or set Phil's house on fire?"

"You're right. We don't know his plans. Only that he has no intention of getting caught. Whatever he's up to, he'll try not to get famous in the act."

Ashley stares at her hands, twists her gargantuan diamond engagement ring. "All right, I'll try to sweet talk Phil into meeting with you and the FBI before the clambake. Don't be surprised if Phil balks. He's working out last-minute details on an acquisition. Said he doesn't have a minute free before the party. Plus, he's hired a boatload of extra security for the weekend. He'll probably just assign a couple of men to shadow Ernie and the two of us."

Ashley sighs. "What Phil won't do is throw out a guest. Not unless the FBI's ready to cart the man off in handcuffs. Lots of media have come to cover the wedding. If you're wrong, and this supposed terrorist is innocent, Phil could be made a laughing stock."

Ashley pauses. "One more thing I can guarantee. Phil won't cancel one second of our wedding weekend. The money's spent. Lots of it. The only thing Phil hates more than public ridicule is wasting a penny of his money."

After Ashley leaves, we keep our seats in the clubhouse lounge. Grandma Myrt rolls her eyes as Dad and I simultaneously whip out cellphones to check for missed calls or texts.

Dad looks up. "Kylee reached Agent Minton and the head of Jade Pointe Security. Agent Minton and at least two more agents will arrive before seven o'clock. The security director is putting his staff on high alert. Good news."

I have a text waiting, too. Mimi remembers the leader's spider tattoo. Great! She can back me up. I reply to her text, "Call the FBI. Ask for Agent Minton."

I start to type more when Dad jumps up, knocking our table and spilling the remains of the drinks we ordered to hold our clubhouse seats.

"Damn it. Knew I shouldn't leave that hard-headed woman alone. Just read a second text from Kylee. She saw Connor sail off in *Seaduction* and decided to hide out on River Rat to watch for his return. Once Connor disembarks, Kylee plans to do a quick search of *Seaduction*. She sent the text an hour ago. Nothing since.

"What in heaven's name is she thinking?"

# Chapter Eighty

## The Leader

*Friday Afternoon*

The minute I arrive at Phil's house, Saffron holds her hand out, palm up, and wiggles her fingers. Oh, crap, can't believe I forgot her earrings.

When I mentioned paying a quick call on Mother, Sis asked me to retrieve a pair of earrings she left in Mom's sitting room. "I'm sure they'll still be on that side table, along with another inch of dust."

I gently close Saffron's wiggling, give-it-here fingers. "Sorry, Sis. Found the earrings right where you said, but left them on *Seaduction*. I'll get them in the morning. Promise."

Sis pouts. "Be a good brother and go get them now," she pleads. "They go perfectly with tonight's outfit. It's not even five o'clock and the clambake doesn't start until seven. Plenty of time to go back. Not like it'll take you an hour to get dressed."

She stretches to scrub her knuckles across the top of my head like she did when we were kids, and I was a runt. "Men are so lucky—no elaborate hairdos or make-up."

I force a smile. Saffron's correct that I only need five minutes to change clothes for the party. However, I do have other time commitments. The flower lady said she'll start arranging displays a little after six. I need to "accidentally" bump into her and help carry her flowers to the stage. Before then, I need to brainstorm a perfect way to sucker the cadet brat into ingesting the drugs.

Guess I can think on my options while I fetch Saffron's earrings. "Okay, Sis, I'll get the earrings. Will have them back to you by seven o'clock."

Playing errand boy means I'm out of Phil's house, and Sis can't try to sidetrack me with some other request when it's time to be a flower delivery boy. Before I leave, I retrieve the bomb and fake phone from my suitcase and store them in my dry bag. Won't come back to Phil's until I've "set the stage" for my special finale.

At the marina, I get lucky. There's a parking space near my section of the pier. I'm almost to my boat when a fisherman two slips down calls out, "Hey, think you've got company. Heard a woman calling your name as she hopped aboard your yacht. She might have left, but didn't see her go."

"Thanks." I mask my anger with a chuckle. "Always enjoy unexpected company, especially company of the female persuasion."

I know the visitor isn't Sis, and, for obvious reasons, I didn't invite a date to Phil's wedding. It must be the Kane woman, the younger one…the retired investigator. What does she hope to find? Is she snooping alone? The woman and that teen's father seem joined at the hip.

I climb aboard. Careful to make my landing silent. While my non-slip deck shoes are quiet, I take no chances; slip them off. My stockinged feet glide soundlessly on the polished decks. I fully intend to surprise my uninvited guest.

*Where would she go?*

My stateroom. I make it my first stop. A faint noise comes from the master bath. A drawer snicking shut? The bitch is rummaging through my things. Damn it! The wig's in there. Should have tossed it. Has she found it?

I carefully peer around the corner to see if she's alone. Multiple mirrors and the shower stall's glass door make every corner of the master bath visible. She's all by her lonesome. My wig peeks out of the open bottom drawer. When she stoops over to open a backpack, her jacket rides up.

*Nice of you to bring me a weapon.*

I slip around the door. She's too busy gloating to pay attention, to hear me. As she straightens, my reflection in the mirror will deliver the bad news. By then, it'll be too late.

I pounce. Slam my body into her. A sharp huff. Good. Knocked the breath out of her. I use my torso like a battering ram three times, hard as I can. Then I ease off to wriggle my hand between us and snatch the gun from her waistband.

In the mirror, our eyes meet. The snoop whips an arm back like she's winding up for a fastball pitch. I catch her arm as it shoots forward. She frantically claws at me, trying to reach my face and blind me. One fingernail digs into my cheek.

*Damn, she's feisty.*

Good thing I have a considerable height and weight advantage. I smash my body into her once more. As her hips grind against the counter's hard marble, she cries out.

*Can't have her screaming.*

Mr. Fisherman might decide my female companion isn't enjoying herself. I grab the back of the Kane woman's neck and straight arm her head into the mirror. The glass spiderwebs. She's stunned, but still conscious. I see her blink.

*Use the gun.*

I grab her jacket collar with my left hand and yank until she starts to choke. Gives me time to grip her gun like a club. I mimic the bitch's wind-up and slam the gun butt into the crown of her head. A satisfying whomp. Her body slumps. I check her pulse. She's alive. Just out cold.

I drag Kylee into my stateroom; toss her on the bed. While I'm not into bondage, I know tying a spread-eagled person's arms and legs to a four-poster effectively transforms the subject into a submissive. Just need rope, and, like every mariner, I have an ample supply.

*Should I risk leaving her alone?*

Given my karma, she'll come around and try some fancy defense moves they teach in the military. Better to settle for what's at hand.

I stuff a washcloth in her mouth. Slip the tie out of my bathrobe's loops and secure her hands behind her back.

Immediate problem solved, I relax and dump the backpack's contents on the bed. Nothing inside except my razor, card keys for Jade Pointe Inn rooms, and her cellphone. Nice of the Kane woman to leave it switched on.

I thumb through recent texts—incoming as well as sent.

*Gee, Ted, sorry you're so worried about your honey.*

I compose a text and hit send.

*Kind of me to set up a family reunion.*

Now, how do I move Ms. Snoop from *Seaduction* to her boat without attracting attention—or straining my back?

Well, she is a piece of trash. On lengthy cruises, I use a commercial trash bin to offload garbage and bring back supplies. The round container is about three feet wide and more than four feet tall. Best of all, it has built-in wheels. While she's not exactly a petite, delicate flower, the bin should be big enough to stuff her in like a human pretzel. I fetch the bin, roll it to the side of the bed, and tilt it. Once I drape Kylee's legs over the side and grab her belt, gravity does most of the work.

After I snap the bin's sturdy latch in place, I notice Kylee's backpack. Not enough room to stuff it in the bin with her. Have to dispose of it later—after I wheel her over to the River Rat. The woman's treasure hunt has changed my priorities. I need to dispose of Kylee, her mom, and the Welch troublemakers.

I whistle as I roll the bin down the ramp and onto the pier. Have just started pushing it along when I feel a vibration in my pocket. My personal phone, not my burner. I stop. The ringtone says it's Saffron.

"Hey," I answer. "Don't get your panties in a twist. I have your earrings. I'll be back at Phil's before you need to leave for the beach party."

Saffron laughs. "You always think you can read my mind. Not why I'm calling. Looks like we may be in for more excitement tonight. Overheard Ashley telling Phil that the lady whose house burned down claims a terrorist is on the guest list. Apparently, the old lady refuses to tell Ashley his name because it's someone Phil would never suspect. Who do you suppose it is?

Can't imagine any of Phil's friends or business acquaintances hooking up with Neuter1."

My grip on the phone tightens. Maybe if I break it in two or chuck it in the water, the bad news will end.

"The old lady's dotty," I reply. "If you'd told me she thought a neo-Nazi was attending, I'd give it more credence. But Neuter1? No way. Sis, I need to go. See you in a little bit."

I'm ready to roll the bin again when I hear the whine of a boat motor.

# Chapter Eighty-One

Grant

*Friday Early Evening*

Dad's hands are shaking as he texts Kylee. No answer. Aggravated, he switches to a phone call. "Kylee, pick up. If you get this message, call me—immediately."

He disconnects. "I'm going to the marina. I'll check the River Rat first. If Kylee's not there, I'll search *Seaduction*."

Grandma Myrt grabs Dad's arm. "Believe me, I know my daughter can be infuriating, but she isn't stupid. If you storm in, not knowing the situation, you might make matters worse. If Kylee's not aboard the River Rat, call security, Ted. Let them investigate."

"And tell them what, exactly? That I think Kylee is guilty of breaking and entering. I imagine that felony applies to yachts as well as houses. Or, should I say I'm convinced the boat owner's a terrorist, who'll make sure Kylee never snoops again?"

Grandma Myrt folds her bony arms across her chest. "You can do better than that, Ted. Say you heard a loud noise followed by a scream, and you're afraid someone may be injured inside the yacht. Ask for a welfare check. If Kylee's alone and unharmed, she'll come up with an excuse for being there."

Before Dad can reply, his phone beeps. "Thank God, it's a text from Kylee."

He reads aloud. "Left yacht. Need u 3 aboard River Rat." Dad's eyebrows practically meet as he reads the last sentence. "Now!"

Mom shakes her head. "Un-uh. Doesn't sound like Kylee. If she's in trouble—which the text implies—she'd never ask us to join her."

Dad nods. "I agree. She'd give some clue about the situation. I kid Kylee about her compulsion to explain her reason for any request."

My mind spins back to Q, the Neuter1 leader, telling his stooges to send phony texts using Mimi's and my phones.

"Connor used this tactic before—faking texts for misdirection. Bet he's at it again. That means he has Aunt Kylee's phone. Does it mean he's captured her, too?"

"Afraid we have to assume that's the case," Dad answers. "Wish I knew what our next move should be. Obviously, Connor wants us all aboard the River Rat. Kylee may already be tied up there. Do you suppose he's starting a new hostage collection?"

Grandma Myrt's eyes squeeze shut like she's fighting a migraine. "Connor's no longer interested in taking hostages," she says as her eyes snap open. "If he caught Kylee snooping, he has to assume all of us know who he is, what he's done. He can't leave any of us alive. Imagine he wants us all in one spot to arrange some sort of mass fatality."

Dad nods. "I agree. But, if he's holding Kylee inside the River Rat, I have to try and save her—even if it's a trap."

Grandma Myrt almost smiles. "Why not use the tactic I suggested before? Ask security to do a welfare check, but, this time, on the River Rat. If Connor sees a security officer coming, he'd probably make a run for it."

Dad shakes his head. "No. We might be sending an officer to his death. Maybe Connor's rigged the boat to explode a couple of minutes after anyone sets foot on deck. That would be just like that bastard. I can't ask anyone else to take that chance. I'm going. Alone. You two will *not* go with me. If I don't return…if anything happens, tell the FBI and the security officers what happened."

I feel sucker-punched. "No! Dad, that's crazy. I don't want to lose both of you!"

"I'm going," Myrt announces in her don't-sass me voice. "Ted, I know you love Kylee, but she's my daughter. If Connor pulls something and I die, my life will be cut short a few years, not the decades you have left. You're brave, and you love Kylee. I get it, but listen to your son. Think about Grant."

Myrt chuckles. "Imagine Connor's face if he is aboard the River Rat, waiting for all three of us. I'll be happy to inform him that if he harms Kylee and me, he'll create two smart, vengeful enemies who'll hunt him to the ends of the earth."

*Damn. I don't want Grandma Myrt to go, either. And I bet Dad won't let her play the martyr.*

# Chapter Eighty-Two

Kylee

*Friday Early Evening*

**M**y head pounds. A half-second later, my entire body signals distress. I'm folded like an accordion. Ankles twisted. Knees bent. Thighs pushed against my calves. My eyelids are lead weights. I struggle to force them apart. Blink. Blink. The effort rewards me with the view of a sooty black void.

*What the hell? You idiot! You let Connor catch you.*

I can't see. My jaws ache. Can't close my mouth. Can't spit out the gag.

I remember Connor's face in the mirror. Eyes glaring as he battered me against the edge of the vanity. I try to straighten and lift my head. It bumps against something. A ceiling? No, it gives, flexes.

I shift sideways. My nose collides with a cool surface. Not metal. Softer.

I wriggle my fingers. My arms may be tied behind me, but my fingers can explore. I touch something fuzzy. Definitely cloth. Maybe I can find the end of whatever Connor used to tie my hands.

Yacht owners know about ropes. Why didn't he do a better job tying me up? There's enough slack to jerk my hands apart. I try a second time, hard as I can. The cloth binding stretches. One more fast yank. Okay, the fingers on my right hand can reach the knot above my left wrist. If I have enough time, I can undo it.

Suddenly, my body tilts forty-five degrees, and I'm bouncing up and down. Takes a couple seconds for my mind to catch up. Connor's wheeling whatever he's stuck me in along the pier. Each time the wheels hit the edge of a plank, the vibrations travel up my spine.

Connor's voice penetrates my prison. *Crap.* Don't know if he's on his phone or talking with one of his thugs. His words run together in an indistinct rumble. Need to stay quiet. Can't let Connor know I'm conscious.

Where is he taking me? And why?

My plastic coffin tilts again. A one-hundred-eighty-degree pivot. A U-turn. We're heading back. Did he forget something? Change his mind?

Is this good news or bad?

# Chapter Eighty-Three

## The Leader

### *Friday Early Evening*

Damn the luck. Couldn't that cutter wait five more minutes?*

Lettering on its hull proclaims the cutter speeding toward the docks is the property of the Beaufort County Sheriff's Department.

I don't think anyone on her deck has spotted me. The cutter's at least two-hundred feet out. She'll throttle down to idle soon. Even so, the boat will dock before I can make it to the River Rat. Can't have anyone see me hauling a big-ass container aboard the bitch's boat. Especially law enforcement.

In public appearances, the acting sheriff makes no secret of his dis-like—okay, hatred—of the Kane woman. Still, can't count on him or his officers to turn a blind eye to my whereabouts shortly before she dies on her boat.

Best to take Kylee back to *Seaduction*. But then what?

Think! According to Saffron, old lady Kane's already warned Phil about a terrorist parading as a guest. I have to strike tonight. I just need to be quick and get rid of all hard evidence. Nobody would convict me on the say-so of a teen who *thinks* I talk like a terrorist.

Of course, Kylee's testimony would change that. She's part of the "evidence" I need to disappear. But my plan to stage one of those inexplicable murder-suicide tragedies is no longer possible. No way to make it look like Kylee shot her loved ones before turning the gun on herself.

Maybe a drowning? Seems an appropriate end for a Coast Guard vet. Good thing my yacht's near the end of the pier. The cutter's headed to an empty slip at a pier two fingers away. Once it docks, *Seaduction*'s bow will be in a blind spot for anyone on board.

What would happen if I use my yacht's lift net to lower the trash bin in the water? Most likely, it'll bob like a cork before it starts to sink. But I can speed things up. Drill a hole in the lid to let the water fill faster. She'll drown as the bin sinks out of sight inside the confines of the net.

After I deliver my wedding present, I'll return and pull the net. Once I remove Kylee's gag and my bathrobe tie, I'll let her body float free. It'll look like she stumbled, hit her head, and fell in the drink. The bump on her head and seawater in her lungs should convince the coroner to call it an accidental drowning.

I'll keep Kylee's gun for the time being. Might come in handy. However, her phone and backpack are problems. Could throw both in the ocean, but someone might fish them out and sound an alarm before I extract her corpse from the bin. Okay, take the battery out of the phone and leave it in the backpack. There's a big construction dumpster a mile or two down the road. I'll dump the damn wig there as well. As long as it's not found on *Seaduction*, the wig can't incriminate me.

# Chapter Eighty-Four

Kylee

*Friday Early Evening*

I sense Connor's rolling me up a ramp. Are we back on *Seaduction*'s deck? Wish I could tell if he's nearby. Just when I begin to hope he's gone, I hear footsteps.

*What's that noise? Sounds like an electric drill.*

My God, he's drilling a hole in the lid. Does he think I'm dead, that he needn't worry about drilling a hole through my skull?

Light begins to leak inside. I scrunch as low as I can to bring every inch of my flesh as far from that drilling din as possible. A pain shoots through my left calf. The cramping burn makes me want to scream. Surely, Connor can't see inside, but I shove my hands out of sight in case. He can't know I'm untied.

Why is he drilling a hole in the bin? I'm willing to bet it's not to provide me with fresh air. It's a perfect circle about four inches across. A hole-saw attachment? He revs up the drill once more, and the whirring blades bite into the plastic again.

The hole's now twice as big. Makes it easier to see my container's interior ridges and to make out Connor's words as he mutters to himself.

"Drowning. They say it's like going to sleep. Better than being blown apart. A Coast Guard retiree should appreciate burial at sea." He sounds amused. "Should you wash up in time, your family might even have a body to bury."

He whistles a tune. Then sings a stanza, "Anchors aweigh, my girl…."

The bin tips onto its side. So, instead of being right-side up, I'm lying down on my back. The container starts to roll downhill. I use my arms the best I can to brace myself in position. Still, I bounce around like a Mexican jumping bean inside a perverted carnival ride. I feel the bin lift off the ground. A swinging sensation makes my stomach somersault.

Connor chuckles. "Goodbye, Kylee. Too bad you'll miss tonight's fireworks. Should be spectacular, given my unique contribution to the grand finale. Like you, Phil Graham won't have a chance to appreciate the final glorious burst."

The swinging sensation stops. The bin's still on its side, and the tumble has put the hole in the lid below me. Icy water surges in, adding a new source of pain as it connects with the back of my neck.

*That madman is going to drown me.*

I wrestle my hands to my face and wrench the gag from my mouth. Need it closed before the water level rises. I could scream. But who would hear? Connor?

Screaming won't bring any rescuer. If I want to live, I need to save myself.

# Chapter Eighty-Five

Grant

*Friday Early Evening*

Before we climb in our complimentary golf cart, Dad whispers, "When we get to the River Rat, hold onto Myrt while I run inside." Thirty seconds later, Grandma Myrt grabs my arm. "Whatever your Dad said, don't you dare!"

*I'm faster than both of them. I'll just make a dash for it.*

Dad claims the driver's seat, and Grandma Myrt sits beside him. I hop on the backward-facing rear seat, and we're off like a shot. Paths connecting the inn, clubhouse, marina, and main road curve every which way to let drivers change course. Our cart swerves to take the first off-ramp within a miniature version of an interstate cloverleaf.

In the dark, overhead lights brighten the cloverleaf's intersections. I see someone else is in as big a hurry as we are. He's got one souped-up golf cart. Didn't know they could go so fast. As the speeder zips by on a parallel path, light reflects off an item in the cart's backseat.

"Dad, stop!" I shout. "Kylee's backpack. It's on that golf cart."

Dad pumps the brakes. "What are you saying?"

"That golf cart that shot by like a bat out of hell. Kylee's backpack was sitting in the back seat."

"How could you possibly tell?" Grandma Myrt asks.

"Kylee really liked mine, so I gave her one just like it for her birthday. I put the same big, reflective sea turtle on the side."

"Did you see who was driving?" Dad asks.

"No. And I wouldn't have seen the backpack either if I hadn't been sitting backwards. But you can bet it was Connor."

"Which means he's not waiting to blow us up," Grandma Myrt comments.

"True, but he still could have rigged an explosion," Dad adds.

"Not on his own yacht," I put in. "We should visit *Seaduction* first. He's clearly not there, and maybe Aunt Kylee is. Or he may have left clues about his plans for the River Rat."

"Good idea," Dad says.

*And it postpones my need to race Dad and Grandma to the River Rat.*

After Dad parks the golf cart, he turns to Grandma. "Myrt, please listen. I want you to sit tight out here as our lookout. If you see Connor—or anyone—headed toward *Seaduction*, call. If you come along, we're more vulnerable. I know you don't want to hear it, but you'll slow us down. Okay?"

"Okay, I get it. I'll behave."

Once we're on the docks, I look right, then left. While no one's nearby, several people are chatting in the parking lot. Good thing they're nowhere near Grandma Myrt. One of them looks like the acting sheriff.

Best to keep out of his sight.

# Chapter Eighty-Six

Kylee

*Friday Early Evening*

Seawater's pouring in, pooling beneath me and soaking my back. Still, I can breathe. A pocket of air is trapped above me. It won't last long. I lift my head and gulp in deep breaths.

I shiver. Can't help it. The icy water triggers involuntary gasps. Stay calm.

At least hypothermia's not a worry. Though exposure to cold water makes bodies lose heat much faster than the same air temp, I'm not going to lose consciousness. From my Coast Guard days, I know these coastal waters never drop below the low-sixties in late November. Cold but not deadly.

*Loss of air is an entirely different matter.*

I need to shove my way out of the bin before it completely fills. I brace my feet against the bin's bottom, bring my arms to shoulder height, and thrust against the lid with all my might.

*Shit!* I just succeeded in speeding the flooding. My push slightly lifted the flexible top, breaking the seal with the rim to let more water rush in. But the bin's sturdy latch didn't budge.

Damn. Haven't enough strength to pop the latch.

The hole! Of course. Is it big enough?

I cup my right hand, snake it through the hole. The plastic's rough-sawn edges act like fingernails and draw blood. Don't be a wimp. I have to wiggle my forearm through the hole, all the way up to my elbow. That'll let me bend my arm so my fingers can search the rim.

My fingers scrabble over the container's lip. I find the latch and yank up. No luck.

Water covers my mouth. It'll be over my nose in seconds. I force every ounce of energy into popping the latch. Give it up, you sucker!

It moves. Can I punch free now?

Yes! I'm out.

I exhale and swallow water, not air. My lungs feel like they'll explode. Which way is up? Dammit. The inky underwater world offers no hint.

I see a pinpoint of light. Must be light from the pier. I kick and stroke. Once, twice.

I break the surface. Sputtering, coughing, but sucking in oxygen.

*I love the water. Love air even more.*

# Chapter Eighty-Seven

Grant

*Friday Early Evening*

"Do we search together or split up to finish quicker?" I ask as we climb aboard *Seaduction*.

"We stay together," Dad answers. "If Connor or one of his thugs shows, we're better off together."

We're still standing side by side near the stern when a loud splash breaks the quiet. A big fish? Not likely so close to the docks. I hurry to look and beat Dad to *Seaduction*'s bow by a couple steps. One of the pier's overhead fluorescents acts like a spotlight. It's no fish.

"Aunt Kylee!" I shout. "Geez, what happened?"

Dad almost knocks me overboard in his rush to see. "Kylee, grab that net beside you. We'll pull you up."

Kylee coughs, shakes her head. Treading water, she can't quit coughing long enough to speak. She flings an arm away from the net. "Throw...life... buoy," she chokes out.

I see the ring buoy and toss it, holding tight to its attached rope.

"Hold on," Dad calls to Kylee. "Put your arms through the ring. We'll haul you up."

Once she's close enough, Dad slips his hands under Kylee's armpits and lifts her onto the deck. She looks like a drowned rat. Well, more like a drowned cat with her curly white hair plastered to her head. Blood tints the water that trickles down her cheeks.

"How badly are you injured?" Dad demands. "You're bleeding."

"Head cuts always bleed," she sputters. "May have glass in my hair. Not hurt bad, considering Connor almost succeeded in drowning me."

Kylee coughs up more water. "We have to stop him. Connor's going to detonate a bomb. Tonight. Fireworks finale. He'll kill Phil Graham and anyone near him."

"The fireworks aren't supposed to start until nine o'clock," I say. "It's only six-thirty. The party hasn't even begun. We have time."

"Enough time to leave you with a doctor," Dad adds.

Kylee vehemently shakes her head, flinging water like a cocker spaniel. "No way. Just find me a towel, dry clothes, and a phone. Bastard took my gun...cellphone...backpack. Have to call. Agent Minton...should be on the island by now."

Dad wraps his arms around Kylee as she shivers. "All right. A towel, dry clothes, and a phone, coming up. And while we do your bidding, explain what the devil possessed you to sneak aboard Connor's yacht."

"Thought he'd left," she mumbles. "Yeah, stupid. Let's get out of here before he decides to come back to confirm I've drowned."

# Chapter Eighty-Eight

Kylee

*Friday Early Evening*

C an't seem to stop shivering, though I about rubbed my skin raw, toweling dry. With no time for a hair dryer, I'll have to rock a drenched-poodle look. More bad news—the slinky pantsuit I brought for tonight's clambake isn't going to keep me warm.

I glance around our suite's bedroom. Aha! I tug the comforter free of the bed. At least I can huddle inside it in the golf cart. Too bad we're stuck with open-air transport.

"Sure you don't need help?" Mom calls from the suite's living room.

"I'm fine. Coming out now."

Grant bursts out laughing when I emerge, trailing my quilted bed comforter like a bridal train.

"You look like a kid playing at being queen." Grant chuckles.

"Then treat me like royalty, or it's off with your head," I snap back. "Ted, did you reach Agent Minton?"

"Left voicemail and sent a text. Surely, she'll check her phone soon. Maybe, she's waiting for your cell number to pop up—which it never will. I did get through to Savercool, the Jade Pointe Security director. If he spots Connor, he'll keep an eye on him, but he wanted no part in detaining Phil's son. Though Savercool has the power to arrest lawbreakers inside Jade

Pointe, he reports to the HOA. Since Phil's the HOA president, Connor's dad is his boss. The director won't make a move just on our say so."

"I phoned Ashley," Mom adds. "No point keeping Connor's Neuter1 alter-ego secret now. Not sure the young woman believes he tried to kill you, Kylee. She thinks it may have been a 'misunderstanding.' In Ashley's world, Connor is the antithesis of a Neuter1 believer."

I nod. "Not a surprise. I agree Connor's no Neuter1 crusader. He appropriated the label to deflect suspicion."

"Wonder what he'll do when he sees you, Aunt Kylee," Grant says. "Maybe Connor will think you're a ghost."

"Hope so. I'll do my best to make him think I'm more terrible than Banquo, the bloody ghost only Macbeth could see."

* * *

Grant drives the golf cart with Mom at his side while Ted and my borrowed comforter shield me from the wind whipping across the backseat. While there may be no Lowcountry cliffs for villains to stampede horses over the edge, its knolls can offer long views of surrounding flat lands and the endless sea. Topping one such knoll, I'm awed by an ocean of twinkling lights. Hundreds of boaters have come to witness the promised fireworks. In doing so, they've created their own fairyland.

Bang! Startled, I jump sideways and grab the golf cart's sidebar to steady myself.

*Did Connor decide he couldn't wait for the finale?*

Ted tightens his arm around my shoulder. "Not an explosion. Some boater got bored by the long wait and offered up an appetizer. Must have brought his own supply of sizzlers. That boom originated at sea."

My frazzled nerves aren't amused.

Grant slows our cart. "We're almost to the clambake. Security folks are checking invitations. Did anyone bring ours?"

Mom groans. "No. I forgot. But we may still be royalty. Phil hasn't had much time to downgrade us to peasant stock for maligning his only son."

A private security guard approaches. "Good evening. May I see your invitation?"

Mom switches on her fluttery, sweet-old-lady act. "Oh, my, oh, my. So sorry. Since the chemo, my brain's a sieve. Bad enough being older than dirt. Must we go back to the inn? We're Phil and Ashley's guests. Could you maybe see if you have our names—Myrtle and Kylee Kane, and Ted and Grant Welch?"

"Yes, ma'am." The guard straightens. For a moment, I think he'll salute.

"Miss Ashley told us to extend you every courtesy. I'll park your cart for you. Do you need any other assistance? If you'd like to avoid the buffet lines, we can find you comfortable chairs and have waiters deliver your food and drinks."

"That's so sweet, but we're fine," Mom coos. "I have this young man's arm to lean on. Looking forward to mingling with the guests. Are Phil and Ashley here?"

"Yes. They're walking about, greeting friends. I'm sure they'll find you."

As Mom totters from the golf cart, I whisper in her ear. "Laying it on awfully thick, aren't we?"

"Worked, didn't it?"

The clambake's a mob scene. Looks like every one of the one-hundred and fifty invitees showed. Conversations blend into a buzzing noise, a gigantic hive. The hum is punctuated with higher-pitched clinks. Crystal tapping crystal. No paper cups for this crowd. One sound is missing—children's laughter and shrieks. Thank God it's an adults-only affair.

"Okay, try to look casual," I say.

Despite our desperation, our search needs to appear like an aimless ramble until we find our FBI friends and accuse Connor of attempted murder. That should give them grounds for an immediate arrest and keep Phil, Ashley, Ernie—and any neighboring guests—from becoming active ingredients in the evening's big bang finale.

If we can't get the FBI to help, we need to find Connor and take him by surprise. Can't let him spot us first. The man still has my Glock.

The romantic beach setting looks an unlikely stage for murder. Outdoor "rooms" are petitioned by strings of soft, multi-colored lights looped between poles. The candlelit ambiance is great for mood, bad for picking faces out of the crowd. The guests aren't cooperating either. They refuse to stand still. As soon as I scan faces in one cluster, two newcomers join, and three walk away.

"I see the acting sheriff," Ted whispers. "Ibsen's maybe a hundred feet to our right. Maybe Agent Minton's with him. You know how he'll react if he sees all of us stampeding his way. If I go alone, maybe he won't notice me."

"Okay," I reply. "We'll circle counter-clockwise, looking for the FBI and Connor."

I only make a couple yards of progress when someone bumps into my back.

"Oh, sorry! I tripped." The voice issues from a face hidden behind a long, flower-filled basket. A solid clue.

"Is that you, Sally?" Despite the circumstances, a laugh bubbles up. "Trying to take me out before next week's tennis match?"

Sally Wilson arranges fresh flowers every week for Kay's B&B, and I play tennis with her most Thursdays on the Yacht Club's clay court. Sally's a third-generation member of the Lady's Island institution.

"Oh, Kylee. Didn't mean to stagger into y'all. It's so crowded, and I'm running late. Have this one last piece to place." Sally giggles. "How come your hair's wet? Did you make someone mad enough to keelhaul you behind the River Rat on your way over?"

"Long story. Know you're in a hurry. Us, too. Promise I'll catch you up later. We're looking for Phil's son, Connor Cassidy. Do you know who he is? Have you seen him?"

"The hunk?" Sally wiggles her eyebrows as she shifts her cumbersome floral burden. "He's here. Saw him twice tonight. Looking quite delicious. Last time was maybe thirty minutes ago. If I had a thing for younger men and a few less wrinkles, I'd make a play for him. As it is, I'll settle for arranging his flowers."

Grant offers to hold Sally's flower basket for her. I wait for the arm-to-arm transfer, then ask, "What flowers? Are we talking about the same guy?"

Sally looks almost as puzzled as I am. "Think so. Phil's son, Connor, visited my workshop the other day. Wanted to know how I plan for big events. Asked lots of questions about this shindig, and his mind didn't wander like most men's. He's planning his own extravaganza and wants flowers. Curious about how I decide where flowers should go."

"Where did you put arrangements tonight?" My question comes out as a bark, sharper than I intend. "And where did you last see Connor?"

Sally frowns. "What's going on? You're scaring me. I've already placed the stage and buffet flowers. Finished the stage's floral border just before the string quartet set up."

"Did you see Connor near your flower arrangements?"

"The first time I saw him, I was setting up for the party. He helped me carry flowers to the stage. I used a stretchy net to twine flowers and shells into a whimsical podium wrap. It'll be the focus when Phil and Ashley come on stage to say a few words. Connor helped me attach the net to the podium." Sally sounds exasperated. "Is that a crime?"

*Yes, probably.*

"Sally, sorry to be abrupt. Promise, I'll explain later. Where does your last display go? Not near the stage, right?"

"No. It's for that bar station over there." She waves toward a small kiosk-style bar.

"Okay. Do me a favor," I plead. "Whatever you do, please, please stay away from Connor and that stage."

Grant shifts the flower basket. Forgot we'd left him holding the posies. "Grant, why don't you help Sally with those flowers? I need to get to the stage as fast as I can."

Sally's expression says I'm bonkers. In one breath, I warn her to stay away from the stage; in the next, I'm headed to it. Too bad. Hope I get the chance to explain later.

I catch glimpses of the stage as I elbow through the tightly-packed bodies. Pushing through the crowd, warring perfumes exacerbate my headache. While Connor did me the courtesy of ramming the crown of my head into his mirror instead of my face, my brain isn't celebrating the collision.

The string quartet's music is piped over a PA system to reach all corners of the beach. Still, the sound quality changes the closer we get to the source. Finally, I'm close enough to see the polished shoe of the string quartet's cellist as he taps his foot to keep time.

Grant's rejoined Mom and me. Even with a limp, he moves quickly. We're within perhaps fifteen feet of the stage when my arm's clamped in an iron grip. Yanked backwards, I struggle to stay upright.

Ted gasps as he tries to catch his breath. "Hold up, Kylee. The FBI agents weren't with Ibsen. I pulled Deputy Owens aside without Ibsen spotting me. The deputy says Ibsen quarreled with the FBI agents on the boat ride over to Jade Pointe. The feds split from Ibsen as soon as they landed."

I nod and tell Ted about our encounter with Sally. "I think Connor hid the bomb on the stage," I finish. "When Connor thought I was unconscious, he rambled on about Phil not enjoying his role in the fireworks finale."

"We need a distraction," Ted says. "Something to bring the authorities here and, at the same time, move people away from the stage."

I smile. "Mom, you ably demonstrated your thespian talents with that security guard. How about hamming it up even more?"

Predictably, Mom grins.

# Chapter Eighty-Nine

Kylee

*Friday Early Evening*

We delay the start of our charade until we shove our way within a few feet of the stage. Since the target of the bomb, Phil, isn't nearby, we figure this spot's safe for the time being. Connor wouldn't waste his bomb on us peons, would he?

"Help! Help!" Mom screams and clutches at her chest. "My heart."

She theatrically goes limp as Grant catches her and gently lowers her to the ground. "Please, everyone, back away," Grant yells. "Stay back! The woman needs air. Call for help!"

Pop! Pop! Pop!

"A woman's been shot!" a musician shouts from the stage. The violinist knocks over his music stand in a mad dash to the steps at the rear of the stage.

I search for a sign that someone besides Mom has fallen. "What the hell? Was someone shot?"

"No. Dammit," Ted swears. "Fireworks. Someone set off firecrackers when Myrt went down, and that panicked musician thought it was gunfire."

A dozen voices pick up the raucous cry. "Gun! Gun!" These human mockingbirds don't care the what or why of the noise. They just repeat it over and over in an ever-growing echo chamber. People stampede—or try to—in the crowded space. Not the way we hoped to coax people away from the danger zone and clear the area next to the stage.

The sky erupts in bursts of yellow, green, and red. Fairy dust thrown by an unseen giant. A rocket's high-pitched whistle as it zooms into the sky signals a coming multi-cluster display. The fireworks barge must think it's been given a go-ahead. The aerial light show has started in earnest.

I tear my gaze from the heavens to the turmoil here on earth. Mom's abandoned her feint and bolted upright to a sitting position. Grant helps Mom to her feet as I blink, attempting to clear the strobe-light effect on my vision. The bolting party guests have left us standing alone.

Ted grabs my arm and points. One man isn't retreating. He's barging toward us. The acting sheriff. Has Ibsen been tipped about the bomb's location? For a second, I hope he's trying to be the hero, save the day by grabbing the bomb and hurling it into the sea.

No such luck. Ibsen halts when he reaches our little tableau. He shoves his face an inch from my nose and screams, "Don't you ever stop causing trouble?" Spittle flies from his lips. "What d'you hope to gain from your mother's heart-attack act? The way the old biddy popped up says it's a total con."

Over Ibsen's shoulder, I spot two men walking briskly toward the stage. Phil and Ernie.

"Don't go on the stage!" I yell. "It's not safe."

Ernie cuts me a poisonous look while Phil ignores me. My warning cry does affect one person. It pushes Ibsen over whatever edge he teeters on. He roughly grabs my arm and reaches for handcuffs. Ted's having none of it and punches the lawman in the jaw. Ibsen drops the handcuffs and grabs his Taser. Ted jerks and twitches as he falls to the ground, and Grant rushes to join the fray. Straight into one of Nick's furious fists.

"Stop!" I yell at the stage. "Phil..."

My next words are drowned by Phil's booming voice. He's at the podium, speaking into the mic. "Friends, stop running. There's no gunfire. It was just firecrackers. Don't panic."

*Dammit.* Phil's exactly where Connor wants him. I spin away from the stage, search the retreating crowd for Connor. I spot him in the crowd's far-left fringe. He raises his cellphone high like he's taking a photo.

"There's a bomb! Get down!" I scream as loud as I can.

I circle my arms around Mom and carry her to the ground with me, using my body to cushion her fall. Ted and Grant are already down—courtesy of Nick's Taser and left hook. I move my arms to shield Mom's head and my own.

I tense, anticipating the explosion. My terror isn't misplaced. The wait is short. A flash sears my eyelids. Everything's blood red. The blast's whomp assaults my ears as the ground beneath us trembles from the shockwave.

Then, the quiet's absolute. Nothing.

*Am I dead?*

I feel Mom's quaking arms. Her fingers scrabble over my face. Like me, she wants assurance. Proof of life.

"It's okay," I say the words, though I'm sure she's deaf, too.

I squeeze her hand and struggle to my feet.

Nick Ibsen's mouth is wide open. I can tell he's screaming. But I can barely make out a mewling sound. I read his lips. "I'm hit! I'm hit!"

I look for some sign of his injury and see none. He must have taken a hit in the back. I grab Nick's shoulders and roughly turn him. A substantial piece of stage shrapnel sticks out of his butt. Giddy with relief, I'm on the precipice of a laughing jag when I see the devastation on the stage.

Phil and the podium no longer exist. There's a gaping hole in the stage. But, toward the back of the stage ruins, Ernie slumps against a steel strut. His arms are moving. He's alive. I force myself to move. I need to try and help Ernie.

A hand clamps my shoulder and holds me in place. I see Agent Minton's lips move. I know she's yelling at me, but her words arrive as broken whispers. "Have Connor…safe now…help get Ashley away."

Ashley is running toward the stage when I capture her in my arms and turn her from the bloody scene. "Phil's gone. Don't let this be your final memory."

Sobbing, Ashley collapses in my embrace.

\* \* \*

The bedlam lasts a good two hours. Phil's private security force rushes a doctor to treat Ashley for shock and return her to the mansion. EMTs treat everyone who suffered shrapnel wounds or got hurt in the stampede. While Phil's dead, Ernie's the only other person seriously injured by the blast. A helicopter has ferried him back to Beaufort Memorial.

Mom, Ted, Grant, and I are unscathed, with a few minor exceptions. Ted's finally stopped twitching from his introduction to a Taser. And Grant will return to the Citadel with a black eye. It appears Nick can still pack a wallop. My hearing's improved to the point I can make out every swearword Mom utters about the asswipe acting sheriff for punching Grant. Me? I'm gleeful Ibsen won't be able to sit for days, maybe weeks, to come.

When Agent Minton has a short break, she sends us back to the Inn, adding she'll fill us in on Connor's capture when she can. Until she shares details, we only know that Connor's in handcuffs and he's still breathing.

It's approaching midnight when Shirley Minton's knock wakes Mom from what she calls a power nap and jolts Ted and I from our post-shock stupor. Of course, Grant's wide awake, busy texting with Mimi and sending selfies of his badge-of-honor black eye to his buddies.

While the FBI agent waves off an offer of a drink, she gladly sinks into one of the cushioned club chairs. "I'm sorry we couldn't act on your information in time to save Phil." She sighs. "It would have helped if the acting sheriff had let his men join our search for Connor. Ibsen was in full denial mode, insisting your claim that Connor tried to kill you was bogus. We didn't find Connor until he triggered the bomb. When he saw us coming, he pulled a gun."

I cringe, knowing he had my Glock.

Agent Minton seems to sense my horror. "Don't worry. Connor never got off a shot. We wrestled him to the ground before he could do any more damage. Not that he hadn't done enough."

"How's Ashley doing?" Mom asks.

"The doctor sedated her. When I spoke with her, she begged me to make sure you all know how much she appreciates your attempt to prevent this madness and Phil's death. I'm sure she's fast asleep now. It's time for you to call it a night, too. We'll talk more tomorrow. Take your statements then."

# Chapter Ninety

Kylee

*Saturday Morning*

We're still ensconced in our fancy Jade Pointe digs. We hope to head to Beaufort tomorrow morning. But, for the time being, the FBI insists we stay put. Agent Minton is determined to document every second of last night's horrors. We ordered breakfast in our suite to avoid the reporters swarming the premises looking for people to provide eye-witness accounts.

"Do you think we should reach out to Ashley?" Mom says. "Offer condolences and assure her we'll pay for all our Jade Pointe expenses. Phil's death will leave his estate and finances in a mess—not to mention leave Ashley out in the cold."

I know Ashley is devastated, but there's a delicate balance between giving someone the alone time they need to grieve and providing comfort. "Don't think she has any family here to console her. We can leave word we're thinking of her and ask if there's anything we can do. Let her decide if she wants to see us."

Since Connor stole my phone, I make the call on the suite's landline. A man—the butler?—answers and says Ashley "isn't in residence." I hope that doesn't mean she had to be whisked off the island to be treated for shock.

There's a knock at the door. Ted walks over and asks who it is. We're not opening the door to anyone except the FBI.

"It's Ashley."

We all recognize her voice, even if it has a tremble today. When Ted opens the door, a security guard escorts Ashley inside and glances about. "I'll be right outside when you're ready to leave," he says as he exits the suite.

Ashley looks fragile and sorrowful but unbroken as we take turns expressing our sorrow at her loss. When Mom pledges to pay all our expenses, Ashley actually smiles.

"I won't hear of it. Money isn't a problem. You tried to stop Connor, and I'll be forever grateful. If it weren't for you, I'd have joined Phil on the stage when the fireworks ended. And I'd be dead along with my husband."

*Husband? Not fiancé?*

"Don't worry about the money. I'm sure my husband's finance people will sort it out quickly."

"You were already married?" I blurt out.

"Yes, a month ago in a civil ceremony, right after I signed the prenup. Phil wanted the blow-out wedding to make a big splash in the press before he launched his campaign to be South Carolina's next governor."

I'm stunned. "You didn't want the big wedding?"

"I didn't mind." A shy smile flits around her face. "It was fun planning it."

\* \* \*

Once Ashley leaves, we sit in shock.

"All of Connor's schemes to kill Phil and prevent the wedding were pointless," Grant says.

"Yep," I agree. "And three people are dead. Connor's the one responsible for Carrie's heart attack, his Neuter1 follower who died in the wrecked van, and Phil's death."

Mom smiles. "At least Agent Minton has promised her report will document our efforts to stop Connor and save lives. That should prevent the acting sheriff from shifting any blame our way."

Grant lifts his orange juice glass. "Good reason for a toast. Not champagne, and I'm too young to legally drink it anyway. But I think a toast is appropriate."

"Here, here." My voice joins Ted's and Mom's.

"To my awesome, kick-ass family," Grant says. "I love you all."

# Epilogue

## Grant

### *Spring Break*

I drive down the street where Grandma Myrt's house once stood. All traces of it are gone, and they've started building its replacement. It'll be months before it's complete and Grandma can move in—if she ever does.

She's awesome. Says Hullis Island tongues wag incessantly about her shacking up with Frank, who invited her to stay with him in his big four-bedroom house as long as she wanted. Apparently, they're compatible roommates since they've been living together for months and Grandma never mentions looking for other digs.

On the phone, Myrt told me she's delighted to compete with Kylee as a source of sex-related scandal. "And here I thought I was much too old to be a sexy strumpet!"

I park and walk to Frank's front door. Grandma Myrt's arms wrap around me before I have a chance to knock. Amazing, someone so old and skinny can wrap her arms tighter than a giant octopus.

"Come in, come in! Cookies will be out of the oven in two minutes. And I've got you all to myself for at least an hour. That's when Frank, Kylee, and your dad are supposed to show up for dinner. Tell me all about school. You still happy to be at the Citadel?"

I answer all her questions before I make any attempt to ask my own. And I have plenty. Dad has kept me up-to-date on what's happened to Connor and the deluded Neuter1 thugs who kidnapped Mimi and me at Thanksgiving. Connor, who's in jail and awaiting trial, gave up his followers' Nashville hideaway, hoping it might take the death penalty off the table.

Dad also shared that Carrie's heirs abandoned all plans to sue his company, Kylee and Howie Quinn, over the woman's heart attack. But Dad doesn't talk much about what's going on with his HOA clients and where his own romance might be headed.

When I finally get a chance, I turn the tables on Grandma Myrt, "What's happening with the Hullis Island HOA? Are you still on the board?"

"Yes, much to Cliff's chagrin." She chuckles. "My friends Martha and Ruth have stayed on as well. I planned to resign once we arranged a vote on the fate of the island deer, but the folks who resigned didn't raise their hands to re-up. Serving on the board isn't my favorite thing. But if folks like me, who think HOAs should be run as mini-democracies, don't step up, we get what we deserve."

I grin. "Have you had the deer vote yet?"

"Yes, sir. The planned hunt was soundly defeated. The majority supported a plan to thin the herd through attrition and a variety of birth-control measures."

"Dad hasn't told me what happened at that other HOA where the inmates took over the asylum. Is he still managing Satin Sands?"

Grandma Myrt chuckles. "Yes, once Roger Roper found he couldn't bully his new board members, he resigned. But, like any bully, he'll be back."

"Speaking of bullies, what's Nick Ibsen doing? Dad told me he withdrew from the sheriff's race."

"Sure did." Grandma smiles. "A video of him howling over his butt injury went viral. He was humiliated. He also wasn't keen to answer any more reporter questions about our ability to locate the hostages and figure out Connor was the Neuter1 leader when he was clueless. To save face, he left the race."

"I'm kind of surprised. I figured Ernie would find some way to spin everything one-hundred-eighty degrees and make Ibsen a hero."

"Might have happened if Ernie was at his scheming best," Grandma adds. "But his chickens have come to roost. While he's mostly recovered from his bomb blast injuries, he's fighting sexual harassment lawsuits, and he's been indicted for insider stock trading. Couldn't happen to a nicer guy."

I smile at Grandma. "You still staying in touch with Ashley?"

"Sure am. She's no dummy. Just lacking experience. She'll do fine. She's a natural peacemaker. She even reached out to Saffron. Since anyone involved in a person's death can't benefit from his estate, Ashley and Saffron will inherit the entire Graham fortune. Connor won't get a dime. Unless Saffron pays for his attorney, a public defender will handle his trial. All his grand plans are cold as the ashes from my house."

"Okay, I have one final question," I say. "When will I get the wedding invitations for you and Frank and Dad and Kylee."

Grandma Myrt rolls her eyes and swats my arm. "Mind your p's and q's, boy. You worry about your own love life. Did you ever buy those chocolates for Mimi?"

# A Note from the Author

My love affair with the South Carolina Lowcountry made it a no-brainer to pick this location for my retired Coast Guard heroine's home. The dozen years we lived in the Lowcountry are chockful of fond memories. My biggest challenge was inventing names for fictional HOAs, since most of my original ideas were already taken.

While I'm positive Beaufort County has no more homeowner association (HOA) feuds than other regions, the number and diversity of single-family home and condo communities made it perfect for this series. I also should note that my fictional acting sheriff is just that. He is not meant to reflect on the competence of any law enforcement officer (LEO) or the professionalism of the Beaufort County Sheriff's Office. However, if I let my fictional LEOs promptly solve local mysteries, my heroine would have nothing to do.

How do I feel about HOAs? Like all human collectives, their potential for good or harm depends on the ethics, personalities, and agendas of those in power. I admire the vast majority of individuals who volunteer for HOA boards and committees. I've met many wonderful people while serving as an HOA secretary, vice president, and president. Fortunately, for my series, I've also come across a few less than altruistic owners who are quite adept at generating the conflict every mystery novel needs.

# Acknowledgements

Thanks to Wendy and Jeff Wilson, my only ocean-going sailor friends, for taking a gander at my boating terminology and cleaning up misnomers. Also, kudos to area harbormasters for patiently answering questions about yachts I'll never own. Appreciation is also due Mary and Imtiaz Haque for sharing the marvelous world of birding enthusiasts. I also want to thank long-time Botany Bay lover Cecil Lachicotte for helping me sharpen my visual recall of the entrance to this intriguing nature preserve. Wally Lind, Senior Crime Scene Analyst (Retired), is owed gratitude for his "explosive" help—not all bombs are equal. Rob Spencer, Chief Boatswain's Mate, Ret., continues to coach me on Coast Guard operations.

I can't say enough about my faithful newsletter readers and Facebook friends who join in my book-related contests. On this go-round, Ken Frank won the Name-A-Yacht contest with his suggestion of "*Seaduction*," while author Martha Thwaite Weeks won the Name-An-Island contest with her "Spoonbill Island" submission. Use this link https://tinyurl.com/news-subscribe to sign up for my newsletter.

As always, I'm indebted to fellow authors, friends, and family who serve as critique partners and Beta readers. Their input is invaluable. Hats off to Tammy Nowling, Howard Lewis, Robin Weaver, Lorraine Quinn, Ann Chaney, Cindy Sample, Donna Campbell, and Danielle Dahl.

Level Best Books, my publisher, and editors Harriette Sackler and Shawn Simmons also deserve credit for suggestions that improved the final copy.

Finally, thanks to my husband, Tom Hooker. Our multi-mile walks often include "what if" plot and character discussions with Tom serving as an honest sounding board for my fledgling ideas. Thank heaven for a husband who shares my love of reading!

# About the Author

A journalism major in college, Linda Lovely has spent most of her career working in PR and advertising—an early intro to penning fiction. Neighbors To Die For is Lovely's tenth mystery/suspense novel. Whether she's writing cozy mysteries, historical suspense or contemporary thrillers, her novels share one common element—smart, independent heroines. Humor and romance also sneak into every manuscript. Her work has been recognized as a finalist by such prestigious awards as RWA's Golden Heart for Romantic Suspense and Thriller Nashville's Silver Falchion for Best Cozy Mystery.

A long-time member of Sisters in Crime and former chapter president, Lovely also belongs to International Thriller Writers, Mystery Writers of America, and the South Carolina Writers Association. For many years, she helped organize the Writers' Police Academy. She lives on a lake in Upstate South Carolina with her husband, and enjoys swimming, tennis, gardening, long walks, and, of course, reading.

To learn more, visit the author's website: https://lindalovely.com

SOCIAL MEDIA HANDLES:

Newsletter Signup: https://tinyurl.com/news-subscribe

Facebook: https://facebook.com/LindaLovelyAuthor/

Twitter: https://twitter.com/LovelyAuthor

Goodreads:
https://goodreads.com/author/show/4884053.Linda_Lovely

Amazon: https://amazon.com/author/lindalovely

Barnes & Noble: http://www.barnesandnoble.com/s/Linda+Lovely

BookBub: https://bookbub.com/authors/linda-lovely

AUTHOR WEBSITE: https://lindalovely.com

# Also by Linda Lovely

1st HOA Mystery: *With Neighbors Like These*

Marley Clark Mysteries: *Dear Killer* and *No Wake Zone*

Brie Hooker Mysteries: *Bones to Pick, Picked Off,* and *Bad Pick*

Historical Romantic Suspense: *Lies—Secrets Can Kill*

Smart Women, Dumb Luck Romantic Thrillers: *Dead Line* and *Dead Hunt*